DECEITFUL VOWS

SHANDI BOYES

COPYRIGHT

Photographer: Wander Agiuar

Cover Design: SSB Covers & Design

Editor: Courtney Umphress

Alpha Reader: Carolyn Wallace

Proofreading: Lindsi La Bar

ALSO BY SHANDI BOYES

Denotes Standalone Books

Perception Series

Saving Noah *

Fighting Jacob *

Taming Nick *

Redeeming Slater *

Saving Emily

Wrapped Up with Rise Up

Protecting Nicole *

Enigma Series

Enigma

Unraveling an Enigma

Enigma The Mystery Unmasked

Enigma: The Final Chapter

Beneath The Secrets

Beneath The Sheets

Spy Thy Neighbor *

The Opposite Effect *

I Married a Mob Boss *

Second Shot *

Trey *

The Italian Cartel

Dimitri

Roxanne

Reign

Mafia Ties (Novella)

Maddox

Demi

Ox

Rocco *

Clover *

Smith *

RomCom Standalones

Just Playin' *

Ain't Happenin' *

The Drop Zone *

Very Unlikely *

False Start *

Short Stories - Newsletter Downloads

Christmas Trio *

Falling For A Stranger *

One Night Only Series

WANT TO STAY IN TOUCH?

Facebook: facebook.com/authorshandi

Instagram: instagram.com/authorshandi

Email: authorshandi@gmail.com

Reader's Group: bit.ly/ShandiBookBabes

Website: authorshandi.com

Newsletter: https://www.subscribepage.com/AuthorShandi

DEDICATION

To the reader not afraid to
arch over her man's knees.

NICKNAME GLOSSARY

милая means darling.

Лисичка means little fox (which is a chanterelle in Russia).

Долбоеб means fucker.

PROLOGUE
ANDRIK

Almost five years old...

"Twik. She's coming."

Cold air makes crazy bumps on my arms when Mommy runs past me so fast you'd swear Anoushka, my nanny, was chasing her down with a scratchy, sodden washcloth.

"Quick, Andrik." Mommy's smile when she spins to face me makes my heart thump. I love it when she's happy. It makes me happy too.

I run faster than my feet ever thought possible and then leap into her arms as we reach my bedroom. You'd never know my face is covered with chocolate icing for how tightly she pulls me into her chest. I'm making a mess, even more than I did when I snuck a big bite of my birthday cake just as the baker finished icing it.

It was delicious, and I can't wait to share it with my friends tomorrow.

"Where should we hide, Andrik?"

I laugh like my mommy is as silly as she is pretty when she

throws up the covers on my bed and points to the floor underneath. We'd never fit. There are too many monster trucks under my bed to squeeze in two whole people. It is also the first place Anoushka would look.

I always hide there.

Not anymore. I'm a big boy now.

Well, I will be tomorrow.

I'm turning five and about to have the best birthday party in the world. I'm not the only one who thinks so. All the kids from my hometown want to come to my party—even the ones who made Mommy cry when she found out about them.

I have three brothers, but I am the only one who grew inside my mommy's tummy. She said Daddy has a condition that makes it hard for him to be faithful. I don't know what faithful means. It seems important to Mommy. Anytime she talks about it, she gets wet eyes. She also makes me promise at least once a month that when I find someone I want to love more than I love her—which will *never* happen—that I'll be faithful to them.

Maybe being faithful means that when I want to have babies, I will only have them with one person. I could be wrong, but that's very unlikely. My mommy says I'm very smart. Only when I make steam come out of Anoushka's ears do I take after my daddy.

I don't like when my mommy cries, so anytime we talk about my brothers, I tell her she has nothing to worry about. I'll never love anyone more than I love her, but if that ever changes, I *will* be faithful.

Life is too short to think about ifs and buts.

My mommy says that all the time.

You make a plan and you stick to it.

That's her second favorite saying, so I do exactly that. I snatch up Mommy's hand and race for the closet I had planned to hide in when I dashed out of the kitchen with sticky hands and a mouth full of cake.

We almost make it, but my legs are too tired from all the running I did earlier. My grandfather's house is ginormous. It would have been quicker to run home than to the room I always use when we visit Grandpa. The last time I tried to do that, the secret service agents who follow Grandpa everywhere he goes got mad at me.

I promised them I wouldn't do it again, and I like to keep my promises. They make my mommy happy, and that feels like my job lately.

I giggle, squirm, and squeal when Anoushka wraps her arms around my waist and pulls me back. My screams are loud enough to wake my grandpa, who went to bed ages ago, until Anoushka's washcloth takes care of the mess Mommy's shirt missed. She attacks me with the washcloth like she did in the bath, and I laugh so much I almost pee my pants.

I would have if Mommy hadn't saved me.

She scoops me into her arms and blows raspberries onto my tummy until the thump I mentioned earlier makes me deaf. I feel warm and fuzzy when she places me in bed. I don't think it has anything to do with the thick covers. It's how she looks at me when our eyes lock and the pretty sparkles that dance through her eyes when she tells me she loves me.

"I love you too, Mommy," I reply, yawning.

I've been waking up too early. It isn't my fault. Party preparation takes time, and I overheard someone telling Daddy that Mommy did not have much time left, so I had to help.

After fixing my hair into place, Mommy twists to face Anoushka. "We will save the Big Angry Bear for tomorrow night." Her eyes are back on me, happy and glistening. "Someone seems a little tired. I doubt he will make it through story time."

I yawn again, proving Mommy right. I'm not surprised. She is smarter than me. I'm so tired she only rakes her fingers through my messy dark locks a handful of times before my eyelids grow heavy.

"Go to sleep, Andrik," Mommy whispers. "It's your big day tomorrow, and I can't wait to share it with you."

Her hands are so gentle that not even the excitement that I'm about to turn five stops my eyelids from closing. They flutter shut just as a big booming voice asks to speak to Mommy.

"In a minute," she replies, her voice as soft as her hands. "I promised Andrik that I would put him to bed." She sounds distant even with her hands still in my hair. She must have turned to face the person. "When you make a promise, you keep it." Her breaths tickle my ear more than the dark hairs curled around it. "Don't you, Andrik?"

I nod for half a second before falling asleep.

I shouldn't have skipped story time. I badly need to go to the bathroom. My tummy is making noises like the Angry Bear in my favorite bedtime story. I don't think it liked my cake as much as my tastebuds did.

Mommy said I shouldn't eat sweets before bed or they'll give me a tummy ache.

Mommy was right.

After crawling out of bed, I go to the bathroom in the hallway. I don't have a bathroom next to my desk like in my bedroom at home. Mommy said Grandpa's houses are massive but old. She said when they were built, they had a stinky pan under all the beds for guests to do their business.

That's another reason I'll no longer hide under a bed.

People once put their poop down there.

That's gross.

I'm about to enter the bathroom a few doors down from my room when I hear shouting. That happens a lot at Grandpa's house, especially between my mommy and daddy. The mean voice doesn't sound like Daddy this time. It is deeper and weird, like one of my brothers' moms. She's from another country, so she doesn't talk like us.

I race for the stairwell when Mommy shouts, "No. I can't leave him. He needs me. And you promised. You said if I married him, I could stay."

Whatever the man with a big round tummy tells her makes her mad. She doesn't keep her hands balled at her sides like she does when she shouts at Daddy. She slaps him hard across the face.

I can't see his face since he's so tall, but the crack sound makes it obvious that she hit him—as does the way he grabs my mommy's arms. He digs his fat fingers in deep, and tears burst into my eyes.

He's hurting my mommy, and it makes my chest ache so much that I forget I need to poop. I race down the stairwell with an angry roar and barge away the man with a hairy top lip from my mommy.

He doesn't budge an inch.

I'm not so lucky. He hits me so hard that the red ring on his pinkie finger cracks my cheek and sends me sprawling backward.

I'm not exactly sure what happens next. A weird click sounds through my ears a second before my vision is blocked by the shirt Anoushka wears anytime we stay at Grandpa's place. She has to wear it to make sure the secret service knows she is the help.

She isn't the help to me.

She is family.

"It's okay, Andrik," Anoushka assures me when I try to check on my mommy.

Anoushka must have raced us up the stairwell, as the man who hit me is below me again, surrounded by people in black suits and shiny shoes. Only one pair of shoes look like my mommy's.

"Mommy!" I shout when she walks away with the man who hurt me.

She wouldn't do that.

She would never go with a person who hit me.

She once told Daddy she would kill him if he ever hurt me.

"Mommy! Don't go with him. Come back!"

I fight and fight to get out of Anoushka's hold. She never lets me go. She holds on tight until the wetness on my cheeks makes me so tired that I don't care if I wake up with pajama pants just as messy.

1

ZOYA

Present day...

*M*y focus should be on the almost restraint-like stirrups protruding from the end of the bed I'm seated on, or how my backside is clinging to the minute strip of material maintaining my modesty. The only thing that demands my attention when Dr. Hemway enters his examination room, however, is the location of my underwear.

Excluding a patient gown, I'm naked from the waist down, chilled from an AC set far too low for the icy conditions outside, yet my focus is fixed on whether I remembered to hide my panties when the nurse exited to give me privacy so I could switch my regular clothes for ones made from tissue paper.

Excluding the receptionist, everyone in this office has seen what I'm working with—inside and out—so why do I care if Dr. Hemway sees the skimpy material a fashion lover classified as panties?

It's a paranoia most women have when visiting their gynecologist, though it should be as regular as brushing my teeth for me. I've been poked and prodded for years. It started the week I got my first period, which was at the disgusting age of eleven, and although I could have ended it when forced to move out of my home at the tender age of fifteen, the pain associated with my diagnosis wouldn't allow it.

Endometriosis has been kicking my ass for over a decade, and it has gotten to the point I can no longer ignore it.

I shift my eyes from my handbag that I hope is concealing panties I only ever pull out when I want to pretend I'm enjoying the rollercoaster ride known as adulthood, when Dr. Hemway sighs.

He's reviewing the results of the laparoscopy surgery I undertook two years ago. I was meant to return for the results the following week, but with finances tight and the outcome not overly concerning for someone missing their maternal gene, I put it off for as long as possible.

I wouldn't be here if I didn't feel like I was going to perish from excessive cramps and abnormal flow every twenty-eight days or if Dr. Hemway allowed phone consultations.

"Is it bad?" I ask, too impatient to wait.

He peers up at me, his kind eyes glistening with concern now instead of the disappointment of my prolonged lack of contact. "I've seen worse."

He hits me with a look I can only assume a father gives his daughter when he's about to deliver bad news, before he sits on a wheely chair and rolls closer to my bedside. I'll never experience his expression for real because I've never met my father. He left before I was born, which is ridiculous to admit since my baby sister is six years younger than me and has an identical bloodline.

"But there are no guarantees the endometrial tissue hasn't extended past your uterine wall. It could now be in your fallopian tubes and ovaries as well. I will have to order additional tests."

"Could that be the cause of the additional pain I'm experiencing?"

He twists his lips before slowly shaking his head. "Not necessarily. The severity of the diagnosis doesn't often correspond with the pain allotment. Even someone with minor scarring can face immense pain."

I jerk up my chin in understanding. When I was first diagnosed with endometriosis, the damage was minimal, even with my pain threshold being recorded at an eleven out of ten.

After placing my patient record on top of the torture instruments every woman hates, making me hopeful the nurse's assumption he'd want to examine me is fraudulent, Dr. Hemway wheels closer.

"If you would rather skip additional tests, we have a handful of other options at our disposal."

I wait, not needing to encourage him to continue. He loves to talk, and although I'd prefer he remain quiet while examining me, his ramblings give me something to concentrate on other than the pain.

"Oral contraceptives to control your hormones, or progestins to stop your menstrual period entirely. Another laparoscopic ablation or a laparotomy." His expression changes, cautioning me to catch my breath before I lose the chance. "Or, depending on the severity of your pain, we could consider a full hysterectomy."

The last option is new. He's never mentioned it before. It announces that my options are becoming more limited the longer I ignore my diagnosis and that I was stupid for leaving my condition unmanaged for so long.

"A *full* hysterectomy?" I murmur, needing a moment to think. He nods. "Would that make me...?" I struggle to find which word to go with first. Pain-free should be at the top of the list, but unwomanly is the only word my brain conjures.

Women are constantly judged on their ability to rear offspring.

In my family, your entire existence is based on your fertility status. When my body failed to uphold my mother's belief on what makes me a woman, I was discarded like a broken toy.

I can only imagine her response when she learns I may have to remove "the one thing that makes me a woman" to live a pain-free existence.

Dr. Hemway must see something I didn't mean to express. "A hysterectomy is our *last* option. Before committing to that course of action, we have many routes to explore." I discover the reason for the unease in his tone when he murmurs, "But they *all* come at a cost, Zoya."

Embarrassment colors my tone. "How much?"

He appears as ashamed as I am about discussing finances while I'm not wearing any panties. His deep timbre just hides it better. "The hormone therapy I would recommend for someone in your stage of prognosis commences at approximately two thousand six hundred."

"For the entire treatment?"

My heart sinks to my feet when he shakes his head. "Per month."

"Per month? That's over thirty thousand a year! That might be chump change to you, but I didn't even earn that much last year."

I don't earn a third of that now, but I will save that embarrassment for a day when my legs aren't minutes from being encased in stirrups.

"A hysterectomy won't be any cheaper. You'll require a stay in the hospital, then a similar hormone replacement therapy to slowly ease you into menopause."

"Menopause?" My voice replicates someone who has been repeatedly punched in the stomach. "I'm twenty-seven. I should be swinging from the rafters while having the best sex of my life. I'm not meant to let my vagina wither away like an overcooked clam."

"Vaginal dryness can be corrected with creams."

"Please don't," I beg.

Dr. Hemway was there for me more than anyone else when hormones switched me from a chubby-faced child with piggy-tails to a raging lunatic who flew off the handle as often as she cried herself to sleep, cradling a hot water bottle. I can't discuss *this* with him, however.

He will never be a man who can take a hint. "With the right preparation, sex shouldn't be painful. If you're experiencing pain during intercourse—"

"I'm not," I assure him, my cheeks inflaming. "Well, I assume I won't."

I don't need to look at him to know he's giving me his *please explain* face.

I hold out for almost thirty seconds before the wish for a father figure has me blubbering out a confession I haven't even shared with my best friend. "I haven't had sex in a long time."

"Why?" If his voice were any higher, it would reach the moon.

"Because you said it would be painful, and I'm in enough pain. I don't need more added to the over-stacked pile. Especially not for a guy with a peanut for a cock. Why bother?"

"I said sex *could* be painful. It was merely a warning, not an advisory to give up sexual activities as a whole." He hits the nail on the head when he unearths the real reason for my unexpected sabbatical from an activity I should crave more than my next meal. "Despite your mother's beliefs, your fertility challenges do not make you less desirable, Zoya." An unexpected parcel of laughter rumbles up my chest when he murmurs, "To some men, you are all the more enticing."

"Spoken like a true forty-six-year-old bachelor."

I call myself a selfish cow when he replies, "Forty-seven." He nudges me with his elbow before moving for his famous wall of pamphlets. "Don't feel guilty. My last two laps around the sun seemed to have taken twice as long as the previous forty-five." He plucks a brochure about living with endometriosis out of the stack before spinning to face me. "I guess that's a consequence of having more people cherishing each day instead of the standard one."

My heart does a weird flippy thing when I spot his loved-up expression. "You found your Achilles' heel."

I sigh like a simp when he jerks up his chin like I asked a question. "She's smart, beautiful, and strong."

"She'd have to be to put up with you looking at vaginas all day."

That gets a laugh out of him. For as long as I've been sexually active, I've riled him about being single because no woman would be strong enough to endure the profession he chose to specialize in.

As the years passed, his status never changed, so I wondered if I was more on the money than my teenage self realized.

"I think you'd like Kiara." Fondness glistens in his eyes when he adds, "She reminds me a lot of you." I realize he means more on paper than personality when he hands me a brochure on the best sex positions for people with endometriosis. "So if you won't take my word that sex doesn't necessarily mean pain for endometriosis sufferers, perhaps you will take Kiara's word for it."

He sits behind his desk that's butted up to the chair concealing my underwear to jot down some notes in my medical file. He refuses to use electronic devices for anything. It is paper all the way or no records at all.

"She swears by pages seventeen and thirty-three."

My cheeks inflame for an entirely different reason when I flick to the pages stated. The people who put together this brochure left *nothing* to the imagination. It has some of the best not-suitable-for-work art I've ever seen, and I read graphic romance novels like a gym junkie devours protein.

Dr. Hemway rips a handwritten prescription off a pad most doctors stopped using years ago before spinning to face me. "This is a cheaper alternative to the hormone therapy treatment you require." Before I can snatch the paper out of his hand, he tugs it away. "But you need to be aware that this trial hormone therapy is still under provisional testing. It has not yet been endorsed by the drug administration company. It may not work." Honesty echoes in his tone when he says, "But anything is better than the nothing approach you've been using for the past two years." He writes out another prescription. "Continue taking oral contraception for the first few months to ensure adequate protection is maintained while your menstrual cycle is suppressed."

"I'll still get my period?" I sound disgusted. Rightfully so. I am. If I can't get pregnant, why should I suffer through menstrual cramps and bleeding for days on end?

He doesn't look up while answering me. "For the first few months, yes, but they will slowly subside before eventually stopping altogether." Now he peers at me. "Hormone changes that occur during your menstrual cycle can make the endometriosis pain worse. By stopping them, your pain should decrease. Once it is manageable, we will look at laparoscopic ablation again."

"How much will that cost?" My desperation for a pain-free existence sneaks into my tone. I could barely afford my last surgery bill, however, and I had medical coverage through my employer. I don't have that anymore, so I can't act like he works pro bono.

"The costs can vary, but since the physician determines billing, I'm sure we can come up with an arrangement that will suit us both."

I appreciate Dr. Hemway's honesty. If anyone other than him had spoken those words, I would have taken them the wrong way. Since the doctor has looked out for me more than any other adult in my life, I dip my chin in gratitude.

Continued causes for appreciation roll in when he nudges his head to my handbag before he says, "While you get dressed, I'll let

Melita know that I accidentally double-booked today and that you were gracious enough to agree to reschedule your appointment for next month."

Tingles bombard my nose as stupid tears form.

By saying he double-booked, I won't have to pay for my appointment. That may not seem like much to most people, but when you're between jobs and struggling to pay rent, saving two hundred dollars is a godsend.

I'm also super appreciative that he isn't planning to examine me today.

I've avoided his office like the plague for the past two years because I usually always leave in more pain than when I arrive. Dr. Hemway isn't necessarily rough. He just has giant hands that should have had him rethinking his profession long before medical school.

"Thank you."

With a dip of his chin, he accepts my gratitude as if it is worth more than the consultancy fee he missed out on today before he exits his office, leaving me to change into the underwear I hid so well in my handbag it takes me almost five minutes to find them.

The delay in my arrival at the reception desk has Dr. Hemway looking at me more suspiciously than I'm used to. The groove between his brows deepens when I trip over my tongue upon spotting the patient the nurse is calling into his consulting room.

Good lord, I've never seen such a handsome specimen. His hair is inky and thick enough to lose several fingers in it. His tailored suit showcases every spectacular ridge of his body, and his cut facial features and icy-blue eyes would have even the most menopausal woman believing dryness would never be an issue for her.

This man is divine—and he knows it.

His smug grin enlarges the longer I stare, and the egotism beaming out of him turns so catastrophic that if we were in a nunnery, several women would clutch their pearls.

I'd be frustrated about the I'm-a-hussy vibes I am throwing out if he weren't tossing out as many come-get-me feelers. He's eyeballing me with as much interest as I'm serving him, and it sets my pulse racing.

My insides tap dance in victory when his prolonged gawk sees him crashing into the pamphlet table the receptionist restocks each morning. If he were watching where he was going instead of checking out my ass, he wouldn't have knocked over the sex education pamphlets he should hand out before every hookup. One glance at his sinfully handsome face demands a safe-sex refresher.

Upon hearing the faint giggle that announces I love that I have his head in such a tizzy he almost tumbled, the unnamed man bows his head in defeat before he follows the nurse to Dr. Hemway's office.

Only after the quickest glance back my way does he enter the sterile-scented space as requested by the nurse.

I take just as long to return my focus to Dr. Hemway. "Sorry, what did you say? I was..." My words trail off when I can't find an appropriate excuse. Admitting I was eye-fucking a stranger in an OBGYN office seems a little perverse, even for someone as confident as me.

Why would he be here unless it is for the first half of Stoltz and Hemway Obstetrics and Gynecologist Services?

Unless he's a traveling pharmaceutical representative?

His suit screams corruption, and drug reps are as corrupt as they come.

Mindful I will only get answers from one man. I flick my eyes to Dr. Hemway and then ask, "Is that man a patient of yours?"

"Who?" His blasé response proves there's more to his chosen profession than he lets on. Even when the very epitome of a man is in the same room as him, his confidence doesn't wither in the slightest.

I nudge my head to his now-closed office door. "The adonis who was just shown into your consultancy room."

Since he is still lost, he checks his old-school booking calendar for the patient listed underneath my name. He has such an informal booking process all his patients' appointments are made with their given names. The one penciled in for the final appointment of the day is under Andrik.

Dr. Hemway's expression returns to the concerned, fretful one he wore when he first read my results before he slams his planner shut. "That's confidential." He guides me to the side of the waiting area. "As is anything you tell me."

He builds the suspense so well I am tempted to ask if the cream he mentioned earlier also works for your mouth. Mine is suddenly parched.

"Why today, Zoya? You've been dodging my calls for months, so to say I was surprised when I saw your name listed on my schedule today is an understatement."

"I was... uh... I..." *Come on, brain. You're usually more quick-witted than this.* "The pain was reaching a level I could no longer ignore." Since that isn't a lie, it doesn't sound like one.

Some of the concern on Dr. Hemway's face clears. Not a lot. Just a little.

"That's it? That is the *sole* reason for your visit to Chelabini today?"

I start my lie with a head bob. "Yes."

He sees through my deceit instantly, and the disappointing flare it blazes through his eyes cuts through me like a knife.

"I was also hoping to see Aleena. It's her birthday today."

Aleena is my baby sister. I haven't seen her since her last big birthday, and although I will most likely be turned away again today like I was two minutes into her eighteenth four years ago, I couldn't let her day slip by without acknowledging that I want to be a part of her life.

When I walked out of our family home twelve years ago with a broken heart and a bag full of dirty clothes, I was walking away from our mother's expectations for our lives, not her.

It was never about her.

Even with Dr. Hemway's brooding mood announcing his patients' confidentiality is of the utmost importance to him, I can't help but ask, "Do you see her? Does she still come here?"

It takes him half a beat to answer, and his reply fills me with more relief than panic. "No." My relief morphs into hurt when he murmurs, "But I specialize in infertility, and Aleena has never had..."

"To worry about that," I fill in when words elude him. I smile to assure him the sympathy in his eyes isn't necessary. "Two very different women cut from the same cloth." He looks like he wants to strangle me when I push the boundaries of our friendship even further than a mishap in billing. "Has she visited Dr. Stoltz at all the past four years?"

"Zoya—"

"You don't need to give me any details. Just a simple yes or no answer."

His delay this time around has me sitting on pins and needles. The additional niggle to the constant pain forever invading my body is worth it when he abruptly snaps out, "No."

Who knew one tiny word could offer so much relief? The weight on my shoulders seems manageable, and the curdling of my stomach simmers to barely a boil.

My reprieve is short-lived.

Dr. Hemway piles a heap of uncertainty back on when he hands me a card with an appointment for next month, along with a brochure for post-operative care following laparoscopic ablation. It reminds me of the hell I experienced two short years ago.

"You won't be able to drive for a week or two, so you will need to organize to stay somewhere local after the surgery again." I haven't even combed through the minimal list of people I can rely on when he continues speaking, halting my search. "Kiara and I will happily accommodate you if you don't mind nine p.m. bedtimes and watered-down whiskey."

His offer knocks me back a step, but I hide it well. "You had me until watered-down whiskey."

He returns my smile before lowering his eyes to his business card. "My phone number is on the back. I'm only a phone call away if you have any issues, day or night."

I'm saved from looking like a sentimental shmuck by one of Dr. Hemway's colleagues asking to have a word with him.

He signals that he will be with him in a minute before returning his focus to me. "Do you have any questions?"

The seriousness radiating out of him has me wanting to say something inappropriate. The reminder of his loved-up expression earlier stops me.

"I think you've covered everything. For what you missed, I'm sure your brochures will make up for." My dramatic fan of the pamphlets I'm referencing isn't as stellar since I left one-half of them on the desk in his examination room.

Dr. Hemway will always be the only man who can read me.

"I'll grab it," I say, interrupting his request for the receptionist to return to his examination room to gather the brochure on preferred sex positions for endometriosis patients.

"Are you sure?" he checks. "Usually the nurses have to drag you into my examination room kicking and screaming."

"Because you get too much pleasure torturing your patients with below-freezing duck bills and unheated lube to buy heat-able instruments." My twenty-seven-year-old head pays more attention to the quickest flash of heat that creeps across his cheeks than my seventeen-year-old head ever would have before I remind him that his colleague is waiting for him. "I've also taken up enough of your unpaid time."

"All right," he caves. "But if you don't arrive for your appointment next month, I'll take a temporary placement at Myasnikov Private. There's no reason for you to live in pain, Zoya, and if the only way I can prove that to you is through forced intervention, I'll do that. You're not just a patient to me. You are family."

I never thought I'd get hit with the feels during a trip home, but his last two comments smack me in the gut with sentiment.

He waits for me to jerk up my chin before he farewells me with a smile and then joins his colleague at the side of the reception desk.

I'm tempted to leave without the brochure he handed me in the examination room. My wailing libido just refuses to accept another voiceless promise.

It has been issued many false pledges the past two years. Almost every one of them involved sex.

I don't bother knocking when I reach Dr. Hemway's examination room. His last patient of the day is the very essence of a man, so there's no way he'd be in a room devised solely to remind women why we will always be the superior race.

If we can survive missed medical advancements for hundreds of decades, we can survive anything.

My breath catches in my throat when my intuition leads me astray. It isn't solely the rarity of my misassumption leaving me breathless, but also the brochure the mysterious stranger is perusing. He's stopped at page thirty-three, and his head is as angled as the modified doggy-style position the cartoon characters have adapted.

Since I skipped the examination every woman loathes when

visiting her gynecologist, my mood is playful. "It's all about modi-
fying the incline of entry," I murmur, startling him. "Well, that was
my take on the position the first time I took it in."

His angered expression slackens when he realizes who is
approaching him unannounced, altering to magnetism. I've never
met a man with so much natural arrogance. It should suffocate in
the examination room's sterile confines. All it entices is excitement,
however.

After a second rake of my body, as lengthy as the first, Andrik
asks, "Have you tried it?"

His voice makes the hairs on my arms stand to attention and is
so thick I'm convinced he is a born and bred Russian. I don't hear a
hint of another accent.

I'm saved from being baked under the intensity of his watch
when his snarled top lip reminds me that he asked a question.

I shake my head, too enamored by my body's reaction to his
voice to formulate a better response. It is like hot chocolate sauce
drizzled over a generous helping of whipped cream—too sinfully
delicious to warrant only one taste.

Andrik seems pleased about my nonchalant reply of my pitiful
sex life, so it is only fair that I rile him. "More because I'm having a
hard time moving past page seventeen's suggested position."

It takes several abated breaths for him to remove his eyes from
mine so he can flick through the extensive brochure at a slow,
leisurely pace.

I can tell the exact moment he reaches page seventeen. Not only
do his nostrils flare, but so does the crease in his trousers.

After working his jaw from side to side, he returns his eyes to
mine. Their sheer authority would usually raise my hackles. Today,
they achieve the impossible.

They make me horny.

"I would congratulate your husband... *если бы я верил, он дает тебе то, что тебе нужно.*" He returns to English when my expression announces that I struggle to decipher Russian. "He isn't, though, is he?" My heart thuds in my ears when he steps closer. Barely two feet of air is wedged between us, but his slow, prowling steps make it seem much more. "Or you wouldn't look at me how you are."

"How am I looking at you?" I know how. I can feel the lust doubling the thickness of my veins, feel it slicking my skin with sweat. I've just always believed in playing hard to get.

I'm also not sure he is a man I should mess with.

He's standing in an office predominantly designed for women, yet oozing enough testosterone to make hormone therapy unnecessary.

Andrik's arrogance feeds off the tension bristling between us. It bubbles it to the point of no return before he says with a smirk, "Like you know no man will ever fuck you as well as I will."

Sweet lord, his mouth is as filthy as his words make my panties, and although I'd usually give as good as I get, their unexpected dampening has me failing to come up with a single retort.

My silence doubles his egotism. "Even if you try to tell me I'm wrong, I'll know you're lying, *милая.*"

"Darling?" I roll my eyes. "Please. You know *nothing* about m-me—"

I choke on my last word when he interrupts. "I know you wouldn't need a brochure to tell you what feels good if you were my wife." He stands so close that I can't suck in a full breath without my nipples grazing his chest. "You'd only ever need me."

Goose bumps trek over my skin at the image he paints. He has the confidence to pull off his claim, and the looks, but we're interrupted by a familiar voice before he's given the chance.

"Is everything okay?"

Andrik's eyes shoot to Dr. Hemway for the quickest second

before he trains them back on me. His gaze is darker now, more morose, conveying the misery in his tone when he replies, "Why wouldn't it be? Did you not hear the news? My life is only just beginning."

He doesn't wait for either Dr. Hemway or me to reply. He stalks through the door separating Dr. Hemway's consulting room from his examination room, immediately dispelling a hunger strong enough to break through the fear I've been hiding behind the past two years.

2

ANDRIK

*a*s I watch the blonde hustle to a rusted car parked at the back of the lot, I feel Dr. Hemway's eyes on me. He's probably wondering why I've brought the murkiness of my industry into his sterilely clean world instead of waiting for him to come to me as agreed.

I've asked myself the same numerous times in the past hour.

No reasonable explanation appeared other than impatience.

I'm now skeptical that is the sole cause of the changeup.

People fall to their knees when they see me coming. They don't return my watch like the blonde did. They're usually too fearful of the repercussions their unwanted gawk would demand to unearth if my look is in covetousness or disgust.

They cower away. Wither like a picked flower left in the midday sun.

The blonde did no such thing.

She made me look like a *дурак* who's never sampled a cunt, much less an untouched one.

Her laugh when I ran into the pamphlet table like a soft cock...
fuck.

It made me the hardest I've ever been.

She doesn't fear me—not one bit—and the knowledge has me
torn on how to respond. I want to bend her will, but is that solely so
she will be in a better position to take my dick between her pouty
lips?

Ten minutes ago, I would have said my interest in her had
nothing to do with the way her nipples budded against her shirt
when I couldn't conceal my wish to kill anyone who had ever placed
her in the position displayed on page seventeen. Now I'm struggling
to conceal the interest in my voice when I finally answer one of Dr.
Hemway's numerous silent requests as to why I have arrived at his
office.

I spin to face him like our meeting was scheduled for 6 p.m. this
evening instead of 6 a.m. tomorrow morning. "Is she—"

"No." His clipped tone already has my mood skating from the
playful, harmless bachelor I wanted to fool the blonde with to the
calculated, menacing business mogul everyone in my realm encounters daily, much less what he says next. "She isn't a good candidate."

"Why?" My curt reply announces I hate urging responses. If you
can't be upfront, move aside and let someone else do what you can't.
Don't make me pry answers out of you unless you want to leave our
exchange with fewer fingers.

I work my jaw side to side when Dr. Hemway reminds me why I
selected him for this assignment. "It's confidential."

I need discretion. His inability to break doctor–patient confidentiality is the sole purpose I scoured his personal life for something I
could use to blackmail him. But I'm two seconds from breaking the
fingers that had me so incensed with jealousy I entered a sterile
room to see if the blonde's presence altered its scent as well as she
did my personality with something as simple as a sideways glance.

The equipment at the side of the bed appears untouched.

The good doctor should consider himself lucky.

I'm not sure what my response would have been if I had discovered the sordid thoughts in my head had been accurate.

With Dr. Hemway unwilling to give me answers, I seek my own. It is how I have operated over the past thirty years.

The chunky patient medical file on the desk could be for anyone, but the way Dr. Hemway shoots up from his chair when my eyes stray to it announces it belongs to the blonde.

Acting like a maniac instead of a future contender for the presidency, I force Dr. Hemway back into his seat when he attempts to rip Zoya Galdean's file out of my hand. After I pin him to the backless chair, red-faced and angry, I flick through the extensively documented record with my spare hand. It reveals that Zoya is twenty-seven and a multifaceted foreigner, as indicated by both her accent and unique facial structure.

Although my focus should be on Dr. Hemway's disclosure that Zoya isn't a good candidate for my current political campaign, I center my focus on the personal side of her medical record.

My grip on Dr. Hemway's throat loosens enough for him to breathe without a wheeze when the name cited in the next-of-kin section is also foreign and female.

No spousal details are supplied.

I'll still check, though. Spousal indiscretions aren't my forte. I'd rather take out Zoya's significant other before fucking her.

After will make it seem as if my interest is based on more than lust.

"Is she married?"

My back molars grind as deafeningly as the pompous antique clock in the reception area when silence is the only answer I am given.

"Is. She. Married?"

Spit sizzles on Dr. Hemway's face with my words. It would have been followed with blood if I hadn't spotted the faintest shake of his head.

He's obliging—just.

With my reputation too fearful for Dr. Hemway to budge an inch from his chair, I use the hand once pinning him to his seat to hasten my search through a file decades in the making. It starts before Zoya was of age and was added to regularly up until two years ago.

"Did she visit another gynecologist during the discrepancy in her record?"

Dr. Hemway's voice is husky either with annoyance or because of the grip I had on his throat. "No." I don't care about the cause. I am just grateful he's finally taking me seriously.

"Was she with child?"

Again, his answer is short and blunt. "No."

When I glare at him, warning him my patience is stretched thin, he wets his lips before he thumbs the green tab in Zoya's record and opens it to a report from two years ago.

It is filled with jargon anyone outside the medical profession would gloss over, but one word stands out above the rest: *infertile*.

"Now do you understand why she isn't a good candidate?"

He slams Zoya's file shut like I'm not two seconds from prying his fingernails off with tweezers, before he covers it with a stack of twenty. These have Polaroids attached to the front, and although the women featured are gorgeous in their own right, they don't spark a tenth of the reaction Zoya forced from me when she sauntered to the receptionist desk.

She has an almost clumsy walk, like the top half of her body is too heavy for the rest. When she reached the waiting area of the reception room, her spine straightened and her shoulders rolled back to showcase the spectacular reason for her weighted steps.

In less than a second, she forced the sadness in her eyes to fade into the background with a bright smile and presented a completely different persona.

She's a chameleon. A puzzle I want to solve. But even admitting that is ludicrous. Centuries of traditions are on the line, years of planning. I can't throw that away for a woman I've just met.

Not today.

Not ever.

I deserve answers, and as much as I wish Zoya Galdean could help me find them, her patient file advises that she can't.

That doesn't mean she can't answer the many pleas of my cock, though.

Perhaps that's what I need? I need to fuck her to get her out of my system. Then my head will switch back to game mode, and the plans I've been working on for the past thirty years will be closer to transpiring.

Ignoring the screaming denials of my cock that one taste will never suffice, I enter the consulting room next to Dr. Hemway's examination room to collect my suit jacket.

As I stuff my hands into the starched sleeves, I spin to face the doctor, who's never been more quiet. "Scrap what you have and start again."

"What? Are you insane? That list took weeks—"

I interrupt him before his denial of my demand has me reaching for my gun. "The women you selected are boring. Lackluster." *They didn't inspire a single twitch of my cock, let alone the pandemic of throbs Zoya's giggle caused.* "I'm going to be stuck with her for possibly years, so I want some sort of"—I'm tempted to punch myself in the cock for the choice of my last word—"spark."

He waits for me to adjust my collar before returning my attention to what it shouldn't have deviated from for a single second. "You asked me to find a candidate capable of birthing you a healthy offspring." His following statement exposes he has more gall than

I've given him credit for. "If you want spark, you should have black-mailed a matchmaking service provider."

"Scrap what you have and start again." I speak slower this time, more deadlier. It announces I am not asking him to do this. I am demanding it. "Once you have compiled a more suitable list, forward them to this address." I remove a gold-embossed business card for the latest hotel added to my extensive real estate portfolio and place it on his desk. "Leave it with the receptionist. I don't want to be disturbed."

I'm halfway out the door when Dr. Hemway's ethics get the better of him for the second time today. "She's too smart to fall for your tricks."

I smirk evilly. "I can only hope you are right."

3

ZOYA

My mother's scowl is hotter than the overdoor heating installed to warm up her guests enough they'll dodge the hypothermia her frozen heart lures. It's meant to reduce the likelihood of an illness from a high probability to a slight possibility. With her narrowed eyes bolstering the unnatural setting, there's no chance I'll leave our meeting with frozen digits today.

Even more so since my blood is still thick with lust.

I was disappointed when Dr. Hemway interrupted my exchange with Andrik, though in a way, I was also relieved. I've always said you can tell a man by his suit. Andrik's suit screamed trouble, yet I seemed more frustrated than thankful when he failed to follow my exit from Dr. Hemway's office.

My mother's nasally snarl steals me from my uncalled thoughts. "I've been waiting for you to show up." Unlike Andrik, her voice is a mix of accents. The most notable is American, though an array of European nations also feature.

When she spins on her heel and walks away, neither inviting me inside her home nor demanding my removal, her now head maid, who has served her in various roles over the past almost three decades, sees it as a wordless acknowledgment that I've been granted five minutes of her time.

After handing Stasy, my once nanny, my coat, I trek through my mother's mega-mansion until I find her in the den, serving herself a generous nip of gin.

Shock hardens my features when she tilts the bottle my way in silent offering.

I thought hell would freeze over before she would ever treat me amicably.

When I shake my head, she *pffts* me. "It's not like the occasional treat will cause more harm to your insides."

Her sneered comment hurts, and although I didn't come here to argue about my inability to give her endless grandchildren, I can't help but remind her that endometriosis is a genetic condition. "That means I must have gotten it from you or a direct ancestor of yours."

Her huff pierces my ears, reminding me I'll be long buried before she will ever take the blame for any part of my infertility woes. "You now have four minutes. Make the most of them since they'll likely be your last. Thirty and unmarried is no cause for celebration."

"I'm twenty-seven," I remind her when her glare announces my unmarried status is the reason for her final sneered comment. "And single by choice."

She huffs like she doesn't believe me before checking her watch, hopeful four minutes have whizzed by in a second.

Since she is as unfair as she is unmotherly, I get to the point of my visit. "Aleena—"

"Is enjoying her birthday with her friends." A flare I don't recognize darts through her eyes. It is doused as quickly as her courtesy. "I'll be sure to tell her you stopped by to offer your felicitations." When she waves her hand through the air, Stasy appears out of nowhere. "Please show Ms. *Galdean* the way out." She growls out the last name I chose when she forced me to change my name so my infertility wouldn't stain her "good family name."

It isn't Stasy's fault my hackles are raised, but I can't help but yank out of her hold when she gently grips my elbow and guides me toward the exit.

"Aleena isn't a child anymore. She will soon realize that this"—I wave my hand around the home that will forever be colder than grand—"isn't the norm. We live in the twenty-first century, where girls aren't raised solely to be wives and mothers. They can be anything they want to be. Nikita is a doctor, a fucking good one. And—"

"She is lonely, sad, and depressed. That is *not* someone you should be looking up to, Zoya." She brushes off her skirt like my spat words dotted the decadent material with more than spit. "God forbid we will have a replica of her mother running around. That woman was nothing but trouble."

"How was she trouble? Unlike you, she loved her daughters and her husband. She would have done anything to ensure their happiness."

Her stare turns steely as she glares at me like she hates me. It hurts as much now as it did when I was a child who could never do anything right, but since my confidence is boosted from my flirty exchange with Andrik, the scold won't be permanently disfiguring.

I take a moment to recall the purpose of my first invitation inside her home in three years before saying more respectfully, "I would like to see Aleena. She is my sister, and I want to be a part of her life."

My mother's pause for contemplation pinnacles my hope that there's only one way for it to go when she responds with the same snarky tone she always used when I was a child. "Just because you want something doesn't mean you can have it." She steps closer, hovering over me and reminding me I didn't get my short height from her. "As you said previously, Aleena is now an adult. Who she invites into her life is *her* choice. I can't force her to let you in, Zoya."

"I'm not asking you to force her. I just want you to step back and let her decide."

"What do you think I've been doing the past several years?" *Intervening*, I attempt to reply, but she continues talking, stealing my chance. "I've asked Aleena numerous times if she would like me to initiate contact with you. She always answers the same way." Her following words cut deeper than her vicious smirk. "She has no interest in befriending the person who stole her first real boyfriend."

She could only shock me more if she slapped me in the face. "I offered Bayli a ride home after *you* kicked him out. I didn't steal him."

"That's not how Aleena sees it."

"Because she has you muttering in her ear. You always pit us against each other. You want us to hate each other because, for some stupid reason, you blame us for your inability to keep your legs closed anytime our father came sniffing around."

I lied earlier. I see her slap coming from a mile out, and I'm still shocked by it. It rockets my head to the side and leaves a nasty red imprint on my cheek.

There's no remorse in her eyes when I return my head front and center. No pleas for forgiveness. She looks like a cat staring at an empty bird aviary because she knows I won't fight.

If I fight, I'll lose Aleena entirely. The sporadic contact I get every now and again is nothing spectacular, but it is better than having no contact at all.

"Tell Aleena I was here." With my tone more angst riddled than I am aiming for, I tack on a quick, "Please," before I farewell my mother with a dip of my chin and shadow Stasy out of the den.

Once I am confident we're without prying eyes, I pull out the birthday card I had hoped to hand deliver and slowly veer it toward Stasy. It's plumped out with a handful of the letters that were returned to my apartment unopened and unread over the past year.

"No, Ms. Zoya. Please don't make me." Her English is broken, but I have no trouble understanding the pure agony in her tone. "Mrs. Sakharoff be mad. She won't forgive." She pushes the card back my way. "I no do it. I want no trouble."

"But..." I hate myself for pushing. The worry in her beautifully unique eyes reveals that every word she speaks is true. Her fret is very much warranted, and I hate it even more than how quickly I backtrack on the sole purpose of my visit to Chelabini. "Okay. I'm sorry. I shouldn't have asked."

Her relieved sigh hits the back of my neck as she assists me into my coat. Once it covers my shoulders, hanging lower than they were minutes ago, she spins me around to help pull my hair from the collar.

"It's okay. Leave it. I don't need to impress anyone." My low words expose my confrontation with my mother hurt me more than I will ever admit.

I could beg that woman to love me. I could fall to my knees and promise a loyalty she would never be able to replicate, and she would still turn me away.

That's how much she hates me.

"Goodbye, Stasy."

An icy breeze cools my mother's handprint for half a second before a warm hand curls around my elbow to tug me back into the overheated foyer.

I peer at Stasy with my brows stitched when she hands me a business card for a local hotel. I'm not looking forward to the three-hour drive home. Beggars can't be choosers, however. I can't afford a dingy motel on the outskirts of town, let alone one with business cards with elegant gold-embossed font.

My eyes shoot up to Stasy when she says, "You should stop in for tea. *Медовик* best in the country." My heart beats double-time when a rare smile raises her cheeks. "Source very reliable. She knows her cakes."

Aleena is obsessed with the creamy honey cake our mother would only let us eat on special occasions. She was adamant the repercussions of a regular sugary treat would make us more undesirable than a possible infertility issue.

The last time I had a slice of *медовик* was on my thirteenth birthday. I saw it on the table at Aleena's sixteenth and eighteenth birthday parties. I was removed from the festivities before I could pass on any verbal well-wishes to the birthday girl, much less sample her favorite cake.

At her sixteenth, I was tossed out with a man I discovered was Aleena's first official boyfriend. During the twenty-minute drive to Bayli's home, I learned that he and Aleena had been dating secretly for six months. Aleena had hoped introducing Bayli to our mother during her birthday celebration would force her to take the news of their union with more acceptance.

If Aleena had told me about her plan, I would have suggested that she continue keeping her relationship status a secret.

For the short time I was with Bayli, he seemed like a typical high school jock. He was also polite, well-spoken, and on course for an above-average GPA.

He merely lived four miles in the wrong direction.

Middle class is not good enough for a Sakharoff. Upper class barely makes the cut. If your family's bank accounts are below eight figures, you will never be invited into my mother's tight inner circle.

I'm drawn from my thoughts when Stasy taps her finger on the business card now trembling in my hand. "Go here. Have cake with the birthday girl. Smile."

I nod. "I will."

Any type of affection is frowned upon in my family, but before I can consider the consequences of my actions, I throw my arms around Stasy's neck and hug her fiercely. I melt when she hugs me back.

After an embrace warm enough to restart my frozen heart, I murmur, "Thank you."

I race out of the cold and sterile mansion I'll never call home before Stasy or my mother can see the tears threatening to spill down my cheeks.

4

ANDRIK

The rusted shell of Zoya's ride is surprising when I pull my prototype Marussia sports car to the front of the address I memorized from her file. I have mansions dotted across the country, and a handful of my grandfather's residences could be mistaken for castles, but I'm still in awe of the size of Zoya's home. It is vast, with multiple stories and a long line of garages that no doubt house as many foreign cars as the homemade models my marketing team is endeavoring to get off the ground.

I climb out of the driver's seat of my low ride at the same time the front door of the suburban mansion pops open. I'm not surprised to see a middle-aged man dressed to the nines. Tuxedo-donned butlers are the norm in this part of Russia.

"Sir," the man greets, his chin lowering to his chest in respect. "What a pleasure it is to welcome you to the Sakharoff residence."

His wordless acknowledgment that he is aware of who I am isn't shocking—my face is as notable as my notoriety—but his introduction to the residence I am being invited into is.

I don't know why I am surprised. Women aren't seen as an equal commodity in my industry. Rarely are they permitted to speak their father's name, much less attach it to their given name, so Zoya having a different last name from the owner of her house could be a common practice.

My fists ball, ready for warfare, when "Kazimir, darling" pierces my ears.

I should have realized no one with this type of wealth would reference me any other way.

My given name is veiled with centuries of wealth and political mongering. It has also been the name of our president for over seventeen years and is only ever used by people who know of me instead of truly knowing me.

When a woman in her mid-fifties floats across veined floors, I stop seeking familiarities I may have missed since my dick took center stage during my entrance to the mega-mansion. She has unblemished skin and a fit body, but even while seeking a one-night-only acquaintance, I will never overlook my sole requirement.

I don't fuck women old enough to be my mother or young enough to be my daughter, meaning Mrs. Sakharoff tiptoed over the cutoff line in the past year or two.

"I'm so glad you've finally accepted my invitation." Mrs. Sakharoff leans in to kiss my cheeks, shrouding me with the perfume she put on in a hurry. It has that recently sprayed scent and is still wet on her neck. "How is your father? His campaign? Well, I hope."

"He is good." My reply is abrupt. I didn't come here to talk about my father or his bid for an office closer to my grandfather's grandeur one. Only one thing is on my mind. Or should I say, one person? "Is Zoya here?"

Mrs. Sakharoff balks for the quickest second before she murmurs, "Who, dear?"

I wait for her to excuse her butler from the living room before following her to the liquor cabinet so she can pour herself a generous nip of clear liquor. "Zoya. This is the address cited on her medical record."

I'm not a man who will ever tiptoe around, particularly when it is something I want.

I want Zoya—desperately.

"I met her earlier and would like to finish the discussion we commenced before we were interrupted."

"You saw this address on... *Zoya*, was it?" she checks. When I nod, she continues. "If you saw this address on Zoya's medical record, you must have been perusing it at Stoltz and Hemway."

Again, I nod, hopeful it will hurry her along.

I am not a patient man in general, and my interest in Zoya has siphoned the cup empty.

"Then there's the cause of the mix-up, dear. My daughter attended an appointment there earlier today. Perhaps some information in their patient records got mixed up." She screws the cap back onto the engraved bottle before pivoting to face me, nursing the overzealous serving as if it is a glass of water. "She was previously outside the criteria you had set, but made the cut earlier today." She checks her watch, her smile picking up as she says, "At 11:03 a.m., to be precise."

"Today is your daughter's birthday."

"Yes," she answers as if I was asking a question. I wasn't. "She just turned twenty-two, making her, no doubt, an ideal candidate for your current political campaign."

"Just," I quote, my annoyance picking up.

A woman's warmth wrapped around my cock for the first time just shy of my fourteenth birthday. I am now thirty-five. That puts a twenty-two-year-old on the cusp of being young enough to be my daughter.

"I'm not being biased when I say she is exactly what you are seeking."

Mrs. Sakharoff drags her finger along a long line of photographs on the mantel before she stops at one that looks recent. All the pictures are of one girl. A young blonde-haired, blue-eyed preteen with an almost doll-like complexion.

"My youngest daughter is well-spoken, smart, and reared for a dignitary." Her eyes return to mine. "She is aware of her self-worth, but even more than that, she understands her place." My neck thrums when she murmurs, "She is also untouched."

As she hands the framed photo to me, the butler announces that Mrs. Sakharoff has a guest. She looks panicked until he adds words to his interruption. "The birthday girl has returned."

"Lovely." She snatches the frame out of my hand and returns it to the mantel before twisting me to face the formal entrance of the living room. "Her beauty can't be captured in an image. It is far better to witness her loveliness in person."

I'm about to snarl out a warning for her to remove her hands from my back before I use more than words to remove them, but the clumsy stumble of a platinum blonde halts my words.

My cock pays more attention to her near trip than the generous swell of her breasts, and her staggered walk has me convinced it wasn't the addresses muddled up in Dr. Hemway's patients' records.

It was their names.

I'd be a liar if I said I wasn't hopeful their diagnosis was also awry.

"They didn't have *медовик*, so I got *пирог с ревенем* instead. I hope that's okay."

"Not now, dear. You have a guest waiting for you." After blocking the blonde from my view for the quickest second to snatch a boxed cake from her hands and place it on the mantel, she introduces,

"Arabella, darling, please meet Kazimir Dokovic, grandson of our beloved president, and hopefully your soon-to-be husband."

Introducing me as a descendant of my grandfather instead of the architect behind one of Russia's largest and wealthiest entities would usually raise my hackles to the point of no return. But since my ego is leading the procession of democracy today, I grind my back molars together before stepping closer to the blonde who's had my cock in a constant state of erection for the past hour.

Her chips have been bartered.

Her hand has been exposed.

The game is over... until her chin lifts enough to expose her eyes.

They don't hold Zoya's intensity.

Her grit.

They're as dull as every other pair pinned to the patient files Dr. Hemway compiled over the past month. But since they're also not attached to a word that could end my crusade before it has truly begun—*infertile*—I accept the hand she is holding out in offering and return her sheepish grin as if I'm a wolf willing to hide under a sheep's skin.

I'm not, but there's no need to announce that just yet.

"Kazimir Dokovic. It is a pleasure to meet you, Arabella."

5

ZOYA

"*A*re you sure you don't want me to refrigerate that for you?" The bartender, who has been serving me water for the past four hours without a single grumble of annoyance, nudges his head to the giant slice of *медовик* I purchased from the restaurant of the Broadbent Hotel.

It cost me a fortune since they had to make it fresh, but because I was just as confident my effort would be returned tenfold, I acted like the dip in my bank balance was half what it was.

It seems as if karma took the night off.

I haven't seen hide nor hair of Aleena, and I sat at this end of the bar because it had an uninterrupted view of the only restaurant in a fifty-mile radius that serves freshly made *медовик*.

"It's looking a little worse for wear," the bartender continues, reminding me that he asked a question.

"That's the design. Its sour cream and condensed milk combination resembles curdled milk." When he screws up his nose, I laugh. "Sounds disgusting, but it is actually quite delicious." He gives me a look as if to say, *Are you gonna cough up the goods?* "I would if it was mine. I bought this for my sister."

He stops looking like he's on the verge of dying when my last word echoes in his ears. "Your sister?"

"Uh-huh. It's her birthday today. She's twenty-two and supposedly so in love with this hotel's *медовик*. If I were to find her anywhere today, it would be here."

"Oh..." The shortness of his reply and the fact he is a stranger shouldn't make it seem as if he said so much more than he did, but you'd swear he didn't shut up until he was blue in the face.

"What?"

Remorse darkens his eyes. "There was a group of girls in earlier when my shift started." He lowers his focus to the container I'm sheltering like a bodyguard would a pop star. "They were seeking a slab of that but left with some other sickly combination and a heap of attention." His jaw tics when he scans the patrons surrounding us. "Almost as much attention as you've been getting for the past four hours." He returns his eyes to my face before dragging them down my body. He looks closer to my age than the thirty bracket I was placing him in when his teeth catch his lower lip, and he murmurs on a moan, "*Almost.*"

I'd usually be flattered by his compliment. I'm just too disappointed to respond how I generally would. Furthermore, even with hours whizzing by fast enough to make me dizzy, I haven't been able to get my exchange with Andrik out of my head. It keeps leaking through the cracks and has me scanning the crowd as often for a dark-haired man as I've been seeking a blonde-haired beauty.

After swallowing my disappointment, I ask, "How long ago did your shift start?"

The bartender checks the time while tossing a tea towel over his shoulder. "Almost eight hours ago, which means I'm only half an hour from clocking out." His eyes display his interest, not to mention his smile when he asks, "Are you sure you don't want to share that? I can rustle up some forks in my apartment. It's only a couple of miles from here."

I'd feel bad turning him down if he didn't have the gaga eyes of a buxom trio at the other end of the bar. They've been eyeballing him all evening and seem more than eager to try out the position I falsely claimed I was a pro at earlier today.

"I'm—"

"About to break my ever-lovin' heart."

It is evil for me to smile. It can't be helped, though. You can't hear the playfulness in his tone. It has me on the cusp of believing a night with him would be worth the possible discomfort I'll face when I finally build up the courage to test Dr. Hemway's theory that not all endometriosis sufferers endure pain during sex.

He slides a napkin with his digits on it across the sticky bar. "In case you change your mind." My smile notches my cheeks higher when he moseys to the other side of the bar while saying, "I'll even kick them out of my bed mid-deed if you're not into sharing."

"And if I was interested?" I ask, doing anything to keep the tension off the fact that I turned down an invitation from a devilishly good-looking man for a stranger I'll most likely never see again.

The bartender groans before he grips his chest like his heart can't possibly sustain more damage. "I'd die a very happy man."

He winks like he has the world at his feet when I slip off the barstool and store his number in my pocket before he gives the buxom trio the star treatment they've been seeking for the past several hours.

I smile, glad someone is getting their rocks off tonight, before I head for the exit.

I'm about to break into the foyer when the bartender's deep rumble stops me in my tracks. "They restock the dessert cabinet every day at midday." He waits for me to crank my neck back to face him before saying, "That's what they told the blonde in the middle of the pack when she wasn't as adamant as you that she must have that specific cake."

His reply announces he was watching me longer than I was seated in his bar, awaiting the arrival of my baby sister. I let it slide, however, since he's given me hope I may still see her before returning home for another long stint of absence.

"I'm guessing I am gonna see you tomorrow?"

I don't take even a second to consider my reply. "Your guess would be correct."

The trio's lips drop into a pout when he devotes his attention back to me enough for them to lose the heat of his gaze. "Where are you staying?" My brow barely lifts when he attempts to eradicate my confusion. "You're not a local. If you were, I would have sniffed you out years ago." He takes a moment to relish my furled lips and then adds, "And you're not a hotel guest, or you would have taken advantage of the canapes and free booze offered after four p.m. every afternoon, so where are you gonna rest your head for the night?"

Bartenders are like hairdressers—they know everything. Trying to deceive them is just foolish, so I be honest. "I was planning to drive home. Now I'll probably just find a place to stay on the outskirts of town."

By place, I mean a truck stop or a gas station, where I will sleep in my car with the tire wrench hidden under the hoodie I'm going to treat as a blanket.

The bartender, still nameless, sees through my lie in under a second. "Truck stops ain't no place for a lady." I'm already stammering for air from how easily he read me, so you can picture my gasping state when he says, "You can crash at mine."

Not paying attention to my headshake, he snags a set of keys from beneath the bar and then tosses them at me.

I either catch them or let them fall to the floor.

I catch them. It doesn't mean what the trio at the end of the bar thinks.

I'm not going home with him.

"I'm not... I can't." That whiny brat with a voice oddly similar to mine had better quit stuttering before I smack her. "Thanks for the offer, but I'll be fine."

"You either stay at my place, or I'll spend the night circling the truck stops, seeking you in the..."—he twists his lips as he contemplates—"rusted white Lada Niva you're getting around in that is most likely older than you." I snap my mouth shut. "Your stingy ass is as uneager as the rest of us to pay the valet parking rate here, so you parked behind me in an alleyway a couple of blocks up."

I don't feel threatened by him. He doesn't give off dark and dangerous vibes like Andrik, though it won't stop me from saying, "You said you arrived for your shift eight hours ago." He nods, unknowingly inching toward my trap. "So how did you see me park behind you a little over four hours ago?"

I assume he's seconds from being snared by my trap. I'm poorly mistaken. "Do you really think I'd park my custom Irbis in an alleyway without making sure she was wired up to the hilt with surveillance?"

I have no clue what an Irbis is, but it is clearly important to him. He switches the football on the TV to a live feed of the alleyway two blocks up from the hotel.

"Hey!" a fellow bartender shouts in frustration. "I was watching that."

"Now you're watching my bike," Bartender One replies, his tone firm enough for his colleague to back down on his campaign in an instant.

Bartender One's motorcycle replicates a Harley Davidson. It is all black with chrome features. It's a sexy bike—even more so when featured next to my bomb, which is one coastal visit from being completely rusted out.

After admiring his favorite mode of transport for a few more seconds, he tells the complaining bartender to snap a picture of the tags on his bike.

When he does as asked, Bartender One nudges his head to me before saying with a smile, "Now her."

"I don't conse—"

Too late.

Bartender Two takes my picture without consent.

"Are they clear?" Bartender Two jerks up his chin before spinning his phone screen around to get Bartender One's approval. "That's as clear as a glass of water not removed from the Hudson." He gets off track as quickly as I do when I find something interesting. "What phone is that? It takes a damn good picture. I can even see the tiny little freckles adorning her adorable nose."

When I realize what he is doing—killing my suspicion with compliments—I pull the damp dish towel off his shoulder and throw it in his face.

"Delete that," I demand, pointing to Bartender Two, "before I show you what happens when I don't consent to having my photo taken."

His Adam's apple bobs up and down before he attempts to delete the image.

I say *attempt* because Bartender One snatches his phone out of his grasp before he can. "If you delete the evidence of our blistering yet somewhat one-sided exchange, how will he rat me out to the po-po if your name shows up on a missing person's report tomorrow?"

I am completely and utterly lost. Mercifully, he is better at reading my confused prompts than my not-interested ones. "Lync's got my plates and your image stored in his phone, so if you fail to show up tomorrow to meet with your sister, he has all the info he needs to finally see me in cuffs."

"I'd do it, too," Lync assures me. "Mikhail hasn't shut up about his bike since he bought it." He leans in closer. "That was a very long six months ago. So you can be assured I'll do *anything* for a couple of hours of peace."

I fight to hide my smile when Mikhail rolls his eyes before switching the television program back to football. A penalty shootout has Lync passive in under a minute, and all of Mikhail's focus back on me. "Take a right at the end of the alleyway. After a second set of lights, you'll see a glass-and-steel building half a click up. You can't miss it. I'm in the penthouse. If you'd rather keep your visit under wraps, park in the underground garage and take the service elevator to the top floor. This code will get you inside my apartment." After flipping over my hand, he writes a four-digit PIN code onto my palm. "It changes anytime it's used, so if you are planning to leave and come back, collect the key from the entryway table first."

"Why would I leave?" When he smirks, I free my foot from his trap. "I'd have to arrive before I could leave, and that is *never* going to happen."

"It's happening," Mikhail argues. "And to make sure, I'll treat the Triple Threat Team to a hotel room for the night." He flashes dimples as he nudges his head to the trio awaiting his return. "Then there will be no chance I'll accidentally stumble to my bed in the middle of the night for a late-night snuggle." His smile grows. "I've been caught out before. Consequences of having only one bed and a marshmallow heart."

"Offering strangers your bed for the night nothing out of the ordinary for you, Marshmallow Man?"

He bops my nose with his pen, instantly weakening my defenses. "I only do it for the girls I like." The pen clatters into a stack of twenty when he tosses it into a holder at the side of an ancient cash register. "And you've got me fascinated as fuck." His nose screws up like it's an effort to deliver his next words without vomit. "But I'm starting to think not all my interests center around me." He signals to a patron demanding attention that he won't be a minute before training his eyes on mine. "You good?"

I want to say no. I want to tell him he's crazy to invite a stranger into his home, but something stops me. I just have no clue what it is, so instead, I nod, preferring to lie without words.

6

ZOYA

"You can't seriously be contemplating this," I murmur to myself as my rust bucket slowly pulls up to a massive steel-and-glass structure taller than the clouds.

Mikhail was right. You can't miss his building. It's huge and impressive, with a doorman and a team of valets who are so eager for me to move on one walks up to my driver's side window before I reach the line several other vehicles are vying for.

"Can I help you, ma'am?"

White air puffs from my mouth as I wind down my window. "Uh... I didn't mean to come this way. I am seeking the service entrance."

An expression crosses his face I have no issue deciphering.

He thinks I am him—that I'm the help.

"Past the potted hedge and to the right."

I drink in the hedge before asking, "Is that the closest exit?"

He either doesn't hear me or is too rushed off his feet to act cordially. "Past the hedge and to the right," he repeats before he races to a flashy car cutting the line.

I can't see who is seated behind the wheel. He must be famous, because camera bulbs flash as often as the motorists he cut off toot their horns.

"Ma'am," a second concierge says, startling me, "I need you to move, please. You're creating a fire hazard."

A fire hazard in a driveway?

Too frazzled by the frenzy occurring around me to argue, I mouth an apology before seeking an opening in the long valet line. My gears crunch when I find a small gap between two low-riding vehicles that appear almost futuristic. LEDs light up the underbelly of their over-polished shells, and their pistons hiss with only the slightest compression of their gas pedals.

My engine is so old it chokes and splutters more than it purrs.

It's more like its owner than I previously realized.

I plan to zip out of the line and back onto the street with the rest of society, but the traffic only flows in one direction—to the underground parking lot.

I grow so dizzy following the procession of designer cars to the lower level of the lot that I either pull over and settle the rush of nausea it's caused or spend the remainder of my night cleaning vomit from my clothes.

Sweat dots my neck when I park in the first available space. It is meant for electric vehicles requiring a charge, but I don't care. Rules are meant to be broken, and if a bend in the road saves me from an unwanted barf-fest, I'll be the first to explore it.

The reminder sees me snagging the keys I left the Broadbent Hotel with, and my phone from the middle console, before I head for the elevator marked Personnel Only.

I jump out of my skin when the elevator call button fails to illuminate no matter how many times I jab it. It isn't my annoyance of its faulty nature causing my skittishness. It's the husky voice projecting from a speaker next to my head startling me.

Mikhail chuckles at my frightened response before he repeats his request for me to place the key he gave me into a slot at the side of the elevator's checker plate doors.

"If any rando could ride the service elevator, I'd have to get more than one bed."

I realize he's watching me when his laughter deepens after I roll my eyes.

"There you go," he murmurs when the twist of a key illuminates the elevator button. "You'll be as snug as a bug in a rug in no time." Either more time passed than I realized, or the trio's eagerness to get Mikhail alone saw him leaving his shift earlier than planned, because there's no denying the sorrowed whine of three thirsty women at the end of his sentence. "Not you guys. Jesus. We just got here." His voice loudens, announcing his focus is back on me. "You good, Sunshine? The girls are getting impatient."

I gag. What's with the nicknames today? I went from having none to multiple in hours.

I'm also jealous. Not of Mikhail moving on after my rejection, but that he's having the fun I swore I would have when I gave up stability for the right to make my own decisions.

If I had followed the life plan my mother had devised for me, I wouldn't have needed to work a day in my life. My husband would have been as old as he was decrepit. Since his age would force him to overlook my fertility issues, the societal standards of the rich would permit me to display only graciousness.

I glare at the speaker box when Mikhail asks, "Do you need a cuddle or a shit? I've not quite worked out your expressions yet."

My reply instantly halts his chuckles. "I need to get laid."

"Then why the fuck am I all the way over here instead of in my bed, working out your best O face?"

With the ease of our conversation making it seem as if we've been friends for decades, I shrug. "It probably has something to do with your marshmallow heart. I'm not a fan of soft and gooey things."

"That's the only soft and gooey thing you'll get from me, sweetheart. The rest is hard, thumping, and—Jesus fucking Christ, Kitty. You know my cock is attached, right? It isn't detachable like the big black beast Jasmina is whirling around her..." A moan cuts him off this time instead of an impatient woman. "Sunshine, I've got to go. Help yourself to anything you want. Nothing is off-limits." As he pulls his phone away from his ear, I hear him say, "I don't recall giving *any of you* permission to start without me."

I stop staring at the speaker box like podcast voyeurism is my kink when the elevator dings, announcing its arrival on my floor.

I've barely stepped inside when its doors slam shut and it begins its climb to the penthouse. I didn't even need to select my floor.

Stupidity smacks into me hard and fast when it stops its climb only one floor later. A man grumbling his frustration about being stalked by the paparazzi enters the confined space at the speed of a bullet being dislodged from a gun.

He's so riled up that we ascend three floors before he realizes he has company. My unexpected presence causes the hairs on his nape to bristle, and the anger teeming out of him makes the conditions unbearable.

"If you're a reporter hoping for an exclusive, you entered the wrong fucking elevator." His last three words are roars, but I pay the most attention to the molten lava hotness of his voice.

I've heard it before, only hours ago, and it was as dangerous to my libido back then as it is now.

I can't move, speak, or think.

All I can do is fight the urge not to melt like a popsicle on a hot summer's day.

"All requests for an interview are to be directed through my office." As Andrik spins to face me, his heated words batter the brushed steel casing of the inner walls of the elevator. "You do *not* approach me in private."

When his eyes lift and lock with mine, their sheer fury buckles, replaced with intrigue. He stares at me as if I am a mirage.

Then lust takes hold.

"Zoya."

I'm as stunned now as I was when the icy-blue eyes and cut jaw his voice conjured slowly presented as he spun around.

How does he know my name?

We didn't exchange introductions.

Andrik's eyes bounce between mine for several heart-thrashing seconds before he asks, "What are you doing here?"

"I... ah..." Mikhail's keys jangle when I brush away a bead of sweat the unbelievable heat in the elevator caused my temple, and they break through some of the lusty fog Andrik's closeness incites. "I'm returning these to a... *friend*."

I can be forgiven for my stumble of Mikhail's title.

He was a stranger only hours ago.

As was the man whose anger returns to the boiling point so fast steam almost billows from his ears. "You know Mikhail?"

"Uh-huh," I answer, a better response above me.

I don't work well in the heat. It is one reason I frequently return to Russia even with opportunities abroad far exceeding any I'll receive locally.

I also struggle leaving my best friend behind, and the toil worsened when she practically lost her parents within days of each other.

When Andrik works his jaw from side to side, its crunch returns my focus to the present. He drags his hand across the bristles covering a majority of his panty-wetting jawline before he attempts to force words through the tightness. "Enough for him to give you private access to his penthouse?"

"Uh-huh," I repeat, too focused on unearthing what has caused the fury in his eyes.

Mikhail offered me his bed for the night, not his hand in marriage. Andrik's spasming jaw and narrowing eyes would have you convinced otherwise.

"That's surprising."

"It is?" I reply, stupidly wanting to continue our conversation since my ego is feeding off the tension it is creating.

"Uh-huh," Andrik mocks, his tone low. "Because he only ever gives access to the girls he wants to fuck." He steps closer, brooding and looming. "*Again*." His expression is as ugly as his words, but it still makes me squirm. "So what number is this, Zoya Galdean? Date two, three, or four?"

His words get hotter and deeper with each one he speaks, and they make me so reckless I foolishly fall for the ruse that he's more jealous than angry.

"I'm not exactly sure. Does the consummation of a meal count as a date? Or only if an orgasm is achieved?"

"If?"

His brows are too pinched to show the laughter in his eyes, his expression too taut, but I don't need to hear it to know of its arrival. It batters my chest with its rumbles.

That's how close he stands when he murmurs, "There are no ifs, милая. Not when you're fucked by a real man."

He grips my chin and shoves my head to the side before he drags his nose down the pulse in my neck. When he reaches the risqué neckline of my shirt dusting my collarbone, he growls. Its deep rumble skates through my veins before clustering in my needy pussy.

"Which I'd say you haven't experienced in a long time. *If* ever."

Hating that he is mocking me, I attempt to push him back. He doesn't budge an inch.

He leans in deeper, dampening my panties to a point I can no longer ignore. "Do you want me to show you the difference, милая? Or shall I skip straight to demonstrating how to get past page seventeen?"

His reminder that I'm so broken I need a brochure to enjoy something many people take for granted intensifies my mood.

When denied, even by my own doing, I get bitchy.

"And have you steal the honor Mikhail has worked so hard to achieve? Don't be ridiculous."

My body tingles when he inches so close I can feel the anger my statement caused him all over me. "Lie to me again and I'll take you over my knee."

"Who said I am lying?"

My insides clench when he licks his lips before he lowers his eyes to my nipples budded against my shirt.

Mercifully, I'm saved from needing to explain my stupidity by the elevator arriving at the top floor.

If only something so simple could save me from myself.

"Good evening, Mr...." He seems more pleased I don't know his last name than disappointed. "I hope your night is as pleasant as mine is about to become."

I wish I could stay so his growl could glide across every inch of me instead of solely my face, but with the elevator doors beginning to close, I have no time to spare.

I duck under Andrik's arm and hightail it for the exit, almost in the clear before my wrist is snatched and I'm yanked back with a rueful tug.

Instincts have me rearing up for a fight. My hand sails wildly before I can consider the consequences of my actions. It slaps Andrik so firmly across the face that his head slings sideways.

It does little to loosen his grip on my wrist, though.

It firms to the point of being painful, and the frozen state it prompts sees not a single protest fired when he pins me to the internal wall of the elevator by my throat.

His grip isn't painful.

It is the most erotic way I've ever been held.

As he stares down at me with flaring nostrils, I try to work out why he isn't responding how he should be. He should be pissed I struck him, or at the very least, warning me of the consequences that will occur if I do it again. His reaction, however, is on the opposite end of the spectrum. He's smiling, and lust flares through his eyes so potently I do the last thing anyone should do when they've caught the focus of a madman.

I kiss him.

7

ANDRIK

*S*weet. Fucking. Damnation.

One glance seared my soul, but one brush of a pair of pouty lips seals my fate.

Zoya Galdean is going to ruin me.

No ifs.

No buts.

She will ruin me, but I refuse to withdraw.

Honey lips, pert tits, and a heat I'm so impatient to have wrapped around me I don't think about my little brother and how he only ever hands his keys to the girls he truly likes, or the deal with the devil I initiated today that should have my cock withering away instead of knocking at my zipper, vying to get free.

I don't think about anything but the number of moans I can entice out of Zoya with a sloppy, messy kiss and how far she will let me take this now that she's had a taste of what I can offer her.

When I pull her body flush against mine, she moans, as impatient as me and just as ready.

It isn't solely the scent I smell shadowing her panties announcing this. The wetness that coats my fingers when I slip my hand under her skirt and rub my fingertips over the sensitive flesh between her legs is also telling.

"Fuck, милая. Is all this wetness for me?"

I don't wait for her to answer me.

She'd only lie, and then I'd have to punish her.

I'd rather have her limp with sexual exhaustion than a tanned ass, so I inch her off the handrail hindering the natural roll of her hips, and then slowly slip a finger inside her.

"Tight. So fucking tight."

My thumb circles her clit, once again stealing her rebuttal.

"Don't be ashamed. The tighter you are, the fewer men I'll have to track down once I've had my fill."

She watches me with hooded, dilated eyes as I slowly pump in and out of her. I don't do gentle. Lovemaking isn't my specialty, though the flare of Zoya's nostrils when I treat her with a delicacy she was certain I didn't hold has me in no hurry to mix things up.

I take my time, loving how her cunt sucks at my finger as freely as her delicious scent lingers in my nostrils.

"How many men am I seeking, милая?"

I slant my head to hide my smile when she says with a moan, "None."

Lying to me is usually punishable by death.

She won't face the same level of wrath—purely because I know she is lying for me, not the insolent fools who let her go. She's afraid my jealousy will have me pulling on the reins, stopping a train God himself couldn't slow.

She has no reason to fret.

Even as I was placing the pieces on the chessboard for a verified win, she didn't leave my mind for a second. I palmed my cock as often today as I did the first time I visited a strip club.

I was eleven during my inaugural visit to my uncle's club, so I had the perfect excuse for my dick popping up to say hello.

Today, I had no damn excuse.

And the remembrance pisses me off so much I get arrogant.

"One?"

I watch Zoya like my palm isn't coated with her juices, and her moans don't have me on the cusp of coming in my pants like a soft cock who has never sampled an untouched cunt.

When her face gives nothing away, I say, "Two?"

She doesn't twitch, glower, or flinch.

She just moans.

"Three? Are there three notches on your bedpost, *милая*?"

I finger fuck her harder when a flare darts through her eyes. It isn't a confirming glint, more a flicker announcing I'm getting close to her body count.

"Four?"

Her eyes snap to mine so fast I get the answer I'm seeking without a word spilling from her lips.

She looks embarrassed. It better be because she's worried I'll think her count is too high and not because she's ashamed of the low figure she amassed in the prior decade or so.

I won't handle the latter.

Jealousy has never been an issue of mine. That could be more because virgins were always my top pick.

I never had an interest in another man's leftovers.

I can't say the same now.

I'll still seek names. It just won't be until I've finished making Zoya scream mine.

I don't bother hiding my smile when Zoya strives to keep things even between us. "What about you? What's your count?"

"Does it matter?" I ask while swiping my thumb over her clit.

"Y-yes," she stammers out, her breathing picking up. "If you know mine, it's only fair I know yours."

"There you go with that *if* again, *милая*."

The wetness of her arousal almost drowns out her groan when I work her harder, faster. I toy with her clit until I can add a second finger to the mix without hurting her. Then I return my attention to our conversation.

"If is an uncertainty, a doubt."

When her back rests on the wall of the elevator as she struggles to fill her lungs with air, I tilt her hips higher, opening her up to me.

"It doesn't belong between us. This"—I palm my cock, which is throbbing with so much want a circle of wetness is just left of the tip —"this is the only thing between us, and not even it is an uncertainty." She whimpers desperately when I growl out, "You will take my cock. Every. Hardened. Inch." Then she shudders when my lips brush the shell of her ear. "And then you'll thank me for the orgasms that rip through your body by giving me the name of the *Долбоеб* who did you so wrong you thought abstinence was your only option." We moan in sync when her pussy clenches around my fingers. "He's the only one I won't take my time with. Because if it weren't for him, my kill count for one night may have notched higher than my one-night body count."

Zoya's cheeks burn with embarrassment, brighter and stronger than before.

Or is it jealousy?

We skipped official introductions, so I haven't paid enough attention to her quirks to be able to decipher them just yet. My sole focus has been on concealing my jealousy.

Since I've done a shit fucking job, I stop beating around the bush and get to the point.

"Four is manageable, *милая*. I can deal with four." I lean into her so closely her nipples scrape my chest with every breath she takes. "Six?" My tsk rumbles through both our chests before it vibrates my lips. "Don't test me on six because I can guarantee neither you nor him will survive the outcome."

8
ZOYA

My life was just threatened by a man with his hand down the front of my panties. The same man who has no qualms announcing he keeps a tally of his bed companions *and* his kills, yet the only response my body elicits is devastation when he removes his fingers from my pussy and pops the glistening digits into his mouth.

I've always been a little wild, but this is batshit crazy.

He *threatened* my life. I shouldn't be skimming over that fact. He's handsome as sin and has desire pulsing through my body in a way it's never experienced. Still, morals need to enter the equation somewhere. Lust can't always take center stage.

"I... um. I forgot to remove my phone charger from the port in my car. It'll drain the battery if I don't—"

Stupidly, my knees pull together when Andrik growls partway through my excuse to leave.

I wait for the spark it caused to diminish before correcting my error. "It *will* drain the battery, so I *must* remove it."

After licking his fingers clean like they're coated in cake batter,

Andrik tugs down my skirt until it returns to its pre-whore length. Then he places his hand on the curve of my back and guides me out of the elevator.

"I'll send someone down to do it. Though it won't really matter. You won't be driving that piece of shit for much longer."

"Because?" I ask, too shocked to wade through my confusion alone.

He drops his eyes to mine. They're still full of the lust that saw me toppling into ecstasy with only the lightest of stimulation, but something deeper and more tangible is darkening them. "Because that make and model isn't safe. I'll organize an SUV or a hybrid with a higher safety rating."

I sound nowhere near as smart as my GPA indicates. "You're going to buy me a car?"

"Yes," he answers casually.

"Why?" I talk fast when I'm nervous. "And will that be before or after you track down the *Долбоеб*"—my attempt to mimic his accent is horrendous—"who saved you from needing to have a quintuple-some to keep your reputation intact?"

Of course he veers for the part of my statement that has nothing to do with the threat of murder. "Quintuplesome?"

"I couldn't think of a name for a threesome with two extra participants."

He opens a door at the end of a long hall, dropping my jaw. This place is massive—well outside even my mother's range. I don't get the chance to enjoy the splendor.

"You could have said a gangbang, *милая*."

"And you could have just shut up and made me come instead of worrying about men previously not up to the task. Alas, I've yet to meet a man who uses the brain above his shoulders when he's—"

I snap my mouth shut before I can dig my hole any deeper.

"When he's...?" Andrik pushes, looking smug. "Fucking?

Consuming? Rocking someone's entire existence with only his fingers?"

His smug expression grows when I bark, "I was going to say, 'when he's too hard to think straight.' But if you're seeking a pat on the back you've been denied since birth, we can go with whatever you want."

His husky laugh makes me hot, and I hate myself for it. I'm meant to be finding a way out of his clutch, not doubling my wish to stay. "I don't know whether I should teach you some manners with my hand or my cane."

Cane?

He said cane, right? I didn't mishear him. My pulse is still thudding in my ears, so a mishap is easily excusable.

Our entrance into the living room of the penthouse apartment assures me I don't need my hearing tested. A lady is kneeling on the floor in the middle of the opulent space. She's naked, her head is bowed, and her hands are balanced on her trembling thighs, palm side up.

Even to a BDSM novice, her pose is obvious.

"Leave. Now."

Andrik doesn't need to ask me twice. I hightail it to the door, almost beating the brunette who moves like the wind—silent yet swift.

"Not you."

Andrik tugs me back with the same cruel yank he used in the elevator, so naturally, my instincts respond with the same level of violence.

Again, my slap turns him on more than it annoys him. The front of his pants tightens as the most wickedly evil smirk makes his face even sexier.

"Shouldn't that be the equivalent of eye-rolling to you?" I didn't read as many romance novels as Nikita did during college, but I'm reasonably sure slapping is a no-go for a submissive to do to her dom. "Was she your sub?"

"She doesn't matter."

His curt reply announces his lifestyle status isn't up for negotiation. I can't help but push, though. "I'll take that as a yes." I hook my thumb to the door his submissive just raced through. "I'm going to go."

"Sit, *Лисичка*."

I continue walking as if I'm not the least bit curious about his changeup in nicknames.

"Now!"

I'm not given the option to keep walking this time. He tosses his suit jacket onto an armchair before he bands his arm around my waist and pulls me back until I land in a secondary chair with a clatter.

When I kick and punch, several of my blows make contact. He doesn't react negatively until I drag my nails down his cheek. "Settle down before I take you on the very fucking floor she was most likely kneeling on for the past sixteen-plus hours, awaiting her master." He grips my face firm enough for his nails to dig into my cheek but not enough to leave a mark before he forces my eyes back to his. "I didn't order her. She was most likely a gift. A welcome home present, as such. Tonight is the first time I've laid eyes on her."

There's too much honesty in his narrowed gaze for me to dispute, and Andrik knows that.

He's as smug now as he was when I failed to announce a single protest to him slipping his hand inside my panties.

"Not that you would have cared if she was mine."

My heart thuds in my ears when he falls to his knees, forcing a gap between my thighs with his wide frame.

"You like that I picked you over her, that I didn't even look in her direction."

He drags the back of his hand down my panties that are so soaked they erotically display the lines of my pussy.

"Because you know as well as I do that no woman could *ever* compete with you."

He *tsks* me again. Its rumble rolls through my throbbing clit when my desire to ease the ache between my legs sees me minimizing my thigh gap.

After pulling them back to his desired width, he says, "I worked for that scent, so I deserve to cherish it."

His eye contact is too intimate when he watches me over the heavy rise and fall of my chest as he drags his nose down the seam of my panties.

It doubles the slickness between my legs in an instant and has me on the verge of begging.

I won't, though.

If I talk, I'll moan, and that will only be seen as a victory to a man as dominant as Andrik.

After hooking his index finger into the lacy hem of my panties, he slowly peels it away from my weeping sex. "Is that where you went wrong, милая? Did they leave you unsatisfied because you were too afraid to tell them what you wanted?" His eyes are back on me, hooded and heavy. "What you craved." He doesn't wait for me to answer. "You don't need to be afraid. I have no trouble following directions."

His smirk—kill me now.

It has me so horny that I can't think of a single thing that doesn't include his mouth on my pussy in some way.

"When it comes to sex. I wouldn't test my patience outside that realm, though."

He bends his head low, bringing his mouth closer to my pussy. As you can imagine, that halts any anger I'm experiencing for being underhandedly threatened again.

I shouldn't be doing this. I should have stopped it the instant he slid his hand under my skirt, but the need is too perverse. Too dangerous.

Living without sex is a tormented existence no woman should be forced to endure, and although Andrik gives off the vibe of a man who chews through women as often as he makes money, this battle is bigger than any I've experienced.

I'll never win.

I also want him—everywhere.

There's no denying that when I jerk up my hips, mashing my panties-covered pussy with his mouth. I'm brimming with so much sexual energy I almost freefall into ecstasy from his nose ramming into my aching clit, so you can picture how hard it is for me to hold back when he goes to town on my pussy.

He sucks on my clit, scrapes it with his teeth, and then plunges his tongue deep inside me.

"Keep your eyes on me," Andrik demands when my body goes so pliable under his touch that my head thrusts back.

The hungry, desperate look in his eyes when our gazes collide is almost my undoing. Sexual energy charges through me, leaving goose bumps in its wake. I shudder from its intensity and then gasp when the briefest brush of his hand along my thigh doubles my efforts to keep a rational head.

"Oh, my sweet *милая*. Those men were fools."

One hand shoots to his hair while the other turns white from my grip on the armchair's rolled wooden arm when he slides his thumb through the mess his tongue made. He wets it with my arousal before he uses it to toy my clit into a hardened bud.

"You smell so fucking delicious. *Taste* so fucking delicious. They were just too selfish to ever discover that, weren't they?"

I don't get in a single headshake before he backhands my clit, sending my mind as spiraling into the abyss as my lie. I've had men go down on me before. It was more of a lick-and-spit routine to make me wet enough for penetration. It was never about my pleasure.

I doubt it was even for theirs.

"Foolish, insolent men who won't be missed when I wipe their existence from society."

As quickly as a bid for clemency forms for men I'm unsure deserve his leniency, it disappears. Arrogant Jerks seems to have been my flavor of the month when I dated, but that isn't the cause of my backflip. It is the way Andrik buries his head back between my legs before he tugs me off the seat until the only thing keeping me suspended is his face.

As I balance on his face like a cowgirl riding a mechanical bull, he eats me with a skill set I've never experienced. He drags his tongue the entire length of my pussy before he circles it around my clit and uses it as a guide to suck the nervy bud into his mouth.

I lose my battle when his teeth prove pain can have a place beside pleasure.

As my body convulses through its first non-solo expedition in over two years, I come with a breathy moan. The crest of pleasure tumbling through my womb is long and stimulating. It revitalizes a part of me I tried to tuck away over a decade ago and has me vying to never let her slip away again.

I've just got to survive this orgasm first.

It is intense, blistering—the best I've ever had.

The tingles refuse to stop when Andrik positions me back onto the armchair before he stalks to the other side of the room while undoing his button-up shirt. He has such an arrogant walk. Chest puffed, signature angry sneer every dark and dangerous man should have, and an aura of power.

He screams sex and intrigue, and I'm too trapped under his spell to consider an escape plan.

"What are you looking for?" I ask when he searches the coffee table drawer, a side drawer, and several boxes on an entryway table.

He mutters, "Finally," a second after popping open the lid of a trinket box on top of the grand piano.

I reach my own conclusion when he heads back my way. The foil disk in his hand can't be mistaken, not to mention how he rips it open with his teeth while his free hand works his belt through the loops of his pricy trousers.

A condom.

Pleasure still blazes through me, burning me from the inside out, but now I'm also worried. The girth plumping out the crotch of Andrik's trousers can't be missed. He's hard and jutted, and I struggled to accept his fingers without pain, so questioning my ability to take his cock is understandable.

It is huge, fat, and does that boing every girl fantasizes about when they conjure up the man of their dreams as he yanks his boxers past his trimmed yet still mannish balls.

I am confident it will not fit inside me.

"Andr—"

"Page thirty-three will have to wait."

After sliding the condom down his lengthy girth, he looks up at me and winks. I almost climax again. His confidence is as thrilling as the veins feeding his magnificent cock.

"As much as I want to watch you ride my cock as well as you did my face, I want to drink in your expression the first time you swallow my cock more."

He shrugs off his button-up shirt and toes off his shoes before he grabs a handful of pillows from a three-seater couch. After tossing them onto an expensive-looking rug, he plucks me from the armchair like I don't weigh a thing, and then he undresses me.

He takes his time, savoring every moment, until I'm standing before him in a pair of lacy panties and heels I'm confident were designed to pierce a man's ass while he fucks you hard and fast.

Andrik smiles, convincing me that he heard my inner monologue, before he walks me toward the fort of pillows.

"Sweet... *lord*..." I push out between big breaths when a second after he lays me onto the rug, he returns his mouth to my pussy.

He doesn't bother slipping my panties to the side this time. He sucks my clit through the drenched material before he uses their scantness as a tissue to mop up some of the mess inside.

For several long minutes, he feasts on me with a skill that suddenly bombards me with jealousy and until his name is added to the guttural moans ripping from my throat.

Then he does it again—minus interfering panties this time.

I'm so limp and pliant after the umpteenth orgasm courses through me that it takes several long seconds to realize he paid more attention to the brochure in Dr. Hemway's office than he made out.

After pocketing my panties with no concern that they're the only pair I am traveling with, he positions me as per the cartoon character instructions on page seventeen. Instead of stuffing pillows under my hips on a bed, he does it on the floor of his living room, and he kneels between my legs instead of standing at the foot of the mattress.

Doubt creeps through my veins, turning them icy.

If he's following the recommendations of the brochure, does that mean he knows about my condition? Is he aware that I am broken?

He couldn't. Otherwise he wouldn't look at me like he does. No one has ever looked at me with so much desire. Don't get me wrong, they liked what they saw and came quick enough for me to never doubt my attractiveness. They just had that disappointed, this-will-only-ever-be-a-one-night-affair expression seconds after finishing.

Andrik is making out like page seventeen is foreplay, and we will explore other positions later.

I shoot my eyes to Andrik's face when he braces the crown of his thick cock against the opening of my pussy. He doesn't wait for permission to enter me. He slowly notches in, his speed and eye contact as painful as the burn of his stretch.

I'm drenched front to back, but no amount of wetness could prepare any woman for a man of his size. He is bigger than any man I've been with and shockingly more gentle.

I didn't think he had it in him. He portrays a man who likes to fuck. Hence my body tightening instead of loosening when he notches in the first couple of inches, so to say I'm shocked is an understatement—a big one.

"Christ," he hisses like a snake. "You're so fucking tight."

With one hand under my hips, lifting them higher, he sinks in another couple of inches before flexing his cock.

Shockingly, I moan. He's deeper than I've been taken, filling every inch of me. Other than the burn of being stretched beyond my limits, the pain is bearable. Pleasurable, even.

"It must be the position."

It dawns on me that I said my thought out loud when Andrik replies to it. "Or perhaps because I didn't come within two seconds of being strangled by your cunt, милая. A lesser man wouldn't have been able to hold back." Desire races through my veins when he mutters under his breath, "Doesn't mean I will go any easier on them." He rakes his eyes down my body, his trek starting at the area where we're intimately joined before arriving at my eyes. "Just the thought of them seeing you like this—"

A throaty groan cuts off his reply. I don't know if it came from Andrik or me. His fast grip of my throat could have forced out the last of the air in my windpipe, or the swiftness of his moves when he raced to grip my throat could have mimicked the sound of someone gasping for their last breath.

His grasp on my throat is firm but not painful. It is an erotic hold that has me as desperate to be ravaged as I am for my next breath. It increases my wetness enough for Andrik to pull out to the tip without hindrance, and although his reentrance is faster than his earlier endeavor, it is still at a painstakingly slow pace that shows mammoth constraint.

His body shakes as he tries to hold back the urge to drive into me like a madman, and his fight is my undoing.

I want to be taken hard and fast, fucked so dangerously my cracked insides will have nothing to do with an infertility diagnosis.

I want him to claim me.

When I say that to Andrik, his fingers curled around my neck flex as a Russian cussword leaves his mouth. The primal urge to fuck is beaming out of him, his restraint at its last tether.

He wants this as much as I do. There's just something holding him back.

I think I know what it is, and I can't help but use it to push him over the edge.

"Unless you want to reserve the glory for Mikhail?"

My scream echoes around the penthouse apartment when he thrusts into me with one ardent pump. He takes me to the base of his cock, eliciting a combination of moans, pain, and tingles.

They're all as frantic as the rest. I can't get enough. I feel used and dirty, but I also feel like this is what my body was designed for. To be pleasured and to give pleasure. It isn't just a vessel of parenthood. It is much more than that.

"Yes, Andrik," I hiss through lips that are suddenly bone dry. "Fuck me."

He drives in and out of me, pinning me to the mountain of cushions that are soon replaced with his arm when he loses control. They're no match for the power of his grinds, flattened with every perfect pump.

"This..." I meet him grind for grind as he thrusts harder, faster.

He uses every muscle in his body to command every nerve I own. "This cunt... this scent..." I almost vault out of his arms when he backhands my clit with his last word. "They're going to ruin me." Tremors of an orgasm surface faster than I can contain when he locks his eyes with mine and says, "You're going to ruin me, Zoya Galdean. However, I'd still sign up like a schmuck time and time again anytime it is placed up on offer."

An orgasm pulses through me, but he doesn't stop. He continues plowing into me until the wetness slicking my skin matches the slippery mess between my legs.

Andrik is wearing a condom, so all the hot dampness coating my pussy, ass, and thighs is mine.

I'd be embarrassed if it didn't drive him wild. The wetter I become, the harder he drives into me. He fucks me into oblivion until all I can do is surrender to the madness.

I shove my head back and scream through a blistering of stars, certain the only person about to be ruined is me.

9

ANDRIK

*M*y steps into the living room of my brother's penthouse slow when I detect I am being watched. Being eyeballed like I perform tricks for coin is nothing out of the ordinary for me. People as old as dirt and as fresh as a newborn baby forever watch me. It started at my fifth birthday party and has continued to grow along with my reputation for being a tyrant of a man over the past thirty years.

It is the disapproval in the gawk, however, that has me on the back foot.

People are usually too scared to project their wrath in my direction, even when I am the perpetrator of their suffering.

There's only one man foolish enough to not hide his disdain.

My little brother, Mikhail.

His shirtless torso is leaning on the overhead cupboard in his industrial-sized kitchen, and he's nursing a mug of freshly brewed coffee.

I don't need to ask if he knows I used his bachelor pad for the very reason he purchased it. I felt his beady eyes on me seconds after he engaged the alarm on his prototype motorcycle.

The first emotion he portrayed when he learned his bed was warming two bodies instead of one was smugness.

It was quickly followed by annoyance.

I thought it was because he believed his sheets were smeared with the cum of the woman he left kneeling for hours on end to test her obedience, but learn otherwise when he nudges his head to a wad of envelopes on the kitchen island.

"They were delivered to the hotel this morning. Figured you must have been here since you failed to show up at the bar last night."

He folds his arms over his chest, doubling my smirk. Intimidation is not Mikhail's forte. He can charm the panties off any lady he wants, but he's shit at staining the briefs of our competitors. It's why he sticks to the operation and maintenance side of our company's extensive real estate portfolio.

I'm the muscle *and* the brains.

"What the fuck are you doing treating my crash pad like a brothel, *brother*?" He spits out his last word like we won't have words about it later. I don't tolerate disrespect from anyone... *except from perhaps her.*

"You told her she had free range." I fan my hands out like the pompous prick my mother's disappearance caused me to become. "I took full advantage."

I laugh when my reply angers him enough that he grips the lapels of my suit and pulls me to within an inch of his face.

He can be angry all he likes. He knows as well as I do that Zoya wasn't interested in what he was offering.

I combed over the footage of their first and *only* meeting for hours this morning.

The truth never wavered.

Mikhail invited Zoya here because he knew I wouldn't be able to resist, so he has no right to be angry that I acted *exactly* as predicted.

When I say that to him, he loosens his grip before pushing me back with enough force that I crash into the island.

As I glare at him, I straighten my suit jacket while striving to fight the urge to settle our disagreement with my fists. It wouldn't be the first time we've come to blows. Doubt it would be the last.

"When did you realize she was who I was seeking?"

I called Mikhail during my drive to the Sakharoff residence. I wanted to know if Zoya was local, and if she was, how the fuck did she fly under the radar for so long? I haven't classed Chelabini as my hometown for years, but my family is well-known here. My call went to voicemail. The interrogation I hit his voicemail with, however, remained on point.

I smirk when he answers, "You wear desperate as obviously as every other man." He places his mug into the sink before spinning to face me. "But I guess that's over with now? You never hang around long after the deed. I was surprised to find you still here this morning." His expression doesn't match his tone. He looks cocky but sounds uneased.

"Perhaps," I shockingly reply.

I'm usually out the door before my cum has cooled in the condom I knot and take with me, so perhaps Mikhail is right. Maybe something is off-kilter with me, but sitting around and talking about it is the equivalent of sawing off my cock and handing it to my competitor's wife instead of fucking her with it as well as I plan to fuck over her husband—lackluster and pointless.

Mikhail doesn't feel the same way.

"Perhaps?" His voice is loud enough to wake half the continent. "What do you mean *perhaps*?" His eyes widen as his mouth gapes. "You're still going through with *that*?" He nudges his head to the wad of envelopes Dr. Hemway must have delivered before the sparrows woke when he spits out the last word. He must read something on my face I didn't mean to express. "Are you fucking insane? You got the cream of the crop and enough chemistry to rival an atom bomb, but you're going to toss it aside for a spineless *слизняк* born solely for procreation?"

Now it's my turn to pin him to the kitchen cabinet. I don't give a fuck what he calls the women bred to line their parents' pockets with money. It is his mention of the sparks firing between Zoya and me that I pay the most attention to.

I tighten my grip around his throat before leaning in close enough for my spit to sizzle on his red cheeks. "You better not have seen a single snippet of her skin or not even your last name will save you."

Mikhail likes to fuck. When he's not fucking, he likes watching other people fuck. He has all his favorite possessions wired up with surveillance for that exact purpose. My cock was just too fucking obsessed with how good Zoya smelled to remember that last night.

It still is.

"I didn't see shit. I turned off all surveillance when she slapped you." It is not the time for my cock to twitch. It can't be helped. Zoya's gall is one of her sexiest assets, not that I will ever tell her that. "But I saw enough to know you're a fool if you think you can replace her with one of those... *robots*."

Since I observe nothing but truth in his eyes and tone, I let him go. It is a fucking hard feat. My blood is boiling black. I'm struggling to work out which way is up. Now is not the time to fuck with me.

"I'm not letting her go for anyone." I should have taken more time to consider my next sentence before expressing it because it sounds wrong even to someone as unapologetic as me. "But I won't get the answers I'm seeking without someone who can supplement what she lacks, so I'll—"

"Supplement what she lacks?" Mikhail shakes his head in

disgust. "Fuck, Andrik. Here I was thinking you were *nothing* like them." I've been called every name you can imagine, but his scold burns hotter than any before it when he sneers, "How fucking wrong was I?"

I want to tell him he is wrong, or better yet, ram his words back into his throat with my fists, but since I stupidly care for the brat who's refused to let me forget a single birthday since my mother's disappearance thirty years ago, I veer our conversation in a way I never anticipated it taking.

"Zoya is infertile."

Mikhail balks for half a second before understanding settles on his face.

What the fuck?

"It kind of makes sense." He shrugs like what he's implying is as regular as brushing your teeth every morning. It's fucked to admit I agree with him when he adds, "She would have been shacked up and knocked up years ago if she didn't have any... *issues*." He wets his lips like he is remorseful for his last word, but regretfully, he doesn't keep his mouth shut. "Fortunately for me, I have no intention of following *their* rules, which means ankle biters won't enter the equation when I woo her back into my bed, minus my spineless brother—"

My fist cracks into his nose before another word seeps from his lips, and it takes everything I have not to hit him for a second, third, and fourth time when he remains quiet.

Although the blood gushing over his lips could excuse his lack of retort, I don't believe a bloody nose is the cause of his silence.

He's pleased I reacted how he wanted me to—because it is the only thing that will convince him that I haven't become a direct clone of our father.

While pretending a hundred thoughts aren't running through my head, I work my jaw side to side. Not all my thoughts center on how deep I'll bury Mikhail if he tries to make true on his threat. They just take center stage.

After a beat, I ask, "Do you have any pain medication here, or do I need to get some delivered?"

"It's fine. It doesn't hurt," Mikhail lies, assuming I'm seeking pain medication for him.

I'm not.

"It isn't for you, dipshit, though you should probably take something." The pretentious gleam I'm striving to ignore in his eyes flares brighter when I mutter, "It's for Zoya."

I've had women say they couldn't walk straight for a week after being bedded by me.

This is the first time I've cared if the rumors are true.

"Top left." Mikhail nudges his head to a cupboard behind me before he moves to fetch a tea towel for his nose and a clean mug out of the dishwasher I stacked last night for Zoya.

A coffee pot suspends midair when I say, "Orange juice. She can swallow them with orange juice."

He takes my snappy tone in stride with only the slightest grumble. "If you want to make your cum taste sweeter, you're meant to drink pineapple juice, fuckface."

"Citrus juice alleviates the pain associated with her condition—"

I snap my mouth shut way too late.

The cat is out of the bag.

I seek Mikhail's nuts in his throat when he says in a high-pitched tone, "You researched her condition?"

"No, I didn't."

He doesn't believe my lie for even a second. "Is it reversible?"

"No."

Again, he sees straight through my lie I'm not even sure is a lie.

From what I researched last night, the prognosis of Zoya's diagnosis differs between patients. Some have no trouble getting pregnant with a bit of help. Others never will.

"What does she have to do to fix it? Surely orange juice isn't the only solution."

I snatch the glass out of his hand and fill it with fresh OJ. "Nothing. There's nothing she can do."

"Can you even lie straight in bed anymore, Kazimir?" He uses my given name on purpose. He wants to piss me off. "You have the girl of my dreams in my bed, yet you're acting like she's far from your highly impeccable standards." He air quotes his last three words. "Fuck the bro code. You didn't give a shit about it last night when you noticed she had my keys, so why should I give a fuck about the two minutes of attention I'll need to award her with to help her get over you?"

There's nothing nice about my hold this time around, nothing brotherly to it. It is the grip of a murderer, and one that leaves my little brother so breathless he scratches at my hand, certain he is moments from death.

Once his lips turn a fascinating shade of blue, I loosen my grip. Not a lot. Just enough to ensure his panic is low enough he will hear the sheer honesty of my words. "If you touch her, I *will* kill you."

For some insane reason, I want to protect Zoya. The easiest way to achieve that would be to keep her as far away from my family as possible.

That isn't something I can do.

Zoya Galdean is mine, and I'll annihilate anyone who implies otherwise. I just can't announce that publicly until I fix the monumental fuckup I initiated last night that has nothing to do with bedding the woman I'm certain will destroy me.

10

ZOYA

*a*n unusual aroma wakes me. It isn't unpleasant, more unexpected. It is citrusy and fresh, a stark contradiction to the smells I'm accustomed to waking up to in my apartment.

My building is on the worst street in Myasnikov, yet probably the safest.

Greed is a slavery that will never entrap the poor.

After scrubbing a hand over my eyes I'm certain are a mess, I peer in the direction of the scent. The fruity fragrance makes sense when I discover an oversized glass of orange juice on the bedside table. It is butted against an unopened packet of pain medication.

My body is sore enough to warrant intervention, just not in the way I expected when I gave in to my desires last night. I thought the pain would be unwanted because I never anticipated for it to be a pleasurable throb.

My muscles are sore, but it is more in response to the number of orgasms I experienced than the side effects of endometriosis.

Last night was amazing, and although some could say my high

rating could be attributed to a long abstinence from sex, I'm doubtful.

Andrik rocked my world, proving his cocky statement in Dr. Hemway's examination room was true.

No man has ever fucked me like he did, and I doubt any man after him will compare.

Is it wrong of me to contemplate future bedmates so soon after my last conquest? I would have said no if I'd detected an ounce of Andrik's presence in his home. If the lack of arrogance in the air is anything to go by, he left hours ago.

Although caffeine will always be my go-to pick-me-up, I swallow two pain tablets with a mouthful of orange juice before slinging my legs off the edge of the bed and taking a leisurely stretch.

I'm as naked as the day I was born, which means there's no coverage for the mess my condition caused the no-doubt three-thousand-plus thread count sheets.

I had no clue I had bled last night. Not the slightest bit of disgust crossed Andrik's face when he plucked me from the living room floor and walked me to the kitchen to quieten the loud demands of my hungry stomach.

He was so attentive and sweet while replenishing the energy he had exhausted that the shock of the unexpected treatment saw us undertaking round two shortly after the first round had wrapped up.

That time, dessert was consumed on the kitchen counter.

Page thirty-three was as mind-boggling as the cartoon characters portrayed, and it had me swooning like crazy.

I passed out from exhaustion on Andrik's mammoth bed seconds after the umpteenth orgasm careened through my body. I'm reasonably sure Andrik was on the brink of exhaustion with me, but I can't attest to that. That's how out of it I was.

Mercifully the smears of blood on the sheets are faint. Not faded enough for me not to strip the bedding and search for a washing machine, but they're not so horrific that I'll need to purchase a new set.

"Come on. There has to be a laundry room here somewhere," I murmur to myself when my search of every nook and cranny surrounding the living room comes up empty-handed. There are a hundred spots to hang a coat, but not a single washing machine to be seen.

When I return to the bedroom, lugging the sheets I stripped from the mattress, I sling my eyes to the massive walk-in closet. I only saw one-half of it when I snuck into the bathroom in the darkness of the night to pee away any possible nasties. What I saw was impressive. The room has side-by-side walk-in closets that lead to a bathroom as large as the living room.

I didn't see a washer–dryer combo, but my visit was shrouded by darkness. It's large enough to hold a concealed laundry area, so I head toward the opening wide enough to park my car between.

I'll never be more grateful for a king-size bed when I'm greeted upon entering the walk-in closet.

"Hey there, Sunshine."

As Mikhail pulls a pair of jeans over his ass, sans underwear, I tug the sheets in close to my body—my *naked* body.

Mikhail's grin he fails to hide with a tilted chin announces he heard my gulp. He acts ignorant, though. "Do you always strip the bed after messing the sheets?"

"I... We..." Once again, that stumbling idiot better step back before I smack her. "What are you doing here, Mikhail?" Like a freight train missing the station, the truth smacks into me. "There aren't two penthouse apartments in this building, is there?" He shakes his head, leaving the excavation search for my brain up to me. "Andrik was so—"

"Andrik?" Mikhail interrupts, his brow high.

My mouth gapes as horror rains down on me.

Did I invite a stranger into Mikhail's home?

The hits keep coming.

Did I sleep with said stranger in Mikhail's bed?

I refuse to mention the other numerous surfaces we treated like a set of a porn movie franchise, or I'll never leave our exchange with my dignity intact.

Mikhail's silence bombards me with confusion. Anytime I'm confused, I turn into a blubbering idiot. "He knew the code. He let us in. I assumed this was his penthouse."

I'm seconds from falling to my knees and begging when Mikhail's ruse is broken by a hefty stint of laughter. "He knows the code because his tech company designed the system installed here."

"So you know Andrik?" Please excuse my daftness. I only got a few hours of sleep, and my brain is still in a lust haze.

I breathe out a sigh of relief when Mikhail jerks up his chin, but I still feel terrible that I treated his place of residence like a whore house. I'm also going to need to replace his sheets. Washing them was satisfactory when I thought they belonged to the man partially responsible for the stains. I can't continue with that ruse now.

"I honestly thought this was Andrik's place. I would have never—"

"Stop," Mikhail interrupts, padding closer like he has no idea I'm naked behind heavenly layers of softness. "You've got nothing to apologize for."

"I used your home as a—"

"The very thing it was purchased for." He smiles and winks, and although they shouldn't, their friskiness conjures up memories of the dark and dangerous man I was wrestling last night. "I didn't have the laundry installed next to the bedroom for no reason."

He skirts by me to open a double glossed door at the other end. It exposes the washer–dryer combination I was seeking.

Mikhail takes a moment to relish the gratitude on my face before flicking his eyes to a dresser on his right. "My old college shirts will still swamp you, but I was a little scrawnier back then, so it'll look more like a dress than a potato sack." He nudges his head to the bathroom I visited last night. "Spare toothbrushes are in the second drawer, hair dryer is under the vanity, and any folded towel is unused."

He's about to give me privacy I'm not sure I deserve before he remembers something that sees him spinning like a ballerina. "There's a handful of girlie shit in the bottom drawer of the vanity. If they're not to your satisfaction, I can go grab you anything you need."

I'm lost to what he's referencing. Girlie shit could mean anything. Makeup. Deodorant. Those annoying floss sticks Nikita is rarely without. There are literally millions of things he could be referring to.

My cheeks turn the color of beets when he lowers his eyes to the sheets I'm clutching.

On darker sheets, the micro smear wouldn't be noticeable. On pure-white sheets, it stands out like... You get the picture.

"I'm sure whatever you have is fine. I'm not menstruating. It's a side effect of a broken... *vagina.*"

Someone dig a hole so I can bury my shameful face in it.

I'm too weak from embarrassment to do it myself.

Mikhail must have a ton of sisters. He shrugs off my embarrassment as if it is as weightless as a midge before he heads for the exit. "All right. Cool. Though you should probably keep that"—he waves his hand at the lower half of my body—"between us. Andrik's head is big enough. He'll have trouble walking if he learns he broke your pussy."

He twists his torso to face me, his smile matching the one I'm struggling to keep under wraps. He reminds me so much of Nikita. If I didn't believe opposites attract, I'd be introducing them at the first available opportunity.

Nikita needs someone who will fight tooth and nail to protect her, and although Mikhail's guns look capable of taking down a mountain lion with one punch, the dusting of a bruise under his eye weakens my hypothesis.

He'd fight to the death, but I need to be one hundred percent confident he'd win before I ever recommend him to Nikita.

Mikhail shifts my focus back to him. "While you shower, I'll cancel the truckload of chocolate I ordered to tame the beast I thought was pulverizing your uterus and replace the extravagance with a table for two at Tsar's." It's already a fight to hold back my grin, and I lose the battle when he says, "We need to fill our bellies before our second stakeout, and what better place to do that than at the very restaurant our target is scheduled to visit."

Almost an hour later, I exit Mikhail's bedroom under the whistling approval of its owner.

"Hot fucking damn, Sunshine. My shirt has never looked so good." When he signals for me to twirl around, I can't help but oblige. I still feel horrible for overstretching his hospitality, so I'll be just as indulging while vying to show my gratitude. "This is hot..." He tugs on my high ponytail. "And this is hot..." His college shirt I knotted into the middle of my stomach with a hair tie is awarded its own yank this time. "But when they're combined with that..." He playfully growls when his eyes lower to the pleated skirt I'm wearing sans panties since Andrik appears to have taken them with him. "Fuck me. Naughty is the *only* appropriate word."

I smile to express my thanks for the confidence boost before I drop my eyes to his mug of coffee. "Would I be pushing the boundaries if I asked for one of those?"

Mikhail cranks his neck to the kitchen island before replying, "Not at all." He makes me a coffee with the same flare Andrik used last night to make us dinner, before almost handing it to me. I say *almost* as he pulls it back before I take it. "Did you finish your orange juice?"

"Orange juice?" I murmur, acting stupid.

I'd rather portray an idiot than a lovesick chump who thought her one-night-only bed companion left her post-sex recovery supplies.

I can't believe I thought the juice and tablets were from Andrik. I've never felt more foolish.

My daftness works a charm on Nikita, but Mikhail needs more than puppy dog eyes to pull the wool over his eyes. "You didn't raw dog those fuckers. They're the size of horse tablets and taste just as nasty."

I pout like a child when he returns to his room to fetch the barely touched glass of orange juice.

"Drink this. Then you can have as much coffee as you want."

"I'm not really a fan of orange juice," I say through twisted lips.

"And I'm not a fan of emptying used condoms out of my trash cans after a one-night stand I was excluded from, but you don't see me complaining, do ya?"

I snatch the glass out of his hand and down the entire contents, hopeful the ghastliness of the pulp sliding down my throat will excuse the look of repent trying to cross my face.

I'm not apologetic he was left out of the festivities. I regret that disappointment was the first emotion I felt upon being reminded again that last night was a one-night-only affair.

I'm not looking for anything permanent—it isn't in the cards for me—but I'd be a liar if I said I wouldn't take Andrik up on any offer he tosses my way.

Last night was so unreal my uterus isn't the only thing shuddering in the aftermath of its brilliance. My entire existence is reeling.

When Mikhail winks at me after I hand him the empty glass, I realize I'm getting played by more than one source.

"You play dirty."

He couldn't look more shocked if he tried. "We met yesterday, so how are you only just noticing this?"

Realizing I must match wit with wit, I reply, "Probably your marshmallow heart. Soft men usually play it safe, so you caught me off guard. It won't happen again."

I return his wink before helming our exit. Tsar's sells coffee. That isn't the sole cause of my eagerness to visit the Broadbent Hotel, though. I'm also hopeful the boutique bordering the overpriced restaurant stocks underwear. Aleena exhibits the innocence I was unfairly stripped of when my worth was valued on my fertility status. Meeting her sans panties would only give our mother more reason to burn bridges.

"As I said yesterday, my heart is the *only* thing soft about me." As he shadows my walk out of his apartment, Mikhail's eyes flick up to the camera in the corner of the large space for the quickest second before he says, "But I'm sure you're aware of that now since you've seen me naked."

He guides me into the elevator before I can offer a rebuttal.

11

ANDRIK

My fists ball when the security server monitoring Mikhail's apartment displays an error. I'm meant to be going over last quarter's profit and loss statement with the CFO of my company, but I've spent the last forty-five minutes scrolling through the surveillance I had my security team hack into minutes after arriving at my hotel for a meeting I couldn't get out of.

As he advised earlier, Mikhail shut down the cameras inside his penthouse. My security team had them back in operation up until two minutes ago. I got kicked out a second after Mikhail announced Zoya had seen him naked, and no matter how much code I fill the screen with, it won't come back online.

"Why isn't it fucking working?" My anger is too high to contain for a second longer.

Mikhail won't touch Zoya. He's too cunning to play a hand he knows will only ever win him a bullet hole between his brows, but there wasn't an ounce of untruth in his eyes when he leered up at the camera before making his bold statement.

That fucker pranced around Zoya naked, most likely during their lengthy exchange in the walk-in closet and bathroom facilities that have no cameras, and the knowledge of that has the gun on my hip as heavy as it was when my surveillance team caught him removing the note I'd left with Zoya's orange juice, requesting for her to wait for me at Mikhail's apartment.

Melor, my CFO, looks at me as if I've lost my marbles.

I'm on the cusp of agreeing with him.

I don't pine over women. I sleep with them and then move on. That was the principle of finding a reared-for-the-task bride for my latest campaign. There's just something about Zoya that flipped my life plan on its head.

I want to blame Mikhail's interest in her. He can rile me like no one else can because he knows he'll never be buried in a shallow grave others would face for their insolence. I can't, however.

I researched Zoya's condition for hours last night.

I stalked social media for the hope of unearthing the fools she'd previously permitted in her bed.

I slipped back between the sheets before pulling her into my arms to catch a couple of hours of sleep while spooning her like a soft cock.

Mikhail was there for none of that.

It was all me.

Yet for some fucked-up reason, I wouldn't change a single thing about last night.

Well, except for that one part I'm still endeavoring to fix.

I'm reminded that I asked a question when Melor endeavors to answer it. "The figures are good, Kazimir. Profits are on a steady inc—"

"Not the figures. I don't give a fuck about the figures." That's a shock for everyone in the room, including me. Money usually comes before anything and anyone. "I'm talking about the surveillance in Mikhail's building. Why can't I see what's happening in the elevator?"

My answer comes from the man I make sit in on my meetings so my wealth never extends further than this very room. "It's being blocked by a portable dirtbox."

Thank fuck Konstantine isn't a man I have to pry answers out of. He coughs up the goods as regularly as he beds hookers.

"It impedes camera frequencies and phone signals. Pretty much anything with radio waves with one click of a button." My jaw firms to the point of cracking. "Mikhail was seeking one a couple of weeks back. Right around the time you started that..."

His words trail off as his eyes stray to the stack of files I left Mikhail's apartment with. I have no intention of using them—my grave has been dug. I merely didn't want to leave Mikhail with more ammunition to use against me.

He's already got the charm that makes the ladies weak at the knees.

I just don't see his gimmicks working on Zoya.

She doesn't want a sentimental schmuck who'll make her breakfast in bed and massage her feet when they're sore. She wants to be taken hard and fast. Fucked. She wants to be claimed by a madman who'll send hitmen to her exes' doors because he can't stand the thought of any man seeing her how he saw her last night.

I will do precisely that once I find them.

Zoya's online presence is as limited as my patience.

"Can you work past the block?"

I slam down my laptop screen with so much force it cracks when Konstantine shakes his head. "I designed it so it can't be overridden. Its range is short, though."

I doubt it is as short as my temper.

"The server will resume broadcasting the instant he is twenty feet out of frame."

It takes me longer than I care to admit to work through the barrier Mikhail is attempting to throw up. The delay ensures it is nothing short of brilliant. "Extend the brief I gave you this morning. Add any discrepancies to our servers to your reports. I want to know if a camera is offline for even a second."

When I couldn't find any information on Zoya this morning, I put a tail on her instead. She'll be able to move freely, but each step will be monitored.

Well, they would have been if my punk-ass brother hadn't tossed himself into the ring of a fight he'll never win.

Konstantine jerks up his chin before his focus shifts to his laptop. He only types one line of code when a clear warning to pull in my theatrics smacks into me.

"Who is this girl, Kazimir?" My father stands from the chair he begrudgingly sat in at the commencement of our meeting and paces closer to my desk. "Is she someone we need to be worried about?"

He says *we* as if we're a team, completely neglecting how often he's only ever looked out for himself since I was five.

Unsurprisingly, his comradery doesn't linger for long.

"Do I need my team on this?"

"No." I almost use my frequently spoken "she's no one" line. I don't see it playing out how it generally would, so I devise another tactic.

I fucked up by exposing my hand, but they don't call me The Fox for no reason. I'm sly, intelligent, and adaptable—more cunning than anyone in this room. And it is proven without a doubt when I say, "She was placed on my radar when she was spotted with Mikhail's keys last night."

Just like that, my father's interest wanes.

"Mikhail?" He chokes on laughter. "All this worry for a bitch in heat hoping to sink her hooks into a Dokovic nowhere near the top of the pyramid." Huffing, he returns to his seat, unbuttoning his suit jacket on the way. "I give it until the end of the week before her cum melds in with the other hundreds of samples smeared on his sheets."

He drags his eyes across the room, missing my spasming jaw. I thought leaving Zoya to rest was the amicable thing to do. I like my women floppy with sexual exhaustion, not genuine fatigue. I didn't consider the possibility of another man smelling the delectable scent of her multiple arousals.

That man may be my brother, but the itch to kill still floods my veins when I imagine him dragging his nose across the sheets we made sticky with more than sweat.

"Half of the Chelabini female population has been in Mikhail's bed at some stage over the past six months. Promiscuity is the *only* trait he inherited from me."

My father's snarky comment gets a laugh out of the fools unaware of the repercussions they'll face for siding with him. The only people not grinning are Konstantine and me. We know he's not finished yet. His "solutions" always include bloodshed—even for a son he considers below his league.

"Still, I'll get someone on my team to unearth where her interests lie."

His hand freezes halfway into the breast pocket of his jacket when I snap out, "I said no. I've got a handle on it."

My father takes a moment to authenticate the legitimacy of the threat in my tone before he removes his hand from his pocket and slumps low in his chair. "I'm just trying to be helpful."

He isn't, but I'll pretend that this is the only lie he's ever told me by focusing my attention on Konstantine, who's been inconspicuously trying to obtain it for the past two minutes instead of my gun.

Upon realizing he has my focus, Konstantine spins his laptop around to face me. Hundreds of cameras monitor the guests and staff of the Broadbent Hotel, so the pattern of their failures over the past five minutes announces one thing.

Zoya has landed on my turf.

Unfortunately, so the fuck has the devil I've been avoiding this morning.

12

ZOYA

I'm hesitant to hand my coat to the hostess of Tsar's. The wind today is like ice, but that isn't the cause of my hesitation. My coat's hem sits halfway between my knees and my ankles. My skirt's hemline is far more indecent. It will be a struggle to sit without exposing myself, and the boutique beside the restaurant is closed until two.

Yesterday, I didn't care about the scandalous rise of my skirt's hemline.

Today, I can't stop playing Andrik's threat from last night on repeat.

Six? Don't test me on six because I can guarantee neither you nor him will survive the outcome.

A shiver runs the length of my spine.

Don't ask if it is a good or bad tingle, as I won't know how to answer you.

Mikhail's floppy hair tickles his ears when he slants his head my way. "Will you be right for a tick? Lynx is being a demanding diva."

I return Lynx's wave from across the hotel foyer I'm praying

Aleena will visit sometime today, before I nod in silent assurance to Mikhail that I'll be fine on my own. I have been for the past twelve-plus years, so I'm sure a few more minutes will be no hard feat.

"It will give me the chance to call Keet," I reply, hating that he seems hesitant.

I thought I displayed an air of confidence I wasn't reared to have.

Mikhail has me wondering if it is a ruse.

"All right." He nudges his head past the check-in counter. "You should probably head toward the back, though. Reception is shit near the bar."

He's preaching to the wrong person. I missed three calls and six text messages from Nikita yesterday while waiting for Aleena, which added a ton of worry she doesn't need to her shoulders.

I wait until Mikhail is halfway across the foyer before heading in the opposite direction. I know Nikita's number by heart, but since it is my most frequently called number, I hit her name at the top of my call list and then raise my phone in front of my face.

Nikita answers two seconds later. "You were half an hour from being featured on the side of a milk carton."

I sigh, loving how much she loves me, but I wouldn't be me if I didn't stir her. "Was it a paid gig? If so, I'll call you back in an hour."

Her laugh is lyrical gold—as is the question she asks next. "Is it pathetic to admit I already miss you like crazy?"

"Not at all. I'm extremely missable."

The torn sheets she can't afford to replace crinkle around her body when she rolls to project her voice away from the living room she shares with her grandparents. Their apartment is a one-bedroom dump, yet it is still ten times better than the place I call home.

"Gigi was extra talkative last night since she didn't get to unload all her shenanigans on you."

We giggle in sync when Gigi's snarky tone rumbles through our phones. "I heard that."

I lower my voice like my next lot of words are full of deceit. "I told you she isn't deaf. She just pretends she is so we'll talk freely around her."

Nikita nods before she slips her hand under her cheek. She looks exhausted. That's expected for any third-year surgical registrar. Her tiredness exceeds her counterparts since she works the equivalent of a full-time job on the side to stay one step behind her grandfather's medical bills.

Yes, behind.

His medication costs more than her supervisor earns, but he will never be without it.

We will both make sure of that.

I just need to find a job so I can contribute.

Since that hasn't been an easy task to cross off as I would have liked, I offer moral support instead. "How is Grampies today?"

Her love for the grandfather she was forced to share with me when we became friends shines brightly in her eyes when she smiles. "He's having a good day. He misses you too."

I sigh like a sentimental schmuck. "I'll be home soon. I just figured while I'm here, why not give it one last shot?"

She knows who I'm talking about without me needing to spell it out. "You don't have to convince me. Take all the time you need." A spark of fear darts through her eyes. "Just be safe."

"I always am."

She spots my deceit from a mile out. Mercifully, I'm saved from explaining myself by Mikhail returning to my side.

"I need to go. Mikhail is here." When I twist the phone screen to face Mikhail, he poses for the numerous screenshots Nikita takes. She isn't storing them for future self-pleasing expeditions. She's compiling evidence in case I go missing for real.

Further proof that her and Mikhail are too alike to ever be an item.

"I'll call you when I leave."

Nikita nods before telling me she loves me.

I return her declaration of love with the addition of an air kiss before disconnecting our chat.

"Brother from another mother?" Mikhail asks when he spots the adoration adorning my face.

Nikita is one of the strongest women I know. She just has no clue of her worth. I'm hoping to change that. I am just a little lost on how to go about it.

His face screws up when I reply, "Do I look like I have dangly bits between my legs?"

"I can't tell from this angle." His smirk gains him the worship of dozens of thirsty eyes. Not all of them are feminine. "Maybe you should let me check?"

I punch him in the stomach, winding him.

I wait for him to catch his breath before nudging my head to the bar brimming with hotel patrons despite the early hour. "Is everything okay with Lynx?"

My screwed-up expression jumps onto his face. "Two bar staff called in sick, and he's having trouble finding replacements."

When he leaves it there, I say, "So you're going to ditch our brunch and help out your work friend, right?"

"Fuck no," he instantly replies. "What kind of host would I be if I only fed you a glass of orange juice and half a shot glass of cum for breakfast?"

My elbow gets friendly with his ribs when his mouth falls open from my lack of objection. I ate more than cum, but it was the most delicious item on the menu, so I keep my mouth shut.

"Now his hesitation to leave this morning makes sense."

"You spoke with Andrik this morning?" I almost said, *He was hesitant to leave?* But I went for the line that wouldn't make me seem pathetic.

"Uh-huh," Mikhail replies, guiding me inside Tsar's. "Who do you think gave me the shiner?"

Once again, I take the non-desperate route.

It is a challenging achievement with how high my shock is.

"I assumed the Triple Threat Team liked it rough."

"Oh, they did."

His moan at the end of his statement has me tempted to pluck an umbrella from a stack near the hostess desk. Above-par batting averages may be the only way I survive the stampede we're about to face.

"But Andrik has a temper as short as a matchhead." A smirk curls his lips. "I may also get pleasure out of pushing his buttons."

We're seated at a table with a prime view of most of the hotel's foyer. Mikhail waits for me to sit before he removes a napkin from the hostess's tray and drapes it across my thighs, ending their uncomfortable press.

Once I'm suitably covered, he leans in close and whispers, "He took your underwear, didn't he?"

His words are soft enough for only me to hear. They cause a fiery heat to creep across my cheeks that colors my tone with just as much vibrancy. "Will you call me a hussy if I say yes?"

"No." He sits across from me before accepting a menu from the smiling waitress introducing herself as our server. Her roguish blush is as evident as mine when she drinks in Mikhail's handsome features. He doesn't pay her an ounce of attention. His focus is solely on me and my possible confession. "But it will tempt me to ask what makes you different from the rest. He's usually a fuck-'em-and-leave-before-they've-finished-shuddering kind of guy."

My stomach gurgles. I downplay it as hunger. "Can we eat before you tell me exactly how many times Andrik has used your private abode as a whore house? I'd like to have something to bring up when I vomit. I have issues with dryness." The heat on my cheeks doubles when he chuckles. "Not like that." I pick up the napkin and toss it in his face. "You're disturbing."

"And you are even more feisty when you're embarrassed." He leans back in his chair so the waitress doesn't bump into him when she fills his glass of water. "Maybe that's what attracted Andrik to you? My brother usually goes for the demure, quiet ones. You wouldn't fit that criteria even if you had one foot in the grave."

Brother?

As my eyes zoom over every morsel of Mikhail's face, I'm steamrolled with stupidity. The signs are in black and white for all to see, yet also not.

They're night and day.

Light and dark.

Similar yet unique.

They're the very definition of a brother from another mother. I'd put money on it.

Mikhail quirks a brow when I say, "Now your lack of fear makes sense," demanding further explanation. "You'll survive his threat of disembowelment since you're blood."

"Blood isn't always thicker than water." He leans forward until his elbows balance on the tabletop. "And do you care to elaborate on what his threat entailed?" I don't believe him for a second when he smirks. "I'd like to know which buttons to avoid."

He wants to direct his arrow straight at them, not away from them. His smirk announces this, much less the menacing glint in his eyes.

I thank the waitress for filling my mug with a steaming hot brew as Mikhail's curiosity gets the better of him. "He threatened future bed companions, didn't he?" When I give him a look as if to say, *I'll never tell*, he murmurs, "You don't need to confess, Sunshine. The truth is all over your face. I'm just trying to determine why he'd say that and then do what he did."

I'm lost but too exhausted to excavate with the intelligence it deserves. "What did he do? Leave me to pre-scrub your sheets before placing them in the wash because I had no clue you were related?" I hit him with a pointed stare. "You could have told me he was your brother. Then I wouldn't have broken a nail wrangling a fitted sheet off your ginormous mattress."

He laughs. It is unexpected from how uneasy the groove between his brow makes him appear. "And let him steal the honor I worked so hard to achieve? Don't be ridiculous."

The coffee I'm slowly sipping means it takes me longer than I care to admit to recall where I've heard those words before. It makes me sick when I unlock the vault.

My voice is too loud for our public setting when I ask, "You were watching us?"

Mikhail nods.

He. Fucking. Nods.

I appreciate his honesty, but still, I'm shocked by his nonchalant approach to his reply.

His eyes bulge when he understands the cause for my kick under the table. "Not *that*," he pushes out quickly. "What the fuck is it with everyone today thinking I'd get my rocks off watching my big brother..." He refuses to say his last word. He swallows the bile it instigated before lowering his voice to a more respectable level for our audience. "I saw your exchange in the elevator." His words quicken when my snarl causes me to bare my teeth. "The pre-slap part of your exchange. Jesus, Sunshine. I'm not a complete fucking creep." When I *pfft* him like I'm unsure if I believe him, he says, "I'm trying to be honest with you. I thought you'd rather that than base our friendship on the lies he must have tossed out to get you to—"

He snaps his mouth shut like he said too much.

It's too late for him, though.

His hand has been shown.

"What did he lie about?"

"Nothing." He sits straighter and clears his throat. "I'm talking out of my ass."

"You'll be talking out of your ass with my foot lodged up it if you don't go back to the honesty route you were endeavoring to get off the ground only seconds ago."

I mimic his earlier pose. Elbows on the tabletop, eyes full of sorrow. It displays that I won't let him fob off my interrogation any more than I won't hate him for his brother's actions.

His delay in responding is the equivalent of kneeling on shards of glass. It hurts, but not as much as his confession. "He's married." To ensure I can't use the excuse of bad hearing for any future stuff ups, he repeats, "Andrik is married."

13

ANDRIK

"You're married!" My father's eyes fling from the simple gold band Mrs. Sakharoff shoved into my palm last night, now circling Arabella's ring finger, to me. "When? How? You said you weren't ready."

I wait for my staff to leave as per the demand of my hand thrust before answering, "I changed my mind."

Well, I had.

Arabella presented as the perfect reared-to-serve-my-ruse bride. Then I spent the night ravishing a woman who made me wonder if vengeance is for the weak.

I assumed Zoya would be the wildcat I'd suspected she'd be, but then I'd move on like I generally do. How was I to know one taste would never suffice? Or that it would change my plans in an instant?

I had no clue she'd place me under a spell that would fog my perception so well I thought I could end an agreement with a sternly worded email.

I requested a suspension on the paperwork that shouldn't have been filed until Monday morning, confident it was an easy fix.

Demands work in business, so why shouldn't they also work in my personal life?

You can save your lecture. It seems karma has come knocking to gnaw my ass.

I work my jaw from side to side before getting to work on settling my father's skyrocketing blood pressure before he goes into cardiac arrest. "Paperwork was endorsed yesterday—"

"After a whirlwind three-month courtship and permission from her guardian," Mrs. Sakharoff interrupts, following the plot we devised on a whim last night.

Our union needed to look legitimate, or it would be utterly pointless, so we spent more time tying up the loose ends that would have seen it ending sooner than planned.

My family would have never believed I married a stranger during a drunk, drug-fueled bender. I'm more astute than that.

Furthermore, those types of marriages don't last in my family.

It wouldn't have ended with an annulment, though.

Bullets are cheaper than losing assets that took centuries to earn.

"Did you at least demand a prenup?"

I glare at my father, disapproving of his wrath but conscious he has a right to be angry.

It won't stop me from badgering him, though.

"Do I look like a braindead idiot?"

He doesn't hide his nod, and I can't kill him for it.

He didn't lie, so I have no foundation to punish him.

"The contract we endorsed stated a monetary amount for the dissolution of the marriage. Despite the shortness of our union, I will abide by that term."

My father's cheeks redden, loathing that I'm handing over money to which he has no claim.

I earned the millions in my bank accounts, so I can spend them however I see fit.

"And the rest? What happens with that?"

Mrs. Sakharoff's tone better take a seat before I remind her that she is *not* running the show around here, and neither is the woman she thrusts in front of her like I won't kill her just as fast.

Arabella means nothing to me.

She was the commencement of answers I will devise another tactic to unearth.

It appears her mother believes differently, though.

"The consummation of your vows could have evoked an additional clause."

"I didn't touch her." I sound disgusted by the idea, and Arabella doesn't miss that. Tears dust her lower lashes as her face turns ashen. I'd hate that I've upset her if I actually cared. Since I don't, I keep my tone blunt. "So any clauses you're referencing are null and void."

I was too generous with my assumption of Mrs. Sakharoff's age when she screws up her face while shouting, "Your marital contract demanded haste."

"Because I'm not getting any younger," I fire back, needing to say something to lessen the suspicion on my father's face. It isn't my clock I was watching when determining the terms of our contract. It was my grandfather's. "And neither the fuck is my grandfather."

I age a decade in a second when victory flares through Mrs. Sakharoff's eyes. "So you can understand why we put *immediate* measures into play to ensure we'd meet the terms of your contract in a timely manner."

What is she saying?

Is she implying what I think she is?

Did she use my fucking sperm to impregnate her daughter earlier than the stated timeline in our contract?

I wasn't lying when I told Arabella and her mother that our union would never be about love. They believe it is for the massive payout I'll receive from my grandfather's estate when I create an heir to the Dokovic lineage that has ruled this country for over a hundred years, because that's what I want them to believe.

It's about far more than political power, but they're not privileged enough to be informed of that. I haven't even told Mikhail, so why the fuck would I mention it to someone I hired to help me?

Mrs. Sakharoff scoffs when I say, "I don't believe you." For the first time, fear crosses her face when I stand from my chair and bang my fist on my desk. "And it will be in your best interest to remember what I do to people who lie to me."

"What reason does she have to lie, Kazimir?"

I shoot my eyes in the direction of the Russian voice steeped with history. It doesn't belong to my father. It is projecting from his phone on the coffee table in front of him.

It belongs to my grandfather.

"She had a signed marital contract that stated your wish for an heir, so the federation had no reason to send her away." My jaw tightens during his last sentence.

The public believes the president runs our country. The president and his minions know differently. The federation was once the most ruthless and largest organized crime syndicate in the Soviet Union. Now it is the crown of the Russian political conglomerate.

Don't misconstrue what I'm saying. Bratva members and politicians have worked side by side for centuries. Now, more times than not, they're the same people.

Same suits.

Same arrogance.

Same end game.

Power.

The federation is the peak of the food chain for the entirety of Russia. Nothing said or done under its canopy occurs without its complicit consent—not even the conception of a future presidential candidate.

My contract with Arabella was meant to unearth the main players so I could implode the organization from the inside out, one hierarchy at a time.

That's how much I despise following a life plan devised for me before I was even conceived, and having the only person I've ever loved so cruelly stripped from me.

My mother wasn't waiting for me when I galloped down the stairs on my fifth birthday like my stomach didn't have me wanting to fold in two from being forced to hold.

She was nowhere to be seen, and despite how often I told my guests that she didn't just "leave" as implied, no one believed me.

I had to endure a group of strangers singing happy birthday to me before I was forcefully walked to my room and told not to come out until I had an attitude adjustment.

If it weren't for Anoushka, I would have starved to death.

That's how stubborn I was.

That's how stubborn I still am.

I am Kazimir Andrik Dokovic the Eighth. I don't answer to anyone, so how the fuck did I, in fewer than twelve hours, lose sight of a hate so deeply engrained I've carried it with me for over thirty years?

It shouldn't have left my sight for a single second.

I won't make the same mistake twice.

I just need to fight fire with fire, and the best way to do that is to remember a promise given thirty years ago is still valid today.

"My anger is not directed at the federation." I have to work my following lie through a tight jaw. "It is from the remembrance I forgot to have them vet the future First Lady of our great nation."

Arabella gleams over a title she will *never* see.

I want our family name to return to what it was initially about.

We're gangsters, not political mongers who will do or say anything if it guarantees a vote.

I just can't announce that until I ensure the procedure Arabella undertook last night won't have me breaking the only promise I ever issued directly to my mother.

"If unvetted endorsements are the cause of your backflip, you have nothing to worry about." Mrs. Sakharoff steps closer. "Arabella was reared for precisely this. She is well-educated, can cook and clean, and her political viewpoint will forever match yours." She tugs her daughter forward, oblivious that her praise is weakening her confidence instead of expediting it. "She is also fertile."

"Unlike the woman you spent the night with." My grandfather's chief of staff continues talking, drowning out the brutal snap of my back molars. "So enough with the unnecessary drama. The federation approves of your connubium. However, there are a handful of infractions we need to iron out..."

My grandfather rejoins the conversation. I don't hear a word he speaks. I'm too busy plotting the demise of the leading players to listen to the demands given by faceless voices.

I knew they were watching me, but I had no clue it went this deep. Zoya's fertility issues were only unearthed yesterday, so how the fuck does an organization with millions under its control know about them?

Dr. Hemway is my first guess.

He'll be the first on my hitlist too if my theories stack up.

The rest of the insolent fools thinking I'm a puppet they can make dance on demand will soon follow.

I just need to unearth who they are first, which could be impossible without Arabella's help.

Regretfully.

14

ZOYA

*M*ikhail slices his hand through the air, wordlessly advising the waitress that we're not ready to order yet, before he returns his eyes to me.

I'm not exactly sure how long I've been frozen with shock. I doubt it is close to minutes, but it feels like a lifetime.

My first response to Mikhail's confession is anger. Then it simmers to redemption. I didn't technically do anything wrong—all that weight belongs on Andrik's shoulders—but I still feel like I need to defend myself.

"I didn't know he was married." I swallow the burn hitting the back of my throat before correcting myself. "That he *is* married."

Mikhail exhales deeply, grateful my shock has lifted enough for me to speak. "I know that. I just hope you know I was also unaware." My brows furrow. Mercifully, he endeavors to eradicate my confusion without me needing to speak. "His nuptials are so recent that news about them only started circulating hours *after* I texted him to meet me at my penthouse. My message was delivered mere minutes after you left the bar with my keys."

Even with my confusion as thick as a slab of concrete, his confession slithers through the hairline fractures several tedious minutes of drilling established. "You set us up?"

I don't know whether to scoff in disbelief or anger when he bobs his chin.

"I knew he wouldn't be able to help himself."

"Am I meant to take that as a compliment?"

It takes everything I have to keep my hands balled in my napkin when he nods again. "You were good for him. He was different this morning. Happier. He was so fucking light on his feet he practically floated."

"That probably has more to do with the fact he blew his load all over your sheets." I'm a snarky bitch when I'm angry, and Mikhail is learning that the hard way. "More than once."

When I leap to my feet and march to the front of the restaurant to fetch my coat, no longer hungry, Mikhail races to catch up with me. "Running won't fix anything, Zoya."

"What exactly am I meant to be fixing, Mikhail?"

If he says his brother's infidelities, his left eye will be as shadowed by a bruise as his right.

I am startled by the first contender on his list. "You." He loses me after that. "Him." A hint of vulnerability dulls his bright eyes when he murmurs, "Me." He wets his lips as I stuff my hands into my coat. "There's more to his sudden wish to wed than he will ever let on, but I won't find out what that is without your help. You are the first person to push Andrik off his life plan. You made him remember that he's human."

I like Mikhail. He's the kindest stranger I've ever met, but only yesterday, he was precisely that—a stranger—so it isn't my job to fix his family's woes.

Furthermore, I have enough of my own family drama to contend with. I can't accept more.

When I say that to Mikhail, he uses my wish for a healthy relationship with my sister to his advantage. "Then stay for your sister. It is barely eleven. She's still got an hour before she can damage her insides with multiple forms of curdled cream."

"And risk a possible run-in with Andrik?" When shock that I read his game plan so easily forms on his face, I let out a long-winded breath. "You shouldn't wish that on your worst enemy, much less your brother." A rebellion streak fires through me when I mumble, "I might ball my hand this time."

Mikhail is clearly aware of his brother's hankering for violence. "It's worth a shot. It worked well for you last time."

I "*Ha!*" in his face. "So well I was forced into adultery. Excuse me if I don't rush to sign up for that again."

I only get three steps away from him when his murmured comment stops me in my tracks. "Even if it will see him leaving his wife for you like he did this morning?" He waits for me to twist to face him before saying, "I only learned that he was married because his secretary attached his annulment paperwork to the quarterly business statements instead of the financial reports only ever compiled on Andrik's laptop since he doesn't trust anyone else with them." He steps closer, his walk back to its cocky strut. "You rocked his world so fucking well that the first report he pulled up this morning was how to annul a marriage contract instead of the financials keeping his bank balance in the billions."

The mention of his wealth is unnecessary because no amount of money can excuse Andrik's mistake. He lied—point blank. And as much as my ego is desperate to be stroked, I don't want it coming from a taken man.

My mother's violative relationships exposed that if a man can cheat on his wife with you, he can cheat on you too. There is no loyalty with cheaters.

Realizing nothing he could say will erase years of teachings,

Mikhail rubs his hands together before saying, "Will you at least let me buy you breakfast?"

"I'd rather push your courtesy for a ride back to my car." It is chilly out, and although Mikhail's building is only a few miles from here, I don't want to walk. Anger hardens your muscles even more than multiple orgasms.

He looks like he wants to argue.

Mercifully, he doesn't.

"All right." He accepts his jacket from the smiling coat clerk and puts it on. "But we're stopping at Vai Me! on the way for supplies. I'm fucking starving, and you haven't had nowhere near enough caffeine to work through the pile of shit I just dumped on you."

The flashes of multiple cameras pull me from my stupor state. They race for the vehicle too low to the ground for Mikhail to use the drive-thru at his favorite breakfast haunt before shoving them into Mikhail's face and mine as if we're doing something more interesting than lugging bags of fat and salt-laden fast food into the foyer of his building.

The first few questions are about me and what connection I have to Mikhail. His lack of comment soon shifts their focus to Andrik.

"Mikhail, do you have any comments on your brother's recent relationship status update?"

"Are rumors of a rift between your grandfather and your father true?"

"How did your brother keep his relationship under wraps for so long?"

"Will you be attending the wedding?"

Questions are flung at us so hard and fast that they meld into one.

Thankfully, a combination of security officers and valet attendants stop them from entering the foyer of Mikhail's building.

I'm left defenseless when we reach the private service elevator I only agreed to ride since I left my keys in Mikhail's penthouse, though.

Before I can fathom what's happening, my wrist is seized and I'm yanked into the elevator car with so much force orange juice and flavored iced tea spill over the rims of the plastic cups they were served in, dotting my open-toe heels and ankles.

The stickiness is bad enough to contend with, so I won't mention my response to the discovery that Mikhail wasn't pulled into the carnage with me.

He's still outside the elevator, standing just back from the rapidly closing doors I'll never reach before they snap shut.

I glare at Mikhail's snickering face in warning of the wrath I'll rain down on him once I'm freed from this hot box before I spin to face the cause of the sweat beading on my neck.

As suspected, Andrik is standing opposite me, raking his eyes up my body.

He takes his time assessing me, doubling the anger slicking my skin with sweat.

Justice gets served when his eyes finally make their way to my chest. I don't know the university's emblem slashed across the front of the shirt I borrowed from Mikhail, but Andrik clearly does. It firms his jaw to the point of cracking and has jealousy roaring through his body—jealousy he has no right to have.

After lifting his eyes to my face, he loosens the inflexibility of his jaw with a quick grind before he says, "You need to tell my brother you're not interested." When I roll my eyes in silent assurance that he has no right to bark orders at me, he lowers his tone from menacing to downright dangerous. "Let me rephrase. *Tell* my brother you're not interested." He steps closer, swamping me with his delicious scent. "Or I'll make you watch when I remind him how serious my threats are." The droplets of juice the lid caught are soaked up by his business jacket when he leans in so close his hot breaths revamp my hunger. "Your tally will never reach six, *Лисичка*. Your body count ended the instant I laid eyes on you." A smirk curls his lips at one side. "Now it will only ever travel one way." A shiver involuntarily runs through me when he murmurs, "Dead men don't count."

"Is that what you tell your wife so she sleeps better at night?"

Andrik is not a man I should mess with. He's dark and dangerous, the epitome of threatening, but for some reason, I don't fear him.

"That all your mistresses are dead, so they don't count." I tilt nearer, bringing our eyes so close that our noses touch. "Slashing their self-worth to nothing isn't killing them, Andrik. It simply frees them of men like you."

His anger is so white-hot the iced tea is no longer iced. "My wife—"

"So you admit it? You're married."

"Yes," he answers bluntly, his voice disgusted. "But that doesn't need to change anything between us."

"It doesn't?" If my voice gets any louder, I will sustain permanent hearing loss. "How silly of me. I assumed that the vows you exchange automatically take you off the market when you get married. Now that I know that isn't true, I have no reason to fret matrimony. I can fuck as many men as I please both before and after I replace you."

I took it too far, and I realize that long before Andrik's hand shoots for my throat.

After using his grip to pin me to the wall, he squeezes my windpipe tight enough for me to drop the drinks I was carting for

Mikhail but not firm enough for no air to seep through the minute gap.

"Choose your answers very wisely, *милая*, because my leniencies have reached the end of the line today."

His fingers around my neck flex, proving he still has some morsel of control. I can't say the same. His hold is so possessive that I'm more horny than scared.

"Do you understand that I will kill *any* man you place between us, regardless of his title, status, or reason for being between us?"

His fingers flex again to ensure his firm grip isn't behind the delay of my head bob.

They're not. I'm just a stubborn fuck who shouldn't be turned on by his possessiveness, but for some strange reason, I am.

When I eventually nod, his nostrils flare in victory.

"So what will that make your count when you take your last breath?"

"Five," I squeak out slowly.

"Five?" he double-checks, his arrogance tripling. I nod again, and the smirk it produces would convince any woman that adultery isn't so bad. A minuscule of attention far exceeds none. "It's not five, *милая*." He crowds into me so closely I am confident he is seconds from finding out I'm not wearing any panties. "Because, as I said earlier, dead men don't count." When he wets his lips, his tongue also moistens mine. That's how close he's standing. "So what will your number be?"

I want to say there's a lengthy delay between his question and my answer, but that would be a lie.

I answer so fast I'm more angry at myself than Andrik.

"One."

"One," he repeats, pleased. "And what is the name of that chosen one?"

My delay is far more respectable this time around, but it is still shamefully honest. "Andrik."

"Andrik." He says his name with a throaty purr like he's only ever heard it screamed in ecstasy by me.

As he smirks in victory, he moves his thumb counting my pulse from my neck to my lips. He drags it over them in arrogance like they're not bone dry before he returns it to my neck, several inches lower this time. He brushes it past my collarbone and then drops it to my budded nipple.

"It's cold, so maybe you should turn the elevator's main power back on so we don't freeze to death."

I don't need to look at his face to know he is smiling.

I can feel it.

"You're cold?"

I nod, uneager to test his leniency with a worded lie just yet. I'm also not sure I can speak through the lustiness scorching my throat.

"How?" He doesn't give me a chance to answer. "You're so hot with lust that if I were to slide my cock inside you right now, you'd scald—"

"Off any nasties your inability to keep your dick in your pants might cause your wife?"

I said he could make any woman believe adultery is okay.

I am *not* that woman.

He smirks like I struck him, so I make right of the injustice.

I slap him.

The triumph I feel when his head rockets to the side only lasts a second. That's how fast he advances on me without warning.

In less than a heartbeat, I'm re-pinned to the wall of the elevator, and my mouth is being ravished by the man I swore only minutes ago I'd never let touch me again.

Andrik kisses me as if he can't breathe without his mouth on mine while he removes the bulky jacket stopping our bodies from completely joining.

The kiss steals away every negative thought I'm having. A deep, lush embrace that surges both my heart and clit into a chaotic beat. It is greedy and devouring, so you can imagine how hard it is for me to pull back.

It is a battle I win—just.

"Stop." What should be an affirmation comes out sounding more like a moan. "I don't want this."

There's no doubt my last word is a moan. It can't be helped. Andrik's growl when he slips his hands under my skirt to grip my bare ass warrants nothing less than a desperate, needy rumble.

He knows I'm bare under my skirt, and like all cocky, arrogant men, he assumes I went without panties for him.

"Andrik…" I push out breathlessly when he falls to his knees and shoves up my skirt.

The more I try to push down the risqué flare, the higher he hoists it.

Within seconds, it is caught in the knot of Mikhail's college shirt, erotically exposing me, and Andrik absorbs every minute detail.

"Christ. I fucking knew you were drenched for me."

He backhands my clit before a single lie can fire from my mouth.

When he rubs his fingertips over my opening, my clit's throbs match the brutal drumming of my heart against my ribs.

My defenses weaken more with every subtle touch, but I try to remember my objectives.

"We can't. You're married."

"It's an arrangement." His hot breaths batter my sex as he talks fast and without hesitation. "A tactically laid out ruse. It's not this." He lifts his eyes to my face. "She isn't you." Vulnerability fires through his hooded gaze. "And since you are… *you*, I won't break my promise."

Again, confusion slaughters my smarts.

I stop thinking with my head when that happens.

When Andrik's fingers finally shift their focus to my clit, I balance on my tiptoes. He massages the nervy bud with steady, unhurried swivels, tightening my core and removing the last of my objections my confusion didn't wipe.

"She will *never* see me like this." The pad of his thumb rubs my clit as he peers up at me over my thrusting chest. "On my knees, desperate to please."

I lean my back against the wall and grip my breasts, desperate to ease the ache of their heaviness when his words stimulate my clit as much as his assurance does.

"I'd never had an interest in pleasing a woman orally until I tasted you."

My knees almost buckle when he replaces the pad of his thumb with his tongue. He swipes it across my clit, triggering a throaty moan, before he gently sucks it into his mouth.

Everything tightens as my objections float away.

I couldn't stop this even if I wanted to, so I may as well enjoy it.

I know. That's a pathetic excuse. But can you judge me until you've endured the same? A sex god is on his knees, eager to please me. He exudes masculinity and intrigue and has so much confidence that in this very moment, he owns me.

The knowledge should clam me up, but it does the opposite.

I come with a hoarse cry, my limbs shaking as Andrik's name rips from my throat.

"Yes," he growls against my shuddering clit.

He guides me through the hysteria engulfing me with needy licks, sucks, and scrapes of his teeth before he rebuilds the wave that only recently crashed by standing to his feet and freeing his fat cock from his pants. It's beaded with pre-cum and throbbing with want.

"She will *never* have this. I promise you that."

A surge passes between us, its current so electrifying that I believe every word he speaks.

We lunge for each other at the same time. Our teeth collide as violently as the crest of his cock breaches the opening of my vagina a mere second after he curls my legs around his waist. He's so impatient he knifes his hips upward without warning, impaling me with one urgent thrust.

Pain blisters through my veins. It only lasts as long as it takes for Andrik to remember one of the drawings in the brochure in Dr. Hemway's office. He adjusts my position in an instant. My back braces against the wall, and my hips tilt before he fists the base of his cock with his free hand.

His fist represents the cock pillow the male cartoon character wore, meaning I now only have to acclimate to his girth and not the entirety of his lengthy cock.

The change-up doesn't dampen a single spark firing between us. They launch through the air as regularly as the sweaty claps of our bodies colliding while we fuck like we have no control over anything.

He pounds into me, his hips churning with every thrust to ensure the crest of his cock hits the sweet spot inside me.

"Yes," I moan before encouraging him to go harder. To take me faster. "Fuck me, Andrik. Make me yours."

He pulls me away from the handrail before bouncing me up and down his rigidly thick cock.

I scream as he powers into me. His balls slap my ass as he fucks me with everything he has, making me feel invisible.

I have no shame. No guilt. I've completely forgotten how we got here and the angst that began our exchange. Nothing but my next climax is on my mind.

"Yes," Andrik grunts as the waves crash to shore.

My vision blurs as tingles race over my skin, leaving a trail of goose bumps in their wake. I tremble through a climax so strong the frantic sucks of my pussy as pleasure convulses through it bring Andrik to release.

Blood roars through my ears when he shifts his hips upward before he stills and jerks.

His cum spurting hotly inside me is the first reminder we didn't use protection.

The sheer ownership on Andrik's face is the second.

15

ANDRIK

*I*t took me offering a majority share to Brody's, the bar inside the Broadbent Hotel, and a no-touch promise for Mikhail to agree to deliver Zoya to a location that would offer discretion so I could discuss my dilemma with her like the astute businessman I'm meant to be.

In under ten seconds, I blew my pledge to keep my hands to myself.

Her smell.

Her lusty eyes.

That fucking shirt... *Christ.*

I was torn between ripping it off her and leaving it on the floor of the elevator in shreds or smearing it with cum and forcing her to wear it every day of the week.

Even after calling me every name under the sun when I failed to deny my current marital status, Mikhail upheld his end of our agreement. That alone should announce he isn't my competition, but one sniff of his cologne on Zoya's skin sent my head into a tailspin.

It is still reeling now.

I want to bang my chest and tell every man to back the fuck up. I want to make her mine in every essence of the word. To do that, I must turn my back on a promise I made to myself many years ago.

That's not an easy accomplishment.

I don't know a single man who could give up everything he's been working toward for over two decades for a woman he's only known for twenty-four hours, much less a woman going by an alias.

I'm reasonably sure Zoya isn't lying about her given name, but I've had my security team search high and low for a Zoya Galdean over the past several hours.

Their search has yet to yield a single result.

I'm sure I can extract the truth from her. I must keep a cool, calm head, however, if I want to have my cake and eat it too.

I can't do that in a square box that smells of lust and depravity.

Trades on the black market the CIA would cream their pants to net is a walk in the park compared to the effort it takes me to slowly notch out of Zoya and place her back on her feet.

My pupils blow wide when the removal of my cock is quickly chased by a line of my semen dribbling down Zoya's thigh. I'm not shocked. I am fucking stoked. There's nothing more claiming than taking a woman bareback, and although this is the first time in twenty-two years that I've let go of the reins enough to unearth its brilliance, it won't be the last.

No fucking chance.

"I... ah..." When Zoya peers down at the mess before scanning the floor of the elevator for something to clear away the goop, I pull a handkerchief out of the pocket of my trousers bunched halfway past my ass before placing it between her legs.

One touch and she's burning up everywhere, ready for round two.

It was the same last night. Our chemistry is potent enough to fire through hours of exhaustion and numerous demands for sleep. It displays that one taste would never be enough. We require hit after hit, and even then my cravings won't be satisfied.

My cock is thickening now just at the thought of taking her again.

But I need to take this elsewhere.

There are ears everywhere, but they're worse when royalty is in town.

My father will be the next president of Russia, and I'm meant to be his successor. That makes the vultures of the media extra hungry. They dig through trash every morning with the hope they'll find something they can use against my family, so imagine how rampant they'll become if they learn the once deemed "head bachelor of the Dokovic realm" is still playing the field so soon after the federation removed his single status on all his social media sites.

They'd have a field day knocking down my family pegs more than the federation already has, but since I'd rather save the bloodshed for the true culprits of my family's demise, I must play it safe.

After watching Zoya clean up the mess I suddenly want to stuff back inside her, I tug down her skirt before pushing the emergency stop button on the elevator panel.

As the car jerks back into action, I curl my hand around Zoya's. I'm not usually a hand-holding guy, but the surge it causes to her pulse makes it another item I add to my ever-growing list of wants.

"I should probably get something since we forgot to use protection," Zoya says at the same time I ask, "Are you in any pain?"

I mistook her grimace about how lax we were with protection as a hurtful expression.

I'm a soft cock.

What should sound like an assurance comes out shady since it is forced through clenched teeth. "I'm clean, but I can get tested again if you're worried."

My lips twitch when she replies, "I'm clean, too, but that isn't the cause of my worry."

I'm not struggling to hold back a grin. I am fighting not to go on a rampage since the four men she slept with before me are still breathing.

Their conquests were years ago, so I should be able to let it go, but I can't. I want them dead as much as I plan to kill the man my mother struck. Then I'll stop imagining their mocking grins when it dawns on them that they had her before me.

Their time is limited. They shouldn't see that as a godsend. A delay in proceedings only awards me more time to work out exactly how painful their exits will be.

With my mood already injurious, I deepen my annoyance. "Have you ever had unprotected sex?"

"No," Zoya answers after a beat, her tone a mix of confusion and deceit.

"Do I need to take you over my knee, милая?"

I've never wanted to punish someone as much as I do now. My hands are itching to redden her ass with the same fiery burn racing through my veins.

Jealousy is hotter than hell. It is burning me from the inside out, making the small confines of the elevator scorchingly unbearable.

"I haven't. I just..." The fiery hellion I wrangled at the start of our exchange is back bigger, stronger, and angrier than ever. "Did you not use protection because you had a lapse in judgment or because you knew it was pointless for someone like me?" She air quotes her last three words like she struggled as much as I did earlier to find the right word for her fertility issues. "Because condoms aren't solely to lessen the chance of an unwanted pregnancy. They're just as important for protecting the *players* who should have been benched from unwanted STIs."

She isn't angry at me.

She's pissed at how quickly she caved when I fell to my knees.

"Don't be mad, *милая*. You will never win in *any* game that has you slated against me."

Zoya yanks her hand out of my grasp before fanning it across her cocked hip. "Why? Because you will annihilate my smarts with your stupidly perfect hair, sculptured face, and wickedly gifted mouth?" She whacks me on the chest two times, hardening me in an instant. "I'm not a lust-fueled idiot. I have a brain."

"I know th—"

"Then why do you assume you'll always win?"

Her attitude slips back to manageable when I reply, "Because you will never be on a team opposite me long enough to consider defeat, much less experience it. Even if I'm playing in hell, I'll drag you to the fiery depths right alongside me."

Her mouth gapes as her brows stitch.

That was not what she expected me to say.

I use her distraction to my advantage. "But, in saying that, we need to play this game with the tenacity it demands." She's more subdued when confused, so I pile on terms I haven't had time to properly assess. "We need to be discreet. We can't—"

"Fuck in an elevator with dozens of cameras and microphones only feet away?"

I clench and release my fists, fighting not to wash out her filthy mouth with my cum, before I jerk up my chin.

"Why?" she snaps out before I can utter a syllable.

A mask slips over my face. It is two seconds too late for a woman as shrewd as Zoya to miss. She learns the same brutal truth Mikhail is seconds from learning when the elevator arrives at the penthouse level.

I'm a liar in every meaning of the word.

"Mikhail said you were leaving your wife. That you had filed for an annulment."

"I did." Her relief is as short-lived as mine when I thought I could end an agreement with a sternly worded email. "But I withdrew the request an hour ago."

Her slap shoots my head to the side and sends a crack rumbling through the elevator.

It also makes me as hard as stone, but since we're being eyeballed by the very man I threatened to kill if he saw an inch of the skin hidden beneath her teeny-tiny skirt, I lick up the droplet of blood her strike caused to my top lip instead of smearing it across her scrumptious mouth.

It's a fucking hard feat, one I only achieve when I realize Mikhail isn't the only Dokovic watching the farce.

Our father is here as well.

Fuck it.

16

ZOYA

"*L*et me go."

I kick, thrash, and fight with a heap of grit, but Andrik's grip on my waist doesn't budge an inch. He carries me into Mikhail's apartment like I'm seconds from having my blood drained from my veins before he forcefully pins me to the armchair he ravished me on last night.

He's not hurting me, though anyone outside of our duo is unaware of that. Mikhail requests Andrik to calm down numerous times with both his words and his fists before he turns his focus to the man smirking smugly with his shoulder propped on the door-jamb of his entryway.

"Will you say something? This is meant to be a negotiation, not a fucking shakedown."

Andrik appears as shocked by his confession as I am. It exposes he was unaware of the third man's inclusion. He merely hid his bewilderment better than I did.

Since I am no longer fighting him, too stunned by the similarities between the three men to continue fighting, Andrik frees me from his grip before he moves to a bar at the side of the massive living area.

Even knowing he's a cheating asshole won't stop me from admitting he has a sexy walk. It's full of arrogance, as cocky as his leering eyes when I don't immediately race for the door the instant he turns his back to me.

He's watching me in the glass feature wall on the far side of the dining table.

That's why I don't bolt.

I can feel the heat of his covetousness even on the coldest day.

That, and the fact the man I assume is his father is blocking the only exit. His jacket is too bulky to reveal if he is carrying a weapon, and I don't feel like going home with a bullet wound today.

Nikita has enough on her plate. I don't want to add more drama to the overflowing dish.

Andrik takes a hefty gulp of whiskey before spinning to face me. A mask has slipped over his eyes. It is the same one he summoned two seconds too late in the elevator.

"How much?" he asks, his voice flat. I'm lost but am not given the chance to announce my confusion. "Discretion comes at a cost, so I need to know how much it will take to secure yours."

Confusion juts my words. "You want to pay me to keep quiet?"

"Yes," he answers matter-of-factly.

An expression I don't know how to read crosses his face when I say, "You don't need to pay me to keep my mouth shut. I won't tell a soul about what happened between us." I should leave it there. It would be the smart thing to do. But playing it safe is boring, and my life needs some color. "Also, it's a little late to negotiate *after* the deed has been done." I lock my eyes with Andrik's and sneer. "If you were too quick off the mark to get your money's worth, that's not my issue."

Mikhail laughs at the same time the man I assume is his father asks, "You're a prostitute?"

After flicking my narrowed eyes to a pair identical to Mikhail's in every way, I wave my hand at his eldest son, who stands frozen.

Andrik isn't humored like his little brother.

He's angry.

Good.

"Did you miss what he said? He's offering to pay me—"

"For your discretion," Andrik spits out, his anger rising along with his voice. "Not because you had sex with me."

"For *my* discretion?" I drag my hand across my chest that is thrusting so hard I'm on the verge of a heart attack. "I don't need to be discreet. I'm as free as a bird. Single and ready to mingle." Andrik looks seconds from blowing his top, yet I continue to push. "So this must be more about you than me. Who do you need to be discreet for, Andrik? Your colleagues? Your family? Your—"

"His wife," says the man who suddenly appears nowhere near as worried as he was moments ago. "He's married."

I drop my jaw. My shocked act is worthy of an Oscar. "You're married!"

The buzz of multiple orgasms circles the drain when Andrik keeps his answer short and to the point. "Yes."

There are no pledges that his wife will never have him the way I've had him or falsities that promise his marital status is hours from changing.

He hits me with the honesty he should have awarded me last night, even though I'm skeptical it would have changed the outcome.

I didn't look for a ring last night because I didn't want to find one.

My shameful act in the elevator mere minutes ago is proof of this.

With my wounds not deep enough to scar, I dig the blade in

more profoundly, ensuring a lesson will be learned from my stupidity. "Ten thousand should do it."

"What?" Mikhail blurts out his shock instead of keeping it deeply buried like his older brother does.

"That's about the going rate, isn't it? Five thousand per... *indiscretion*." When his father's brows furrow, I lose all my scruples. "Last night was technically two indiscretions, but I'm happy to offer a discount since the elevator romp on the way up was a little quick-winded."

Mikhail's expression is back to humored.

His father's is a cross between frustrated and disgusted.

Andrik's remains unchanged.

He's still pissed as fuck.

So, naturally, I pour salt over his wounds. "I'd rather cash, but if that isn't available, I can take a check."

When Mikhail's father's eyes shoot to him, wide and with shock, he says, "I have around six or seven K in the safe. I could probably rustle up another three or four from last night's takings at Brody's."

The room falls silent when Andrik asks, "Who should I make the check out to?"

He pulls a checkbook and pen out of the breast pocket of his suit jacket. The shock of his offer conjures so much silence the click of his pen as he prepares to jot down my details has my heart attempting to leap out of my chest.

But I'm as stubborn as I am stupid.

"Zoya Galdean." Since I have no intention of entering the prostitution conglomerate, I spell out a last name not on any official documents. "G. A. L. D. E. A. N."

The rip of the check from the checkbook matches the tear that shreds through my heart when he pulls it from its stub and hands it to me before offering to show me the way out.

"I know the way."

"Still—"

I race for the door before another word can leave Andrik's mouth.

Since he sees his son's check as an affidavit of my promised silence, his father doesn't block my exit. He steps to the side, smirking with an arrogance that must have been passed down for centuries.

It is too cultured to have been recently unearthed.

Untrusting of elevators, I throw open the emergency exit door next to the service elevator before I begin a multiple-floor descent.

I make it thirty floors before my legs refuse to gallop another flight. They're still shuddering in the aftermath of two orgasms, but I'm going to pretend anger is the cause of their aching state. It may be the only way they'll keep moving.

A lady dressed as if she is about to attend the opera startles when I exit the emergency stairwell on her floor. I don't blame her. I'm a sweaty, sticky mess that doubles the guilt weighing down my shoulders.

Once again, anger is my excuse.

"I forgot they don't call these buildings skyscrapers for no reason," I murmur when she peers at me in suspicion when I join her in waiting for the elevator. "My planned exercise regimen far exceeded my capabilities."

She smiles. It exposes that she knows I'm a lying piece of shit, but she doesn't call me out on it—thankfully. "Perhaps next time?"

"Perhaps," I reply as the elevator dings, announcing its arrival.

I gesture for my co-rider to enter first. It is stupid of me to do because her generously plump frame blocks the cause of the spicy scent lingering in the air until it is too late.

I'm once again trapped in the small confines of an elevator with Andrik.

Mercifully, this time around, we're not the sole occupants.

Mikhail is here as well.

Although Mikhail looks remorseful, I slant closer to the stranger wearing too much perfume than the man I was certain was more a friend than foe only minutes ago.

Mikhail can't be trusted—and neither the hell can my libido.

Andrik is an asshole, a reincarnation of the devil, yet the first thing my heart did when it spotted him in the corner of the space far more generous than its less stellar counterpart was stutter.

When a breathy cussword bounces off the brushed steel doors of the elevator, I keep my head front and center but veer my eyes to the side.

Mikhail glares at Andrik like he just kicked him in the shin, before he shifts his focus to the woman forcing enough distance between Andrik and me to ensure I will make it through this elevator ride unscathed. "Is that a Rachel Deprovor brochure?"

I glare at Mikhail with flaring nostrils when his question steals the devotion of my only lifeline. "Why, yes, it is. How observant of you, young man. Are you a fan of Rachel Depovor's work?"

I wordlessly plea for Mikhail not to leave me defenseless when our co-rider twists to face him.

After the quickest flash of a remorseful smirk, he answers, "Of course. Did you hear she was having a showing at Br..."

I miss the rest of his reply. I can't hear anything over my pulse raging through my body when a tattooed hand curls around my elbow, and I'm tugged back until my back is splayed flush with Andrik's erratically panting chest.

The zap of our bodies colliding shudders my thighs and causes an arrogant, big-headed smirk to twist Andrik's lips. It takes everything I have not to take care of the pretentiousness beaming out of him with my fists. I wouldn't hesitate if I trusted myself enough not to surrender to the insanity that usually arrives with his punishments.

Since I don't, I keep my hands balled at my sides.

Andrik sounds as disappointed by my lack of retaliation as I feel. "Did you stop because you're worried about the repercussions, *милая*?" His breathy, whispered words floating over my ear send goose bumps racing to the surface of my skin. "Or because you know I will respond *exactly* how you're hoping."

"I'm not hoping for anything." After a breather to settle the spike his growl caused my blood pressure, I say, "I wouldn't want to slap you if you'd stop playing games. You just asked me to leave. You paid me to keep quiet, and now you're... you're..." My words trail off, desperate not to portray the lust-fueled idiot I've been parading over the past twenty-four hours.

He's married. There's no chance of us being anything, so why does my heart believe differently? Why is it making out like he wants me to stay?

"I don't want to be here. I don't want to be with you."

His lips brush the shell of my ear when he asks, "Why?"

The calm, collective way he asks his question skyrockets my anger.

"Because you're married," I answer through clenched teeth, stating the obvious.

Mikhail talks louder when my angered whisper almost regains me the focus of our dressed-to-the-nines co-rider. Her neck cranks my way, meaning he has to get up close and personal with an elderly neighbor.

Once he has her utmost devotion resecured with a heap of attention I'm skeptical she's ever received, Andrik says, "As I stated earlier, it is a contract. A business transaction. It's not worth more than the piece of paper authenticating it."

"Then why did you cancel the annulment?" I sound desperate, and I hate myself for it. But you can't feel the tension brimming between us. It is electrifying. I've never experienced such a crazy range of emotions, and not all of them are based on anger.

Andrik's fingers flattened on the lower half of my stomach drum as frantically as my heart thrashes my ribs when he mutters, "Because I need answers. I deserve them." The sheer honesty in his voice drops it to barely a whisper. "And Dr. Hemway announced yesterday that you can't help me get them."

It takes several floors for the reason of my inclusion in his reply to smack into me. It makes me sick to my stomach.

Mikhail said Andrik's marriage was so fresh he didn't know about it when he colluded for us to meet at his penthouse. That can only mean one thing.

Andrik wasn't at Dr. Hemway's office yesterday to support his wife through fertility challenges. He was there for the exact reason my legs were forced into stirrups when I became of age—to purchase a breeding-approved wife.

Andrik's grip on my arm loosens when our elevator's arrival at the foyer of Mikhail's building presents the perfect solution for me to be free of him.

"I can't give you what you want, so you can either let me go now, or after I tell anyone who will listen that your marriage isn't worth the piece of paper authenticating it." I nudge my head to the group of paparazzi attempting to barge past the security personnel keeping them out of the foyer. "Starting with them."

My threat sounds legitimate since my throat is burning with anger. I've never felt more ashamed than I did when Andrik announced he was no longer getting an annulment. That shame isn't one tenth of the anger I'm currently experiencing.

Not all of it centers around Andrik's betrayal.

My sights are set on someone I've known far longer than him.

"That will make a lot of people angry." Andrik walks around me until his suit-covered body shelters me from the numerous camera flashes bright enough to illuminate the walls of the elevator even with it being in the far back corner of Mikhail's building. "Are you sure you're ready for that level of animosity, *Лисичка*?"

My immediate nod shocks him, much less the honesty in my tone when I reply, "I was born ready for it."

It isn't time for coyness. Despite his best efforts, the smallest grin tugs on Andrik's lips before he steps aside so I can walk out of his life without so much as a backward glance.

17

ANDRIK

*M*y jaw throbs as manically as my cock when Zoya glides past a conglomerate as focused on the bottom line as the federation is. A handful of heads twist her way. They're all male and will be dead by the end of the day if they don't shift their focus off her ass before Konstantine scans their credentials into my database.

Once they're on my radar, they'll only be removed one way.

With a bullet.

Don't misconstrue. I understand their instant fascination. Zoya has a body that should be worshiped for twenty-four hours of every day, but her defiance deserves an equal amount of attention yet seems forever overlooked.

I've always been good at reading people. Zoya's story would have most men backing away with their hands held in the air.

It's a pity for her I'm a stubborn fuck who always gets want he wants.

I want her, so I will have her.

No contest.

I just refuse for it to occur under the eyes of the puppeteers controlling my grandfather's and father's every move. They're coming out of the woodwork faster than I could have imagined when I orchestrated my scheme, making me hopeful it won't be as lengthy as first perceived.

Though I doubt anyone would see a lifetime commitment as a brief proceeding.

After slanting my head to hide my words from my father, who is approaching me as fast as Zoya is endeavoring to get away from me, I say, "She's coming out the west entrance. Mikhail is hot on her tail."

A conceited grin curls my top lip when I recall the cause of Mikhail's slow chase. Since comms were back in operation, we knew who would enter the elevator on level sixty-three before the doors opened, but Mikhail refused to follow my ruse until I kicked him hard enough to give him a permanent limp.

Not even the full deeds of Brody's could get him over the line during our rushed negotiations to find Zoya before anyone in our father's crew.

I should be pleased I pulled the wool over Mikhail's eyes as well as our father's, but I'm not.

I am too tenacious to admit my worries center around Zoya also believing our meeting was solely about a payout for her silence, so I'll blame it on knowing there's currently more than one woman in Chelabini with my sperm inside her.

That's fucked to even consider, and my mother would be mortified.

The remembrance places on my game face with barely a second to spare.

My father is at my side, signaling over a woman most men would hand over a fortune to bed.

Arabella has class, sophistication, and beauty. She just lacks the

tenacity that makes Zoya such a firecracker. There's no stubbornness to crack, no willfulness to bend. She was made to fit the mold
instead of demanding its reproduction to ensure the perfect cast.

She's boring, and I'm a prick who struggles to hide her deficien-
cies when she holds out her hand in offering as any gushing bride-
to-be would when approaching their spouse. I stuff my hands into
my pockets before shifting on my feet to face my father.

"What's going on?" My tone speaks the words I can't say with an
audience. *Why the fuck are you railroading me again?*

This is his third incident today.

There is pushing the limits, and then there is completely over-
riding them.

His interference today is the latter.

My answer comes from a woman who needs to learn her place.
"We figured with the media in surplus from your father's first visit
home in years, that it would be the prime opportunity to announce
your engagement." Dina, Arabella's mother, curls her hand over the
one I left hanging before tugging Arabella in closer like she has
more say than my soon-to-be wife. "Kolya is confident it will
increase your father's lead in the latest polls by two percent."

She gleams like I should be impressed.

I am far from it.

Her response is the exact reason I want to return my family
name to the notoriety it once held. My ancestors didn't hold press
conferences to settle a debate on who is the most powerful. They
battled like Vikings and siphoned enough blood from their enemies'
veins to fill the rivers of Russia.

They could marry who they wanted, when they wanted, without
the absurdity of multiple events in the lead-up to the exchange of
vows they had no plan to uphold.

It wasn't about giving constituencies something to discuss

around the watercooler with the hope of securing their vote at the next election.

They did what they wanted when they wanted.

So as you can imagine, it took everything I had to pretend I'm fine with the federation's decision to refuse to acknowledge any paperwork I endorsed this morning until my family's dynasty receives some sort of shebang from my fuckup, and that a future presidential puppet wasn't conceived last night.

The only reason I agreed to go along with their suggestions was because Zoya was leaving my premises faster than my sleep-deprived head could come up with a better solution.

My smarts dip when I'm tired.

They're wholly obliterated when my dick takes over the reins.

It wants Zoya as much as I do, and although my "marriage" will have her vying to deny her attraction to me, she won't ever pull the wool over my eyes.

Betrothed or not, she wants me.

Her thirst is as obvious as the front row of journalists hoping they're misreading the brief my grandfather's head of staff is giving them. They'd rather I announce a bid for candidacy than an alteration to my relationship status.

Though I doubt either revelation will simmer their efforts for an exclusive for long. I'm propositioned more by members of the media than by any other field.

Freebies from high-end prostitutes is a close second.

Desperate for two seconds of peace so I can work through some of my confusion, I head for the podium-like stage my father's team would have ensured was covered with his campaign flyers seconds after being erected.

Arabella and her mother fall into step behind me when I tap the microphone to announce the start of the conference I was unaware would be occurring this morning, much less with the scent of another woman's arousal on my cock and lips.

With my thoughts immediately veering to how delicious Zoya tastes, I keep my statement as brief as the one Dina issued earlier in my office before I step back to allow the press the opportunity of adding images to the featured stories they'll run within the hour.

When the flash of cameras doesn't reach one tenth of the glare Zoya and Mikhail's entrance caused, my grandfather's chief of staff leans into my side and mutters, "It needs to look authentic. If it doesn't, call this off now and tell your grandfather you've changed your mind. A loveless marriage will turn voters off even more than your father forever knocking up his mistresses."

Word to the wise, don't mock a man who has nothing to lose.

It never ends well.

Kolya is seconds from learning that the hard way before he distracts me by nudging his head in the direction Zoya went. "Let's just hope *they* don't blame her for the first out-of-wedlock bastard birthed into the Dokovic realm if the procedure last night was effective."

He doesn't need to announce who is behind his underhanded threat. The shakiness of his voice tells me everything I need to know.

He fears the wrath of the federation and believes I should depict the same trepidation.

I will never bow at the feet of an organization so cowardly they refuse to show their faces. But since I can't announce that yet, against the protests of my cock and the small snippets of morals my mother drummed into me before she was forcefully removed from my life, I band my arm around Arabella's slim waist and tug her into my side.

A vein in her neck thuds louder than Kolya's relieved sigh when

I tilt our hips with an intimacy only someone who has bedded her would have before I brush my nose against hers.

I inherited many traits from my father the past thirty years. This is the only one I've ever replicated from before my mother disappeared. Despite the many stepmothers I endured during my youth, my father only ever used this move on my mother. It is the perfect skit to have those around me believing I am in love because my father has never loved anyone but himself. My mother, however, let him get away with murder the instant their noses brushed.

The journalists eat up my rare public display of affection. They snap a hundred pictures, and the heat of their shouted words as they ask a range of questions about our "supposed" upcoming nuptials doubles the hue spreading across Arabella's cheeks.

I'm barely touching her, so her mother's claim of her purity must be accurate.

Only yesterday, the knowledge would have sparked a fierce interest in me.

Today, my cock doesn't feel the slightest flutter.

It is as uninspired as the names listed on the files Dr. Hemway delivered to my hotel this morning, and as insipid as my mood becomes when Petr, the man assigned to trace Zoya's every step, announces into my earpiece that he's lost visual of his target.

Arabella squeaks when my grip on her waist turns deadly. I wring it like I want to Petr's neck while my glare at the security camera in the corner of the new apartment block has him coughing up an excuse that makes me instantly hard despite my fury.

"She kneed me in the balls before popping her fist into my mouth." His next set of words comes out with a stutter of a man on the verge of peeing his pants. "I-I didn't retaliate. Bu-but she kneed me hard enough that by the time I caught my breath, she was long gone."

"Kon—"

I don't even get out his entire name before Konstantine announces he is tracking Zoya's movements from when she left the hotel and that he will have an update on her location within minutes. "Where do you want me to send the coordinates?"

With my arm wrapped around the waist of my alleged fiancée, my reply shouldn't be immediate. But it is. "Send them directly to me."

I don't wait for Konstantine to respond before I move away from the media endeavoring to work out the cause of the groove between my brows. He would follow my orders even if it instigated the massacre of an entire family. He's good like that.

Unfortunately, not all members of my team are as observant of the rules. My return to the foyer of Mikhail's building casts numerous shadows on the pristine marble floors.

I haven't even conjured up an excuse to leave, yet Dina is already bitching in my ear about how it'll look bad if I leave now. "Your father—"

"Knows when to shut his mouth," I snap out, annoyed I'm having my authority questioned by someone who should only ever be seen in the background of every frame. "I have an urgent matter I need to take care of."

"Okay. That's fine," Arabella murmurs at the same time Dina asks, "What kind of matter?"

Again, her tone better take a back seat before I place her behind the scenes permanently.

She strives to wipe the fear from her eyes. It is still prominent when she leans in and whispers, "I'm only asking, Kazimir, because Arabella is in a prime ovulation window." I am lost, and for once, I'm glad. "It is the perfect time for conception."

Suspicion echoes in my tone. "As you stated this morning when you used that as your excuse to have her turkey basted with my sperm. You said it was prime breeding time and that you didn't want to miss the opportunity of fulfilling the sole term of my contract at the earliest possible convenience."

My wording choice could be better. I just don't have the time or the patience to flick through a dictionary for a better definition of the jargon she hit me with this morning when she used the procedure Arabella undertook last night as a reason to deny my request for an annulment.

"That is correct," Dina replies, her throat bobbing. "But the attending physician announced that the probability of conception would be higher if... *it* was administered again."

"It?"

My cock shrivels when she thrusts her hand at my crotch. Its withered response isn't solely because it is the first time it's had a wrinkly hand within an inch of it. It is also compliments to what she says next. "He encourages an old-fashioned approach to conception." She grabs my arm and pulls me deeper into the curtains flanking the floor-to-ceiling windows of the foyer. "Arabella is *exceptionally* trained in *all* aspects of matrimony. She is ripe and ready to please."

Ripe?

She's sporting off her daughter's assets as if she is selling me a piece of steak.

After what I've seen in my industry, I shouldn't be surprised. Women are bartered for as often as cocaine is traded. Their value rarely surpasses the white bricks of snow I'd hand over for free if forced to pick between banking its profits or burying my head between Zoya's legs again.

I will *always* pick the latter.

"You just need to give her a chance to show you she will far succeed your greatest expectations."

Before I can remind Dina of the exact wording of my contract with her daughter, Konstantine announces he has unearthed Zoya's location. "She just entered Stoltz and Hemway's office complex. She isn't alone." My back molars crunch when he says, "Mikhail is shadowing closely behind her. Want me to send someone in?"

"No," I reply, aware nothing is done right unless you do it yourself. "I will handle this."

Konstantine hums like he knows a cleanup crew will be called to Stoltz and Hemway before close of business, but then a harsh swallow cuts off its lengthy rumble.

"What is it?"

I'm seconds from signing Mikhail's death certificate, when Konstantine shifts my focus elsewhere. "Man entering at your six. Blue suit. Seedy stache. One too many undone buttons. And a four-carat ruby on the custom piece on his left pinkie." My eyes bounce to each feature he points out as I tighten my jaw more and more. "Does that crest look familiar to you?"

I squint, then cuss. I can't see shit from this angle.

"The sun is—"

My phone buzzing in my pocket interrupts my excuse. With my eyes on the man greeting my father as if they're long-lost acquaintances, I dig my phone out of my pocket, then apprehensively drop my eyes to the image Konstantine forwarded.

Vengeance burns through my blood hot and fast. It isn't an exact replica of the emblem I drew over a decade ago, but it is pretty fucking close.

"Who is he?"

A keyboard being punished sounds before Konstantine's gravely tone. "Running him through facials now."

Forever impatient, I say, "Tell Mikhail to move in closer until I get there."

I don't want to lose Zoya's tail for the second time, but I'm too curious about the unnamed man's identity to wait for facial recognition software to find a match. I've been seeking the owner of a large ruby ring with an engraved family crest on it for over thirty years. It was on the hand of the man my mother slapped mere seconds before she vanished without a trace—the same hand that left my cheek with a hairline scar.

"Warn Mikhail what will happen if he loses sight of her."

"I'll send exterminators to Petr's location now," Konstantine replies, announcing he knows what my unvoiced threat entails. "Anything else?"

Conscious he has eyes everywhere, I shake my head before yanking the bead-size communication device from my ear and dropping it to the floor.

The crunch of its demise is softer than the whack I hit my father's back with before demanding an introduction to the man who has the focus of my entire team.

Even Arabella is gawking at him in surprise, and I'm really fucking curious to unearth why.

18

ZOYA

"*I* thought the tears your colleague shed as he fell to his knees would have warned you to stay away." I bump closed one of the many filing cabinets hidden at the back of the reception desk of Stoltz and Hemway before spinning to face the man whose pricy cologne announced his stalk long before the slow bob of his Adam's apple. "If you're as eager to breed as your brother, I suggest you turn around. It may be the only way your nuts will stay out of your stomach."

Mikhail smiles.

He. Fucking. Smiles.

"I'm not playing, Mikhail."

It only took me minutes to realize I was being followed when I raced out of Mikhail's building, too hot with fury to remember my only mode of transport was parked in his underground parking lot.

I dealt with the tail as I wish I could have taken Andrik down.

I kneed him in the balls.

"I know how serious you are, Sunshine." With his hands held in the air, Mikhail takes a non-defensive step forward. "I just figured if you truly want to remain off his radar, you'll need the help I thought I was offering earlier."

He scans his eyes over the filing cabinets I'm not even one-tenth of the way through. Dr. Hemway doesn't file his patients' records in alphabetical order like every other gynecologist. He has a system that isn't meant to be cracked—or rate women on their fertility status.

I thought he was one of the good guys.

I've never felt more stupid.

Not even Mikhail's betrayal hurt this much, because I understand he must side with his family.

Dr. Hemway was as close to family as I had in my adolescence.

I never thought he would betray me like this.

Mikhail's low tone shifts my focus off my heartache. "There has to be hundreds of patients' files here. You won't find who you're seeking without my help."

"Who said I'm seeking anyone? Maybe I just want to ensure my imprint on society remains anonymous."

I hate the sympathetic look he gives me. It is the same look I was given when the sole reason for my existence was removed from the table and I was overlooked time and time again.

That's why I stupidly crave Andrik's attention. I like that he picked me over anyone else—even his wife. Don't get me wrong. I still feel guilty as hell. It was just nice to be picked first for a change instead of being disregarded like a broken toy.

Childish tears burn my eyes when Mikhail reminds me why I'll never be first. "I saw your face drop when you realized his connection to Dr. Hemway." Again, he doesn't need to say Andrik's name for me to know who he is referencing. "You know why he was here as well as I do."

I hold out my hand, stopping him from coming any closer when an immature tear is close to rolling down my cheek. I should be used to rejection by now. It has been scalded in me since I was eleven. It just hurts being reminded why I was left to fend for myself at fifteen.

I had to do things no child should have to do to survive, yet my mother lived in a suburban mansion with a butler and half a dozen servants.

I doubt I would have seen adulthood if I hadn't met Nikita and her family. They had nothing, yet they made me a part of their family as if their bank balances were garnished with millions of dollars.

The remembrance should end my search and see me returning to the town I now call home.

My mother articulated Aleena's name without a single snarl, so to others, she is clearly not as "unfortunate" as me. It's just my first two years on the streets that taught me even women draped in jewels can still be abused.

Angrily, I brush my cheek to make sure it isn't wet before murmuring, "I need to make sure she wasn't on his list." I stop, breathe, then correct myself. "That she will never be on a list like that."

"Who?" Mikhail asks a second before the truth dawns on him. "Your sister?"

My nod almost sends fresh tears streaming down my face. I hold them back. Just.

Mikhail works his jaw side to side as he contemplates. He wants to offer an easy solution. Since he can't, he goes with honesty. "If she is on a list, you won't find it here." When I huff, he talks louder. "This is the first place men using this type of service would look to undercut the middleman. Dr. Hemway is a spineless leech, but Andrik wouldn't have used him if he wasn't smart."

It takes everything I have not to defend Dr. Hemway. Don't ask me why. I wouldn't be able to give you an honest answer.

"So if you want answers, you need to go to the source of your anger. You need to confront..." His words are traded for a smile as he peers at someone over my shoulder. "You either have balls of steel or I gave your intellect more credit than it deserves."

I crank my neck back so fast my muscles scream in disgust. Dr. Hemway is standing in the alcove of the storage room of Stoltz and Hemway. His nose is bloody, his top lip is cracked, and multiple bruises dot his face and torso. He looks like he's been put through the wringer, but the only emotion I showcase when our eyes lock and hold is fury.

"Was she on his list?"

Dr. Hemway steps back like my question is loaded with more than anger. He looks set to dodge bullets. "What? I'd—"

I cut him off with a roar the most unhinged man in the world would be proud of. "Was she on the approved list you gave your last *client* of the day yesterday?"

His eyes widen in shock. "He told you about that... *assignment*?"

"No. He didn't need to." I step closer to him. "The guilt on your face tells me everything I need to know." I speak slower, breathing through every punctuated word that grows louder with each one delivered. "Was. My. Baby. Sister. On. *His.* List?" I almost say Aleena's name. The only reason I don't is because I don't trust either of these men standing across from me. They trade women. That makes them no better than the scum I was forced to endure when I was kicked out of my home when I was still a child.

"No," Dr. Hemway answers, weakening my frustration by a smidge. "As I told you yesterday, I haven't seen her in years. Not since she..."

"Got your seal of approval?" I ask when his words trail off.

When silence is the only answer given, I'm seconds from discovering if he, like Andrik, also gets horny when struck.

His brief headshake saves his face from additional bruises by the skin of his teeth.

"I've kept her off their lists the same way I have you for years."

I stare at him in shock, unmoving and unspeaking.

He can't be saying what I think he is. I suffer through horrific cramps and nonstop pain a minimum of three weeks a month. Sex hurts. I bleed, for crying out loud.

Although my last two points could solely correspond with having sex with someone as well-endowed as Andrik, my prior two can't be as easily excused.

I'm an endometriosis sufferer.

Shock pummels into me when something Dr. Hemway said yesterday smacks back into me.

The severity of the diagnosis doesn't often correspond with the pain allotment. Even someone with minor scarring can face immense pain.

"You—"

"Kept your sister safe the only way I knew how," Dr. Hemway interrupts. "I logged your results into her file."

Disappointment shouldn't be the first emotion I express.

Regretfully it is.

I'm reminded that Mikhail is in the room with us when he stops Dr. Hemway from approaching me by coughing in silent warning. He fans out his jacket to announce he's carrying. He doesn't trust him. I understand why. I'm having a hard time believing him, and I've known him for over a decade.

My pain is real, so there's no judging that, but if he diagnosed Aleena as infertile to remove her name from a list we were placed on when we were born, why hasn't our mother discarded Aleena like she did me? Why is she still blaming the smudge against our family name solely on me?

I'm happy to take the heat off Aleena. That doesn't mean I'm not also curious.

My eyes float up from the floor when Dr. Hemway whispers, "I want to give you answers, Zoya, but I can't do that right now." I'm reminded he is bruised and battered when the shudder of his words announces how hard his body is trembling. "Kiara"—he chokes on his next two words—"my daughter." His face is the picture of petrified. "I can't lose my family."

I nod in full understanding. I'm here for that exact reason. There's just one thing that is unclear. Why is he here, then? If he's worried about his family, why leave them for something of little importance?

When I ask him that, he moves toward a filing cabinet I was hours from searching before he ruffles through the middle stack. In seconds, he removes three thick files. One I recognize from yesterday. The other two are nowhere near as thick.

After storing one under his arm, he places my patient record on top of the remaining file before he hands them to me. "Now you will *never* be on a list. Neither of you."

A brick lodges in my throat when the shake of my hands rattles my file enough to expose the name of the secondary record.

It belongs to Aleena.

"Thank you," I whisper, still wary but alert enough to know he risked a lot to come here and remove mine, Aleena's, and I assume his wife's files from a stack of thousands that will no longer be monitored by him.

Dr. Hemway cringes like he doesn't deserve my praise before he dips his chin in farewell and hotfoots it to the closest exit—the same exit being blocked by Mikhail.

"Mikhail." My mutter of his name gains me his attention. My reminder of his marshmallow heart frees Dr. Hemway from his wrath. "If you lose that, you'll be no better than them."

After a beat, he steps to the side, giving Dr. Hemway enough space to skirt past, before he joins me in the middle of the storage room.

His walk shouldn't be so cocky.

He's still on my shitlist.

When his eyes drop to the half of Aleena's name exposed by my wonky hold of the files, I pull them in close to my chest before heading for the exit. I got what I came here for, so there's no need for me to continue breaking the law.

"What now?" Mikhail asks after racing to catch up with me.

"I'm going home," I answer before I can stop myself.

My brain is too clouded with confusion to think clearly. I need to step back and look at the entire picture. I can't do that here. The memories are too painful, and I don't trust myself not to demand answers I'm not sure I want to unearth.

My steps across a dusty lot slow when Mikhail says, "He will follow you there."

"No, he won't." I twist to face him. "Because he doesn't know where that is, and you're not going to tell him which way I went."

Again, he slows my steps. "He will log your tags into the transport department database the instant his security team strips them from the servers of the underground parking lot of my building." I hate how much honesty is in his tone when he continues. "If you so much as drive through a toll booth or past an infringement camera, he will learn of your whereabouts."

"Then I'll take the bus," I shout, my anger picking up.

My car is the only thing of value I own, yet the thought of abandoning it isn't the sole cause of my frustration. I'm the most annoyed about the hope Mikhail's warning flooded my veins with.

I can't be attracted to a taken man.

It is morally unethical.

I just wish Andrik was as ugly as a monkey's butt, and that the sheer honesty in his eyes when he said his marriage was a tactically laid out ruse seemed more fraudulent than real. Then I could walk away without the slightest snippet of hesitation. I'd stop second-guessing my guilt as doubt and move on with my life.

"His hacker will infiltrate the bus network as fast as he does any website, social media app, or bank account you use. From what I witnessed, he's snowed fucking under, Sunshine. Buried deep. He won't let you walk away from him." I'm about to yell at him that it isn't Andrik's choice. That he doesn't own me. Before I can, Mikhail's eyes widen and his mouth gapes. "Unless..."

"Unless?" I encourage, desperate to get away from the inane thoughts in my head telling me infertility makes me worthless.

Mikhail digs a small black device out of his pocket. I have no clue what it is, but Mikhail stares at it as if it is the answer of every riddle. "He'll kill me but fuck it." Mischievousness fires through his eyes when he locks them with mine. "It is a little brother's job to make his siblings miserable." His expression takes on a serious note. "And maybe this will replace the hate daggers you've been hitting me with over the past hour back to friendly fire."

I don't hate him, but once again, I'm too confused to express any emotion, much less one that requires a fully functioning heart.

After exhaling his disappointment that I didn't deny his accusation of dislike, he explains what the device is and how it operates. "You can't use it at every location, or he'll track the disruption of intermittence. But if you coordinate its use with visits to less monitored locations, you should be able to make it home relatively unscathed."

"Is there a tracker in this?" I accept the dirtbox he's holding out for me before swiveling it around. It's so small it shouldn't elicit so much power. But I feel stronger just holding it.

Dark hairs flop into Mikhail's eyes when he shakes his head. "No. No one will know where it is used or when. Not even me." When I fail to hide the flare of disappointment darting through my eyes, his lips inch higher. "You know where to find me when you're ready."

"For?" I ask, still too bamboozled to dig through the rubble unaided.

He bumps me like he knows I'm nowhere near as stupid as I am portraying, before he jogs to a car parked a couple of spots up. "This should get you across the country multiple times."

I push back the wad of cash he attempts to hand me. "I can't take your money."

"Why the fuck not?" he asks, his tone serious.

He *pffts* me when I say, "I didn't earn it."

"You reminded Andrik that he is human. That's worth far more than this." His expression switches from serious to playful. "And I don't want you using the excuse you've got no data or some shit like that when you're finally ready to forgive me." The crinkle between his brows is back, deeper and as uneased as ever. "I didn't know they were going to bombard you like that. My father made out—"

"It doesn't matter," I interrupt, too confused to add more to the over-stacked plate. "I'll pay you back." I split the bundle he handed me in half and return the bigger half to him. "So I guess you better give me your number so I have a way of contacting you for your bank details."

You'd swear I invited him into my bed. That's how big his smile is when he plucks a bill from his stack and scribbles his phone number across it.

I roll my eyes when he hands it to me.

Of course, it is the biggest denomination available in Russia.

"What?" Mikhail's grin is brighter than the high-hanging sun. "It's not like you'll spend it." He pops the cap onto the marker he summoned from nowhere before smacking his lips together with a similar noise. "Your eyes didn't get the slightest sugar-baby gleam when I mentioned Andrik's wealth earlier."

"Well-rehearsed on the traits of sugar babies, are we, Marsh-mallow Man?" I ask, hating his dour tone.

I'm reminded that he's been the most honest of the bunch when he quotes, "Will you call me a hussy if I say yes?" When I smile, he nudges his head to his ride before opening the passenger side door in offering. "My coffin has already been chosen, so why not add an extra few nails for sturdiness."

If I truly believed he was in danger, I wouldn't accept his offer.

But since I know the depths one sibling will go for another, I push the button on the dirtbox before sliding onto the passenger's seat of Mikhail's fancy ride.

19

ZOYA

"*H*ey." I lift my chin from my chest before slowly pointing it in the direction of the groggy voice. My lips curl into a grin when I spot Nikita sauntering across the miniscule living room of her grandparents' rent-controlled basement apartment. She looks zonked but works what should be a negative like a model does a catwalk. Her voluptuous dark locks, her soul-searing eyes, and a body that exposes she rarely sits still ensures she will never be classified as ugly.

I bury my face in her scrubs-covered stomach when she wraps her arm around my shoulders and hugs me hello. "Have you been here all night?"

Since I don't want to portray the loser I've been for the past two weeks, I conspicuously peer at my watch before making out I have more of a life than I do. "I popped in on my way home from a night out to check on Gigi and Grampies."

Nikita arches a brow in surprise but doesn't call me out on my lie.

Since I took Mikhail's warning that Andrik would track me down as literal, I haven't been out since I returned home from Chelabini.

I'm a fool.

The only honest thing Andrik said last month were the words he spoke while endeavoring to buy my silence.

The public transport I took home crisscrossed the country, and I utilized the dirtbox discreetly as suggested, but I'm still surprised Mikhail's plan worked.

I'm also disappointed, but since I've lectured myself enough about my stupidity, I'll keep that to myself.

Furthermore, no matter how beaten down someone's ego is, they should never seek a solution for its brokenness with a taken man. I know that better than anyone. The sparks just blind me anytime Andrik is in the same realm as me.

I don't need to worry about that now since I've not seen hide nor hair of him in the past two weeks.

When the whistle of a sneaky breath sounds through my ears, I peer up at the only true friend I have. "Did you just sniff my hair?"

"No," Nikita immediately denies, pulling away. "It's dusty down here. My allergies are suffering."

"Suffering from filling the lungs of a liar."

She rolls her eyes but remains quiet, announcing I'm on the money.

When I follow her into the kitchen for a bottle of the vitamin water she mixes herself from out of date vitamins and a protein powder an over-muscled freak left at my gym six months ago, her inability to be deceitful weighs down her shoulders until she can no longer ignore its heaviness.

"When you go out dancing, your hair usually smells like cigarettes and sweat." Gulps of gross water slide down her throat before she wipes away the remnants from her lips with the back of her hand. "This morning, it smells nothing close to gross."

"That's because your schnozz was shoved too close to vomit bags and poopy bed pans all night. With how many gastro outbreaks you've been handling the past few months, you'd think a colostomy bag smells like roses."

Since she can't deny the truth, she doesn't.

Instead, she shifts her focus to a downfall as deficient as my love life—my employment status.

"How did your interview go today?" Her sympathetic look when I shake my head I can handle. It's her offer after my short announcement of rejection that scorches my throat with bile. "I can lend you—"

"No, Keet." I stray my eyes to the box hidden under the floorboards her sofa bed covers. "That money is for more important things than my energy drink obsession." I talk faster when she tries to argue. "Mr. Fakher also stuffed up the books, so my rent appears in advance. And I handed out a ton of resumes today. It won't be long before something decent pops up. Fingers crossed it is weeks before my building's owner realizes Mr. Fakher can't do basic math."

I could have sworn I owed two months of back rent, but when I tried to hand Mr. Fakher the two hundred dollars Dr. Hemway refused, he acted like my last payment was for a year instead of a measly week.

He seemed skittish. He wasn't as nervous as Dr. Hemway's brief contact during my travels home to announce that he and his family were safe and that he'd be in contact when he could, but there was something off with him.

He's usually cockier—as rationalized as Nikita's next statement. "Mr. Fakher is only fudging the books because he wants to do *precisely* that."

Like a puppy following its new owner, I shadow her steps to the bathroom that's as moldy and damp as the main living area. Nikita's grandfather is in the final stages of his life. Since she wants him to live out his last years as comfortably as possible, most of her earnings as a third-year surgical resident goes toward the medication that will allow that. The rest, and eighty percent of her moonlighting job, goes toward the equipment needed to administer a pain-free existence.

It is a cruel cycle. One I want to contribute to—hence me sneaking in the leftovers from Mikhail's generosity into the box under Nikita's bed the day after I arrived home—but my efforts have been minimal since I don't have stable employment.

Once I secure a job, I'll be able to help Nikita purchase the breathing machine Grampies so desperately needs and pay back Mikhail.

The latter was on my mind when I snuck every bill in my purse into the box when Nikita went to the hospital dispensary to plead for a monthly billing roster instead of bi-weekly. As I watched Grampies's lips turn blue as he struggled to breath, I realized he needed the money now. Mikhail didn't.

At the time, I felt like Robin Hood—robbing from the rich to save the poor.

Now I feel guilty.

Not a lot, but enough for me to yank my phone out of my pocket and scroll through my limited list of contacts. Mikhail's name is just above Nikita's. Random employment agency contacts fill the rest.

God, my life is pathetic.

Nikita coughs, drawing me from my thoughts. I'm lost as to why she looks disappointed. She's dealt with my unemployment woes as long as I have, so she should be accustomed to it by now.

I'm reminded that sleeping in an armchair never ends well when she says, "The one time I attempt a joke and it sails right over your head."

"You told a joke?" She nods, and I stammer. "When? Where? Was it in the last century?"

She ribs me, sending my giggles bouncing around the bathroom. "Haha. You're such an a—"

I save her from swearing since I know how much she hates it. "Fakher. He wants to fuck her." When her brow lifts, waiting for my critique, I twist my lips. "Your joke wasn't bad. Especially considering how long *it* has been for you."

Her groan assures me she knows what "it" refers to. "Don't remind me. It's been so long my uterus probably resembles a shriveled-up clam."

"As long as it doesn't smell like one, we're good."

That gets a laugh out of her.

After she washes the gunk off her face—medical goop, not makeup—she switches her scrubs for pajamas before she slowly trudges toward a bed that should have been dumped onto a sidewalk years ago. "Are you staying?"

She folds down one-half of the sheets before moving to the other side. "I'm good. I've got enough issues to contend with. I don't need to add *that* to the mix." I wiggle my fingers around the lumpy mattress during "that."

When I gather my coat off the armchair I was resting on when Nikita returned from a double shift, she shoots up to a half-seated position. "You can't walk home now. It's dark out."

"Says the lady who just walked home from work."

I love how quiet she is when she's void of an objection.

"And it's barely two blocks. I'll be fine."

"Three miles isn't two blocks."

"It is when you're taking the bus." Before she can argue that public transport is worse than walking the streets of Myasnikov alone, I remind her I have impressive fighting skills. "I'm almost a black belt." I grumble my next words, but it is obvious Nikita hears them. "I would have been *if* Leonard knew how to keep his dick in his pants during training."

Leonard didn't sexually assault me. He simply failed to announce that I wasn't the only female fighter he was giving "free" lessons to. He was already cocky as fuck, but he hasn't quit bragging to his minions about how good of a trainer he is since I left him with two black eyes and a busted nose after walking in on him and his 3 p.m. client.

I closed my fist that time like I should have done in the elevator with Andrik.

I move fast so Nikita won't hear the sigh of my lie as easily as my libido did. "I've also got mace. If my fist doesn't take them down, scorching-hot pepper spray will."

Her delay in replying exposes I am getting through to her. "Z..."

If cramps weren't announcing her sheets are one wayward roll from being massacred, I would have succumbed to her pleading eyes. Since I'm minutes from folding in two from the pain, I tell her I love her before I race through her front door at the speed of a bullet.

It is no easy feat considering it takes a bodybuilder to get her front door to budge from the lip. It's swelled with the dampness I am anticipating to flood my uterus over the next three to five days.

I hold my arm in the air like Nikita can see me when she says, "Message me when you get home," before I climb the half a dozen stairs to the foyer of her building.

It is far ritzier than the basement apartment Gigi and Grampies have been renting for the past several decades. It would have you believing Nikita's family is rolling in money. That was my first thought when she invited me to meet her family years ago.

The mold spores my lungs fight to keep at bay assure me otherwise.

"Thank you," I murmur to the doorman holding open the front door for me.

It's cool tonight, so there's no excuse for my slow pace down the isolated street—except perhaps the realization that I have nothing to race for.

I just walked away from the only people who have ever cared for me.

Nikita and her grandparents are all I have.

And perhaps a rascally faced marshmallow man whose generosity nudged my best friend three months closer to achieving her goal.

Remorse smacks into me when I peer down at Mikhail's name on my phone for the umpteenth time in the past two weeks. He was nice to me—scheming but still nice—yet anytime I've attempted to reach out to him, I've let his brother's actions persuade me against it.

That isn't fair, and it is time for me to stop acting like a spoiled brat who's never experienced deceit.

A grin I only ever showcase when spending time with Nikita stretches across my face when the perfect message to send pops into my head. I take a detour down a side alley so I can snap a picture of the Michelin tire plant that closed its doors several months ago.

With my smile as bright as the moon, I attach the marshmallow-looking Micheline mascot to my outgoing message.

ME:

Reminded me of you.

It's late, so I'm not anticipating for Mikhail to reply. I'm storing my phone away when it buzzes with a message.

MIKHAIL:

He better have a massive steel rod under all those layers of flab or I'm going to feel insulted.

My fingers fly over the screen of my phone.

ME:

> It's hard to tell from this angle. Want me to check?

MIKHAIL:

> Fuck yes! Unless there is actually a dude under that suit. He might not survive your grope.

With my ego desperate for a firm yet still-friendly stroke, I reply.

ME:

> Too much blood deferring from your heart to your dick is dangerous for any man, but I'm sure I will make it worthwhile for him.

MIKHAIL:

> I'm sure you will. But that isn't what I meant, Sunshine.

Another message pops up before I can demand an explanation for his riddle.

MIKHAIL:

> Though I am glad to learn your confidence didn't dip in the slightest after... you know.

I do know.

I wish I didn't, but I do.

That doesn't mean I want Mikhail to know that, though.

ME:

> After???

The vibe switches back to playful when he replies.

MIKHAIL:

Are we really going there, Sunshine? All
right. Bruise my ego some more by making
out you've yet to realize no other man can
compete with me.

My reply is so natural I type it out before my head can formulate
a single objection.

ME:

You sound just like your brother.

My eyes' quick scan of the last word mercifully saves me from
making a mistake. I move my thumb to the delete button instead of
the send.

I'm partway through deleting my reply when my phone
commences ringing. It is a video call request from Mikhail. I
consider pretending my battery is flat since my mood is circling the
drain, but that excuse flies out the window when a message pops up
in the middle of the screen.

MIKHAIL:

Marshmallow Man's rolls are reflective, and
my phone's zoom capabilities are the best
in the country, so don't even try to pretend
your battery is flat.

Mikhail laughs when he catches the last half of my eye roll.
"Some men in my industry would see that as a challenge." He tilts
closer to the camera, filling the screen. "Are you challenging me,
Sunshine?"

Weeks of uncertainty slip away as I reply, "Would you call me a
hussy if I said yes?"

"Fuck no." He looks like he wants to say more, but something
behind my shoulder alters the direction of our conversation. "Are

you outside?" Before I can answer, he asks another question. "What time is it there?"

I cringe. "A little after four."

"In the morning? How many buses did you take to get home?" He slants his head, draws his brows together, and then mutters, "Actually, don't answer that."

I hear the words he didn't speak the loudest, and they hurt.

"He could have found me by now if he wanted to."

Mikhail sighs while sinking back far enough for me to realize where he is. He's sitting on the armchair Andrik placed me on before he suspended my pussy on his face. "I know. I just..." Again, he breathes out heavily. This one arrives with a heap of cusswords. "I don't know what the fuck is going on with him. He's acting like nothing matters more right now than producing the next..."

When my expression announces he's discussing his brother's downfalls with the wrong person, his words trail off.

I smile to assure him I am grateful before telling him I have to go. "My bus is almost here."

"Bus? You're taking the fucking bus at this time of night? I don't care if you live in the safest neighborhood in the world—no one is safe on public transport at four in the morning!"

He *tsks* me when I say, "It isn't as bad as it sounds."

"Zoya... fuck. You're making my hands twitch, and I'm not a man who generally uses spankings as a form of punishment."

"Now you really sound like your brother," I reply before I can stop myself.

The crunch of my back molars is nowhere near as damaging as it could be when Mikhail asks, "Am I meant to take that as a compliment?"

"No," I reply honestly. "But you need to come up with your own material. You're one infringement away from a copyright claim."

He howls like a wolf. I only get to bask in its brilliance for mere seconds. My phone has plenty of battery. It is just no longer in my possession since it is plucked from my grasp seconds after I arrive at the bus stop—stolen along with my purse and the last of my cash.

"Hey!" I scream at the man dressed head to toe in black sprinting in the direction I just came.

I'm about to take off after him, when the faintest sob stops me in my tracks. A woman is crouched next to the scratched display banner edging a recently graffitied bench.

The remnants of the streetlight that usually keep incidents like this on the other side of Myasnikov dot her nonslip work shoes, and the camera dome is covered with more spray paint than the bench she should be seated on.

My heart squeezes when I notice her cheeks are ashen and wet. Nasty red welts circle her wrists and neckline, announcing that the perp stole more than her phone and purse. He took every possession she owned—including her sanity.

"It's okay," I assure her, bending down until we're eye level.

She must have fought her attacker. Her eye is swelling with a fresh bruise, and numerous grazes scrape her legs and arms not covered by her maid's outfit.

Her tremors shudder through me as well as I scan the area, seeking help. When my search comes up empty, I stray my eyes to the emergency assistance button at the end of the stop.

"I'll be right back."

The dark-haired woman shoots her eyes in the direction I'm peering for merely a second before she murmurs, "No. No police. Please." She seems more scared now. "I-I—"

"It's okay," I assure her again, understanding her apprehension. The people who are meant to be the safe option often do not prove they are. "Can you stand?"

"Yes. I th-think so," she stammers out slowly before her work shoes crunch the shards of plastic scattered around her.

"Just take it slow," I plead when she almost tumbles. She's woozy, and I believe the blood seeping from the back of her head is responsible for that. "There's a hospital—"

"No hospital. I j-just need to get home."

"Okay," I repeat, even aware it isn't the answer I should be giving. "Can I help you?" When apprehension is the first thing to cross her face, I say, "I'm here to take the bus home as well. We're probably going in the same direction." Her maid's outfit announces she doesn't belong in this area of Myasnikov any more than I do. "So it won't be any bother."

"Ok-okay," she parrots, making me smile when I recall how often people do that around me. "I ca-can pay your fare. They didn't take this."

It isn't the right time for either of us to laugh, but it can't be helped when she wiggles her bus card.

Not even criminals unwilling to work for what they want are desperate enough to use public transport.

20

ZOYA

*M*ara and I live on the same block. She doesn't normally catch the late bus home, but her boss, who owns an apartment in Nikita's building, was hosting a late-evening event. Mara altered her roster, hopeful the two-hundred-dollar cash payment she'd receive would keep her fed for a month.

The perp stole it along with a necklace she'd inherited from her mother and a fake tennis bracelet her boss had gifted her last Christmas.

Helping Mara kept my veins flooded with adrenaline for the past forty minutes. Now that they've simmered, I realize there are a handful of calls I need to make on a phone I no longer have.

That's what led to me standing outside my building supervisor's apartment, praying he is an early riser.

I'm about to knock for the second time when Mr. Fakher's door slowly inches open. Except it's not Mr. Fakher answering. It is a man who has a far slimmer stomach and a headful of hair.

I inch back to check I'm at the fourth door from the stairwell.

Mr. Fakher gave me directions plenty of times to make sure it stuck, but it's early and I'm tired, so I could have miscounted.

Once I'm certain I have the right apartment, I turn my eyes back to the man who has to be in his early fifties. "I was seeking the building sup?"

He flashes his pearly white teeth before replying, "You've found him." He fans his hand across his chest. "Luka Traite. What can I do for you, sweetheart?"

His sleezy rake of my body during what is meant to be a term of endearment assures me I have the right property. All building supervisors are the same—one immoral gesture from criminal charges.

Although I'd rather brush off his eagerness in the same manner I do Mr. Fakher, I can't. He is my only lifeline to the world outside my apartment walls.

"Mr. Fakher was meant to fix my landline last month."

Luka's brow arches as high as his voice. "You still have a landline?"

"Yes." I don't mention it is because its previous tenant was on life support that required constant connectivity in the event of a cell service failure. The particulars don't matter, and I'm too tired to pretend they do. "But it isn't working, and I don't have access to a phone, so I was wondering if I could use the landline in the security office."

He waits a beat before asking, "What happened to your phone?"

His question exposes he was born in at least the last five decades.

Even Gigi knows no one over the age of ten gets around without a phone these days.

"It was stolen—"

"You got jumped?" He pulls me into his apartment before scanning the hallway like the perp is standing behind me, digging his gun into my ribs. "Where?"

I wiggle out of his hold before answering, "At the Myasnikov Private Hospital bus stop."

"Why the fuck were you at a bus stop?"

I glare at him like he's stupid. "To catch a bus."

His expression matches the one I'm hitting him with. "You'd rather catch the bus than get around in that sweet-ass ride parked in your parking bay?"

I'm lost, and mercifully, I don't need to announce that.

"There's a brand-new Audi in your bay. It was delivered last week." His tone gets more and more suspicious the longer he talks. "I thought it was yours?"

Assuming he's one of those goody two shoes who bring in the police for a minor incident, I say, "I no longer need a parking spot, so I let another tenant use it." He doesn't believe my lie. I don't blame him. It was a doozie. "Anyway, back to the reason for my early-morning visit. I need to borrow a phone so I can tell my friend that I arrived home safely."

"Oh... yep... right. Checking in is good." He coughs to clear the rattle in his throat before gesturing me to take a right at the end of the entryway hall. "You can use mine. It'll be easier than trudging back down the stairs to the security office. The elevator is out."

His mention of the defunct elevator exposes he hasn't worked here for long. It's been out of operation for over eighteen months.

When we arrive in the living area, I scan my eyes over the apartment that is meant to be the pick of the bunch. It isn't. There are no good apartments in this part of Myasnikov. They're all dumps.

No wonder he didn't believe my lie. No one in this part of Myasnikov can afford a secondhand foreign car, much less a new one.

"You can use this while I get dressed."

He hands me a phone that is as dated as the carpet in his living room before he heads for the sole bedroom.

Mercifully, I know Nikita's number by heart, so it is the first number I call.

"Hello," she answers, her tone ripe with suspicion.

"Hey—"

Her relieved breath cuts me off before a heap of words. "Z... You scared me half to death. I thought someone was calling to say you'd been hurt. I'm still your first point of contact, right? I was tracking the bus's route, so I know you only got home ten minutes ago, but you weren't answering your phone, so I panicked and—"

"Breathe, Nikita," I demand when the exhausted whistle of her lungs whizzes through my ears. When she does as asked, I say, "I was helping a fellow passenger. She..."—when I realize my reply will never see me walking the streets of Myasnikov alone again, I alter it—"was a little groggy after a long day, so I walked with her to make sure she got home safely."

"Aww." Since she can't see me, she believes my lie. Her truth-seeking talents aren't as capable over the phone. "That was really kind of you, but I hope you didn't get too close. Multiple cases of gastroenteritis were reported today at Myasnikov Private. It is highly contagious."

"Yippee. No diet for me this month."

She groans before her smarts kick back on long enough to put me on the back foot. "Whose phone are you using? Your number didn't come up."

"Ah..." This lie takes me a little longer to summon than its predecessors. "My building sup's."

"Zoya! If I find out you're paying your rent by—"

A shocked scoff helms my interruption. "My phone went flat, so he let me use his so you wouldn't worry."

She swallows harshly before pushing out the quickest apology. "I'm sorry."

"As you should be." I could leave it there, but that would make my life more boring than it has been the past two weeks. "I stopped turning tricks for coins months ago."

"Z..." What should be a stubborn snap is more a whiny groan.

"I'm joking." *It's more years than months.* "But you can make up for your insult by doing me a favor."

"Anything," she immediately answers, announcing why she will always be my best friend.

"In the box you mentioned earlier is a bill with a phone number scribbled across it. Can you tell me what that number is?"

You shouldn't be able to hear someone's brain ticking over a million miles an hour. I can. But since Nikita will always be more inquisitive than she is stubborn. She doesn't grill me about the extra cash in her cardboard box safe until after she's flipped off its lid.

"Z, there has to be an extra three thousand dollars in here." Ruffling sounds down the line before she asks, "Where did you get this money from?"

"It doesn't matter—"

"It *does* matter," she interrupts, shouting. "I can't accept it."

I'm on the defense immediately. "You can and you will. It isn't up for negotiation. Grampies is my grandfather too, so it isn't solely your responsibility to look after him."

She wants to argue, but since it would break my heart, she remains quiet.

"So can you please get me the number on one of the bills so I can make sure I can keep contributing?"

My voice is on the verge of cracking, and I'm not the only one noticing. Its husky wobble is the sole reason Nikita agrees to my demand with the faintest snivel.

After many rustles, she asks, "Do you have a pen?"

I nod like she can see me.

She must hear its whoosh, as she recites Mikhail's number without additional prompting.

I read it back to her to make sure I have it correct before whispering, "Please don't be mad at me."

I won't survive another rejection, especially not from her. She is using her studies to become something great. I can't even get a job at McDonalds.

My heart stops being strangled when Nikita replies, "I'm not mad. I love you, Z."

"I love you too, Keet." With my voice holding too many emotions, I cut our chat short. "I'll talk to you tomorrow."

She reminds me it is already tomorrow before advising me she will call me before her upcoming double shift. "Bye."

"Bye."

I wait for her to disconnect our call before lifting my eyes to my new building supervisor. He's dressed and looking somewhat relieved—until I say, "Can I please make one more call? It'll be quick."

His eyes lower to the number I scribbled across my palm before he licks his lips. "Sure. That's fine." He nudges his head to the kitchen. "I'll make some coffee."

"I'm fine, thanks. I don't drink caffeine this early."

He mumbles something about it not being for me before he disappears into the poky kitchen.

I dial Mikhail's number I need to memorize since my sweaty hands are already smudging the digits.

He answers not even two rings later.

"You better have good fucking news or I'll—"

"Slay me with your marshmallow heart?"

"Zoya... fuck... Jesus." The revs of a motorcycle lower before they completely end. "What the fuck happened? One minute we were talking. The next minute—"

"You hitched a ride with a man who couldn't tell the difference between a Nokia C12 and the latest iPhone." In case you're wondering, I know the difference but could only afford a Nokia. Although that may now be out of my price range as well. "My phone was stolen at the bus stop."

"You got jumped?" He waits for me to murmur in agreement before asking, "Were you hurt? Did he hurt you?"

"No." His relieved sigh gives me the warm and fuzzies. "But another passenger wasn't as lucky. She got knocked around pretty bad." I turn to face the direction of Mara's building. "She wouldn't let me call the police, so I helped her to her feet and made sure she got home safely."

I have no idea why Mikhail deserves my honesty more than Nikita does. The truth just blurts from my mouth before I can stop it.

"I'm glad you were there to help her and that you weren't injured as well, but Jesus, Sunshine. You scared the shit out of me."

I'm a gooey, sticky mess, but I try to downplay how nice it is to have another person on my side with humor. "I recommend throwing out your armchair. Dry cleaning would be the cheapest option to handle the mess, but who wants to admit they shit themselves?"

Mikhail's laugh roaring out of the building supervisor's phone weakens the worry on my face as quickly as it does the sup's.

21

ANDRIK

"What is the predicted annual revenue?"

When my question is drowned out by the belittled huff of my brother for the umpteenth time this morning, I sling my eyes to Mikhail before arching a brow. He's been pushing my buttons nonstop over the past hour, testing the elasticity of my leniencies more than ever, and it has reached a point I can no longer ignore.

He's being rude, and I'm seconds from teaching him some lessons with my fists.

A bullet would be cheaper, but since the cleanup bill will be about the same, I may as well get some enjoyment from it.

"Do you have something you need to get off your chest, *Brother*?" I spit out his title with the same abhorrent disdain he uses anytime he's addressed me over the past two weeks. "You seem... frustrated." I almost say on the verge of death, but I hold back the verdict I want to rain down on him since we're surrounded by the equivalent of the help.

The Broadbent Hotel has been in official operation for three months, so we're crunching numbers to calculate the timeline from deficit to profit. I, too, would like to be anywhere but here, but when business responsibilities are sidestepped, personal endeavors soon follow.

I can't allow that to happen, so I arrived for our meeting within a respectable time frame considering the commute and have kept an open mind.

Mikhail has not.

"What could possibly be bothering me?" Mikhail's tone is as arrogant as his expression.

"I don't know." Each of my words are punctuated. "Hence me asking if there is anything you'd like to share."

He's here because I gifted him the majority share in Brody's as promised, yet he's acting like I reneged on my offer as quickly as I tried to annul my marriage.

He's being a dick, and we're going to have words sooner rather than later if he doesn't pull his head out of his ass.

"Maybe you're projecting, *Brother*?" He speaks as if we're not in the same room as another thirty people. "You seem to do that a lot lately. Forever pushing your shit onto everyone else."

"Mikhail—"

I cut our father off by slicing my hand through the air.

"Let him speak." I glare up and down at him, doubling the firmness of his jaw. "It's about time he acts like he gives a fuck about anything but the millions *I've* made him." I lean back in my chair before folding my arms in front of my chest. "The floor is yours, Mikhail. Use it for whatever the fuck you want." I continue talking before he can accept the imaginary microphone I'm handing him. "But don't you dare say I've pushed my shit onto you. I have sheltered you from it for years, shielded you from the brunt of what it takes to lead this family. I've protected you—"

"I don't need your protection!" he shouts, standing to his feet and banging his fist on the boardroom table between us. "I can take care of myself."

"Then what the fuck has your panties in such a twist?" I mimic his pose. My feet plant to the width of my shoulders, and the veins in my muscles bulge as I lean over the table like I'm not seconds from dragging him across it and pummeling some sense into him. "What more can I do for you that I'm not already doing? I've given you everything you've *ever* wanted."

Several shocked huffs sound when he mutters, "*After* taking it away."

I stare at him in bewilderment. I've never taken a single thing from him. I've given him everything he has, so why would I then take it away? His claim of thievery is unfounded. Not solely because it isn't theft when you're the rightful owner, but also because I would never steal from him.

He is my blood. My brother. He comes before anyone—*except her.*

My inner monologue trails off when my final two words ring through my head on repeat.

Except. Her.

Dozens of eyes snap to me when my low tone replicates the deathly warning of an imminent hurricane. "Get out."

"Boss—"

"Now!"

Female staff members race for the door first. They're overtaken before they break through the conference room doors by cowards who'll never have the balls to run a company like mine, let alone puppeteer it.

The knowledge sees me flicking my eyes to Konstantine a second before he follows the stragglers out. I don't need to voice my command. He can smell the wish for carnage wafting from my pores, and the rancid scent doubles when I lock eyes with my brother pacing the floor-to-ceiling windows facing the Chelabini business district.

"Speak. Now." I walk around the conference table before butting my ass against the antique trim I wring with my hands. I need to do something to stop them from colliding with Mikhail's face. "And before you give me any shit about projecting, remember who the fuck you are speaking with. I will *not* be disrespected on my turf by anyone. Particularly when that man has no claim to the person he's crowding the plate for."

The tightening of Mikhail's fists during my last sentence tells me everything I need to know. He isn't pissed at me for himself. He's fighting the battle for a woman who hasn't left my mind for a single second over the past two weeks.

I just can't tell him that because it wasn't solely the identity of the man with the ruby ring that tossed my game into an entirely different code. It was what he said while I was proving to him that I'm no longer a kid he can push around anymore that flipped my ruse on its head.

When Mikhail remains quiet, protecting Zoya from me as readily as I'm endeavoring to protect her from my enemies, I get to the point. "Zoya—"

"Got jumped this morning."

I grip the conference room table so firmly that my fingerprints will never be removed from its curved edges.

"She was catching *the bus* home and got robbed by a punk-ass fucking weasel with an ugly face tat."

I try to speak.

I try to reply.

Nothing comes out but angry bubbles of air.

I discover the reason for Mikhail's anger being directed at me when he sneers. "I tried to call you five times this morning. Five. Fucking. Times." He steps closer, his chest raging with anger.

"Where the fuck were you when I needed you? Where were you when my life was turned upside down?"

"I was—"

"Playing house with your pretty little bride in your big ass mansion?" His gall when he steps up to me impresses me. That's no easy feat. "I was there for you, year after year, *Kazimir*"—he spits out my given name with disgust—"but the one time I needed you, you were nowhere to be found."

"Because *I* have responsibilities you don't have! Obligations *I* can't get out of. But you wouldn't know about any of that, Mikhail, because *I* shelter you from that."

I want to pummel some sense into him. Or better yet, force him to walk the halls I must walk for his freedom, but since I can't shift my focus from his confession, I veer the conversation away from my frustrations and devote it to my fury.

"Was she hurt?" My voice is nothing like I've heard before.

I'm shocked I can talk. I've never felt the range of emotions that are walloping me now.

Hate. Fear. Vengeance. They all smack into me. But since this is about the first person since my mother to remind me that I have a heart in my chest, words make it through the rumble crashing down on me and burying me whole.

"Was she fucking hurt, Mikhail?" I scream my question so loud being on the top level of the hotel won't save our guests from hearing my roar.

He waits until my nerves are kneeling on tacks before shaking his head. "No. But—"

"There are no buts... because I leave *nothing* to chance."

When I spin on my heel and race for the door, my little brother is hot on my tail. He jabs his thumb into the elevator call button when we reach the corridor, assuming I'm heading for the foyer. He's dead fucking wrong. There's only one way I am going. Up.

My chopper pilot is already buckled in the cockpit, ready for immediate transfer as requested, but with Mikhail shadowing me, I signal for him to move before I veer for the pilot side of the helicopter instead of the co-pilot's seat.

I've always operated on the notion "the fewer witnesses the better," so this morning's endeavor will follow that concept.

"Fucking Christ," Mikhail shouts when I fully open the throttle and pull up the collective before he's buckled in. "You almost shook me out."

"That was the point," I mutter as I depress the left pedal to counteract the torque produced by the main rotor.

If my blood weren't too hot to think rationally, I'd return to the helipad and force my brother's removal from the cockpit with the same level of violence his confession flooded me with. But since the control I govern my life with has been completely obliterated, I continue en route, making a three-hour commute in barely thirty minutes.

Mikhail doesn't speak a word the entire time. He knows how short my temper is and just how furious the inferno is when ignited. He doesn't want to get burned.

One of Konstantine's subordinates meets me on the helipad of a building in the middle of Myasnikov's business district. It is approximately half a mile from Zoya's apartment.

"Who was assigned watchman of the target last night?"

I stop walking toward Daniil when the familiar scent of the shadow I've struggled to lose for a single second after my mother's disappearance wafts into my nostrils.

It still has that chocolate frosting scent from when he found me hiding in the closet I wish I had made it to before being found by Anoushka. Mikhail was only two, so he didn't understand why I refused to eat the cake my mother had encouraged me to take a bite out of only hours earlier. He devoured his slice before bringing the second biggest piece to me.

He's done the same every birthday since. I just no longer hide in a closet in my room.

Underground fight clubs are more my scene.

After working my jaw to loosen its stiffness, I shift on my feet to face Mikhail. I could order his removal from the rooftop. Since that will steal time away from my objective, I threaten him instead.

"If you breathe a single iota of this to anyone, I will bury you. If it goes beyond this group of people"—I point to Konstantine's lackey, Mikhail, and me—"I'll bury you." Jealousy talks on my behalf during my next warning. "And if I find out you said anything inappropriate to her during what I promise was a brief reintroduction into her life, I will bury you."

Mikhail stares at me for several seconds longer than I'm happy about before a sly grin stretches across his face. "You know whoever said absence makes the heart grow fonder is full of shit, right?" My gun already feels heavy on my hip. He doubles its weight by proving he still has a lot to learn about the woman still unknowingly plotting my demise. "I also don't think she's a girl who'll wait around for you to get your shit together."

"I don't *think* she'll wait for me, Mikhail. I *know* she will."

He looks set to argue, but my patience is stretched too thin. I make a beeline for the steel emergency exit stairwell on the side of the building, grumbling under my breath that Zoya's count will only ever travel one way.

After calling me a cocky fuck, Mikhail assists me in unearthing the identity of the fool who made an erroneous mistake last night. "Who was the watchman in charge of Zoya's surveillance this morning?" He jogs to catch up to Daniil and me before he pulls out his phone and brings up a blurry image of a man who wouldn't rank any higher than a low-ranking gangster. "And has anyone in your crew seen him before?"

"We were assigned this case two weeks ago, but we've not yet had the chance to introduce ourselves to the locals," Daniil replies, his tone a mix of sarcastic and truthful. "I'll run his image through a program to clean it up before completing facials." He scans the image into a black tablet before tapping on the screen. "When do you need it by?"

"Yesterday," I answer on Mikhail's behalf, my voice tainted with guilt.

I fucked up by not personally overseeing the team in charge of Zoya's surveillance, but I wasn't lying when I said my entire plan was flipped on its head. I've been scrambling to make sense of everything since the press conference at the front of Mikhail's building. It's been one fucking thing after another, so I let what I thought would cause minor implications slip.

I won't make the same mistake twice.

"I'll have you a name in under an hour." Daniil's sly smirk matches mine when he says, "But until then, how about we go pay him a visit?"

He double taps the screen, bringing up the name of the man rostered to watch Zoya last night.

I hope Luka Traite kissed his family goodbye before accepting the security contract Konstantine offered him two weeks ago, because it would have been for the final time.

22

ZOYA

*A*s the rotors of a helicopter soar over my apartment building, a knock sounds at my door. I furrow my brows before shooting my eyes to the clock. It's late—*if you're as old as Gigi*—but I'm still shocked to have a caller at this hour. It is 9 p.m.

When they knock again, louder this time, I throw down the tea towel drying the bowl I used when I consumed cereal for dinner, before stomping to the door. Luka has probably realized why Mr. Fakher refused to fix my landline. I've yet to meet a building supervisor eager to assist with *anything* unless the requests are made by a tenant willing to fall to her knees and pay for his help with her mouth.

Since I'm disinclined to sell my body for money, I blurt out the same excuse I gave Mr. Fakher when he came sniffing for rent. "I have a job interview tomorrow afternoon. The employment agent said they'd consider an advance."

I step back, shocked when my reply comes from the last voice I expect. "Any position offering an advance is a sham, Sunshine." Mikhail winks and grins before he enters my apartment without waiting for permission. "Not even hookers get paid up front." My unease weakens a smidge when the tails of his winter coat fan as he spins to face me. "And from what I've heard, they only offer a discount if their client comes in under a minute."

"I didn't say your brother only lasted a minute. I said he was—"

"Quick-winded," he interrupts, too eager to add salt to his brother's invisible wounds to not steal the saltshaker two weeks of whining won't let me hand over without a fight. I doubt Andrik pined over my absence for even a second, let alone weeks, so it is only fair that I brandish invisible weapons when he's thrust back into the forefront of my mind. "Close enough."

I roll my eyes like I'm not loving his playfulness before I close my door and get back to drying the one unchipped bowl I own. "What are you doing here, Mikhail? How do you even know where I live?" My throat grows scratchy when I recall his worries the last time he showed up unannounced. "Did you track my phone?"

I hate having blonde hair—until I need it as an excuse for my stupidity.

How can he track a phone I no longer have access to?

A second dose of idiocy smacks into me when he dumps my phone and purse onto my coffee table before he moves to a wall of dust collectors on the far left of the living room. Don't ask me whose trinkets they are. They were here when I moved in, and since they made the place more alive than its bland walls and stained carpets, I left them there.

When I can't hide my shock that he found the belongings I spent half the day seeking at the many thrift shops dotted across Myasnikov, Mikhail smiles. "They weren't hard to find. And neither were you. The number of the tire plant was in the corner of the photo you sent this morning." He flashes me a playful look that makes his investigation skills seem more flamboyant than invasive. "I'm still waiting on confirmation about how big his rod is, by the way." Then he gets back to the point. "And although there are hundreds of pawnshops in this region, most only accept one phone per customer per transaction." He'd sound posh if he weren't laughing while saying, "And *no one* wants a Nokia. Not even a dealer willing to trade anything to get a new customer hooked on his *cooking*." He air quotes his last word.

Not in the mood to discuss the reason I'll most likely only ever own a Nokia, I poke my tongue out at him instead. It increases his smile, which doubles the depth of the dimples in his top lip.

Their boyish charm reminds me who I am standing across from. It isn't the man who sets my panties on fire with a single sultry glance. It is his younger and much more playful brother.

"There's nothing wrong with being original."

"That's true," Mikhail agrees. "But a Nokia?" He gags. "That's worse than the fake ID you're carrying around. It won't even get you a discount card at Costco."

My eyes widen as my throat dries. "You went through my purse?"

"No," he instantly denies. "I flicked through it to ensure nothing was missing." He wets his lips before rubbing his hands together. "There wasn't much to go through. If it weren't for the IOU slip a dick turd left that gave specific step-by-step details on how to go from Apartment 12A to Apartment 4B, I wouldn't have known this was your building."

I'm reasonably sure he's lying, but since I only have a handful of brain cells to work with from a long night of tossing and turning before walking for miles since I couldn't afford a bus fare, I act as if I didn't notice the increase in his pitch during the delivery of his lie by drying my spoon and placing it into the cutlery drawer.

Mikhail isn't as eager to let bygones be bygones. "Do you often get rent reduction offers in the form of directional maps to a man's bed, Sunshine?"

"Not often." I ease the disappointment crossing his handsome face by murmuring, "Only at the end of every second month. No one pays in advance anymore. Not even hookers."

His laughter rumbles through my ears as I pop open my purse to check how long my mourning should last. I didn't have a lot of funds, but the leftovers of the severance pay from a bar that closed a few months ago were enough to get me by for a couple of weeks. I noticed its absence this morning when I purchased an off-brand cereal instead of the one with nuts I really wanted.

I'm anticipating every denomination to be minuscule, so you can picture my shock when I notice several high denominations stuffed between their less-craved counterparts.

Several thousand, to be precise.

"Mikhail..." I murmur on a groan when the truth smacks into me. He didn't go through my purse to snoop. He garnished the limited funds I had inside with a much more impressive figure. "This isn't mine. I had two hundred at the most."

When I thrust the bundle, minus a handful I won't live without, toward him, Mikhail holds his hands in the air while stepping back. "That ain't mine."

I glare at him, calling out his lie without words.

"It ain't," he says again. "This is the first time I've seen those bills. I swear on my mother's grave."

When he draws a cross on his chest, my heart sinks. "Your momma is dead?"

I want to smack myself up the back of the head. I'm not good with words, but it is worse when I am hungry. Still, that question was a doozie even for my food-deprived brain.

"I'm sorry. I lack empathy when hungry."

"It's all good, Sunshine. I'm not offended." He spins back around to face the mantel full of ornaments. "It is a little hard to be when you have no clue what you're meant to take offense to."

His reply riddles me with confusion, so instead of continuing with my quest for him to take the money my purse has never had the pleasure of housing, I dump it and the bundle of cash back onto my coffee table before sitting on the ripped sofa.

My need to know everything ruefully gnaws at me, but miraculously, I remain quiet, leaving the floor to Mikhail.

He accepts the invisible microphone I'm offering him thirty seconds after spinning around a porcelain duck so its beak faces the wall instead of me. "My ma disappeared when I was four."

When he shows me a duck identical to the one he just spun around yet three times dustier at the back of the stack, I shrug before signaling for him to get back to his confession instead of the stupid ornaments that hold not an ounce of sentimental value.

He places the dusty duck in front of the newer one before doing as suggested. "She was pregnant." He scratches his head. "I'm not exactly sure how far along. It would have been a few months, as she'd learned the sex of the baby not long before she disappeared." I'm shocked when delight is the first emotion he expresses upon announcing he was going to have a baby sister. "We have a long succession of boys in the family, so I was looking forward to having someone not related to me by blood to pummel." My brows barely join when he commences eradicating my confusion. "She would have had boyfriends, and it would have been my job as her older brother to vet them. I doubt there would have been a better way to do that than with my fists."

I love his protectiveness.

It makes me swoon—maternally not sexually.

My heart does its second drop of the night when he mutters, "I would have been a good big brother."

Would have?

Mikhail must hear my silent question, because he jerks up his chin before his focus returns to the trinkets. "It's weird to think I could have been batting you off me with a stick instead of the other way around." His smile reflects in the mirror above the dust collectors he's rearranging. "I couldn't have dated my little sister's best friend. That's just nasty." He treats my ornaments as if they're his own before cranking his neck back to me. "In case you're wondering, I have no issues accepting my big brother's leftovers—"

I hook a pillow off my couch and throw it in his face before he can finalize his reply.

It has Mikhail laughing like we weren't discussing missing family members as the rotors of a helicopter hover closer than ever.

23

ANDRIK

*W*hile cursing Mikhail to hell, I slam down my laptop screen. "I knew this was a bad idea. He was meant to return her belongings, not debug her fucking apartment."

I'm not speaking to anyone, but Konstantine replies as if I am. "He won't touch her. He only wants to protect her."

There lies the issue of my jealousy.

For the first time in my life, I don't want to saddle the white horse my brother uses to ride in and save the day. I want to straddle the beast and slay the dragon before rescuing the princess from the tower.

I want the accolades I never waited around for even after my greatest victories.

I want to be the hero of the story instead of the villain for a change.

But I can't alter a story when not even half of it has been written.

My narrative is still in the plotting stage. There are *many* pages left to comb through. So as much as I want to skip to the alternative ending I never saw coming while suffering through a prologue no child should have to face, I need to give this tale the chance it deserves.

I must see it through—even if it kills me.

"Reestablish surveillance at the earliest convenience. I want eyes on Zoya twenty-four-seven." By I, I mean *I*. "Make sure I am the only person who has full access to her surveillance feed. The fewer people aware she is being monitored, the less likely the feed will be infiltrated."

Konstantine lifts his chin, his eyes never moving from his laptop screen. His inability to maintain eye contact makes sense when he asks, "And Mikhail? What do you want me to do with him?"

It takes a long time for anything, excluding death, to enter my head, and even then, the plan is indicative. "I will deal with him."

I don't know how or when, but I'm sure we will eventually come to a head over his inability to follow orders.

I'd just rather it be when he's not grieving.

Even my strength struggles to reach its full potential when my head is buried in the remorse of my past, hence my lack of involvement in organizing surveillance for Zoya.

It is easier to deny your every want when it isn't being flashed in your face.

One sniff of Zoya's scent in her apartment and I once again wanted to backtrack on every decision I've ever made.

I would have if I hadn't been called by my family's physician minutes after tracking down the thug who mugged a woman by knifepoint before adding Zoya's minimal belongings to his takings.

I'm needed at home.

If I weren't, my head would already be buried back between Zoya Galdean's legs.

My cock's twitch of conformation is responsible for my next demand. "I want our team based out of Myasnikov until informed otherwise. What happened this morning cannot occur again."

"Okay," Konstantine says before he shocks me by questioning my directive. He usually never seeks confirmation of my orders. He follows them to a T, conscious of the downfall if he were to stray from them for a single second. "But can I ask why?"

"No, you can't."

I'm not being arrogant. I honestly don't know why I'm suddenly mindful of Zoya's security. I would like to blame the low-ranking gangster whose death will spread caution across the globe of the consequences of messing with her. Ethics won't allow it.

I want to protect her as desperately as I want her to scream my name, but both tasks will be difficult to achieve if I don't bridge the three thousand miles between us.

Chelabini was my hometown growing up, but last month was the first time I'd been there in years. I have too many skeletons there, too many ghosts.

I refuse for Myasnikov to be stained in the same manner.

"I will instruct Anoushka in the morning to start arrangements to transfer our home base. We will join you in Myasnikov at the earliest possible convenience."

Stealing Konstantine's chance to reply, I exit my chauffeur-driven ride seconds after it pulls to the entrance of one of my many palatial mansions. My brisk departure saves the driver from shutting down the engine, which means Konstantine can begin an immediate departure to Myasnikov.

Help flounders when they spot me coming. I'm not a kind man, and their scramble to act busy announces I am not afraid to show this.

"Andrik," a familiar voice greets a second before she commences removing my coat.

Anoushka was the longest serving nanny to the Dokovic clan before I promoted her to my head of staff. Her title and longevity in my inner circle give her the right to call me Andrik. Only those closest to me are privileged, and they're mindful it isn't to be used anywhere that could have it overheard.

The remembrance announces my car's weave through the manicured lawns of my mansion had the effect I was aiming for.

It is just Anoushka and me in the entryway of my home.

"Where is my father?"

Anoushka shakes out my coat to rid it of the sprinkles of rain I gathered during the short trek from the driveway to the main house before she hangs it in the coat room. "With Zakhar in his room." Her smile is gentle. "Zak has been asking for you all day." The drop in her smile softens the lines sprouting in the corners of her glistening eyes. "You were gone longer than expected."

"I had business to take care of."

Anoushka dips her head in understanding.

The witch outstaying her welcome doesn't.

"Business where?" Dina saunters into the foyer, nursing an overzealous glass of gin. "Your secretary said she hasn't seen you since your meeting this morning." She spins the watch too large for her rake-thin wrist until it displays the time. "That was over thirteen hours ago. What could possibly take that long to finalize?"

"I can think of a number of things," I mutter, my tone hinting at just how deprived she makes my thoughts. "But none I need to discuss with you."

She scoffs but doesn't dare to continue badgering me. It won't end well for her, and her wish to remain at her daughter's side as negotiated in our contract reminds her of that fact.

After wordlessly cautioning Arabella to bring her mother into line, I head for the west wing.

Yes, my home has wings.

No, I will never have the need for the thirty-plus rooms they house.

The grandeur of my home is part of the gimmick I am forced to portray.

It is a prop—as are the people I invite inside. They're all part of the plan. Only one person is excluded. The little boy swamped by a hospital bed he hasn't left in months.

I had originally intended to make him part of my ruse, but just like Zoya, he imprinted himself on my soul in less than a heartbeat, so he will be protected just as fiercely.

"I might have believed you were sleeping if your nose wasn't twitching like a rabbit," I whisper in Russian. "Sweets are like hearts. Designed to be devoured. So why don't you stop pretending to be asleep and see what I brought home for you."

Zakhar's lips twitch into a smile before he slowly opens his eyes. There's so much pain in his baby blues, so much hurt, but he smiles large enough to showcase his wobbly tooth is holding on by a thread.

You're not the only one, tooth.

"How is your tooth still in your mouth? I told Anoushka to put concrete in your cookies. It should have yanked it straight out."

My eyes shoot to the side when a low voice mutters, "He's been too unwell to eat." My father moves out of the shadows he was hiding in, his agility too silent for a man of his size. "He's barely keeping down water."

I try to make out his comment didn't dry my throat too much for me to speak. "That's because it's water." I shift my eyes back to Zakhar. "Real men don't drink water. We drink vodka from goblets carved out of our enemy's bones."

"Like our ancestors did," Zakhar adds, playing his part of the ruse we've perfected over the past two weeks.

"That's right." I move to the bar a notable Russian is never without, where I pour from a crystal decanter filled with filtered water instead of the alcohol my veins are currently demanding. "Water won't give us hairs on our chests and our..." I finalize my reply with an arched brow.

Zakhar giggles like he's not on his deathbed when I pull a face like Anoushka is two seconds from swatting the back of my head.

I hand him one of the glasses I filled and clink it with mine.

"To Russia," I cheer, my full-blooded accent on display.

"To Russia," Zakhar mimics before he swallows barely a mouthful.

"More, Zak. You don't want the one measly little hair Mikhail has on his chest, do you?"

The weight on my shoulders slackens when he fires back, "No. But I don't want to be a gorilla like Па, either."

"A gorilla? You think Pa is a gorilla?" When he nods, I mimic the slow stomp of a ridgeback before tickling his ribs. "He's only a gorilla to make sure his hands are big enough to tickle your ribs until you pee your pants."

He bucks and rears like it's not taking everything he has to respond to my tease before he shouts for a clemency I rarely give. "Mercy! Mercy!"

I'm not usually a man who offers leniencies, but since it is for him, I pull back my hands before telling him to finish his "vodka."

"We need you as fit as a fox..."—we lock eyes over the rim of his glass—"and as hairy as one too."

24

ZOYA

*N*erves tap dance in my stomach when I veer my borrowed ride down a paved driveway that stretches for over a mile. We're only forty miles west of Myasnikov, but I had no clue their wealth extended this far. Mansions are dotted on pristinely maintained acres, and several of them have helipads and Olympic-sized swimming pools as one of their many features.

When the tension gets the better of me, I check the address the employment broker wrote down with the one cited on the GPS. It is a match.

The knowledge does little to settle my unease.

It feels like I'm driving toward a tornado instead of away from it. The hairs on the back of my neck are standing to attention, despite the wetness of my nape, and a peculiar sensation is making my stomach a swishy mess.

My jitters are understandable when you learn of my past. I've yet to meet a pleasant rich person. Still, I usually portray an aura of confidence. I haven't been this nervous since I showed up at Aleena's twelfth birthday with ripped jeans and a handmade card.

I breathe out a handful of butterflies in my stomach when a message from Nikita pops up on the screen of my ride's fancy navigation system.

> KEET:
>
> Chin up. Chest out. You've got this.

I picture her eye roll while speaking my reply to Siri.

> ME:
>
> It's a PA position for a man overcompensating for his peanut cock with a massive mansion. I've totally got this.

After slowing the roll of the tires, I snap a picture of the huge country estate coming up over the horizon and attach it to my outgoing message before continuing down the winding driveway.

A reply from Nikita pops up on the dashboard screen two seconds later.

> KEET:
>
> Holy marshmallow. Is that a palace?

Her inability to swear reminds me of how I got a last-minute placement on an interview schedule finalized before I had submitted an application.

The resident of this huge stately manor is a friend of Mikhail's. He said she usually replaces her rotation of personal assistants with a temp agency, but with a move in the works requiring new contacts, she branched out to the employment agency I've been seeking guidance from for the past fourteen months.

As a long line of garages comes into sight, I convey my requests to Siri.

"Hey Siri, send a message to Mikhail."

If Siri didn't work the same in every country, I'd struggle to understand her reply. "*Что бы вы хотели сказать?*"

"What field does KADOK Industries specialize in?"

Siri repeats my message before asking if I want to send it.

I answer yes.

"Done."

While waiting for Mikhail's reply, I summarize my own response.

The gardeners maintaining the impeccable lawns are wearing sun-safe long-sleeved shirts and pants as expected. The man jogging toward me to park my car is more casually dressed than showy. His dress shirt is ironed and tucked in, but his ensemble is minus the jacket and tie most old-money staff have. It announces the owner of KADOK Industries grew his wealth himself or his family's wealth is relatively new—say the last century or less.

As I arrive at the front of a large rotunda-style entryway, a valet opens the door of my borrowed ride. "Interviews are being held in the state room in the east wing."

He chuckles when I request to be directed to the north so I can work out which quarter of this architectural wonder may be the east wing.

I settle on brand-new money when he places his hands on my shoulders to twist me to face north. Touching is a big no with old money—even when they pay for precisely that.

After sending a quick message to Nikita advising I will buzz her once my interview is over, I toss my phone and purse into the glove compartment before heading in the direction another half a dozen women are walking.

I grimace when I recall how badly I bombed during my last group interview. I don't do well in group situations. I'm usually too busy watching for the knife that is forever directed at my back when the competition realizes my Es are natural instead of paying attention to the interviewer's questions.

As I enter a set of French doors on the heels of a brunette with long legs and a gorgeous designer skirt, I adjust my bra straps before rolling my shoulders forward.

I really need this job, so if I must act like I was gifted a flat chest from my mother, I'll work it like a pro.

I'm greeted in the foyer of the east wing by a lady with a bright smile and a thick wad of papers weighing down a flimsy plastic clipboard.

"I don't see your name on my interview schedule, but if you're prepared, we can slot you in with these candidates." After pinning my recently updated resumé to the top of her stack, she peers up at me to check my response.

"Prepared for...?" I'm lost, and my low tone proves it. "My employment agency forwarded my resumé earlier this week. That one is the most up to date." I point to the lonely sheet of paper she didn't even glance at during the "that" part of my reply. "Was there something more I was meant to do?"

She smiles at me as if I am daft.

For once, I feel as if her judgment is accurate.

"Most applicants prepare a routine."

My bewilderment continues. "On how fast they can type?"

She throws her head back and laughs. It is as refined as her glamour portrays. She is a beautiful woman, but miraculously, she doesn't appear snooty.

After saying she'll hire me no matter how uncoordinated I am, she guides me through another pair of French doors. The clothing of the applicants I followed moments ago is more risqué now than earlier, and a handful are doing stretches that make my groin ache.

"What exactly does KADOK Industries stand for?" I ask after watching one applicant strip down to a sequined pair of panties.

That's it.

That is *all* she's wearing.

"KADOK?" The blonde's eyes widen before she rushes me out of the room now filled with more naked bodies than clothed ones. "You're meant to be in the *west* wing. This is... ah... auditions for a new cabaret club." She summons a man with a cut jaw and tattooed neck to her side with a flick of her wrist before she instructs him to take me to the west wing.

"If you're busy, I can find my own way. I'm an hour early, so I have plenty of time to... mingle." I mentally smack myself for the lack of confidence in my tone before admitting the real reason I want to stay. "If *that* doesn't work out"—I hook my thumb to the west—"how much does *this* position pay?" I point to the floor.

My head slings to the side when a deep, gravelly voice says, "Not enough for you to even consider."

A brick lodges in my throat when I come face-to-face with Andrik. He's dressed similarly to the last time he bombarded me. His scowl is even sexier than his designer suit, and don't get me started on the rest of him.

My memories must have been courteous by only reminding me of ten percent of his sexiness.

This man is fine, and he knows it. His smirk when he catches my admiring stare announces this, not to mention the flattening of the ironed creases in the crotch of his pricy trousers.

"What are you doing here, Zoya? This is private property. You have no right to be here." From his tone alone, it is easy to decipher that "private property" stands for "my wife's home."

With words evading me, the blonde jumps in. "That's my fault." The rake of her nails over his chest boils my veins with jealousy. They appear friendly—*very* friendly.

Oh. My. God. Is she the wife?

"I told the valet to send all the busty girls my way." Andrik's eyes follow hers down my body. "I forgot other interviews were being conducted today." I don't know if it is envy or suspicion blazing in her eyes. "She's too pretty to be a secretary."

"She is," Andrik agrees, stupidly falling into her trap. I don't care how cocky you are, *never* compliment another woman in front of your wife. "But that doesn't answer my question." He moves away from the blonde, his stalk both dropping her hand from his chest and doubling my heart rate. "Why are you here, at my family's estate, today of all days?"

"I'm here for a—"

"No," Andrik denies before I can give him an excuse.

"My employment agen—"

"No," he mutters again, his jaw ticking as rapidly as my anger rises.

He's acting like I'm the adulterous half of our duo, and it shreds my last nerve.

I act out when railroaded.

"Mikhail invited me here." He's already folding from my metaphoric punch to the stomach, so I double his bend. "He wanted to show me his old stomping ground. Something about wanting to recreate the first place he ever got..."

I make a gesture with my tongue and the inside of my cheek no woman over the age of seventeen should use. It makes the blonde's smile blinding enough to pay only the slightest bit of attention to the fierce red coloring of Andrik's face.

"So I guess I better get a wiggle on. I'd hate to be late for our..." —I tap my finger against my lips and arch a brow—"*sixth* date in the past month."

I run in heels. My getaway isn't pretty or fast, but it is effective.

I almost make it back to Mikhail's car parked behind a long line of sports cars before my inability to act my age catches up to me.

I'm flattened to the door of my borrowed ride by a big steaming

Russian. My lungs strive to fill with air half a second before Andrik's hot breaths bead condensation on my nape.

"Think very hard before speaking because your antics have gained you the eyes of over a dozen men I *will* kill when I am forced to respond to your lie with more than words." When he slants his head to align our eyes, anger is there, but that isn't all they display. They also show jealousy he has no right to have. "Why are you here?"

He doesn't deserve an explanation, but if I don't say something, my panties aren't the only thing about to be massacred. Our argument has gained us many eyes, and there was nothing but utmost certainty in Andrik's tone when he snarled his threat.

"Mikhail—"

Men scatter in all directions when Andrik pulls away from me with a growl. He tugs me to the hood of Mikhail's car and arches me over it.

I don't register him pulling up the hem of the business skirt I only ever wear to interviews until the cool breeze floating over my backside offers an immense amount of relief to the burn of his first spank.

He spanks me as if I am a disobedient child, and I love every damn minute of it.

Regretfully.

Tingles race across my skin as throaty, dirty moans form low in my throat. It takes everything I have not to release them, but I attempt to hold some of my pride.

After a dozen swats, the hand turning my backside red switches from punishing to soothing. Andrik rubs my stinging globes, his fingers lowering with every gentle stroke.

"Fuck, милая." His husky words float over my back when his fingertips brush past the opening of my pussy.

I'm wet.

Ashamedly.

"N-not for you," I stammer, fighting with the last morsel of rebellion I have.

After angling his body so I'm blocked from the main residence by his brooding frame and awarding me a smirk that announces I'm five seconds from being spanked again, Andrik slides his hand under the damp material clinging to my pussy and circles his thumb over my clit.

"You like being punished by *me*."

He isn't asking a question—he's stating a fact. But I still rear up, fighting like hell to prove him wrong. "As much as I'd love having my wisdom teeth extracted."

His laugh makes me hot all over, and when he places even more pressure on the nervy bud stealing my smarts, my willpower bends.

"Your clit is so hard that one flick of my tongue over it would have you screaming my name loud enough for Myasnikov residents to hear."

"Y-you wish."

He acts as if I never spoke.

"You're drenched for *me*." When he uses his spare hand to force eye contact, my thighs press together. Gone is the menacing madman hell-bent on vengeance. Replaced with a man with his head stuck in a lust cloud. "Aren't you, милая?"

He makes sure I can't reply by dedicating a heap of attention to my clit. He sweeps his thumb over it while maintaining eye contact.

His heated watch is almost too much. Too explosive. *Too untamed.* It courses desire through my body so uncontrollably that the only objections I manage are the ones warning my head that I will never forgive myself if it ends this now.

I should hate how good he makes my body feel.

Guilt should be my strongest emotion.

Regretfully, it isn't.

It is taking everything I have not to come, and I'm not the only one noticing.

Andrik slides his fingers through the folds of my pussy, doubling the sticky residue coating his palm, before he asks, "Who owns this cunt, милая?"

He flicks my clit harder when I remain quiet. He bends my will by sliding two fingers inside me. His growl when my pussy sucks around them makes me whimper. He takes them deep, bruising me with his touch as much as he claims me with it.

"The word you're seeking is 'you,' милая."

"Fuck you."

I feel his smile more than I see it.

You can't miss the heat of arrogance, and I can no longer maintain eye contact. It is too intense and primal and has me the most conflicted I've ever felt.

"It'll be my pleasure, милая." Andrik pushes into me so deeply the imprint of his cock will be embedded in my ass for eternity. "But first, I need you wet enough to take me."

"That isn't what I meant. I don't want th-this."

My stuttered response has him seeing straight through my lie, much less the sound of my arousal as he pumps in and out of me.

He toys with my clit while finger fucking me at a slow, leisurely pace like he has all the time in the world. He knows every button to push, and within minutes, I roll my hips in rhythm to the frantic pulse of my clit.

I'm wet enough for signs of an imminent climax to be unmissable and to make a mess on the front of Andrik's pants, yet his pace doesn't hasten in the slightest. He takes his time, not needing a worded confirmation that he owns both me and my pussy.

He drives me to the brink until stars form and his name sits breathlessly on the tip of my tongue, and then he teases me with an underhanded promise I shouldn't crave but desperately want.

"Do you want me to make you come now, *милая*, or once my dick is buried deep inside you?"

"Now," I beg, arching up on my tippy-toes. "Please."

"Please, who?"

I grit my teeth, hating how fast his name almost whips out of my mouth.

This isn't how I envisioned our reunion. He's meant to be huddled over, gripping his crotch, not cupping mine. He's the enemy. The monster. A cheater. He isn't supposed to have the ability to turn my brain to mush.

"St-stop."

Andrik impedes my wish to flee by pressing down on the middle of my back with his spare hand before he shifts the sole focus of his thumb to my clit. My thighs shake as rapidly as my pulse surges through my veins. I snap my eyes shut and bite my lower lip, hopeful a snippet of pain will slow the freight train of desire racing through my veins.

My hands ball so I don't scratch the pricy paintwork of Mikhail's car when Andrik grinds his thick cock against the seam of my ass. I can feel its throbs and the wetness pooled at the end. I can feel every perfect inch.

Pleasure courses through me as I thrust my head back and whimper. My climax is right there. Within grasp. Then Andrik freezes, and the only tumble I endure is the brutal fumble of my morals.

"No. Please."

The surge of my pulse when he arches over me almost drowns out his repeated question. "Please, *who?*"

"Andrik! Please, *Andrik.*"

My womb spasms when he growls out in a gravelly tone, "There's my good girl."

With his chest swollen with smugness, he pushes two fingers

back inside me. Wetness coats his palm when the greedy rock of my hips forces him to pick up speed. He fucks me with his fingers while moaning in approval of my impatience.

I'm on the edge of hysteria, racing for the finish line again in no time. Then, without warning, Andrik once again removes his fingers from my pussy. This time, he doesn't keep them teasingly close. He pulls his hand out of my panties before taking a giant step back, unpinning me from the hood.

My first thought is hope. Andrik has the skills to bring me to climax with just his fingers, but his cock deserves its own unique category. It is the stuff of magic, and I'm dying to feel the stretch of its brilliance again. But my optimism soon slithers to despair when Andrik tugs down my skirt while grunting that my application to work at KADOK Industries has been declined.

"What...?" I spin to face him, horrified my legs aren't in the process of buckling out from beneath me. "You can't... I did as you asked... Why?"

My questions are barely decipherable, but they are answered in the most horrifying way—with the same mask Andrik wore in the elevator when I learned he was no longer filing for an annulment.

It proves our exchange isn't about untapped desire hotter than the sun.

It is about punishment and authority.

Power and conviction.

He's reminding me that although I will never own him, he will forever own me.

"Fuck you, Andrik..."

I hate myself even more than I already do when I can't add his surname to my scold. I don't Skype, Snapchat, or FaceTime. I don't even have an Instagram account, for crying out loud. I keep my imprint on social media minimal so I don't have to worry about the ghosts of my past finding their way back to me via their invisible footsteps.

"Fuck you and your brother and your stupid-ass power trip."

I push him away from me before tossing open the driver's side door of Mikhail's suddenly less-appealing ride to retrieve my belongings. It is only a charging cable, an outdated phone, and a purse with minimal funds, but I own them, so I refuse to leave without them.

"The closest town is twelve miles away," Andrik announces in a low, thigh-quaking tone when I hotfoot it toward his long, winding driveway.

I don't spin around to see his response when I flip him the bird a second after I commence aerating his pristine lawn with the four-inch heels of my stilettos. I don't need to. The heat of his snarl will keep me warm during the long trek home, not to mention the absolute fury that blackens my veins when disappointment is my first response for his lack of retribution.

25

ANDRIK

My eyes flick from Zoya's rapidly dwindling frame to a fleet of SUVs rolling through the front gates of my palatial mansion when Mikhail finally answers my call. "You've reached Brody's. How can I help you?"

"Are you a complete fucking idiot?"

I don't give him a chance to answer because I don't need to hear his words to know that is precisely what he is.

His breathy chuckle tells me everything I need to know.

"Or are you so determined to make my life a living hell that you're willing to drag her to the fiery depths alongside me?"

My annoyance grows, and I hate that I don't need to say Zoya's name for him to know who I am referencing. "Anoushka said you are seeking a new PA for this region. Zoya studied—"

"We are seeking a new PA for this region because the last one asked the wrong houseguest why I was paying the rent of a one-bedroom apartment on the outskirts of Myasnikov when I own multiple estates not even a twenty-minute drive from there." When he remains quiet, not quite putting the pieces together as fast as

I'd like, I spell it out for him. "She asked Arabella, who doesn't have a single fucking thought without running it by her mother first. The same fucking woman who has our father eating out of her palm."

"Fuck."

That's it. That is all he gives me.

Then, after numerous cusswords, he says, "I wasn't thinking."

"No, you weren't."

And neither the fuck was I. I'm not going to tell him that, though.

My plan was to move closer to Zoya's location to protect her, not pin a target on her back, but even something billed as a country escape was impossible to implement with the federation and my father breathing down my neck.

My every move is being scrutinized, and I hate it almost as much as I loathe the devastated look Zoya gave me when I had to pretend she's nothing but a prop for me to fuck with.

I didn't lie two weeks ago when I said she hasn't left my head for a single second. She's in every frame, but I'm not the only one playing her features on repeat.

Her name has been tossed around too often over the past month for me not to pay careful attention to every mutter.

If I hadn't looked up with a second to spare, I would have been busted violating the very woman I'm endeavoring to hide.

I can't fight fire with fire when Zoya is directly in front of me. It isn't possible. I'm not thinking about vengeance or the possible retaliation I'll face when they find out the man my mother struck didn't die of natural causes.

Nothing but the thrill of the chase is on my mind, and how much I crave my middle name being spoken by Zoya while she's in the midst of ecstasy.

But as quickly as the wish to make her climax burns through my veins, so does the remembrance of the last time I failed to protect the only person I truly cared about.

As much as I should hate to admit this, Zoya's fiery attitude attracts me more than her vulnerability. I love that she's willing to push the boundaries and that she has the gall to pull off a raid not even the world's deadliest assassin would consider.

She won't just slap a man who does her wrong.

She will wholly fucking destroy him.

But I can't stomach picturing her enduring the same outcome of my mother.

That's why I need to toe the line while endeavoring to unearth the key players of the federation. I need to play this game with the integrity it deserves, and so the fuck do the people who are meant to be on my side.

"You almost put her in their direct sight, Mikhail."

"Only almost?" Mikhail queries, hearing what he wants to hear.

I shift my eyes from the SUVs coming to stop under the large canopy that is usually bustling with employees but now resembles a ghost town to Zoya's shadowed figure. She's visible enough for a trained sniper to take her out, but barely a speck for someone with aged eyes.

My grandfather is a fit man for his age, but he can barely see two feet in front of him.

Thank fuck.

Arabella's vision is far more percipient. After exiting the door I tore through when my intuition had me tracking Zoya's location faster than the reports of numerous surveillance cameras being taken offline, Arabella follows my gaze over the rolling hills before trudging to my side without the giddy anticipation of a soon-to-be bride.

As I curl my arm around her waist, weakening the narrowed glare of my grandfather who is watching the farce from his office window, I twist us away from a planned meetup the federation organized before shifting my focus back to my conversation with Mikhail.

"To maintain his cover, Konstantine will drop her off at the closest truck stop. Find a way there before them or start digging your grave."

I'd rather Konstantine take Zoya back to her apartment, but since he is the only man on my team I trust to guide my next move, I can't instruct him to do that. I need Mikhail to step in, not only to take the heat off me, but also from Zoya.

If they think she was here for Mikhail as she lied about earlier, her arrival today won't be second-guessed. My family's estates are as much his as they are mine, so it is a pliable cover.

"I'll be—"

I disconnect our call before all of Mikhail's reply leaves his mouth. I'm too hot with vengeance to hear any more of his excuses, and too fucking hard from the scent of Zoya's arousal on my palm to have any conversation, much less the one I'm about to endure.

"Kazimir, darling, come meet our guests." Dina ushers me over as if we're standing in the driveway of her home before she introduces me to two men I swear I've seen before. "Please meet Dr. Abdulov and Dr. Azores."

I shake the middle-aged men's hands before shifting on my feet to face the additional three who appear to have more authority singularly than Dr. Abdulov and Dr. Azores combined. One has a large scar down one side of his jaw and carries himself with a confidence that announces he is rarely without a weapon. He's most likely the protective detail, though I will save my judgment fully for after Konstantine has arrived.

My intuition has been impaired the past few weeks, so I'm not as trusting of it as I once was.

With the trio not eager to offer an introduction, I tighten my jaw before gesturing for them to enter my family's country manor as if they're wanted guests. They're not, but since I must move in silence until I can announce checkmate, I pretend they are.

When Arabella and her mother shadow their steps, I beat them to the door before spinning to face them, blocking their entrance. "Did they get everything needed?"

"Yes," Arabella answers softly, her head faintly bobbing.

Dina remains quiet. She doesn't need to speak for me to hear her accusatory tone. Her brow is as spiked now as it was when she demanded they travel back to this part of Russia with me so Arabella could attend an appointment with a dress fitter favorable with the stars.

I initially told them no, that any appointments they need to attend to can be done in-house—it will make any possible media leaks about her identity less likely. Then I remembered Arabella isn't as schooled at hiding her expressions as her mother is. She's far easier for me to read, so I wanted to witness her first interaction with my grandfather in person, desperate to know if they'd met previously.

She gushed as most people do, and almost stumbled while reaching out to accept the hand he was holding out for her, but she seemed more concerned about impressing him than impressing the bigwigs strategizing his every move. That's all the proof I need that she's not yet wholly under the federation's thumb as the man I killed last month made out.

"Would you like to see the designs on the shortlist?" Arabella asks, drawing me back to the reason I'm barricading the entryway. "They're all beautiful and will pair well with any tuxedo coloring you choose, but I'd like you to have the final say on the dress I'll wear on our big day."

She stops rummaging through her oversized purse when I shake my head. I don't need to approve the designs she picked because I have no intention of seeing her in any of them. The devastation that flared through Zoya's eyes when she thought Vanka was my wife assures me of this, not to mention the recent news that Arabella's first attempt at conception was unsuccessful.

The test results emailed to me this morning were fresh in my mind when I suspended all the scheduled insemination dates slated in our contract. It was mere minutes before I detected Zoya's presence.

I still plan to implode the federation. I just need to change tactics to make sure their downfall occurs without unnecessary casualties.

A handful of matters need to be finalized before I can publicly announce my "separation," starting with the meeting being delayed by a woman with no authority questioning mine.

With time not in my favor, and my mood souring, I get to the point rather snappily. "Since there is no reason for you to be here anymore, I will request Anoushka to organize you transportation home."

Arabella has more gall than I give her credit for. "I'd rather stay." When her interruption raises both my hackles and my brow, she pushes out quickly, "I was hoping we could confirm some wedding plans while we're here. A beautiful chapel twenty miles from Chelabini is usually booked out years in advance, but they said they could adjust their schedule for—"

She is cut off by the last person I expect. "Not now, dear. It is clear Kazimir has important business matters to take care of." While adjusting the collar of Arabella's dress, Dina *tsks* her as if she is still a child. "You should not encroach on his time more than necessary, especially for things of little importance."

"I wasn't meaning to be a pain. I was just..." Arabella looks as confused as she sounds. "I'm sorry," she eventually settles on. "I will do better."

Her apology doesn't appear to be for me, but since I don't have time to remind a grown woman that she doesn't need to obey her parents' every demand, I dip my chin before telling her I will be in contact shortly.

Arabella replies. I miss what she says since Dina commences a brutal dressing-down a mere second after I enter an estate that's been in my family for centuries with them on the outer, as I hope they'll soon be permanently.

26

ZOYA

"Thank you so much."

For the first time in the history of hitchhiking, my savior dips his chin in gratitude for my praise before he signals to veer back into the heavy flow of traffic on I-25.

I can't recall the last time I wasn't expected to hand over a sexual favor for a two-minute trip, so to say I'm shocked he drove me over twenty miles without a single innuendo exchanged would be a major understatement.

I'm flabbergasted.

It isn't like it would have been a hard feat. The driver is sexy, and I'm hyped up on the endorphins my stomp over Andrik's manicured lawns didn't deplete in the slightest. They're thrumming through my body like I wasn't rejected like a broken toy, and not even the fury I feel when I lock eyes with a familiar pair over the roof of my savior's car trumps the knowledge that only Andrik could douse the flames his presence ignites.

When Mikhail smirks like he knows none of the redness on my cheeks is from embarrassment, my first thought is to run.

It's a pity for him I'm hormonal all year round instead of twelve precise weeks.

Gravel kicks up around my feet when I make a beeline for the man who dumped me in the Pacific Ocean's equivalent of shit creek without a paddle. It dusts my shoes with dirt. I'm not bothered. The sooty coating protects the velour material from the droplets of blood that drip from Mikhail's nose when I sock him in the face.

"Whoa. What the fuck?" Mikhail stammers as he staggers backward.

My hit didn't drop him to the ground as I'd hoped, but I get mammoth satisfaction from the red ooze dribbling from his nose.

"If this is about your dilated eyes and sweaty neck, you need to step the fuck back, Sunshine. I didn't know he was going to be there."

When I rear my arm back for another punch, my stance showing I'll accept nothing below a knockout this time, he partially backtracks on his lie.

"*This* time. I didn't know he was going to be there *this* time."

"You sent me to his home! Of course he was going to be there."

"He has hundreds of homes. A dozen in this state alone. How was I to know—" His words cut off when I attempt to strike him for the second time.

He catches my fist seconds before it collides with his nose and then uses his grip on my hand to spin me away from him and yank me back until I'm cocooned by his body.

If he thinks our difference in height and build will protect him from my onslaught, he's dead wrong.

I headbutt him before stomping on his foot. Then I bob low, bump him back half an inch with an ass nudge, before slamming my elbow into his crotch.

Now he drops like a bag of shit.

"Jesus... Christ... Sunshine. You got me in my left nut." His face reddens more with each word he speaks, growing along with the painful glint in his eyes.

It almost has me feeling sorry for him.

Almost.

As I race for the closest trucker, I say, "Stay out of my life, Mikhail."

He wheezes, coughs, and sputters before he shakes his head. "I... can't... do that, Sunshine."

I whip around so fast my hair slaps my face. "Why? Because you get pleasure tormenting me?" When he remains quiet, guilt stealing his words, I thrust my hand in the direction I came from. "He's married, Mikhail, so why do you keep dangling him in front of me like that doesn't matter?"

"Because it doesn't." For someone with one nut now larger than the other, he talks remarkably fast. "She doesn't mean anything to him. He doesn't love her. He—"

I jump the gate with my reply to ensure he can't try to convince my heart that any of its foolish notions over the past month are plausible. "Then he should leave her." I get two steps away before the man-hating devil on my shoulder demands the chance to be heard. "Or better yet, she should leave him. Even if there is a prenup, they rarely protect adulterers. She could take him to the cleaners, and I'll be more than happy to testify on her behalf to make sure she gets every penny she deserves."

Mikhail smiles, and it instantly conjures up memories of the man I'm endeavoring to hate.

Bastard!

"You don't mean that, Sunshine."

"Wanna bet?"

After hitting him with a scorn hot enough to burn, I recommence my travels.

I barely get two steps away when four short words immediately end my campaign to escape. "Zoya. Is that you?"

I crank my neck to the voice so fast that I almost give myself whiplash. Unfortunately, the platinum-blonde locks and unblemished face I am seeking don't belong to the voice's owner, but she is a very close second.

"Shevi?" I murmur, unsure if my rummage through the tumbleweeds in my head is up to the task so soon after a near orgasmic eruption and mental meltdown.

Shevi has been Aleena's best friend since kindergarten. The last time I laid eyes on her, she had braces and pigtails. She wasn't the exotic beauty standing across from me now.

"Yes." She gleams. "I can't believe you remember me."

I'm taken aback when she races for me before throwing her arms around my neck and hugging me tight. The only female affection I've received in the past twelve years is from Nikita, and she's stingy when it comes to friendly PDA.

After embracing me long enough for Mikhail to make a full recovery, Shevi inches back until we're eye to eye. "I'm sorry we missed you at the fitting. Aleena..." Her pause gives my heart time to recover from the mention of my baby sister's name. "Gosh. Not even those handful of times we managed to sneak out tainted how angelic she looked in her dress." She bumps me with her hip. "The dress fitter didn't even ask if she should consider an ivory gown instead of the pure white Dina demanded." She rolls her eyes like I do anytime I mention my mother's name. "Even though I despise her more than chicken strips with no ranch dressing, I couldn't disagree with her decision. The dress she picked for Aleena is perfect. She is going to be the most beautiful bride."

"Aleena is getting married?" The words shoot out of my mouth before I can stop them. I'm too shocked to play the cool cucumber I'm meant to be when associating with my little sister's best friend.

"Yeah... ah..." Shevi's sigh rustles the hair clinging to my neck. It isn't hot. I just haven't cooled down enough from my exchange with Andrik just yet. "I'm sorry. I assumed you knew. It's new. Her fiancé is..."

I wait and wait and wait for her to continue.

It is a very long thirty seconds.

"He's handsome," she eventually settles on. "And rich. And—"

"Is she happy?" I interrupt, more concerned about Aleena's well-being than a stranger I will most likely never meet.

Shevi's eyes flick past me for the quickest second before she faintly nods. "Yes. She's happy. *Very* happy."

The weight of a mountain shifts off my shoulders, and tears prick my eyes. Those last two words are all I've ever wanted. They bring so much closure and make up for the horrible things I had to endure to achieve them.

"I'm sorry, Zoya, I have to go." Shevi signals to a man at the end of the lot that she won't be a minute before she gives my hand a gentle squeeze. "But we will talk more soon." She smiles. It is full of hesitance. "We have a heap of wonderful events coming up, so I am sure we will bump into each other again." After a final squeeze, she murmurs goodbye before hotfooting it to the dark-haired man waiting for her.

I'm so stunned by her confession that my sister is getting married that I don't object to Mikhail butting shoulders with me to watch her exit. We stand in silence for several long minutes, the quiet only ending when a truck driver sounds his horn, requesting we move from the middle of the dusty lot so he can exit without running us over.

"Can I—"

"Nope," I answer before Mikhail can finalize his question, walking away from him.

"He'll—"

I silence him with an action this time instead of words. I hold the dirtbox he gifted me last month in the air before clicking the button.

I told myself I was being neurotic when I put it in my purse. Andrik hadn't made a single effort to find me.

Now I realize it was the smartest thing I've done all month.

27

ANDRIK

"*G*o back."

Konstantine scrubs at his tired eyes before doing as asked. We've been working nonstop for the past eight hours, attempting to infiltrate a system the world's greatest hackers invented, so I shouldn't be surprised that what should have been an easy task to end our day took a dramatic turn.

"There. Just before Mikhail ducks behind the pillar."

I should have realized Zoya has too much gall for Mikhail to subdue. There's only one man capable of breaking her will.

It isn't my little brother.

My chest stops expanding like a peacock's feathers when Konstantine murmurs, "Holy fucking shit."

He cleans up a portion of the footage Mikhail has been capturing since he commenced following Zoya home hours ago. The images are grainy because the dirtbox Zoya is utilizing as her own personal cloak of protection requires Mikhail to maintain a decent amount of distance. *Finally.*

"That's—"

"Irina Ivanov," I interrupt, my tone announcing my disbelief.

Irina is the mother of Maksim and Matvei Ivanov. Although she now goes by her maiden name, the surname cited on all her official government records is known across the globe. She is Bastian Fernandez's first wife—heiress to one of the most notable Italian crime syndicates in the world.

Her ties to the bratva are limited, but with Matvei's shrewd business skills having him in favor with many mafia families, and her eldest son's business dealings across the globe reminding the federation that the bratva isn't solely for Russian-born descendants, it is notable enough for my gut to declare caution when Konstantine cleans up the image enough to unearth who she is corresponding with.

Dr. Abdulov must have immediately returned to Myasnikov Private Hospital after our meeting today. The footage is time-stamped only an hour after he left.

"He couldn't be that stupid, surely." Konstantine leans low in his chair before folding his arms over his chest and crinkling his dark brows. "There's stupid, and then there's *stupid*. That's the latter." He nudges his head to the still image of Dr. Abdulov standing across from a wheelchair-bound Irina at a nurses' station desk in the surgical department.

I shrug. It is unexpected. My replies are usually more cut and dry.

After checking Zoya's feed and noting it is still blank since she charged the dirtbox within minutes of Konstantine advising me it had finally gone flat, I ask, "What can you get me on Irina's admission?" Konstantine's fingers stop flying over the keys of his laptop when I say, "Not what the hospital's information system says." I wet my dry lips before straying my eyes to the command center he set up in the room next to my office earlier today. "From the system we unearthed today."

"You clearly believe he is the latter," Konstantine murmurs when he gets the gist of what I am requesting.

Government staff are the same as politicians. They tell you what they want you to know and only share the truth with those who need to know.

To the federation, that need rarely goes past them.

Konstantine's fingers barely touch his keyboard over the next fifteen minutes. We can't have our infiltration announced or we will be booted out in less than a nanosecond. He needs to follow steps already taken more than create his own. It makes it a slow and tedious search, but the result makes up for the delay.

Irina Ivanov's admission is for the exact reason I accepted an invitation to meet with Dr. Abdulov and Dr. Azores today. Except she isn't purchasing organs. Hers were sold to someone as desperate as me to save a loved one as I am to avenge the death of another.

After a moment of reflection not long enough to ensure I'm not making a mistake, I say, "Get me contact information for Matvei."

Konstantine looks at me as if I have grown a second head. I'm beginning to wonder the same. Maksim has more ties to the bratva than his younger brother does, but that's why I need to go around him. I need to be in favor to someone outside of our realm, and Matvei is the best person to help me establish that.

It takes a lot of fucking gall to potentially hurt the people you're trying to save from the carnage, but if anyone can do it and come out stronger, it'll be me.

With guilt that I'm taking steps that may hurt someone too young to defend himself, I log into the security feed of Zakhar's room a little after midnight instead of slipping into bed with the woman who has my head in such a state that I refuse to wash my hands for the fear of losing her scent.

I'm not surprised to discover Zakhar is actually asleep this time. The pain medication they've been pumping into him via an IV over the past two weeks makes him groggy, but he's been struggling to keep down even water the past two days, so he's more lethargic than usual.

That's how the doctor in charge of his care survived telling me he won't clear him for travel. I pushed to get the answer I wanted how I always do—with violence—but no number of threats rolled the dice in my favor.

Zakhar is too sick to travel. Not even a motorcade of ambulances could guarantee he would survive the three-thousand-mile trip I wanted him to face. He's in his final stages of life, and I feel like a complete fucking prick that I keep placing my needs before his.

If Mikhail had done the same, I wouldn't have a future to contemplate, much less one that involved others.

The motion-detected surveillance camera announces my watch has been busted a mere second before a husky, sleep-deprived voice breaks through the speakers of my laptop. "He's slept more than usual today, but he has also eaten more." Under the watchful eye of a monitoring system mothers-to-be would pay out the eye to have, my father leaves the corner of Zakhar's room where Anoushka set up a cot for him. "I think that's a good sign, but what would I know? I was trained to read a teleprompt from the age of four. That's as far as my skill set goes."

This is the first time he's announced disdain for his life plan.

It isn't something I thought he would ever display.

I guess Zakhar's condition is affecting more people than just me.

As he scrubs at his tired eyes, he inches closer to the camera with inbuilt speakers. "How was the meeting today? Did they have a solution?"

I'm so caught off guard by the genuine hope in his tone that I nod before recalling that he can't see me. "They believe they can find a suitable candidate for Zak."

"But?" my father asks, aware I left my reply short for a reason.

I don't often take the honesty route, but when I do, I leave no stone unturned. "I don't believe they're the right outfitters for the job. Their work is sloppy. They leave a paper trail a mile long, and their candidates aren't worthy of Dokovic ties."

Usually, the mere mention of our family name would puff his chest high.

Tonight, it deflates it.

Since I know why, I say, "I will find someone more suitable."

"We don't have time to find someone else, Andrik." The camera follows his eyes as they drift to Zakhar, who stirs from his roar. "Zakhar doesn't have time. He needs a new heart."

"That I will find him," I shout back, my voice just as loud, my anger as palpable even via a speaker. "But not like this. Not at the expense of everything I've been working toward."

My marriage initially commenced as a way to find out what happened to my mother and why she and the many other women before and after her disappeared either hours after discovering they were expecting a daughter, or within days of their son's fifth birthday.

It wasn't meant to be about appeasing the federation's every want with the hope that they'd supply my half-brother with a heart he so desperately needs.

The only reason I've continued my ruse is because Zakhar's condition is bringing the main players out far sooner than the possible months it could take Arabella to conceive. He's demanding the attention of the hierarchies I will take down. I'm just confused as to why.

Mikhail is closer to the imaginary throne my family governs than Zakhar, but remains so far off the federation's radar he could knock up a dozen hookers and no one would bat an eyelash.

There's more at play here than I am being told, but I won't know what it is until I'm buried so deep in the federation's underbelly they'll never get me back out.

The reminder adds a ton of angst to my voice—angst I am not used to handling. "For how much you are asking of me, the least you could do is trust me."

"I do—"

My huff cuts him off.

He doesn't trust me because he doesn't trust anyone.

It wasn't solely my mother the federation forced from his life. Mikhail's mother walked the same narrow corridor with the same faceless men. It was just a year earlier than planned since the unborn child in her stomach was a girl.

"If he—"

I cut him off again. "There are no ifs. Life is too short for ifs and buts." My eyes bounce between his suddenly wet pair not even a grainy feed can hide when I whisper in a deadly tone, "You should know that better than anyone."

Needing to end our exchange before I'm tempted to express myself how I usually do when snowed under—with my fists—I click out of the feed of Zakhar's room, losing one set of worldly eyes.

The pair I didn't notice straight away are more notable than my father's, more seeped in history. They belong to my grandfather, and although they put my head in as much of a state as Zoya's unexpected visit to his palatial mansion today, I have a solution to my problem. An out for my angst.

I have the perfect outlet for emotions I haven't handled in years, and for the first time in a month, she is only a thirty-minute drive away.

28

ZOYA

My climb into my bed takes longer than usual. I was a little generous with my nips when I cracked open the bottle of vodka I purchased with the hope it would pre-empt celebratory drinks for the position I was meant to secure today.

It would have been commiseration drinks if I hadn't run into Shevi.

That brief encounter gave me something to celebrate, and I never do anything in halves—particularly when my bed is mere feet from my chosen drinking location.

I'm not close to blackout drunk. The buzz is almost as nice as the one Andrik's hand created earlier.

Almost.

My body has been thrumming with unexploited restlessness for hours. I want to blame the thickening of my veins on my first contact with a member of my sister's inner circle in years, but that would be a lie.

The thud of my pulse is sexually related. The heat between my legs announces it, not to mention my head's constant reminder tonight that I have a drawer of apparatuses at my disposal, so I don't need a man to take care of the thrill.

Although annoyed my needs can't take a step back for just one day, I also understand why that is the case. My morals dip when I'm tipsy, but they're wholly obliterated when I'm horny.

If I want any chance of working past my confusion, I need to take the edge off.

Before I met Andrik, I self-stimulated regularly. Often multiple times a day. Now I'm on a climax drought that has me wishing I asked Dr. Hemway for some recommendations when he mentioned creams for dryness.

A tube of lube may be the only way I will get the vault back open after Andrik sealed it shut so cruelly earlier today. I was right there, on the cusp of orgasm, and then he took away all my surf gear and forced me to find my own way back to shore.

Perhaps that's what the extra thump of my pulse is?

Maybe I'm not horny.

Perhaps it is solely fury keeping my head clouded with confusion.

Nope.

The only thing I am is a liar. The quickest brush of my fingertip over my panties-covered pussy proves this. My clit is primed and ready to go, and despite my belief I'd be dryer than the Sahara, the faintest sliver of dampness coats my index finger.

I'm wet and, for once, unashamed by this.

I don't need a man to climax, and it isn't like Andrik owns my orgasms. He doesn't even own me, so how can he claim possession of something that is a part of me?

He can't.

Ignoring the screaming protests of my body that a solo trek will never feel as good as a fire-sparking coupling, I slant my head to peer out my partially cracked-open bedroom door.

I don't know who I am looking for. I've lived alone for years. There's just been a weird feeling in the air over the last couple of weeks. Almost like I am being watched.

To ensure that isn't the case, I plug in the dirtbox Mikhail gifted me four weeks ago to ensure it doesn't lose charge like it did when I turned up at Nikita's work unannounced earlier today.

Once its flashes announce it is in operation, I slide my hand back between my legs so fast that vodka isn't the sole cause of my dizziness. I hate that I'm already wet enough to darken the crotch of my panties with a shadow, but you wouldn't know that for how fast I direct my fingers to my clit. My motivation to bring myself to climax seems more about proving to myself that I still have what it takes to be pleasured, that I don't need a man to make me feel good—especially not a taken one.

After tugging off my panties, I slide two fingers between the folds of my pussy, slicking them with the wetness building more rapidly than any previous solo journey, before firming my clit more with my thumb.

A lazy smile stretches across my face when they don't encounter an ounce of resistance when I thrust two fingers inside myself—forever impatient.

They slide in with ease and feel incredibly arousing.

The buzz they spark through me has me hopeful this won't take long. My first self-pleasing expedition in over a month has nothing to do with pleasure and everything to do with needing sleep.

I'll never be able to help Nikita purchase the breathing machine Grampies needs to live pain-free if I turn up to an interview looking like a zombie.

Yeah, right.

Even when it is of my own doing, I like to feel desired. *Validated.*

I want to be wanted.

It is an annoying crutch I've struggled to give up since childhood.

I doubt it will ever fully go away. I just wish I could mimic how desired I felt when it was Andrik's hand on me instead of my own.

He knew precisely where to touch and for exactly how long. It was like he could read my body and understand its every desire.

Although it is fleeting, he truly makes me feel wanted when his hands are on me.

Cherished, even.

An unwanted shudder shakes my thigh when a stern tweak of my clit has me recalling something he said earlier.

Who owns this cunt, darling?

"Not you," I murmur, more angry at myself than him that he is leading what is meant to be a solo expedition.

He shouldn't be hard to hate. The guilt he makes me feel after every exchange should fester in my heart until it boils over. But no matter how hard I've tried to forget him the past month, he continually pops up. Whether in my dreams or while speaking to Mikhail before he railroaded me without warning again today, he always takes center stage.

I can't let him have this too.

This is the one thing I have all to myself. I don't have to share it with anyone.

I slide my fingers in and out of myself while flicking my clit with my opposite hand. Pleasure jolts through me over and over, but before it can crest and then crash through me, the anticipation I'm attempting to ignite dulls to a simmer, and the urge floats away.

As I drift my eyes to the drawer that's impossible to open without a creak loud enough to wake my neighbors, I push my fingers in and out of my pussy at a frantic pace.

Is that the issue? Do I want to be fucked instead of made slow, lazy love to like I was after Andrik cooked and fed me?

The memory of his attentiveness that night spreads a rush of heat across my chest and puckers my nipples.

"*Yesss*," I moan, hopeful.

I work myself faster, *harder*. I fuck myself with my fingers until stars form and my thighs shake. It is an almost clumsy embrace since my woozy limbs can't keep up with the frantic pace my body is demanding. Each flick, pinch, and thrust brings me closer and closer to the edge.

They just never fully push me over it.

I can't climax by myself anymore, and the frustration has me on the verge of bursting into tears.

With the aggression of a man who forgot to take his little blue pill before his fiftieth birthday sex, I yank my hand out of my pants and then throw an arm over my eyes.

I will not cry over this any more than I'd cry over a man. I just need a moment to gather my bearings and to let the alcohol fumbling my movements burn off enough to find the right rhythm.

I'm not broken.

I am simply drunker than I first realized.

"I can do this. I can make myself come. Andrik doesn't own my orgasms."

My pulse thumps as loudly as my shouted chant when a deep accented voice says, "Do I need to take you over my knee again, милая?"

As my arm falls from my face, my eyes rocket open. I can't see a damn thing. It is dark in my room in general. Tonight, it is pitch black. Not even the streetlights that reflect off the building across from mine sneak through the cracks of my curtains.

Certain my ears are playing tricks on me, I remain quiet while endeavoring to adjust my eyes to the dark conditions.

The scent I refused to wash off tonight adds to the goose bumps popping up over my skin. It isn't solely pricy aftershave. It is a mixture of smells that conjure up memories of sheet-clenching sex, and it sends my head into a tailspin.

I don't need a drawer of sex toys to come anymore. I just need that delicious smell.

No longer capable of playing the daft card, I say, "Andr—"

"Shh," interrupts a whispered voice close enough to announce the cause of the dip at the end of my mattress near my ankles. "We need to be quiet."

As quickly as fret slicked my skin with sweat, anger dries it.

"No. *You* need to be quiet. *I* can do whatever the fuck *I* want."

You shouldn't be able to hear a smirk. I swear I can.

It is so obvious that Andrik is relishing my defiance that it fortifies my determination to give him the full shebang.

"You need to go home, back to your *wife*."

The slip-up at the end of my sentence is easily forgivable when you learn how quickly Andrik can make my body pliable to his touch. His lips barely nibble on my ankle, yet the wave in my stomach is on the verge of cresting.

It almost topples when he says, "I don't want her. I want *you*." His hand slides up my thigh, growling when he realizes I am without panties. "And I will have you. I just need you to be patient until it is safe. Until I can guarantee I can protect you better than I did my mother."

I can't see him, but I can feel his determination. I continue to fight, though, to remember my anger. His rejection hurt me today, and I'm notorious for lashing out when hurt. Why should my quirks be any different for him?

"I don't need your protection. I own a gun, and I know how to use it."

"Good." The level of praise in his gravelly voice doubles the height of the goose bumps dotting my skin. He sounds genuinely pleased. "Perhaps after I've made you come you can show it to me."

I squirm up the bed. "You're not going to make me come. I don't need you to make me come. I'm perfectly capable of making myself come."

Underneath the bedding, his hot breaths batter my skin when he backhands my clit before murmuring, "Lie to me again, милая, and not even my hand marks on your ass will save you from my wrath."

"Who said I'm lying?" I force the words through lips dying to release the moans rumbling in my chest.

Quicker than I can fathom, the bedding is pulled across my body, leaving me exposed and vulnerable.

"This..." I stammer in a sharp breath when his fingers play at the wetness between my legs. "Your hands barely caused a trickle." Again, he backhands my clit, sending a fiery warmth across my midsection. "I've hardly touched you, yet you're already drenched" —my eyes are slowly adjusting. I don't need the room lit up like daylight to know he inches closer before finalizing his sentence, though—"for *me*."

I kick at the heat licking at my feet enough for Andrik to grunt. There's no real power behind my whack. No real anger. I didn't lie when I said my morals are obliterated when I'm horny. They're nowhere to be seen since there was more assurance in his tone than haughtiness.

Part of me is furious I let this get this far. The other part, the clearly unethical part, won't let anything stop it. Shock waves of pleasure careen down over me, making me a shuddering mess, and I am desperate to come. But can I do this? Can I disregard another woman's feelings so my ego can be stroked?

No, I can't.

"You can't be here. You need to go. I don't want you here." With words not getting through to him, I get desperate. "Mikhail could come back at any—"

A hand clamps my mouth shut at the same time a warm and probing tongue invades my pussy. It spears in deep before it does a long, leisurely lick of my insides.

One lick and my campaign to be on the right side of good is undone.

As my thighs sweep open, pleasure cascades down my spine.

Two fingers slip between my legs next. They gather up the wetness before dipping into my pussy at the same unhurried pace of his tongue.

My brain screams at me to buck him off me and make out this isn't exactly what I am craving, but since I am as desperate for him to bestow my clit with a heap of attention as I am to stop this, I breathe through the sensation threatening to swallow me whole and act like the submissive I will never be.

It is an act worthy of an Oscar, but the instant Andrik's tongue curls around my clit, I crumble like a dried mud pie left on the asphalt being run over by a Mack truck.

An orgasm crashes through me as frantically as a tsunami races to shore. It is uncontrollable. Wild. And devastating.

It tells my head what my body was trying to express only moments ago.

That Andrik owns my orgasms as much as he does me.

I will never let him know that I've worked that out, though. The instant he unclamps my mouth, the first thing I'll tell him is that I will never be his.

I just need him to stop eating me. Stop consuming me. Stop making me feel so wanted that I don't care how many baby mommas or wives he ends up with.

He doesn't, though. He continues devouring me as if I am his favorite dessert until I scream his name into the tattooed hand muffling my mouth and then collapse from exhaustion.

29

ANDRIK

I wake with a monstrous hard-on.

That isn't unusual. I am in my peak sexual prime. But this one is different. It isn't morning wood that will go down in a minute or two. It's not even an erection inspired by the hope of sexual gratification. It is my body's response to the closeness of his mate, and how making her orgasm over and over again was more satisfying than any release I've ever achieved.

I wanted to come last night. I wanted to fuck away the frustrations that have been bombarding me for the past month. Like all my greatest plans over the past four weeks, the urge flew out the window the instant I realized why Zoya couldn't bring herself to climax.

She doesn't want some random's head between her legs.

She doesn't even want my brother's.

She only wants mine.

The knowledge had me banging my chest like an ape—and acting like one too.

I wanted to make Zoya scream my name so loud it would ring in my ears for a week. Mercifully, with barely a second to spare, I remembered that my needs aren't the only ones I'm striving to answer.

There are ears everywhere. As stated previously, they more than triple when the king is in court.

My grandfather is in this region of Russia for a reason, and as much as I want to pretend that isn't true for a few more hours so I can relish the taste coating my lips and fingers, I can't.

The faster I play this game, the quicker I will win.

Zoya murmurs when I pull my arm out from underneath her before replacing my chest with a pillow. I'm still mostly clothed. I only removed my jacket when the image of Zoya with her eyes fluttered shut and her cheeks flushed made the conditions too stuffy to ignore. I toed off my shoes a second before climbing into bed with her. The rest of my clothes remained untouched.

It is cool this morning, but a nonoperational AC unit isn't the reason I pull Zoya's covers up tight. It is the beady watch of my little brother. His lower back is balanced on the wrought iron railing of Zoya's shared balcony, and his sleeping pants are low enough to expose he's still not a fan of underwear.

"You don't think you should wake her before sneaking out?" Mikhail asks when I collect the shoes I left near the armchair in the corner of the room.

I join him on the emergency exit stairwell. "No." My reply is curt. It can't be helped. I hate having my authority questioned. It is worse when it comes to Zoya. "She needs sleep. She is exhausted." And how the fuck am I meant to explain something to her that I don't even understand? I tried last night, and I miserably failed to make sense of anything.

I usually strategize my games to the wire, but for the past four weeks, I've been flying blind. I went from caring about nothing but revenge to sheltering so many people I'm worried there won't be enough space for everyone under my umbrella.

I won't lose—it isn't in my vocabulary—but it is near impossible to pull off a solo victory when you're playing a team sport.

Zoya learned that the hard way last night.

I glare at Mikhail when he mutters, "She wouldn't be so exhausted if you told her the truth."

"And what exactly is that truth, Mikhail?" I snap out before I can stop myself.

He doesn't answer me because he can't. I'm sheltering him from the burden until I can ensure it won't affect him how it is affecting me. That he won't face the same level of liability he was forced to endure during his childhood. I need to make sure he isn't burned time and time again like he was when he was Zakhar's age.

Zak is sick. I don't know if he will survive, so why subject Mikhail to the heartache of his existence until I know for sure? He's lost so much already. First his mother and his sister, then any other sibling the federation deemed unsuitable for the Dokovic name. They were all pushed aside and downgraded. Some were killed. Mikhail only made the cut because he was *my* sole reason to obey.

When I rebelled against their rules, Mikhail was beaten as if he were disobedient.

When I refused to eat until someone told me where my mother went, Mikhail's meals were served to the dogs guarding the prison-like mansion we were forced to call home.

When I begged for one of my numerous brothers to take my spot at the top of the pyramid, Mikhail was pushed further and further down the ladder of importance.

He was treated like shit so I would grow up years before I was close to being an adult. I refuse to do the same now that I am one.

The remembrance sees me offering a rare lenience. "She will know the truth soon." When he attempts to interrupt me, I talk faster and with authority. "As will you. But not until I am ready, and not until I am sure you are both protected from any possible downfall it could inflict."

There's no dishonesty in my tone. No deceit. So Mikhail shockingly accepts my word. "All right." He wets his lips like he's preparing for them to be split before saying, "But I want to stay close until then. I want to make sure with my own two eyes that she's okay."

"I won't let anything happen to her."

"I know," he instantly replies, easing my rapidly surging fury. "But still, I want to stay nearby."

My first thought is fuck no, that I have enough issues to deal with without adding my little brother cozying up to the woman who will be mine no matter what, but there's a gleam in his eyes I can't misplace. It is the same glint that formed in them every time he found me in my hiding spot when we were kids.

We sat in my closet some years for hours on end. We didn't speak or play with the hundreds of toys our grandfather bribed us with. We mused over a possible life outside those walls.

It proves he's looking at Zoya now as more of a sister than a prospective bed companion, and that alone eases my hesitation.

"All right," I parrot.

Mikhail looks as shocked as I feel.

This is *not* how I envisioned our next meetup going.

"But not here. Not in this building."

It drove me insane with jealousy when Konstantine announced Mikhail had kicked out the men Daniil had placed in the apartments bordering Zoya's so he could lay down roots.

Just knowing he was under the same roof as Zoya longer than me last night had my arrogance at an all-time high.

"I'll organize you another apartment—"

"I can find somewhere else to stay. You don't need to go out of your way to accommodate me." For the first time ever, he gives me a bit of leeway on the numerous tasks I undertake each day. "I'm sure you've got enough on your plate."

I huff like his dart didn't hit the board before putting on my shoes and tying the laces.

Once I'm ready to go, I commence climbing down the emergency fire exit stairwell. "Give her some space. She'll forgive you when she's ready, not because you try to force her to. She's stubborn as fuck." I could leave it there, but I'll have to kill someone to maintain my reputation if Mikhail were to see my smile. "And buy some fucking underwear. You're meant to garnish their appetite with a sneak peek of what is about to come, not bring out all three courses a second after they sit down."

Mikhail's laugh is still ringing in my ears when I slide into the back door of one of the many maintenance vans siding Zoya's building.

With the amount of coin KADOK Industries has been throwing into this side of Myasnikov, a late-night inspection from a building supervisor was an easy cover. I just had to keep Zoya's moans to a minimum.

That wasn't easy, and the remembrance tightens the front of my pants.

I try to downplay it, though. The last thing I need is for my crew to think I am weak. We're putting in steps for the biggest coup of the century. I can't lose their faith now.

"Anything?"

Konstantine peers up from a laptop he is rarely without. He takes in my crumpled shirt and trousers before slowly shaking his head. "Not a peep."

I sigh, relieved. I took a risk coming here last night. My grandfather is in town, which means the top-tiered members of the federation are only steps behind him, but it had been too long since I'd heard Zoya moan my name and had her heat wrapped around my cock. I couldn't set aside my needs for a second longer.

I ticked off the first half of my wish list within minutes of arriving at her apartment. The latter will have to wait. I want Zoya floppy with sexual exhaustion, not alcohol. Last night, part of our exchange swayed toward the latter.

As I slot into the driver's seat of the van, I say, "Keep ears close to the ground. If news of my visit to this part of town circulates, I'll have Kolya organize a press release."

My father's pledge last election was more affordable housing for his less wealthy constituents. His promise got him elected, so it is only right his favorite son helps him uphold his pledge.

When I check the side mirror to make sure I can pull onto the street safely, a woman in a sparkly gold dress captures my attention. I'm not perving. What interest could I have in another woman when the arousal of the very definition of a goddess is still on my lips? It is recalling where I've seen her before, and how a refresher in my attitude could help me more than disadvantage me that secures my devotion.

"And reach out to Lilia. I need her help with something."

Konstantine grunts in understanding as I pull onto an almost isolated street.

30

ZOYA

*M*y heart beeps in my neck when my brief scroll of the social media site I only joined an hour ago has me stumbling onto an event I've been seeking for the past two days. It isn't "the" event, but it is one of the biggest indicators that Shevi's confession was true, and that nothing that happened after it was imagined as my groggy head tried to convince my heart.

Aleena is getting married, and her bachelorette party is only two short weeks away.

I searched Aleena's name for hours after I woke up to an empty yet spicy-scented bed the morning following my botched interview. Nothing came up. Not a single thing. The search results were as blank as I tried to make my hazy memories from the night before.

I was beginning to wonder if Aleena had changed her name like I had when I was forced to grow up years too soon, and then a similarity for the upcoming nuptials presented.

Almost every article started with the groom's name followed by "and his fiancée." Not even the brides with as much wealth and power as their male counterparts were mentioned by name.

It reminded me that Russia still has a long way to travel before it can remove bigamist from its dictionaries, and although my life isn't close to glamorous, it could be worse.

I could be so worthless to Andrik that not a single article of our quickie marriage made it to print.

I hate admitting this, but when my search of Aleena's impending nuptials failed to yield a single result, I switched my focus to the man responsible for the furious thud raging through my body.

Andrik is a common name in Russia, but its upsurge in popularity over the past twenty years didn't hinder my search. I couldn't find a single press release about his wedding, much less an in-depth article, and mercifully, I located no other "family" announcements, either.

Guilt will always crash down on me when Andrik's devastating blue eyes and cut jaw enter my thoughts, but I'd rather be a mistress than a homewrecker.

My skin quivers with more than annoyance when Nikita sneaks up on me unawares. "Whatcha looking at?"

Once I've ensured my heart stays in my chest, I twist my phone screen around to face her.

Her eyes gleam as brightly now as they did when I arrived with a ton of greasy breakfast treats one of my elderly neighbors was going to throw out if I didn't accept them. She had cooked too much for a family gathering, so she distributed trays of leftovers to everyone in our building. I was still reeling in the effects of a horrific hangover, so there was no way I was going to say no to crispy strips of bacon. It was also nice to shower Nikita and her grandparents with treats for a change. They're usually always feeding me.

"Oh my god. You found it."

My words come out breathy. "It's not the wedding, but—"

"It's close enough."

She slots onto the bed next to me before offering me one of her ghastly vitamin waters. I shake my head, unwilling to test my stomach so soon after its last exodus. I didn't make it out of bed for over an hour yesterday.

When Nikita spots the signs of dehydration my scaly skin is struggling to conceal, she eyes me like she's not above water-boarding me to replenish my body with the fluids it so desperately needs. I accept the bottle and take a hesitant sip.

It isn't as ghastly as I remember, but it isn't great either.

I'd much prefer coffee.

After a handful more sips, I calculate how long it will take for us to get to the Trudny District from Myasnikov, and an approximate cost. Nikita has to come with me. I can't see the guest list since I'm not an official group member, and my ego is too fragile from the multiple hits it has endured over the past month to consider facing my mother alone again.

"You'll have to fly," Nikita murmurs, her mind reading skills at full capacity since we're practically joined at the hip. Her "bed" is as saggy as my couch. "It will take too long to drive, and the cost to hire a car would be outrageous."

She thinks Mikhail's contribution to her grandfather's breathing machine is because I sold my rusted bomb. I haven't had the heart to tell her I left it in the basement of a man's building because I can't trust myself around his brother for half a second. My shameful act two nights ago proves this without fault.

"Not to mention the conditions," Nikita murmurs, returning my focus to the task at hand. "You can't drive in snowy conditions even when it's not snowing."

Since nothing she said is dishonest, I don't argue. Instead, I veer my search to the cheapest available airline before placing two people in the ticket search bar.

"Z—"

"Please, Keet." I peer up at her with big puppy dog eyes, praying they'll be enough to pull her over the fence. "I can't do this without you." I take a breather before announcing the true cause of my worry. "What if she rejects me?"

"For what? Traveling three hours each way every year with the hope of seeing her for five seconds on her birthday? Or for acting like your letters aren't returned unopened every time you send her a new one?" She looks sternly at me. "She has no reason to reject you, Z. And if she tries, I'm not opposed to teaching her some manners."

I shouldn't laugh. She is being dead serious. But I love how much she loves me that my smile radiates through me before I can shut it down.

"But..." I could kill her for the delay. "I promised myself if I were ever given the chance to repay you for getting Professor Kincaid off my back, I'd take it. So..."

I refuse to accept another delay. "So you're going to break out a bikini for the first time in your life to join me in soaking up the rays of the Trudny Peninsula sun?"

"I was going to say..." I don't know who taught her delayed gratification, but I'm about ready to smack them. "So I guess I'm not opposed to using my credit card points to purchase *us* tickets to your baby sister's bachelorette party."

I'm internally screaming, but the rattle of trains rolling over outdated tracks harnesses my excitement. "Are you sure you don't need the points for something else?"

Nikita doesn't live near a train station. That's just how rattly Grampies's chest is when he's struggling through a severe case of pneumonia. While I strived and failed to pretend that I am a morally ethical woman, he had a bad turn. It's been playing havoc with my mind even more than usual.

I really need a job, but the chances of me securing one will be even less likely if I place a stipulation for time off on my application.

"Maybe we should wait for the wedding. There will be more

people in attendance, which means my mother will be on her best behavior."

"But that means there will also be more people between Aleena and you." Nikita plucks up her phone, searches for the group I found, then invites herself to the Facebook group Shevi accidentally made public. "The list of invitees is small. It's intimate and manageable..." Her eyes pop open before her throat works hard to swallow. "*And* it is void of the Wicked Witch."

I scroll the list of ten names at least a dozen times before letting the truth sink in.

My mother isn't on Aleena's bachelorette guest list.

None of her aliases are present.

"We have to go." Nikita's inclusion in her reply already has me on board. What she says next seals the deal. "And while I'm there, maybe I can hand Mrs. Ivanov my discharge plan in person."

She ribs me when I mutter under my breath, "And perhaps she'll be so grateful she will share her marital status with you along with her many millions."

Nikita met a man two nights ago. Her fascination was as instant as his, but unlike me, she didn't immediately act on her impulses. She erred on the side of caution because the man who beguiled her in under a second shares the same last name as one of her patients.

She is a firm believer that cheating is a choice, not a mistake, hence me keeping quiet on my indiscretions with Andrik. I won't survive a scolding by the only person who has ever truly loved me.

Mistaking my sigh as disappointment about the outrageous price gouge airlines have been undertaking since COVID, Nikita tells me to switch my search from paid fares to points. "It's amazing how much further the dollar stretches when it's fake." She nudges me for the second time. "If only everything could be paid for with monopoly money, then we'd be set."

31

ANDRIK

I'm not surprised when Anoushka's tired eyes are the first I spot when exiting Zakhar's room. It's late, but Anoushka doesn't sleep until all the Dokovic children she raised are settled—myself included.

In an endeavor to lessen some of the burden weighing down my chest, I returned home to once again try to convince Zakhar's medical team to move him closer to the base I am endeavoring to set up near Myasnikov.

It only took one glance into Zak's pained eyes to know my efforts would be fraudulent.

He is extremely unwell.

I wait for Anoushka to join me at the side of the den before instructing, "Call Dr. Makarand and request his attendance at the first available convenience." I shift on my feet to face Zakhar's room before breathing out some of my annoyance with a handful of words. "His pain is increasing to a level I'm uncomfortable with."

"It is," she agrees, her tone as low as mine, her shoulders just as heavy. "But Dr. Makarand announced earlier this evening that Zak can't be offered more medication. He has reached his limit."

I cuss before an excuse to shift my rapidly building anger onto someone else forms.

"Dr. Makarand was here earlier?" I'm yelling, and it is unsuitable. I am just too stunned she overstepped my directive to act cordial.

I specifically stated last night that no one was to enter Zakhar's room without my explicit consent. Keeping him hidden isn't solely about his safety. It is one of only a handful of things keeping his will to live alive.

Zakhar is nearly five. That means the woman he asks about a million times a day has mere weeks to live. I was unaware of his existence only a month ago, but that doesn't mean I want him to experience the pain Mikhail and I were forced to endure during our childhood.

"Yes," Anoushka whispers, her head bobbing softly. "He arrived with Dr. Fairmont." Her suddenly wide eyes bounce between mine. "I was of the belief you knew of their attendance today."

She swallows harshly when I reply through clenched teeth, "This is the first I'm hearing of it."

"With Arabella's first attempt at conception unsuccessful, a second round was scheduled for this morning," announces a voice from the side—a voice becoming far too familiar for how agitated it makes me. "It was meant to be after your meeting yesterday, but it was pushed back when Dr. Fairmont was unable to find you to gain your permission for the insemination. Allegedly, he was informed that the schedule in our contract had been postponed."

Dina hands Anoushka her empty gin glass before shooing her away as if she is the help.

She is a paid member of my team, but I will never see her as the help.

She is family—unlike the crustation standing across from me.

"Dr. Fairmont tried to reach you for confirmation, but after seeing how poorly dear Zakhar is, your father figured it was best to forge forward with *your* initially devised schedule." She emphasizes certain parts of her reply to ensure I don't forget who commenced this ruse. "Was that wrong of him to do?" She continues talking before I can tell her that I've murdered people for less. "Time isn't in your favor, Kazimir. Appeasing *them* is your brother's only lifeline." A confidence she shouldn't hold flares through her eyes. "They like my daughter. She is their first and *only* pick. So perhaps you should consider how unpleased they will be if they were to learn that you continue to stain their legacy for a penniless hick from Mysan—"

I pin her to the wall by her throat before all her reply leaves her mouth. There's nothing kind about my grip. Nothing weak. I strangle her with the full intention of killing her.

My anger doesn't center around having my authority overridden. I will get back to that after ensuring Dina is aware that her wealth doesn't make her a better person.

"A penniless hick who has more class in her pinkie than you do in your entire body."

I tighten my grip, loathing the pinkness rimming her lips.

It needs to be several shades darker.

"A penniless hick who could have any man she wants. A penniless hick who can wipe your daughter from my mind with one sideways glance. Is that the penniless hick you are referring to, Dina?" I pull her forward before slamming her back. "If she is who you are referencing, you should bow at her feet and pray for her forgiveness because *if* it weren't for her, I wouldn't know I have a heart in my chest, and you would already be dead."

I had nothing to live for and nothing to lose, so the only thing I feared in the wake of my demise was not taking enough people down with me.

My opinion changed a month ago.

It was approximately twelve hours *before* I learned of Zakhar's existence. How much more proof does Dina need that she placed her chips on the wrong number?

My grip loosens a smidge when a voice full of nobility breaks through the madness engulfing me. "As much as you hate what she is saying, anger cannot excuse the truth." My father steps closer, switching the scent of death leeching from Dina to hope. "Zakhar will not live without the federation's help." He places his hand on my shoulder, squeezing ever so gently. "And neither will you."

I want to deny his insinuation before proving it isn't factual. I want to yell at him to man the fuck up and return the notoriety our family name deserves. But the palest blue eyes I've ever seen stop me.

He shouldn't be out of bed, much less witnessing his brother murder his father.

32

ZOYA

With our search for cheap seats taking longer than expected—even with it still seeing us stuck on a red-eye—I exit Nikita's apartment with her the following morning.

We hug at the front of her building before she heads to Myasnikov Private Hospital for what should have been her first solo shift while I direct my steps to the employment agency whose agents are still angry at me for botching an almost guaranteed placement.

They've never had an applicant turned down by KADOK Industries, and they didn't see the humor when I said I was glad I was their first.

Partway down Jessop Street, my phone buzzes.

"Shit," I mutter to myself when the removal of my phone announces it is switched on and with full service. The dirtbox is flat, which is odd considering I just charged it. Its battery must be fried from overuse. I have been utilizing it twenty-four-seven over the past week.

If only I could silence my moans just as readily.

After taking a mental note to carry a portable battery pack with me everywhere I go, I open my messenger app to see who the text is from.

My pace slows when I notice it is a message from the employment agency I am about to visit.

WORX CONNECT:

> We're pleased to announce you have an interview for a bookkeeping position this afternoon at 2 p.m. A prospective employment package and interview details have been forwarded to your email and the inbox of our app. Good luck.

The message is worded so similarly to the one I had for KADOK Industries that I don't immediately veer for my inbox. I press the number at the top of the text screen and then squash my phone to my ear.

"Worx Connect. This is Marcell. How can I help you?"

I tell Marcell about the text and request confirmation that the placement is legitimate.

"Yes. We're seeking an applicant for a newly advertised position. The hours are flexible, and the pay rate is..." Excitement heats my blood when a whistle finalizes her reply.

"Are there many other applicants?" I don't want to get my hopes up. I've had my fair share of disappointments lately.

"Ah... no. You're the only one."

My excitement takes a back seat for curiosity. "Why?"

Marcell takes my bluntness in stride like it was anticipated. "The position is a little... risqué, so we're struggling to obtain other interviewees for it." After a brief pause, she gets to the point. "It's at Le Rogue."

My throat grows scratchy as my eyes bulge. "The strip club?"

I apologize to a lady I startle with my loud roar before curtseying to a handful of construction workers promising to visit me during my first shift while Marcell hums an agreeing yes.

Once I'm out of earshot of potential future customers, I say, "The text said it was for a bookkeeping position."

"It is. Tasks include payroll, profit and loss, the maintenance and updating of all account ledgers, and..."—you never stop aging, but with how many delays I've faced over the past twenty-four hours, I feel like I am aging at twice the speed of everyone else—"you will be in charge of collecting and distributing the tips between the dancers."

I'm still not seeing an issue, although something seems off. Butterflies are fluttering in my stomach. That usually only happens when my intuition is warning me to be cautious—*or when I'm horny.*

Since that side of my brain has only led me to trouble lately, I ask, "Are there any other vacancies needing fulfillment?" When Marcell sighs, I add, "I'm not saying no. I am merely keeping my options open."

"Oh..." Ruffling sounds down the line. "There's a tattoo artist vacancy in Durando or..."—more flicking—"a live-in maid's position at a—"

"I can't draw, and the only time I wrangle fitted sheets is when I'm being thoroughly fuc—" I stop before I'm forced to find another employment agency to represent me. "I'm not maid material." When Marcell hums in agreement, I breathe out slowly. "So I guess I'll keep my fingers crossed for a good result this afternoon."

She sounds more relieved than shocked. "Wonderful. I'm sure you will do great. This job sounds right up your alley." She has the kind of tone that makes you believe criticisms are compliments. "I'll text you the address so you won't have to scroll through the app to find it, and I'll give you a call tomorrow morning to see how it went."

"Great. Thanks."

Her enthusiasm would usually rub off on me. I'm not feeling it today. It feels like a storm is brewing, but there isn't a single cloud in the sky.

I'm going to pretend it is because you can't experience a rainbow without first enduring the storm, because if I were to share the real reason for the sweat skating across my skin, you'd call me a whore.

"We have two guys on the door every night. Three bouncers backstage, and the bartenders have been trained in dispute resolution." Lilia, the person interviewing me for a position at Le Roque, twists to face me. "I won't lie. It is a little rowdy on the weekends, and although most of the patrons' focus should be on the dancers" —she pushes her glasses up her slim nose as her eyes rake my body —"you may get an equal amount of attention. Are you sure you want to apply for the bookkeeping position? You could make a killing as a dancer."

"I'm sure." My tone is as unconvincing as the one my third building supervisor in the past two months used when he arrived to fix my landline phone.

I have no clue where Luka went. He up and vanished as fast as Mr. Fakher. But Mr. Hernandez was extremely obliging. He even assisted me with a leaking pipe in the bathroom, and not once did he ogle my booty shorts while doing so.

"Okay." Lilia smiles sweetly before asking, "So what do you think? Would you like to join the Le Rogue family?"

Recalling how minimal the job classifications were this morning, I accept the hand she is holding out, without a single snippet of hesitation.

"Great! Let's get you signed up."

Before she can race away, I snatch up her arm. I hate asking for favors so soon into a budding work relationship, but I don't have much choice. My baby sister is getting married, and I refuse to miss out on that part of her life for anything or anyone.

"Is there a chance I could request a small favor?"

Lilia pats my arm, saving herself from a dreaded my-life-sucks grumble. "Of course. But I'm sure whatever you need will be fine. For the right team member, I can make a V look like a U."

I smile in gratitude before following her into her office for my first official placement in over a year.

33

ZOYA

"*D*on't." Nikita cups the single candle in the middle of a cake that looks like a disaster but tastes divine before finalizing her reply. "If you start, I'll start."

"I'm not starting anything." I roll my eyes like the sudden movement won't cause the wetness brimming in them to spill over.

I blow out the candle before Nikita and Gigi are halfway through singing "Happy Birthday."

Even Grampies gets in on the act. His lyrics aren't as clear as his counterparts', but the sparkle in his eyes when he tells me to make a wish as I commence cutting a cake big enough to share with a hundred make up for his lack of singing skills.

"If you touch the bottom, you have to kiss the closest boy."

My laugh is as husky as his words when he puckers his lips. They're cracked from his breathing mask stealing all the moisture from his mouth, but they're the only pair on offer, so I jab the knife in deep before leaning over his hospital bed to let him give me a sloppy birthday kiss.

"Happy birthday, Cheeky Chops," he whispers in my ear before pulling me in for a hug.

"Thank you, Grampies." I wipe my hand across my cheeks to ensure they're dry before twisting to face the woman responsible for the first bit of happy wetness on my cheeks in months. "Where did you find медовик in Myasnikov? I've been searching for it for years."

I wouldn't have bought a slice if I'd found it—I have better things to spend my money on than painful memories—but that doesn't mean I don't constantly scan high-end bakeries for it.

Nikita's brows furrow. "I thought—"

"Who's ready for dessert?" Gigi interrupts while balancing layers of honey-and-condensed-milk cake on her hands.

I shoot my hand in the air like a kindergarten student busting to use the bathroom.

Nikita's response is the opposite of my eagerness. "I'm sorry. I have to go. I can't be late. Dr. Abdulov—"

"It's fine," I assure her, aware I've already taken up a ton of time she doesn't have.

We had a pamper day. It was free since we used supplies purchased before Nikita's mom died. My skin has never felt so lush. It's a pity I have nowhere to show it off.

Not that Nikita is aware of that.

"And you should probably get a wiggle on, too, Z. What time does the DJ gig start?"

I lie about a glamorous life so she won't feel guilty about gifting me a thirty-minute shoulder massage in the dingy bathroom of her grandparents' apartment for my birthday.

Furthermore, Nikita is studying to be a surgeon. Her hands are already miracle makers. The last thing she should feel is shame when offering up their services to a friend who still gives handmade birthday cards every year.

"I think it is around seven. It's one of those secret gigs no one knows about, so the details are a little hush-hush." I said I lie to protect her feelings. I never said I was good at it. "So I guess I should get a wiggle on."

"What about your cake?" Gigi asks, desperate for more of the girl-on-girl time we've had in excess today.

I can't remember the last time we've had Nikita alert and present for longer than two hours.

"It's already curdled. I doubt a few more hours will hurt it."

Gigi leans in to sniff the cake. When her nose crinkles, gratitude sparks through Nikita's eyes. There's nothing wrong with the cake, but by making out it tastes as ghastly as it looks, there will be plenty left for Nikita and me to share tomorrow. Gigi has a sweet tooth, but she's fussy when it comes to the desserts she consumes.

"Thank you for today. I had so much fun."

Gigi returns my hug before she whispers that only a sadist would enjoy a painful wax session. Then she shifts her focus to her blood.

"I'm so proud of you, darling." Stupid wetness mists my eyes for the second time when she cups Nikita's cheeks with her hands before she brushes their noses together.

Eskimo kisses were one of Nikita's mother's favorite ways to say goodbye.

I miss them as much as I do her, so I can only imagine the emotions Gigi's farewell bombards Nikita with.

"You good?" I ask Nikita as we exit the basement apartment shoulder to shoulder.

"Yeah," she whispers softly, her mind deep in thought. "Are you?"

"Of course. Why wouldn't I be?"

She shoves open the door at the side of the main entrance before pulling up the collar of her winter coat to protect her glossy locks from the cool winds. "You waxed."

"Yeah. And?" I smile when she gets annoyed at me for tossing back to her one of the many neuroses she hands me every day, before saying, "Hairy vaginas went out of fashion decades ago."

"Yeah, but..."

I wave my hand through the air, encouraging her to continue.

She follows along nicely. "You're going out tonight. You don't usually wax when you are going out." I realize my excentric personality is beginning to rub off on her when she says, "The only day you get a Brazilian is the day you don't want sex. It's your birthday. You have plans, and you look like that"—she drags her hand down my body—"so why today of all days did you wax?"

It takes me longer than I care to admit to come up with an excuse. "Everyone's pain tolerance is different?" Since my reply is more a question than a confirmation, it sounds like one. "And by the time the concert is over, it'll be close to twenty-four hours since you were up in my business."

She scoffs before walking faster. "I was *not* up in your business."

"You were so far up there I was beginning to wonder if you were giving me a pap smear."

Nikita stops walking and turns to face me. "Talking about pap smears—"

"Nope." I shake my head in disgust. "We're not going there, and you're not doing that. *Ever.*"

"I'm a trained professional."

"I don't care if you are the highest paid escort in the country, you're not sticking *anything* inside me, let alone an ice-cold duck beak and a kitchen scraper. I don't swing that way."

Well, I didn't.

Andrik said he'd kill any *man* who came between us.

He didn't mention women.

It's a pity I love dick more than a Celine Dion mega fan or I could have closed my eyes and pretended mouth stimulation alone would take care of an itch no amount of self-stimulation has scratched over the past five weeks.

My self-loathing party ends when Nikita grumbles, "Says the lady who rode my leg all the way to climax station this morning." She shudders like she walked through a cobweb.

"I wasn't close to climax. Your disgusted howl cut the journey short. I was a mere minute from saving you from the need to shower." When she appears lost, I ask, "Is squirting a medical term, or should I refer to it as—"

Her hand shoots up to clamp my mouth before I get out all my question. Then her motherly eyes hit their full potential. "Because it is your birthday, I'm going to act like we're not having this conversation outside my place of employment. Behave, be safe, and message me when you get home. I don't care what time it is. I'll most likely be awake, anyway."

I pretend that my message isn't ten minutes from being sent since Lilia gave me the night off for my birthday.

My agreeing gesture appeases Nikita enough to lower her hand from my mouth. "I love you, Z." She wraps me up in a warm hug. "Happy birthday."

"I love you too." I return her hug before pushing her into the hospital entrance only used by staff. "Now get out of here before Boris works out why you don't use the main entrance anymore."

Boris is lovely, but if Andrik had his face, keeping his dick in his pants wouldn't be an issue for him. I doubt even his wife would want to give it up.

There's no doubt my wild side is whittling its way under Nikita's skin when she twists to face me just before entering the hospital severely underpaying its staff. "Squirting is the correct medical term, but some people also call it female ejaculation. Women expel fluids of various quantities and compositions from the urethra during sexual arousal and orgasm. There have been several studies conducted on the phenomenon, but most of the researchers were male. They took centuries to find the clit, so I haven't given their findings much thought." She tilts her head and flashes the cutest grin. "Should I consider my own study?"

I twist my lips. "I think you should. But can I suggest a practical approach to your research instead of theoretical? The results will be more accurate that way."

"They would. But then I'd need a research assistant, and I don't see anyone offering their services."

"Except Boris," I correct.

"Except Boris," she parrots.

After groaning, she drops her lower lip, waves me goodbye, and then trudges into her workplace like every man she crosses paths with today wouldn't sell their left kidney to assist her with a study on the female anatomy.

Once Nikita is out of eyesight, I take the most direct route home. It is the same bus I've ridden the past month. Since it is early, it is brimming with people. The ratio of men to women is starkly different, and the handful who appear attached to a significant other don't miss the bounce the potholes cause my chest.

Their eyes do the same boing their children do on the knees of their wives, and it makes me sick to my stomach that their wives gave them something I never could, yet they still gawk like the best they can get isn't directly in front of them.

Don't they know looks fade, but family is for life?

Or was it only my mother who drummed that into her daughters since adolescence?

With my mood no longer playful, I don't realize someone is sitting in the stairwell outside my apartment door until we almost knock knees.

His prolonged rake of my body is as deprived as my fellow male riders, but regretfully, he knows what I'm rocking under my T-shirt, jeans, and jacket combination.

"Vlad." I slow my roll to ensure I maintain plenty of distance between me and the last guy who couldn't find my clit with a map and a compass. "What are you doing here?"

He looks at me in shock. "It's your birthday. As if I wouldn't visit my favorite girl on her birthday."

"I'm twenty-eight." With him lost, I continue. "Where were you when I turned twenty-seven?"

Vlad is the man who had me believing abstinence was the better option. He was the last person I slept with before Andrik, and he only cared about getting himself off, leaving me unsatisfied and sore enough from his jackrabbit moves not to rush out and seek a replacement.

I assumed all bed companions would be like him. Selfish.

Andrik taught me otherwise.

I take some of the anger I should be directing at myself for letting Andrik slip into my head again for the umpteenth time today out on Vlad. "I would show you out, but I'm reasonably sure you know the way."

"Come on, Zoy." His nasally whine annoys me, but not as much as his following words. "We were good once."

"Once," I agree. "Then you snuck out in the middle of the night and I never heard from you again." I could leave it there, but life without drama is dull. "It just happened to be the same night I tried to assure you not all the dryness was your fault. It was, by the way."

He smiles like he doesn't believe me.

It doubles my anger.

"You're an asshole."

I make it to my front door before his sniveling tone ends my steps. "All that mess was my ma, Zoy. I didn't want ankle biters.

Never did. But I was the last of the Stronovics, and Ma didn't want Pa's name to die with me."

The honesty in his tone cools my turbines by a smidge. "So what's changed?"

His smile slips as he rubs his hands together. "I've got a couple of rugrats now, so she's good. She is off my back."

"A few?" My pitch is as high as my brows.

I realize I've forgotten Vlad's quirks when he rubs his hands faster. He isn't gleaming with attitude. He's shitting his pants.

"Yeah... I've got four."

"Four?" I double-check, certain I heard him wrong. "You have four kids?" When he nods, I take a step back. "How the hell did you have four kids in two years?"

He wets his lips, shifting foot to foot. "Technically three."

"Three kids or three years?"

He bows his head like a dog about to be smacked with a rolled-up newspaper. "Three years. Three pregnancies, and one set of twins with a side chick."

It takes my sluggish head a minute to click on, and when it does, it is a devastating blow to my ego.

He cheated on me.

A man who drove his mother's Honda and still lived at home when we dated cheated on me.

What. The. Fuck has my life become?

"I... We..." When violence is the only thought I have for several long seconds, I point to the stairwell. "You should go... or I can't guarantee your chances of further procreation won't lower to zero."

"I was a dick back then, Zoy." He waves to the stairwell like the past is one step behind him. "I've grown. Matured. I've even got a job now. That's how I was able to afford these." He thrusts a gas-store-purchased bunch of flowers into my chest, along with a card. "I made the card because I know how much you like them to come from the heart." Several petals float to the floor when he tugs the card out of the badly wilted arrangement. "And you've been wanting to go to this gig for years, so I asked around and found some tickets."

Too curious for my own good, I accept the card he's holding out and tear it open. I'm surprised when an elaborately gilded ticket falls into my palm. It isn't for the DJ gig I told Nakita about earlier. It's for a sex club Vlad mentioned numerous times during our brief courtship.

He's been seeking an invitation for years but was never high enough on *any* social ladder to be granted one.

"It's for tonight." He steps closer, bringing himself near enough for me to smell his breath. It doesn't smell like whiskey, but something is definitely up with it. "And I really want to experience it for the first time with you, Zoy. It's been a dream of mine for as long as I can remember." When I don't immediately tell him to take a hike, he rubs his hands together like I've already said yes. "The name on the ticket doesn't matter. I checked with the club before I arrived, so all you need to do is get your fine ass dressed and we're good to go."

My eyes shoot down to a name not close to mine for half a second before my knee pops into Vlad's groin. It's the name of the woman I accused him of hooking up with when we were together, except her last name is no longer Berkov. It matches Vlad's surname.

"Fuck... that..." He tries to remain standing tall, but within seconds, the pain becomes too much for him to bear. "I need to sit down for a minute. Can I?" He points to the section of stairwell his ass was warming when I arrived home.

"Take all the time you need, Vlad." I bob down until not even his misted eyes can miss the seriousness in my gaze. "But you better be off my stoop by the morning or I'll invite my best friend over for a game of doctors and nurses." I lower my tone to a deadly whisper.

"Her party tricks involve unclean scalpels." When I recall his personality is the only time I can mention "dick" with an impressive edge while referencing him, I add, "And tweezers. Teeny-tiny peanut-grabbing tweezers!"

Not giving him a chance to reply or defend his manhood, I shove my key into the lock with enough force to bend the metal before I race into the entryway of my apartment, slamming the door behind me.

My back barely braces against the battered wood when I'm confronted by another fool with a death wish. "He's gonna need longer than a minute. But I'm up for a game of doctors and nurses if you're seeking participants."

I glare at Mikhail before twisting the door handle, ruefully yanking open the only entry point of my apartment and then gesturing for him to leave. "You have five seconds to get out of my house before your right nut joins your left nut in your stomach."

He doesn't take my threat seriously. "How'd you know you got my left nut?"

"You told me," I bark out before I can stop myself, "two seconds before you fell to the ground and cried like a baby."

"I know why he did that." Vlad's voice crackles with a sob. "I'm reasonably sure my left nut is gone. Like *gone*, gone." He fiddles with his crotch like it's a bag of marbles. "I can't find it."

"It'll come back down... *eventually*," Mikhail replies before he shuts my door with him on the wrong side of it.

"You're not welcome in my ho—"

"If I can prove I didn't know he was going to be there, will you at least give me five seconds of your time to explain that I'm not setting out to intentionally hurt you?"

I don't back down without a fight. I just fail to mention that my anger is more centered on that the wrong brother showed up to celebrate my birthday.

"It was his home. Whether you knew he would be there that day or not doesn't count. You knew he would *eventually* be there."

Since he can't deny the truth, he remains quiet.

"I guess you no longer need five seconds?"

"I—"

Since I'm feeling hormonal and my ego is obliterated enough to demand privacy, I cut him off. "Goodbye, Mikhail."

"Sunshine..."

I open the door like my heart isn't breaking from the devastation in his tone before stepping back so he can exit without bumping into me.

He stops partway through the door. "If you didn't want him to react, you wouldn't have used me to rile him." He brushes his lips against the corner of my mouth. "You know how to reach me when you need me." He flashes a ghost-like grin, mouths, *Happy birthday*, then gallops down the stairs Vlad is still hogging.

Silence reigns supreme under the healthy roar of a high-powered motorcycle rumbling through my building.

"Is he your boyfr—"

"Goodnight, Vlad."

I close my apartment door before Vlad can voice all of his reply. I can still hear it since the walls are paper-thin. "Can I please get back the ticket to Vixens? If you're not going to use it, I may as well give it to someone who wants it. They're not easy to come by."

I almost tell him to go to hell, but then I remember I'm no better than him.

I'm a cheater too.

He wobbles to his feet when I slide the ticket under the door's lip. He gathers it up before locking his eyes with the peephole I'm peering through. "Would I be pushing my luck to get my leather jacket too?" My sigh is silent, but he must hear its ripples. "It was my pa's, and I thought maybe I could hand it down to my eldest like he did me." After another lengthy delay, his eyes turn pleading. "I swear it'll be the last thing I ever ask of you."

Hopeful he's being honest for a change, I stomp to my room to grab the dust collector hiding in the back of my closet. I find Vlad's jacket in under thirty seconds. It is next to the suit jacket that has a lusty scent as strong now as it was weeks ago.

I run my nose across the pricy material of Andrik's business jacket before my head can demand my heart not to. It smells delicious, and our intermingled scents make me a mixture of angry and hot.

It should be impossible to miss a man you hardly know, but I'd be a liar if I said I hadn't missed Andrik today. His attention is so thrilling that I forget I'm not meant to crave it.

I'm also not meant to throw my friends under the bus with me to achieve it.

Mikhail was right.

I used him to force Andrik to respond.

Since I am mad at myself, I thrust Andrik's jacket back into its spot with the same aggression I used weeks ago. This time, since my hearing isn't affected from the ringing tires rolling over asphalt for twenty-four hours straight, I hear a crinkle I missed last time.

My throat works through a hard swallow when I discover two documents in the breast pocket. The first one is a plain sheet of white paper holding two tickets for the concert I mentioned earlier tonight. The other is an official-looking document. None of the details are filled in, but the terms in black and white for the world to see all point to the same thing.

Andrik's wish for an heir.

As he's hinted at numerous times, he doesn't want his child to be produced the old-fashioned way. His marital contract states with the utmost certainty that the couple's union is not about love. The child's conception, fetal development, and delivery are clinically planned procedures.

Even the mother-to-be's living arrangements form part of the agreement.

There isn't an option for her to share a room with Andrik—nor a bed.

The knowledge makes me smile... until a date on the ledger registers as familiar.

Andrik's reared-to-breed wife was scheduled for artificial insemination on the day I attended my interview.

He was fingering me in the driveway of his palatial home while his wife was being inseminated with his sperm, and it was inside her when he was in my bed, eating me for dessert.

The amount of disrespect is shocking, and it sends my emotions into a debilitating downward spiral.

Andrik isn't demanding discreetness to respect my wish not to be portrayed as a homewrecking whore like my mother was for years. He's rejecting me like every other man has when they realize the only thing I can offer them long-term is me.

That's a slap to the face worse than any I've been given, and it dips my confidence to the lowest point it's ever been.

"Fuck you, Andrik," I lash out, shouting like he can hear me. "I am more than enough. If you're too stupid to see that, that's on you, not me. My fertility status doesn't make me a woman. My body does. My strengths." A fire roars inside me as my ego strives to break through the deluge swamping it. "My ability to do what I want, when I what, for exactly how long I want makes me more a woman than any name you could have placed at the top of your contract."

With my confidence semi-restored, I toss down the document, snatch up Vlad's jacket, and then hightail it out my front door.

An oomph leaves Vlad's mouth when I thrust his jacket into his chest. It has nothing on the holler that leaves his mouth when I pluck the ticket for Vixens out of his hand and then gallop down the stairs two at a time.

We dated long enough for him to recognize when my wild side is coming out.

Regretfully.

34

ZOYA

My enthusiasm wilts like a picked flower on a hot summer's day when we arrive at an industrial building approximately fifty miles from Myasnikov. The wealth of the cars in front of us showcases why Vixens is such a hard club to get an invite to, not to mention how elegantly dressed the people slowly filtering inside are.

I'm treading in water outside my means, but too stubborn to admit that out loud.

"Undo some of your buttons and give me your belt."

As Vlad follows my lead, I remove my jeans and then tease out my hair. My makeup is already perfect from my day of glam, so all I need to do is get my outfit right.

"That's good. You look hot."

I backhand Vlad's chest when his gaze lingers on my thighs longer than what could be classed as a friendly glance.

That is all we will ever be, and it won't be a solid friendship like I have with Nikita. More one where I'll wave hello when he passes by instead of acting like he doesn't exist as I have for the past two years.

"Do I look okay?" Vlad scoffs. "I don't know how a sex club has a dress code. It's not like they stay on long after you enter."

He screws up his nose when I say, "It's a sex club, not an invitation to an all-out orgy."

"A sex club with naked trapeze acts." His wiggling brows are back. "Close enough."

Needing space before my knee finds its way back to his crotch, I exit his car. Vlad bumps into the back of me just as I join the line. It moves fast, and within minutes we enter a space far more elaborate than my imagination could have ever conjured.

The aura of wealth is in abundance, and the scenes dotted through the oversized space are more erotic masterpieces than poorly scripted porn.

"Here." Vlad hands me an all-black mask and a white tablet.

I place on the mask but "accidentally" drop the tablet before kicking it to the other side of the foyer. I don't need a narcotic to keep my veins flooded with energy. They haven't stopped strumming for weeks.

"You good?" Vlad checks.

I jerk up my chin before gesturing for him to lead the way. I'm not a forgive-and-forget person. It just seems the norm for the men to take the lead at this club. A woman on our right is walking a man through the crowd on a leash, and another directly in front is whipping a woman on a cross, but most of the scenes display that the ratio of doms to dommes is one to thirty, if not a little more.

"What scene do you want to check out first?"

I wet my lips while scanning the crowd. It's almost overwhelming. There's so much skin on display I feel overdressed even while wearing a T-shirt as a dress, but it doesn't seem tacky.

It's making me hot.

Mistaking the hue on my cheeks as embarrassment, Vlad leads

us past a glass-wall cubicle where three men and one woman are performing.

As more scenes come into view, he says, "You don't have to participate. You can just watch."

"And if I want to participate?"

I check whose hand is warming my back when Vlad answers, "I'll die a very happy man."

A peculiar sensation prickles the fine hairs on my nape when he directs us into a closed-off room all men entering with us veer for first.

A man wearing a black mask is getting head from a woman with her hands tied behind her back. Her eyes bulge with each deep dive of his cock, and she looks in her element.

Although we've just arrived, it appears their set has been going for some time. The blonde's thighs are drenched from multiple orgasms, and the satin straps of her sequin mask are damp with sweat. Her curvy backside also looks newly paddled.

How do I know she was recently spanked? Her backside is housing the same red handprints mine did for over a week after I left Andrik's country mansion, and they have a freshly spanked appearance with raised red edges.

Over the next several minutes, Vlad and I stand shoulder to shoulder, watching but not speaking.

It is a raunchy scene, but no matter how much my heart pleads for me to look away, I can't.

The blonde is on her knees and bound, though she appears to have all the control. Her every desire is the forefront of her partner's mind. The way he pays attention to each moan she releases while he feeds his cock in and out of her mouth is a sure-fire sign. And let's not forget that she is only on her knees because her every whim was answered, so the focus can now shift to her partner.

Her drenched thighs assure me of this—as does personal experience from not that long ago.

Knowing her needs are being placed before his own is a massive turn-on. I've only had that happen a handful of times. Those experiences were mind-blowing. But I can't think about him now. I'm here to forget him. To move on.

I'm here to let my body's wants be heard instead of having it judged for its "supposed" failures.

I am sick of the negativity I've been forced to swallow anytime sex is mentioned. It is meant to be a beautiful display of how femininity and masculinity blur all barriers, not a chore with one purpose—reproduction.

Even if it is just for a night, I want to cherish how good sex can make people feel, and that it doesn't always come with an agenda of terms and conditions.

The scene before me, the selfishness of pleasure, is something I've always hoped to achieve. To be wanted so fiercely no barrier is too strong to overcome is an addiction more potent than any drug on the market.

I've wanted it forever.

And I had it for half a second.

I shake my head to rid it of inappropriate thoughts before shifting my focus back to the scene playing out before me. My panties cling to the lines of my pussy when the man's grunts increase. He isn't solely responding to how good the blonde's lips feel around his pulsating shaft. He's moaning in response to her eye contact.

She stares up at him, coaxing him to come with a hooded gaze barely seen beneath a silver mask.

My thighs press together when he answers her numerous silent requests thirty seconds later. He grunts through his release, which the blonde swallows without a single objection firing through her hooded eyes, before he demands her to move to a studded chaise in the corner of the space.

They move so fluidly together I wouldn't be surprised to discover they've played together at Vixens previously. They have a spark no amount of sexual chemistry could mimic. Two stars in the sky, perfectly aligning for one hell of a show.

Within seconds, the blonde is arched over the chaise, and the male participant enters her from behind.

"Do they not use protection?" I ask Vlad, my voice barely a whisper, like I'm afraid the couple making me a sticky mess may hear me and stop performing. When Vlad remains quiet, I ram my elbow into his ribs, my eyes unmoving from the erotic imagery better than any porn I've watched. "Vlad."

"Sorry. Ah. What did you say?" His voice is husky with desire.

I understand its roughness. My throat is dry. My pussy, however, is on the other end of the scale. There's something carnal about seeing a man's cock coated in a woman's arousal without the flimsy barrier of latex Andrik forgot...

No, Zoya. You are not *going there again so soon after your last slip-up.*

Striving to keep the train on its tracks, I ask again, "Protection? Do participants not need protection?"

I don't need to look at Vlad to know his eyes are on me.

I can feel the heat of his gaze.

"That's Anya," he announces, his tone pitched in a way that announces his trousers are facing the same tented design. "She's a regular. The men *love* her because..."

"Because?" I ask when words elude him.

Anya is gorgeous, and from what I witnessed earlier, she has no gag reflex and no issue taking every inch of a nine-inch penis, but that doesn't explain the reason she is lax on protection. There are more condoms in crystal dishes around this club than candy buckets at a Halloween party.

Again, Vlad rubs his hands together. This time it seems more sensual than sinister. "Because she's"—he waits a beat before finalizing his reply—"like you." The scene is no longer appealing when he steps close enough I can feel the effect it's had on him. He's hard. "Excluding condom breaks, I've never ridden bareback. I'd love for you to be my fir—"

I shove my hand into his face before he can finalize his reply, and then shunt him back two steps. "You'll lose the ability to ride anything if you finish that sentence."

He smiles like I'm not being serious.

He's dead wrong.

After licking my palm, forcing its immediate removal from his face, he nudges his head to the exit. "Marley's show is about to start. You ain't seen nothing until you've seen Marley hit the bullseye with her..." He makes a hand gesture I would be proud of if it were directed at Nikita. "I want a prime spot, so we need to go now."

"I'm fine here," I reply.

I return my eyes to the scene, needing a distraction before I act hormonal. The fluency of the man's hip thrusts doesn't enthrall me as it did only moments ago. It isn't anything he's doing causing my sudden backflip. It is wondering if the attention he bestows on Anya is solely because he doesn't need to use protection.

Seconds ago, their connection seemed to be a mutual fascination —two magnets unable to pull apart no matter how much they should.

Now I need a little more convincing.

"Are you sure, Zoy?" Vlad waits for our eyes to align again before he says, "Marley gets the pick of the bunch. Her show isn't solely for Vixens' male patrons."

I smile, grateful he is, for once, not solely focused on his desires. But it doesn't alter the facts.

"I'm sure. I'll find you once this set is over."

"All right." He seems hesitant to leave, but the mass exit of the people surrounding us gets his feet moving. "I'll save you a spot."

In minutes, the number of people doubling the humidity of the room halves.

It drops to a scarce few when Anya's partner doesn't immediately exit the chamber-like viewing room with them.

They don't stay to watch how they snuggle on the chaise for several minutes with his cock still pulsating inside her, or how attentive he is with aftercare. They stupidly believe the fireworks are over the instant they're freed from their chambers. They don't realize the chaos their detonation caused to the sky is what the show is truly about.

I'm so mesmerized watching the way the dark-haired man takes care of Anya that I instinctively move closer to the glass separating them from their audience.

The man's doting expression never changes.

Not once.

If he knows Anya is infertile, it doesn't bother him.

He isn't looking at her with anything but lust *and* love.

It is a glance full of admiration, and it mirrors the one that reflects back at me for half a second before the glass wall suddenly darkens and the room plunges into blackness.

Dancing shadows covered half my stalker's face before the lights were switched off, but I'll never forget those eyes or the cut lines of his jaw. Not to mention the smirk that tugged at his full lips when my first thought wasn't to run for the closest exit when our eyes locked for a nanosecond.

I'd bolt if I weren't frozen in shock.

Well, that's what my heart plans to tell my head when guilt eventually surfaces.

It is so dark that I don't realize Andrik is standing behind me until his warm breaths float over my ear. "Aren't I meant to give you a gift today, милая?" The glass gives relief to my overheated skin when he leans into me so deeply I either flatten my breasts against the cool surface or grind against him like a nymph. "It is your birthday, yet here you are, surprising me."

"I didn't know you would be here." My voice is shockingly strong considering how jittery my insides become when he splays his hand against my stomach and draws me back.

"Do I need to take you over my knee, милая?" I curse my lack of attention to detail to hell when excitement is my first response to his threat.

If I had paid more attention to both the ticket and our location, I would have known his next confession before he announced it. "I own this club... and *everyone* in it." My eye roll stops halfway when he whispers, "Including the fool you arrived with."

My throat grows scratchy when I recall the conversation we had when his jealousy got the better of him.

Dead men don't count.

Vlad doesn't deserve my loyalty, but I give it to him anyway. "Vlad didn't touch me."

"Tonight," Andrik agrees as he places something bulky and cool around my neck. "But he has previously." My heart beats in my ears when a second after he clasps what I believe to be a necklace together, he returns his hand to my stomach and growls, "That's enough for me to kill him."

My brain is mush from having him so near, knowing he isn't a man who tosses out worthless threats, and my unexpected gift, so I'm not surprised when my smarts dip to his level. "Then I suggest you double your security. I know where you live, so if you touch Vlad, I'll tell your wife exactly how many *indiscretions* you've had in your *very* short marriage."

He smiles.

He. Fucking. Smiles.

It pisses me off to no end, but no matter how hard my brain screams for my feet to move, they refuse to budge. His quick exploration of my body means his fingers are a mere inch from my clit. They sear my morals as potently as greed does when I notice the size of the massive rock reflecting in the glass wall. It is massive.

Furthermore, I read his contract. I know the terms.

His wife isn't getting this from him.

I shouldn't be either.

Even if it is an arrangement, he has to respect the vows he took —doesn't he?

My brain screams yes. My heart is on the other side of the fence. It is trying to rationalize that his marriage is nothing more than a roundabout way of surrogacy.

It's fucked to think this way, but a straight and narrow path is boring, and I've already had my share of lackluster encounters. Isn't it time for me to live for me?

Goose bumps rise over every inch of me when Andrik's hand slides under my shirt. As his fingertip glides over the soaked seam of my panties, his hot breaths continue caressing my ear. "I'd kill him if I believed any of this wetness was for him."

When he nudges his head to the glass pane separating us from Anya and her partner, I murmur, "It is for hi—"

His hand stills, immediately ending my campaign to dispute his truthful accusation.

I'm not wet because the man doting on Anya is well-endowed and lasted longer than two seconds. My eyes rarely veered lower than his midsection. I was mesmerized by his eye contact and how he made it seem as if Anya was the only person on the planet he was out to impress.

It is similar to how Andrik is making me feel now.

He knows every button to push and for exactly how long. Within seconds, the guilt that forever charges our exchanges lightens enough to blur the line I'm endeavoring to place between us.

As his fingers roll over my clit, his lips nibble on my shoulder. I moan as my hands splay against the glass wall, lost in the sensation of a gifted pair of hands.

"More," I plead desperately, my pussy needing something to cling to as it rides the wave of ecstasy threatening to crest at any moment.

My teeth grit when Andrik breathes heavily against my neck. "More *who*?"

I shiver when his fingers slip between the folds of my pussy and arch upward. He's not quite fingering me, more ensuring I can't deny his need to be reminded of who is helming our exchange.

"More, Andrik. *Please.*"

His lips rise against my nape before he spears his fingers inside me, shoving them in deep. They're so long and girthy that if I didn't feel his fat cock grinding against my ass, I would assume we skipped foreplay.

Andrik thrusts his fingers in and out of me, stroking my G-spot with every precise pump. In seconds, sweat beads my nape and pleasure swells my insides. I can't deny how wet I am. I can feel it slicking Andrik's palm and hear it over my frantic moans. I'm drenched, and at this very instant, unashamed.

"Oh god," I pant when the world commences blurring.

"No," Andrik snaps out against my neck. "Not him. There is only one name you're allowed to scream when you're being wholly consumed. It isn't his."

He finger fucks me faster, harder. He drives me to a blubbering, shuddering mess with rough pounds and curling fingertips.

"Whose name are you allowed to speak, милая? Who is the *only* man allowed to touch you like this?"

"You," I choke out, shuddering through the tingles racing through my core.

"Yes. M*e*." My hands slip against the glass when he demands the name of the man about to make me come all over his hand. "Scream it loud enough for them all to hear."

His "them" mention reminds me of where we are. It doesn't clam me up, however. It makes me feel more wanted. More desired. And it has the crest in my stomach forming so quickly I'm blindsided by a ferocious orgasm before I can force Andrik onto the wild ride with me.

I explode so fiercely stars detonate and the world tilts on its axis. Everything blurs as a fiery warmth spreads from my womb to my limbs.

I cry out loud enough for Anya's partner's attention to divert from her for the quickest second. He stares straight at me as if the glass is no longer frosted. It is a fading glance. As quickly as Andrik's zipper lowering steals my devotion, Anya's tired yawn captures his.

When his admiring glare once again matches the one reflecting back at me, I can't help but seek answers as to why Anya and I are the chosen ones.

"Does he know?"

"Know what?" Andrik's breathing pattern matches mine when he spreads my feet wide with a gentle kick before his fingers recommence their exploration of the heat between my legs.

"Does he know she's infertile?" It is hard to talk. Nothing but moans want to leave my mouth when his fat cock pierces between my wet folds.

Andrik's lips lift against the exposed skin on my shoulder for the briefest second before he answers tersely, "Yes."

"Then why does he look at her how he does?" The words shoot from my mouth before I can stop them. That's how stunned I am that he enters me without the slightest bit of protest from my body.

Our position probably helps. I can't take all of him from this angle, but the inches I can are delicious.

After swiveling my hips, welcoming him in further with only the slightest snippet of pain, I say, "He looks at her like she can give him everything he's ever wanted."

"Because she can," he answers on a moan as he adjusts the tilt of my ass and then jerks his hips upward.

He rubs at my clit, clouding my head with lust so it won't acknowledge the pain of the additional inches my new position allows him to stuff in, but I manage to speak through the fog. "That's not true. If it were, you wouldn't be fucking me in a dark room like I'm a dirty little secret."

When Andrik stills, his cock doesn't display the disappointment of the rest of his body. It throbs as evidently as his jaw. "Don't."

His reply is clipped, and it sets my pulse racing. I don't listen to the silent warning that I'm no longer treading in waters beyond my means, though. I've dived headfirst into the Pacific. "You wouldn't be demanding discreetness."

My last word comes out with a groan when Andrik's hand shoots up from my hip to my throat. He grips my neck tightly, lighting not needed to see the flicker his eyes get when he's being challenged.

"Don't make me ask you again, Zoya. Stop. *Now.*"

I squash my cheek to the glass and sweep open my thighs like I'm not doing everything I can to derail this train. "You wouldn't be hoping the contract you had Mikhail plant would have me believing adultery is okay since feelings aren't involved."

"Stop. This. *Now!* Or your ass will be so red you won't sit for a week."

I don't listen.

I never do.

"How many women have you coerced into your bed with the same lies, Andrik?"

He pulls out of me with a roar, his anger as apparent as the furious stomp of my libido that I've pushed him so hard that his cock is most likely as deflated as my ego. "None!"

"How many payouts have you issued for their silence?"

"None." His reply is a sneer, not a word, as snapped and out of control as the rough yank on my arm to spin me around to face him. "Not. A. Single. Fucking. One. But since you seem to know every-thing about me, why don't you tell me how many indiscretions I've had? You said you will tell my *wife*"—he snarls his last word—"exactly how many. So tell me... how many have I had? One... two... three..." His wild and dilated eyes bounce between mine. "Four? Do you think I've had four, милая? Or did I start my tally too low? Tell me how many women I've slept with since you."

"I don't know how many," I spit out, suddenly disgusted.

I hate the thought of him with his wife, so I don't want to add more people to the crazy notions that haven't quit rolling through my head over the past few weeks.

"I don't know how many women you've slept with since me. But does it matter? Once a cheater, always a cheater."

"I haven't cheated!" he roars, freezing both my heart and my astuteness. "I haven't been with anyone since you." He doesn't give me a chance to respond to the sheer honesty in his tone or to portray my absolute shock. "You've put my head in such a fucking spin that goals I've been working toward since I was five were forgotten in an instant. I backflipped on every pledge I've made in the past thirty years in under twelve fucking hours. Nothing mattered." I hear his jaw tightening more than I see it. "Nothing matters but *you*."

With my eyes adjusting to the dark, I have no trouble seeing the truth in his narrowed gaze when his eyes connect with mine, but I'm as stubborn as a mule, and perhaps a smidge heartbroken.

"You were fingering me while your wife was being inseminated with your sperm."

"No," he immediately denies, shaking his head.

"I saw your contract, Andrik. It stated the date in thick black ink for all to see." I grit my teeth when he continues to shake his head. "Then why did you send me away? Why did you stop? Why did you sneak into my room in the middle of the night under the cloak of darkness?" With my heartache overtaking the zing of intimacy thickening my veins, I blurt out my next question without evaluating the possible consequences it could cause. "Why did you pick her instead of me?"

For the first time, vulnerability flares through his eyes. "I didn't pick her."

"You married her, Andrik! She's your wife."

"No," he denies, talking through a clenched jaw. "She's a prop. A ploy. A measure to get answers. I don't want her." When he steps closer, my heart thuds in my ears. "I want you."

"Don't," I beg when he cups my jaw with the same hand he used to bring me to climax.

He doesn't listen, and as much as I shouldn't admit this, I'm glad.

"And you want me too." His thumb slips over my lips, diverting the pulse deafening me to between my legs. It isn't solely his touch prompting the positive responses of my body. It is also what he says next. "I'll call the wedding off. I will find another way to get answers."

The mask I'm growing to hate as much as I loathe the woman I've become slips over his face quicker than I can snap my fingers when we're interrupted. "Andrik? Are you in here?"

The blonde who was conducting interviews in the east wing pushes open the door, streaming unnatural light into the room and highlighting the manic tic in Andrik's jaw. "Not now."

She takes his snarky tone in stride. "I know you requested not to be disturbed, but it is *extremely* urgent."

The utter desperation in her voice announces the end of our exchange mere seconds before Andrik vocalizes the same. "Mikhail is waiting for you outside." After floating his eyes over my face for the quickest second, he checks that his fly is right before he stalks to the door being held open by the blonde. "Straight home, милая."

"Andrik—"

"Straight. Home!"

He exits first, confident enough in his assertiveness that I'll never disobey a direct order.

It is a pity he's underestimated how stupid I become when pushed down the totem pole of importance.

35

ANDRIK

"What happened?"

My father lifts his hanging head, but my answer comes from Dr. Makarand, who is standing at Zakhar's bedside, looking glum. "My guess is hypertrophic cardiomyopathy. It is when the muscle cells in the heart's lower chambers thicken, causing an abnormal heart rhythm."

His response blindsides me. Not because of what he says, but how he started his reply. "Guess? I'm paying you one hundred thousand dollars a week to *guess* the cause of an almost five-year-old having a heart attack!"

My father signals for me to calm down. I'm too worked up from my fight with Zoya to listen. I have a heap of adrenaline to disperse, and no one to take it out on but the man standing in front of me.

"How much will it take for you not to guess?" I don't give him a chance to respond. "Two hundred thousand a week? Three?" He looks cocky until I say, "A bullet?"

I step up to him, my chest heaving with anger. I'm not solely devastated for what this could mean for Zakhar. I hate that I had to leave Zoya in a vulnerable state.

She should come first, but shit like this is forcing her into the background.

"Will that give you enough incentive to stop fooling around and do your fucking job!"

Dr. Makarand has bigger balls than I give him credit for. "From the whispers I've heard, I'm not the one stalling proceedings."

I crack him in the face, splitting his nose, before my father pulls me away from him.

"Enough!" my father shouts when I shrug out of his hold with my fists at the ready.

Once again, bullets are cleaner. They're less fun, however, and won't dispel half the frustration heating my blood. Zoya's pain when she begged for me to pick her had me ready to pack it all in. It convinced me for once and all that vengeance is for the weak, and that I don't need to hurt the people I care about to find the men responsible for my years of misery. Then Anouskha got word to my lead club hostess that Zakhar had gone into cardiac arrest, and my plan was flipped on its head for the umpteenth time in the past several weeks.

My father slows my steps to Dr. Makarand by muttering, "If you want to take down every man who blames your inability to step back from that girl for the delay in Zakhar's recovery, you may as well start with me." He steps up to me as if my gun isn't as heavy as my guilt. "They've reshaped their rules for you, but you are so hell-bent on bringing them to heel that you're seconds from snapping them." He thrusts his hand at Zakhar's bed. "From snapping him." For the first time in years, tears gloss his eyes. "Is that what you want? Do you want to kill him before he's even had a chance to live?"

"No!" I shout, speaking the truth. "But I don't want to give them everything, either. They will have *all* the control. Every fucking thing I've worked for will be governed by them."

Zakhar needs a new heart. The federation will give him one, but only after I've kneeled at their feet and kissed the family-crested rubies on their pinkie finger rings.

I hate being puppeteered, and the dislike is the sole cause of my next sentence—and perhaps my wish to ensure a feisty blonde knows I will always pick her first. "You wouldn't expect me to offer the same for Mikhail, so why the fuck are you asking for so much this time? You have sons across the country. Children younger than Zakhar, but—"

"I only have one grandson," he interrupts, cutting me off.

I shake my head, wordlessly discrediting his lie. He has grandsons. They may be illegitimate since they were conceived and birthed out of wedlock, but that doesn't dismiss their lineage.

The brisk shake of my head weakens when my father murmurs, "One grandson in direct succession for the throne."

I step back, certain I'm misunderstanding him.

According to the federation, our country's rulers have been predetermined for centuries. For the twenty-first century, it was always going to be my grandfather, my father, me, and then my son. Every detail was meticulously planned—even our births were planned with a twenty-five-year gap. It made the evolution from political underdog to chief commander that much easier.

The lower house in your mid-to-late twenties. Upper house by your fifties. Then on to the top job no later than seventy-five. Their plan meant all bases of politics were covered by the one family.

I threw a spanner in the works when I refused to fall into line. I didn't marry at twenty-four and produce an heir by twenty-five. I fought the system and assumed I had won.

I'm a fucking idiot.

"That's not possible." I shake my head like the similarity of

Zakhar's features are because he is my half-brother like Mikhail, not my son. "I've never had unprotected sex. I took any used condoms with me. I—"

"Had your wisdom teeth removed under general anesthetic just shy of your twenty-nineth birthday," my father murmurs, his voice ashamed. "Thirty was the official cutoff to produce the next president of our great country."

With the roar of a defeated man, I remove my gun from its holster, slam my father against the wall of Zakhar's room, and then pinch his temple with its barrel.

I can't breathe through the anger engulfing me.

I can't think.

I'm so fucking angry it takes everything I have to stop my finger from pushing back on the trigger firm enough to lodge a bullet into his skull.

And he doubles the battle. "This is the rightful order. This is how it's meant to be."

"This is my fucking life! There's no order. No plan. I don't want my life dictated to me."

He must have a death wish. "That choice was taken out of your hands the instant you were conceived." His words rattle along with his teeth when I inch back the trigger until it is almost fully compressed. "The sooner you learn that, the less painful it will be for *your* son."

36

ZOYA

*W*aking up hungover sucks. Bile is burning my throat, my head is thumping, and I'm reasonably sure I've only been asleep for a matter of a few hours.

I wouldn't still feel this drunk if I'd gone to bed eight-plus hours ago. Although I'd give anything for a few more hours of sleep, I've got to pull up my big girl panties and suck it up. This is one of a limited number of downfalls to paid employment.

At least I didn't forget about that.

My memories are shot to hell. Mercifully, it is only for the last fourteen-plus hours.

They're all a fog. I think I warned Vlad of the imminent tornado about to bear down on him before swallowing tequila like it was water to forget my shameful plea to be picked first, but don't ask me to place my hand on the Bible and testify to that.

I truly can't remember. I recall groping, and a leathery strap circling my thighs. The rest of my night is a haze.

I've never had such a bad tequila intolerance. It usually takes a bottle or two to drag me to the depths of memory loss. I don't recall having more than two shots.

After blowing a wayward hair out of my face, I trudge to the bathroom to remove the makeup I shouldn't have slept in. If my pores can't breathe, my body will struggle to remove the toxins I forced it to endure last night, and it will make my recovery that much longer.

The jack hammer going to town in my head means I don't realize the sound of running water is coming from my bathroom until it is too late. A dark-haired devil is in my shower. Regretfully, it isn't the imp my depraved heart is craving.

"Morning, Sunshine," Mikhail croons, not bothering to cover up.

There's enough soap scum on my shower door to maintain his modesty, making the visual more an outline instead of a double-page centerfold spread.

Well, it was until Mikhail switches off the water and steps out of the shower.

He chuckles when I divert my eyes before they can ogle his cock. The naughty vixen on my shoulder isn't understanding of my heart's desire not to be pulverized. She stomps her feet in disgust, certain the visual will outweigh any heartache a quick peek would instill.

Mikhail is more like his older brother than I first gave him credit for. Banging guns, firm pecs, and a six-pack that stole my focus long enough that I can't compare their cocks.

After twisting a towel around his waist, he flicks off the excess droplets of water from his locks with his fingers. It gives it that sexed-up look women love and unlocks my first memory of the day.

"It rained last night."

The scent lingering in the air isn't the sole cause of my sudden recollection. It is also how the wetness removes the natural kink in the bottom of Mikhail's boyish locks.

"It did. We got drenched."

When his lips quirk at the end of his sentence, I arch a brow. There's too much ambiguity in his tone for me to let slide, but I'm too hungover to gently chip at my confusion, so I go straight for the jugular.

"What aren't you telling me?"

Mikhail drags his hand across the stubble on his chin before spinning to face me. "What do you remember about last night?"

"I remember kicking you out." When his eyes gleam, I mutter, "Yet here you are the following morning, acting like my casa is your casa." He looks like he wants to interrupt me, but something stops him. "Then I recall going to Vixens and being bombarded by your brother"—I hit him with the stink eye to rival all stink eyes—"*again*."

"That had *nothing* to do with me. You made that bed when you accepted that douchebag's invite. Then you wholly fucking destroyed it by accepting another dickwad's invitation for some X-rated PDA."

"Huh?" Excuse my daftness. I'm hungover and completely fucking lost. You will barely get two sentences out of me today.

Mikhail smiles like my stupidity is endearing.

It has my elbow desperate to reacquaint with his groin.

Since my expression announces that, he works on eradicating my confusion instead of doubling it. "Douchebag—"

"Vlad," I announce, too hungover to continue working out who is whom on the long list of nicknames he uses.

"Vlad wouldn't take your hint to leave, so you forced the focus off him by..." I can't hear a thing he says. It isn't because my brain is being drilled by the tequila worm I forever swallow because I've yet to learn I am no longer sixteen. It is because he's mumbling.

"Speak up, Marshmallow Man. I'm two minutes from barfing, and you look like the type who sympathy vomits."

His nose screws up before his words come out crisp and clear.

"You forced the focus off Vlad by accepting an invitation to participate in a public scene."

I swallow down the slosh in my stomach a mere second before it makes its way back into the world. "I went on stage?"

"Uh-huh," Mikhail answers nonchalantly.

"And then...?"

Thank god he isn't a fan of delayed gratification. "After you were strapped to a sex swing, three to ten men from the audience raced to the stage as volunteers." I learn he isn't bad at math when he shifts from foot to foot while murmuring, "It was hard to gauge an exact number. Once gun fire rang out throughout the club, things went a little crazy."

My eyes pop.

Mikhail's expression remains neutral.

"The club was emptied in seconds. You were clueless, though." Another memory sparks when he closes my gaped mouth. "And you drool a fuck ton when you're passed out."

I take a moment to sort through the slosh in my head. "Vlad...?"

"Last I saw, he was hightailing it out with the rest of the survivor wannabes." Mikhail looks annoyed. I understand why when he adds, "He didn't even peer back in your direction, Sunshine, so you shouldn't have thrown yourself on the fire for him."

"I wasn't doing it solely for him. It was also for me." Since my reply is honest, it sounds that way. I blow another wayward hair out of my eye before plopping my backside on the closed toilet lid. "I found Andrik's marriage contract last night."

Air whizzes out his nose like he now understands the catalyst of my rebellion, and the genuine shock on his face announces he wasn't the one who placed it in Andrik's jacket.

"It implied that his marriage isn't about love."

Again, he makes an agreeing hum.

It shifts to a shocked huff when I murmur, "And Andrik hinted the same when we... *spoke*. He told me he hasn't been with anyone since me."

It takes him a beat, but eventually, Mikhail clicks on to the cause of my hesitation. "You don't believe him?"

"I want to," I murmur. "But—"

"You've been burned in the past?"

I nod before trying to make my ghosts appear less pathetic. "And it's not like he has a monkey's butt for a face. Even if his wife knows the terms, I'm sure she's trying."

"Trying...?" Mikhail appears utterly lost.

"To..." I make a hand gesture he immediately clicks to.

"You think she wants to fuck him?" He takes a minute to contemplate. "She could be trying, but that doesn't mean he's falling for her tricks."

"He fell for mine last night."

"Because you're you." He gives my ego a moment to bask in the glory of his stroke. "I told you that you changed him. You flipped his life plan on its head."

"He said that last night too." I breathe out slowly before nursing my thumping head in my hands. "And that I've had him backflipping on promises he made thirty years ago."

For the first time since I've known him, Mikhail is quiet.

Several seconds tick by, and disgustingly, the silence adds to my throbbing temples.

After a lengthy deliberation, Mikhail asks, "Can I see his contract?"

Shocked by the unease of his question, I slowly nod. "It's in my room—"

He's out the door before all my reply leaves my mouth.

Either he can speed read or he skims over the prominent parts of the contract like I did last night, because in under thirty seconds, he races for the stairwell, taking Andrik's marriage contract with him and leaving me to wade through my confusion alone.

————

Several hours later, a knock sounds at my door. Since I assume it is Mikhail, I don't bother checking the peephole. I swing open my door, leaving myself defenseless to a brutal onslaught.

It isn't Mikhail or his older brother.

It is their father.

What the?

"Mr...." How do I not know Mikhail's surname yet? My snooping best friend would be horrified.

"Ellis," he introduces, letting himself in. "You can call me Ellis."

"Okay." I sound lost. Rightly so. I am. "How can I help you, Ellis? If you're here seeking Mikhail, he—"

"I'm not here about Mikhail."

He takes in the trinkets on my mantel in a manner his youngest son would be proud of before he turns on his heel to face me. He balks as sternly as I did hours ago when he takes in the massive teardrop diamond on the necklace Andrik gifted me last night. Its heaviness announces its intricate design is made up of a lot of carats. If it is real, it would have cost Andrik an absolute fortune.

I wish I would have realized that before I went gung-ho with a quest to be picked first.

Ellis's voice is full of angst when he says, "I am here about your involvement with my firstborn son."

I wait for him to elaborate, unwilling to tiptoe over the trap he's setting, let alone stomp through it.

It is an extremely long thirty seconds that only ends when I break it. "Andrik—"

"Is married."

I swallow to ease the burn that didn't fully soothe even after emptying my stomach's contents into the toilet seconds after Mikhail left.

That's one part of my conversation with Andrik I haven't been able to brush aside as easily as my jealousy. I thought he was married as implied by Ellis just now, but last night, Andrik spoke as if he's not yet exchanged vows.

I'm so confused it takes Ellis growling at me to remind me that he's standing across from me.

"I am aware of that."

"Yet you still throw yourself at him at every available opportunity."

His tone is offensive, so naturally, I take offense.

"No. I've tried to stay away."

He scoffs like he doesn't believe me. For some reason, it hurts as much as it did when my mother didn't believe a single thing I told her.

"You came to *his* hometown. *His* hotel. Had sex in the elevator of *his* building and let him have his way with you in the driveway of *his* country estate before doing god knows what at *his* club. But I'm meant to believe you're not throwing yourself at him?" He doesn't wait for me to answer him. "How many times has he been here ..."—he screws up his nose like my name leaves a bad taste in his mouth—"Zoya, right?"

My timid head bob makes me feel naked, because although he asks for my name, he refuses to use it.

"How many times has he been here?"

"Your son—"

I learn who Andrik gets his bossiness from when Ellis shouts, "How. Many!"

Just like Vlad, Andrik doesn't deserve my loyalty, but I still give it to him. "None. He hasn't been here at all." My voice is just as loud, my anger just as apparent. I hate lying when I'm unsure if the person I am being deceitful for deserves the intervention, and Andrik's motives have me unsure which side of the fence I should be on.

"So that entails that *you're* the issue, not him." Ellis glares me up and down like I'm dog poo his shoe picked up at the park. "So you also need to be the solution."

"Andrik—"

"Will never get divorced, leave his wife for you, or save you from this." He waves his hand around my apartment. "You are a gimmick. A sex toy with a pulse. You're the whore keeping his sheets warm while—"

I slap the words from his mouth.

He reacts opposite to Andrik when struck. His face reddens with anger as his teeth grit. But I am the only one left gasping for air when he asks, "How much will it take for you to walk away from my son and never look back?"

"I don't want your money."

He acts as if I never spoke. "I can organize transfers to another country, new *passable* IDs, and grant you access to resources you've never had in your life." He bobs down low before whispering in a chilling tone, "I can free you from your cage, little bird. I can set you free."

"I'm already free," I snarl, my tone as deadly as his glare, my anger just as rife. "So get the fuck out of my house before I steal more than just the devotion of your little minions."

Ellis returns my glare for several heart-thumping seconds before he straightens his spine, pulls a business card out of the breast pocket of his suit jacket, and then stuffs it into the beak of the dusty duck Mikhail pointed out weeks ago.

"My offer expires in seven days." He heads for the door while grumbling under his breath. "The next one won't be issued to you. It will be *for* you."

37

ANDRIK

"*A*re you mad?" Zakhar wiggles his tongue around his mouth, wetting it for the long Q-tip a doctor is about to scrape along the inside of his cheek, before he returns his focus to me. "You seem mad. Did I do something wrong?"

"No," I reply, my tone curt and brutish.

When he arches a brow and purses his lips, I mutter a cussword under my breath.

In my anger, I forgot how receptive he is to liars. He can spot a deceitful man from a mile out. I've used his skills to my advantage more than once in the past month and hope to be able to do the same for many years to come.

After attempting to slacken the tightness of my jaw and failing, I say, "I'm not mad at you, Zak. You're not the issue."

Since my reply is honest this time, he believes me. "I'm glad you're not mad at me, but you shouldn't be mad at anyone." He continues swishing his tongue when his words come out huskily. "Mommy says life is too short to be angry." His eyes water when he peers down at the cords taped to his tiny chest. "I guess she was right. I'm not surprised. Mommy is always right. She is *very* smart."

When he tilts his head back as per the doctor's instructions, causing the wetness in his eyes to trickle past his ears, I hate myself more than I ever thought possible.

He is wired up to the hilt with monitors, and on more medication than men twenty times his age, yet I'm more concerned about getting his DNA verified than finding a solution to the predicament I placed him in when I tipped off the Ivanovs about Irina's organs being sold.

Dr. Abdulov and Dr. Azores won't be able to give Zakhar a new heart because they'll be dead by the end of the week, possibly sooner if Matvei passes on the information I gave him to his eldest brother before he arrives in Russia.

Furthermore, I don't need a test to know Zakhar is a Dokovic. He looks so much like Mikhail and me I've often wondered over the past month where the last thirty years went. When I stand across from Zakhar, it's as if I'm back in the closet of my bedroom, hiding from a life I promised Mikhail and myself we'd never have to live.

I had no clue how many lies I've told in my life until Zakhar refused to believe my fib that I replaced Dr. Makarand with a colleague more specialized for a patient with his condition.

From the look he gave me, you'd swear he was conscious when my anger that I'd been manipulated saw me popping a bullet between Dr. Makarand's dark brows.

A rare smile tugs my lips at one side when Zakhar giggles from the Q-tip scraping the inside of his mouth. "That tickles."

Heat colors his face when he hears the response I can't hold back from his croaky laugh rumbling through my chest. It's an expression I gave often before my fifth birthday. It was only ever directed at one person. My mother.

I jerk my chin up in acknowledgement when the doctor who swabbed my mouth earlier like my DNA hadn't been burned off with a gallon of whiskey says, "I'll have the results back as soon as possible."

Once he leaves, I pour Zakhar a glass of "vodka" to help with the tickle the swab caused the back of his throat.

"More, Zak," I demand when he only takes the tiniest sip. "We need you fit..."

"Like a fox," he murmurs, stammering through the spit the slightest slosh of water caused his mouth since he's struggled to swallow the past few days.

His failing heart is his biggest health battle, but its downfall means the rest of his organs are slowly following suit. He is mere weeks from death.

"Like a fox," I quote, struggling to speak through the guilt about the steps I've taken thus far.

Whether he is my son or not, Zakhar is a child. I should have never placed my needs before his. I'm a man. An adult. I'm not a child hiding in a closet, waiting for his mother to come back.

I stop filling a glass with real vodka when someone bursts into Zakhar's room unannounced despite numerous requests from his childhood nanny for him to do the opposite.

Mikhail's eyes widen to the size of saucers as they flick between Zak and me, and his mouth gapes like a fish out of water. In under a second, he sees what I saw—another innocent victim of our father's.

Zak finds Mikhail's expression hilarious. "You look like you need to go poopie."

"I feel like I need to go poopie," Mikhail replies when Zakhar's boyish laugh snaps him out of his trance.

He mouths, *What the fuck?* to me before he moves closer to Zak's bedside.

As he drinks in Zak's undisputed Dokovic features, I signal for the two guards I placed at Zakhar's door to stand down. Mikhail isn't a threat to Zakhar any more than I am.

I can't issue the same guarantee for anyone else currently residing under my roof.

38

ZOYA

*M*y heart whines when I push a bundle of cash to the other side of my desk instead of stuffing it into my purse. The funds I handed a pharmacist this morning were almost in comparison to the stack of cash Mars is clutching close to her chest, but it doesn't alter the facts.

Not a single note belongs to me, so I can't accept them.

Mars earned those tips. I merely tallied them, lodged them for tax purposes, and then distributed them to their rightful owner.

After adding the funds I'd refused into the bundle I just handed her, Mars moans like she hates money. "The bartenders get a share of our tips, so why shouldn't you?"

Not looking up, I reply, "Because the bartenders offer a service. I do not."

"You could."

Now, I look up.

"Don't give me that look." Mars purses her lips in a way I plan to replicate when I'm not exhausted from working nights after spending my days with Nikita's grandparents.

Nikita will never admit it, but we were close to losing Grampies during his last downward spiral. One bad case of pneumonia saw his medication bill doubling, and Nikita's savings returned to what it was six months ago.

Without a proper breathing machine, Grampies's condition will continue worsening, which in turn means he will need more medication.

It is a cruel cycle I don't see us winning anytime soon, but I refuse to give up. Grampies was the first man who was ever kind to me, so I can't turn my back on him like my family did me.

Mars burns off any wetness attempting to fill my eyes before it can make me look stupid. "I've seen the way the patrons stare when Trace takes too long to refill your drink. You could earn triple what you do now and work far less hours."

"Don't remind me."

The salaries at Le Rogue are amazing. My position is the highest paid job I've held since college. My paycheck allows me to contribute to the rent, which my new building supervisor assures me I don't owe since I'm supposedly months in advance, and some of Grampies's ongoing medical expenses, but I doubt that will remain the case when Mr. Fakher's accounting error is unearthed.

It is only a matter of time before I'll owe thousands in backdated rent. I could lessen the anxiety keeping me awake at all hours of the night by being honest with the building sup and organizing a payment plan, but sometimes the best lessons are the ones you teach yourself.

That's how I'm seeing my time at Le Rogue—as a lesson.

Nothing in life comes free...

And when you lay with an adulterer, you could end up surrounded by them.

I don't think any of the Le Rogue regulars are single and ready to mingle. Not even ten percent of the patrons bother hiding their wedding rings, yet they're still one step higher on the morality chart than Andrik.

They keep their extramarital activities away from their home base. They don't flaunt it in the driveway of their mega-mansions for their wives to possibly see, or in a sex club with hundreds of guests only feet away.

"That dick must have been good," Mars murmurs, pulling me from my thoughts. "Because you, my dear sexy friend, could have *any* dick you want, but you seem unwilling to let go of the last dick you had."

"I wasn't thinking about dick."

She *pffts* me before slumping onto the chair opposite me like she's wearing more clothing than she is. One wrong knee slip and I'll see *everything*. "I'm surrounded by unvoiced desires for hours every night. I can read thoughts when it comes to what people are craving, and you, baby girl, are stuck on your ex."

"He isn't an ex," I choke out with a laugh, hopeful it will hide my angst.

I've only known Mars for a week, yet she can already read me like a book. "So there is someone?"

Too tired to lie, I remain quiet.

Mars can never take a hint that you want to let bygones be bygones. "Cough it up. Who has your panties in such a mess you don't want to flash them for 20K for one night's worth of work?"

My eyes bulge at the mention of potential earnings, but her calculations are a little off. "That's only 2K."

She fans the cash I handed her, ruffling her perfect hair. "For my first dance of the night after a three-year stint in the strip circuit. First-timers rake in a fortune. Some pots even go as high as twenty."

"Thousand?" I double-check.

I've been caught out before.

I won't make that mistake twice.

She hums in agreement. "Melita got close to a new record last month. She was a couple of hundred short." She flashes a cheeky grin, doubling my interest. "But between you and me, she more than doubled that when she went home with a John wanting a second viewing."

The longer I remain quiet, the larger Mars's smile grows.

I'm not shy, not in the slightest, but as often as guilt floods my heart, so does Andrik's threat.

Don't test me on six because I can guarantee neither you nor him will survive the outcome.

I tested him last week.

I've not heard a peep from Vlad since, and I've called him over a hundred times.

So as much as a one-time twirl around a pole could help me replenish the funds stripped from Nikita's savings after Grampies's latest health crisis, I don't give it any true thought... until Gigi's number pops up on my phone.

With my heart in my throat, I slide my finger across my phone screen and then squash it to my ear. "Gigi, are you okay? It's late."

"He's struggling to breathe. His lips are blue. I tried to call Nikita. She's not answering. I don't know what to do."

I shoot up from my chair, startling Mars. "Have you given him Epinephrine?"

"I can't. The box is empty." The rattle of an empty box sounds down the line. "There are no EpiPens left."

Panic rains down on me before lucidity slips through the cracks. "Hang up and call an ambulance."

"We can't afford that."

"I'll get the money. I promise you I will. But you need to call them now, Gigi. He needs help you can't give him. He needs *urgent* medical assistance."

Her sob breaks my heart. She knows as well as I do that

Grampies won't make it if she doesn't seek medical help immedi-ately. "Ok-okay. I'll call them now."

She disconnects our call. I race for the exit just as fast.

"Go," Lilia says before I can issue her a single excuse to leave early. "I'll cover your shift."

She accepts my mouthed thanks with a smile before telling the doorman to hail me a cab.

Disgustingly, I arrive at Gigi's apartment at the same time as the paramedics. They give Grampies a shot of adrenaline that spikes his heart rate high enough for the monitors at his bedside to alarm. It also helps him breathe.

His color improves drastically as well.

The opposite can be said for Gigi.

"It's okay," I promise her after wrapping her up in a tight hug. "We will fix this. We will make it right. Grampies will get better. Look." I wave my hand at him resting far more peacefully now that his breathing tube isn't kinked.

I love Gigi with all my heart, but she is a klutz. She meant well wheeling in close to Grampies's bedside to feed him his supper, but she forgot the tubes of the ECOM machine keeping his lungs primed with oxygen are too fragile to be clamped to his bedrails. They're draped across the floor—right where she placed the feet of the dining room chair.

"He's already improving."

"It's not just Grampies." She breathes in and out three times before aligning her drenched eyes with mine. "It's Nikita. She won't go with you when she finds out about tonight. She'll stay and continue working to the bone." I can barely hear her over her sobs when she murmurs, "She can't keep working the hours she's doing. It will kill her even faster than Grampies's condition is taking him from us."

Since I agree with her, I remain quiet.

If I can't scatter some truths throughout my lies, you won't get a word out of me.

"She needs to live, Zoya. She needs to live for her." Tears spring down her rheumy cheeks. "She needs to live the life her mama never got to have."

"She does," I wholeheartedly agree before striving to find a solution and coming up empty.

Gigi doesn't face the same battle. "That's why we're not going to tell her about what happened tonight." She sucks in a big breath, clears her tears with her sleeves, and then peers up at me in silent begging. "Grampies's condition is stable... *despite my stupidity.*" She swallows down the painful sob that arrived with her last three words. "So there is no need to worry Nikita with this."

"She'll—"

"She needs this time away, Zoya. She needs to recover before she burns out."

Once again, I remain quiet, having no defense to argue with. Nikita is a fighter. She will fight to the death for her grandfather, but she is also one shift of overtime from burnout.

She either takes a break or breaks.

If I am forced to pick which break she endures, I'd rather it be the former.

"Okay." I breathe out slowly, nodding. "It will remain between us."

I hate betraying my friend, but I truly believe a little white lie to save someone from a heap of heartache is okay on a rare occasion. Nikita will forgive me. It just won't be until after I have forgiven myself.

Gigi sighs in relief. "Now that you're on board, all we need to do is work out a way to pay for this"—she thrusts her hand at the paramedics still assessing Grampies before twisting her lips—"without Nikita finding out." Her eyes glisten with an equal amount of excitement and tears. "I have some antique ornaments I could sell. We just need to find the right owner. They're an acquired taste."

Her voluptuous waddle to a collection of non-dusty knickknacks on a glass shelf next to Nikita's sofa bed pops the perfect solution into my head.

"I know a way to get funds quickly." When she peers at me with crinkled brows, I recall my earlier pledge that lying is only bad when it's done to cause pain. "I was offered a gig earlier. It is a one-time opportunity, so it pays *really* well." By sprinkling snippets of honesty in a lie, it is far more viable. "It could cover tonight's incident and perhaps a couple of months of medication."

"Really?" Gigi looks exalted, and it has my chin dipping with only the slightest bit of unease.

I doubt my nerves will be as contained when it comes to executing my plan, though.

It's easier to talk the talk than to walk the walk.

39

ANDRIK

"How did you find out?"

After placing a bottle of whiskey on the bar, Mikhail strays his eyes to the hallway of the west wing. I know what door he's imagining without needing to follow the direction of his gaze. My eyes have taken the same route numerous times in the past month, though they never had this level of angst attached to them.

"He looks a fuck ton like you, but he also doesn't. He kinda..."

When his words trail off, I fill in the gaps. "Looks like you?"

He jerks up his chin. "That's why I thought he was one of us." By one of us, he means one of our father's many sons. "So to say I was shocked when you introduced him as your son." He blows out a hot breath. "I've never been more surprised, and I've seen some shit in my time." Guilt flares through his eyes. I understand why when he murmurs, "Have you checked that the claim is legitimate?"

I nod as if DNA test results are immediate. I know Zakhar is my son. My gut tells me this, not to mention how I was immediately compelled to protect him. I've only had that desire once before. It was hours before I knew of Zakhar's existence.

Mikhail's swallow is audible before he asks, "Does Zoya know?"

A huff whistles through my teeth. I should have known his first thought would veer to Zoya instead of the woman he believes I am married to, because I had the exact same response.

When he remains staring, impatiently awaiting an answer, I shake my head. "No one knows, except..." I can't force the remainder of my reply past my clenched jaw.

That's how fucking furious I am. I want to go on a rampage. I want to kill the fools who thought they could play me like this and live to endure the aftermath of their stupidity, but to do that, I'd have to bury my son.

That isn't something I can do. I am my father's son, but he only makes up half my DNA. My mother couldn't even take her anger out on the children causing infinite cracks in her marriage because she knew it wasn't their choice to be born, so there's no way I could treat my son with so much disrespect that it would cause his demise.

Realizing the waters are getting deeper and deeper, I seek help from one of the few people I trust. "Zak needs a heart transplant."

"Okay." Mikhail breathes out slowly like the pieces of the puzzle are slotting together. "We can get him one of those."

"It isn't as easy as it sounds." He waits, knowing there's more. "Not a single operation is performed in Russia without—"

"The federation's tick of approval," Mikhail interrupts, finally clicking on. His eyes flick up this time. "That's why you canceled the annulment? She's their prime pick for the next First Lady." He cusses when I nod, but just as quickly, confusion settles on his face. "But you only just found out about Zak, so what stopped you back then?" I don't get the chance to talk. He's too clued in to my quirks for me to get a word in, and I'm too bristling with anger to hide them from him. "In-vitro fertilization wouldn't have broken the promise you made to your mom, Andrik." I feel like a chump, but his following words make the burn not so scalding. "But I get it. It would be hard to woo a woman while initiating the downfall of another."

Even with him hitting the nail on the head, it takes everything I have to keep my fists balled at my sides.

Mikhail doubles the effort. "That's what you're doing, right?" He tosses down a stapled document I didn't know he was holding until now. "Ten million for each year of marriage after the birth of an heir, capped at fifty million." He already knows the answer to his question, though he still asks it. "How did you know your marriage would only last five years after the birth of your son, Andrik?"

"The same way you knew how to read the terms of my contract, Mikhail." I say his name with the same disdain he used for mine. "Because the pattern never alters. If you give them a son, you get five years. If you give them a daughter—"

"They're both dead."

I don't want to hurt him, but I can no longer continue to carry this burden alone, so I jerk up my chin instead of shaking my head

After a moment to settle his rising anger, Mikhail asks, "Is that what happened to Zak's mother?"

I shrug, truly unsure and too snowed under wondering how I am going to fix my mammoth fuckup to care.

Mikhail will never let me disregard our family's lineage so easily.

He glares until I buckle under the intensity.

"Zak talks about her as if she was a part of his life, but he hasn't given me anything concrete like a name or the location where he grew up. You'd swear he was raised in a windowless room."

My anger triples when Mikhail mutters, "He probably was." He scoffs as if surprised I didn't consider that myself before he gets back to more pressing matters than the identity of a woman with a looming expiration date. "This isn't something I ever thought I'd say, but you can buy pretty much anything on the black market. Have you looked for a heart there?"

"I have," I confess. "But those avenues in Russia became unavailable to me when I drafted and lodged a second annulment earlier this month."

My fight with Zoya wasn't the commencement of Arabella's downfall. It was barely the tip of the iceberg. But none of that matters right now. Getting Zakhar a new heart must be my utmost priority.

"Then we will go to another country," Mikhail spits out as if it is as simple as ordering your eggs sunny-side up instead of scrambled.

"We can't. Zak can barely leave his room, so there's no way he will survive an international flight."

"Then we will bring the surgeon here along with his new heart!"

I understand his frustration. I fullheartedly understand it. But it doesn't alter the facts. "A heart can't survive outside its host for longer than four hours. The longer it is without oxygen, the more damaged the cells become, meaning we could replace Zak's heart with one more damaged."

"Fuck!" Mikhail knocks over the crystal bar no home in Russia is ever without before shooting his hands up to tug at his hair.

He yanks on it firmly enough for my roots to sympathize, his hand only dropping when I murmur, "But I know a way around the block."

He looks confused until I raise my eyes to the floor above us, and then his expression switches to disgust.

He doesn't want to play by their rules any more than I do, but we don't have a choice.

All bets are off once Zakhar has a new heart, though.

40

ZOYA

*T*he loud chatter of the crowd displays why the dancers at Le Rogue are more family than competitors. Mars could have steered me wrong when I asked her advice for getting a favorable outcome for a first-time performer.

She could have pushed me to dance on a Tuesday so her tips weren't reduced further than the long spell in the strip club circuit most dancers face. She didn't because her job description doesn't change who she is.

She is a good person, and so am I.

The remembrance clears away the last of my nerves and has me reared up and ready for my first, but not guaranteed last, performance.

The euphoria is addictive, and the energy is thrumming.

I haven't felt this alive since...

Mercifully, I am cut off by Mars this time instead of guilt. "Are you ready?"

I jiggle my chest before jerking up my chin. "As ready as I will ever be."

With a devilish grin, Mars flickers the lights on the stage, announcing to the patrons that my show is about to begin.

It doubles the muttering and sets my belly ablaze with untapped excitement. Even if I only earn one quarter of Mars's predicted revenue, I will have plenty of funds to pay for Grampies's unexpected in-home health visit, and perhaps add a little garnish to the items I've purchased over the past two weeks for the two women who mean the world to me.

As I approach the wings of the stage, I take in Le Rogue from a new vantage point. Just like Vixens, Le Rogue isn't much to look at from the outside. Its outer shell is old and rundown, and the neon lighting at the front flickers more than the doorman's flashlight when he checks the patrons' IDs upon entry.

The insides of the brick-and-mortar building on the outskirts of town are far more elaborate. The stage is made from a pricy wood you can only import on the black market, the bar is stocked with whiskey that costs as much per nip as an entire bottle at a corner store, and the stage lights are the best money can buy.

Rich clients come here, hence my unexpected nerves.

I squint when the lighting crew switches on the stage's main lights. When I collect the money men toss onto the dancer's feet during each performance, the lights are switched off, so I've never faced the full intensity of their warmth. I'm not complaining. It'll be easier to prance around naked since I'll only be subjected to the heat of multiple ogling stares instead of seeing them directly.

Also, with the temperature reaching roasting, I'm more than ready to remove my first piece of clothing.

"Give them another thirty seconds. The hungrier they are, the better they'll tip." Mars wiggles her brows.

Nodding, I drag my sweaty palms down my pleated skirt. I went for the naughty secretary skit. Mars said it produces the best tips because most of the men who visit Le Rogue work in a corporate setting and fantasize about fucking their secretaries.

The glitter on my chest sparkles under the stage lights when the curtains are drawn, and I'm encouraged on stage by the vocal cheers of the dancers who should see me as competition but don't.

I feed off their energy and burst onto the stage like I was made to perform.

I was. Just not in the way most people think.

As Mars predicted, the crowd goes apeshit when they realize I'm not on the regular schedule. They holler and shout, and before my hands can move for the buttons on the business shirt I tied midway on my stomach, several bills of multiple denominations land at my feet.

They're not close to the amount I'm seeking, but they are a great start.

I move in sync with the music, my set as choreographed as the lie I told Gigi this morning when she busted me garnishing the savings in Nikita's box with the leftovers of my second paycheck.

My shirt falls to the floor with timed perfection. The crowd eats up the hot-pink bra my plain white shirt couldn't conceal before they chant for me to lose it.

I wiggle my finger at them, sending them into an uproar about my inability to follow orders.

More bills float to my feet as I prance to the pole in the middle of the stage. I work it for barely thirty seconds. I don't have the skills to incorporate it into my routine like Mars and the other dancers do, though the crowd of mostly men don't seem to mind. They shout and holler before promising to rain the stage with cash once I lose my skirt.

I can't help but oblige. It isn't that I'm a person who jumps on cue. I merely refuse to miss a timed-to-perfection beat. This routine was devised fast, but that doesn't mean I won't act as if it was chore-graphed by Shakira herself.

I'm having so much fun that it takes longer than I care to admit to notice the dulling of the crowd's chants the longer I perform. The occasional shout hollers between hip thrusts, though they're far and few between compared to when I started.

Desperate to unearth what the hell is going on, and too curious for my own good, I move toward the edge of the stage. Perhaps the lights bouncing off the sequins on my bra-and-panties combination are too reflective for the clubgoers to take full advantage of the provocativeness of my performance.

My stomach gurgles when my vision clears enough to see the first row of chairs. The number of people filling the seats is thin. Barely a backside fills a chair, and the ear-piercing whistle of my shocked sigh loses me the last of the stragglers as well.

"Keep going," Mars encourages when I peer back at her, seeking assistance.

After rolling my shoulders back and sticking out my ample chest, I strut to the side of the stage still in view of half a dozen patrons.

I barely jiggle my bra-covered breasts before the paltry number of guests remaining slim further. They practically sprint for the exit, racing through the doors like recently pronged cattle burst out the gate.

Within minutes, the club is empty.

Not even the male bartenders remain.

Yet my confidence climbs out of the trenches instead of seeking a safe place to hide. The stage is littered with bills, and I have someone so desperate for a private show they've scared off the other admirers.

This may be my biggest payday to date.

I shoot my eyes to the side when a deep, booming clap breaks the quiet. The stage lights hide the man's face from view, but even with his features hidden, my intuition switches my excitement to unease.

Something feels wrong.

Very wrong.

This isn't how my first performance is meant to go.

Artic-blue eyes break past the shadows first.

Then a malicious smirk.

Although they're the same features that find their way into my dreams every night, the lines bordering them keep my heart rate at a leisurely jog instead of a sprint.

It isn't Andrik as my heart is endeavoring to convince my head.

It is his father.

"Brilliant. Wonderful. Keep going."

Ellis moves to the front of the stage before he spins around a chair and straddles it backward. He's so close to the action hotspot that every breath he releases batters my scarcely covered vagina.

When I remain frozen, he assumes my lack of motivation is because he hasn't paid for the honor. With a smirk that is as condescending as it is sickening, he pulls a thick wad of bills out of his wallet before tossing five at my feet.

He tilts his head to hide his smirk when I step back from them like they're covered with the blood of his firstborn son.

"Not enough?"

He doesn't wait for me to answer. He removes another three bills from the stack before holding them out in front of himself. Their denominations are larger than their predecessors, but not close to the amount he'd have to pay to convince me to finish my performance.

He could offer me millions and I still wouldn't take his money.

I have class—it's just hard to demand respect when half your ass is hanging out.

An annoyed huff commences his barter. "Come on, Zoya. I know I'm not the man you were hoping to see tonight, but any money is better than none, right? And you won't get a single penny from him after the stunt you pulled last week."

It takes everything I have to walk away, but he continues to push like I'm not seconds from ramming my fist into his face.

"Two thousand, and you can keep your panties on."

I continue walking.

"Five thousand."

Mars looks set to jump on stage and do my routine for me when the bids keep coming in. "Ten thousand... Twenty thousand... Thirty thousand, and I'll make out to Andrik that not the slightest bit of disappointment crossed your face when you realized he doesn't care enough about you to respond to you selling parts of your body for money... *again*." He snickers his last word like being on the verge of starving to death isn't a valid excuse to get drastic with your attempts to earn some funds.

I shouldn't bite at the bait he is dangling out, but haunted memories are making my emotions too askew not to. "Dancing and selling your body are two very different things."

He looks smug that he forced me to respond, so it is only fair I strive to wipe it off his face.

"I figured you'd know that better than anyone since I doubt a single person has volunteered to slip between your sheets without expecting a payout for the injustice."

I'm lying. Ellis is handsome. He just rubs me the wrong way, and the frustration it instigates has me acting out as if he is the father figure I never had growing up.

He scoffs before hitting me where it hurts. "Doesn't make the truth any less honest." He leans over the chair, freeing his face from the shadows. "You're only ever on his mind when you're directly in front of him." He screws up his face like he vomited in his mouth.

"And even then, the attention is fleeting." His arrogant grin hackles the last of my nerves. "You were in a club designed for sex and sensuality, yet he left after only the briefest brush of your clit because you tried to force his hand. That never ends well."

"He emptied the club with gunfire because he was jealous." I don't need to correct his misinformation on how far our exchange went. That will remain between Andrik and me because it *involved* Andrik and me.

Ellis's laughter is haunting. "You think that was him?" He slaps his thigh like he's at a comedy club, its crack echoing in the empty club. "That was Mikhail playing another trick on his brother. He's always riling him. Your inclusion in their lives merely offered them a couple of weeks of bonus ammunition in the game they've been playing since they were kids. That's it. Nothing more."

When I remain quiet, too annoyed to think of a comeback, Ellis pulls his phone out of his pocket.

"If you don't believe me, I can show you. I've got footage from multiple angles."

I can't see the footage he plays, but I hear gunfire, which is quickly followed by Mikhail shouting for people to clear out.

I'm glad Mikhail stopped me from making a mistake I couldn't take back, but the knowledge it was him also fills me with a ton of confusion.

And anger. So much anger.

I act out when blindsided.

"One hundred thousand in cash, delivered to me, *in person*, by close of business tomorrow night." Ellis tries to speak, but I cut him off. "If you can achieve that, I'll stay away from your son."

With my terms nonnegotiable, I tilt my chin high before exiting the stage with a spring in my step someone who was duped out of a possible ten thousand dollars shouldn't have.

41

ANDRIK

*O*ne hundred thousand in cash, delivered to me, in person, by close of business tomorrow night. If you can achieve that, I'll stay away from your son.

I wet my lips before rewinding the video clip Konstantine forwarded to me this evening. With Zoya's name associated with the footage, I had planned to immediately watch it, but I was approached by a key member of Zakhar's medical team, so I set it aside for when I was alone.

Now I'm glad.

I wear jealous as obviously as every other fool. That's not a look a man should express when standing across from his alleged wife.

One hundred thousand in cash, delivered to me, in person—

I slam down my laptop before I can hear the remainder of Zoya's demand again. Since the cracking of the screen offers little relief to my anger, I send my laptop flying across the room. It crashes into a bookshelf in my office before crumbling into pieces on the floor.

"Why didn't Lilia stop her from going on stage?"

I'm fucking furious Zoya put a price on our relationship, but I also understand that sometimes you've got to fight fire with fire. My father was railroading her. He had her cornered, so she pushed back. Was it in a way I approve of? Fuck no. But that is a matter for us to handle in private, after I've waded through the shit raining down on me, and when there isn't three thousand miles between us.

Zoya's ass will need to travel just as long to recover once I'm done with her.

"Lilia was not aware she was performing until she was already on stage," Konstantine answers, his voice low, as if he knows I'm one measly millimeter from losing my cool.

"How can that be? Lilia—"

"Was given the day off."

"By whom?" Confusion hits me first when he spins around his laptop screen to show me the email forwarded to Lilia this morning. It is quickly replaced with fury. "Anoushka doesn't sign off her emails with her job title. She's family, not staff, so she'd never pretend otherwise." Konstantine jerks up his chin in agreement. "Find out who really sent that email. I want a name by the a.m."

Again, he nods.

His brisk shake does little to hide his smirk when I add another task to his list.

"And send extermination orders for anyone who didn't immediately recognize Zoya. I don't issue no touch orders for fun."

My jaw tightens when Konstantine asks, "The men who stayed after she removed her shirt or just her skirt?"

I could offer leniency. The men who remained seated around the stage wouldn't have seen more than they would have if Zoya was at the beach, but after the day I've had, I'm at my limit of pleasantries. I'm fucking done.

"Both."

Konstantine smiles the way he did when he hand-delivered the last man on the list of names Zoya unknowingly compiled for me when she joined a social media site two weeks ago. Her exes came out of the woodwork faster than I could take them down, meaning someone got word to the final man I need to return her tally to one.

He went into hiding—*went* being the prominent part of my confession.

He'll be dead when I get two seconds to breathe without someone from the federation calculating exactly how much air I'm intaking.

42

ZOYA

I underestimated Ellis's wish to keep me away from his son.

The way he bombarded me last night is a sure-fire sign of his desperateness, so I won't mention his expression as he stands in the entryway of my apartment, glaring at me days earlier than planned.

I thought he'd have the stamina of his eldest son. That's why I was so gung-ho with my extortion attempt. I had no inkling he was a premature ejaculator.

I didn't pluck the date and time I gave Ellis last night out of thin air. This weekend is Aleena's hen party celebration. It was meant to guarantee there'd be three thousand miles between us before the agreed time of our meetup, but he screwed it over by rocking up hours earlier than stated.

That goes against the terms of our agreement, so I am well within my rights to renege on my offer.

"I—"

"Before you say anything, a verbal agreement is as legally binding as a written one." I was planning to tell him to get the hell off my doorstep with a ton of derogative words, but he steals my ability to talk by reminding me I should never jump before looking. "And Le Rogue never closes, so any lawyer could argue that the time stated was wide-ranging for a reason." A smug expression curls his lips at one side. "You also said 'by close of business.' By means—"

"I know the definition of by," I snap out, frustrated.

His smirk grows as he thrusts a plumped-out duffle bag into my chest. It is lighter than what I thought one hundred thousand would weigh. That could be because I'm more measuring the weight it adds to my chest instead of my arms.

I can barely breathe through the pressure.

"I—"

Ellis cuts me off with a threatening tone this time. "Follow our agreement. That is *all* you need to do."

"Or?" I ask, stubborn and confident his threat was unfinished.

I almost fold in two when he murmurs, "Or Vlad's name won't be the only one cited on a missing person's report."

I'm so reeling from his admission that something bad has happened to Vlad that it takes several long seconds for me to realize the only breaths depriving my apartment of oxygen are mine.

The first thing I lose when my mind is spiraling is my smarts.

The second is the ability to absorb intimidation.

Before my heart can talk me out of it, I snatch up my phone and hit the number one spot above my best friend's.

When my call is connected, I don't wait for Mikhail to issue a greeting. I go into full meltdown mode. "You need to tell your father to back off. I haven't done anything wrong." I pace my living room while shouting. "I've tried to stay away from Andrik, but you continually force us back together. Your father doesn't know that, though. He thinks it's all me. I am getting blamed for everything. It isn't fair, Mikhail. He's a fucking moron who—"

"That isn't very nice." The voice interrupting is nowhere near as deep as it should be, and nowhere near as mature. "You shouldn't call people names, no matter how bad they are. My mommy said..."

As the childlike voice continues reprimanding me, I pull my phone away from my ear to check that Mikhail's name is flashing across the screen. It is.

After squashing my phone back to my ear, I ask, "Who is this?"

"I'm Zakhar," answers a boy I assume is around five or six. "Who are you?"

"I'm Zoya. I am a friend of your..." I've never sounded so unconfident. "Is this your phone, Zakhar?"

Even though I can't see him, I'm confident in declaring that he laughs with his whole belly. That's how boisterous his chuckles are. "No, silly. Daddy went—"

"This is your dad's phone?" I ask, too shocked to wait for him to finalize his question.

"No." For one short word, it takes him almost three seconds to deliver it. "This is дядя Mikhail's phone."

My Russian is decent, but it takes me longer than I care to admit to remember that дядя is uncle in Russian.

The knowledge that Mikhail isn't hiding a secret child from me should weaken the churns of my stomach, not triple them. It doesn't. I feel as uneased now as I did in the seconds leading to Mikhail announcing that Andrik is married.

"Is your dad with you, Zakhar?"

"He was, but he went to speak with Anoushka. I think I got him in trouble. I'm not meant to stay up so late, but Daddy said it would be okay. Don't tell my mommy, though. She says bedtimes are important because sleep helps your brain grow." His tone dips as if he is confused. "But sleeping around makes you stupid." My heart beats at an unnatural rhythm when he asks, "What is sleeping around? Is that like a sleepover?"

"Um. Yeah. Kinda." This is not a conversation I want to have with an adult, much less a child, so I strive to end it. "I should probably go. I have a plane to catch."

Zakhar's voice jumps as high as my brow when he squeals, "Daddy! You came back!"

It feels like the sun circles the planet a million times when his wheezy squeals are overtaken by the breaths of a man aware he's about to be caught in a lie. "Who is this?"

I freeze while recalling the last time I heard that clipped, stern rumble.

Its commanding aura usually dots goose bumps across my skin.

Tonight, it cakes it with dread.

I suck in a sharp breath when my caller identifies my gasp as readily as I did his voice. "Zoya."

Just the way Andrik says my name breaks my heart further.

And it makes me angry—furiously, undisputedly angry.

He made me become the one thing I swore I'd never be.

He turned me into my mother.

Andrik must hear the devastation in my breaths. "Zoya, don't—"

"Goodbye, Andrik," I murmur, my tone, for once, full of honesty.

I am done with this game once and for all.

"Zo—"

I throw my phone to the ground hard enough to shatter the screen and pop out the battery before I race into my room to pack the last of my things.

In an ashamedly quick three minutes, all my most valuable possessions are stored in a ripped duffle bag. There are only three items missing from my bag.

The one hundred thousand dollars I had no intention of spending until now, the dirtbox that will ensure I can do it without interruption, and the necklace I'm leaving behind.

43

ANDRIK

"*A*nything yet?"

Konstantine has been with me for years, so he knows who my query centers around even with me not saying her name.

After a quick breath that flares his nostrils, he shakes his head. "You'll be the first I inform when I find her." His next words are barely a whisper, but I still hear them. "Perhaps you should send Mikhail out in the field. It's his dirtbox making my life fucking difficult."

I had considered his suggestion. The thought only lingered for thirty seconds. It wasn't solely jealousy that squashed it like a bug. It was knowing there's no better man to explain to Zoya why I need to continue with my ruse than me.

As I said weeks ago, betrothed or not, she wants me.

She will have me. There's just a handful more obstacles I need to find my way around first.

"If she had kept her necklace on, we wouldn't be facing so many issues."

Yes, I placed a tracker in Zoya's necklace. It wasn't solely to keep an eye on her. It is the fact the diamond would cost over eight million dollars to replace. A tracker lowers its insurance premium.

Yeah, right.

Konstantine only shared the tracker's brilliance with me after I instructed the jeweler to place it in Zoya's necklace.

Konstantine hums in agreement as his focus returns to his laptop. After his brows furrow, he releases the breath he just sucked in.

"What is it?"

Mindful there are more strangers in my house this morning than there has been the prior ten years, he twists his laptop around to face me so I can unearth my own answer instead of him vocalizing it.

With my ruse back in full swing, a handful of Arabella's school friends arrived for her bachelorette party tonight. Although I'm frustrated by how many people are trampling my personal space, this is only one skit of many I'll be forced to endure while endeavoring to secure Zakhar a new heart. It is by far the least harmful since the festivities are about to move to a hotel not too far from my home base. It is the same hotel I have a meeting at with Maksim Ivanov tomorrow morning, though he may need to postpone if the footage Konstantine is showing me is un-doctored.

Matvei must have gotten word to his older brother. Maksim is as gung-ho for revenge as I was only weeks ago, but he's gunning for immediate blood.

"Has his body been found yet?"

The murderous gleam in Maksim's eyes as he guides Dr. Abdulov down an isolated alleyway tells me everything I need to know. Dr. Abdulov won't leave their exchange breathing.

Days ago, I would have been pleased.

Now I feel the opposite.

Dr. Abdulov was an easy solution to my predicament. I wouldn't have even needed to blackmail him to find Zakhar a new heart. He, and many of his colleagues, work for one thing and one thing only. Profit.

There's only one doctor I haven't been able to lure onto my payroll with a heap of coin. It is the same man I let live because he kept Zoya safe before I took over the role I was born to live.

"Send someone to Dr. Hemway's safe haven."

You have no clue how hard it is to send others to do my bidding. It isn't solely the trust I have to instill that they will represent me in the right manner, but also that it makes it seem as if my contact is more a business endeavor than a personal venture.

This is as personal as it gets—in more ways than one.

"Dr. Hemway?" Konstantine checks, lost.

His bewilderment intensifies when I jerk up my chin. "Dr. Makarand said congenital heart defects are genetic."

"So Zakhar's mother couldn't have been properly vetted by the federation," Konstantine adds, clicking on. "They would have never let her get this far if they knew she had a hereditary condition."

"Exactly," I agree. "Someone fucked up. Most likely on purpose. If we can find out who that is, perhaps we can convince them to tell us who else is willing to do the same."

I glare at him when he mutters, "You'll just need to keep your bullets out of their skulls long enough to get answers when we find them." When the heat of my stare becomes too much for him to bear, he huffs out, "I'm not saying I wouldn't have done the same. Dr. Makarand was getting too big for his britches." His dark eyes flick up. "As is he."

I work my jaw side to side when Dr. Fairmont is greeted in the driveway of my home by Dina. She air kisses his cheeks before gesturing for him to come in.

"This is his third visit this week."

"Fourth," Konstantine corrects. "He dropped off some pamphlets yesterday afternoon."

He clicks on his keyboard a handful of times before bringing up the footage he is referring to. The pamphlets are similar to the ones Dr. Hemway gave Zoya during her last visit, but they're excluding risqué cartoon character art.

Does that mean what I think it does? Was Arabella's first attempt at conception unsuccessful for reasons other than me praying long and fucking hard for a negative outcome?

If so, perhaps I should be paying more attention to my wife than the occasional grunt I've directed at her over the past month.

When my eyes dart from Dr. Fairmont to Dina, the heat of my gaze shifts her focus to me. She startles, as if surprised by my watch, before she bows out of our stare down with a faint smile.

That's unexpected. She usually fights tooth and nail to gain my attention, even more so when someone keeping her daughter in my favor is close by.

The changeup ensures I was wrong to place an extra set of eyes on only my father. Dina deserves her own shadow, and for once, that cast won't be instigated by her daughter.

Konstantine looks up from his laptop when I say, "If Dr. Fairmont so much as gets within a foot of Arabella with a vial of my sperm, take him out."

The federation wants Arabella to be their next First Lady. Their terms state nothing about her birthing an heir. Now that I know why that is, there's no longer any reason for me to continue with that side of my deception. I will find out what happened to my mother, and with Zak's fifth birthday looming, it may be soon.

Konstantine's grin leaps onto my face when he mutters, "It'll be my pleasure."

44

ZOYA

*T*here is no better fix for a broken ego than spoiling someone more defeated than you, but I don't recommend indulging when you're spending money you didn't earn.

For how worked up I was when I left my apartment, I'm shocked to announce that my splurge was a little on the lenient side.

I can't say the same for my guilt.

I spend thousands in mere minutes, and although it is already resulting in my best friend getting a taste of the lavish lifestyle she could live if she'd ever consider placing herself first, I still feel like trash.

I guess that's expected.

Homewreckers aren't known for their graciousness.

Also, since I've had plenty of time to contemplate during our flight across the country, I may have overreacted earlier. Andrik's contract blatantly specified his wish for an heir. Why would it be worded like that if he already has a son? It makes no sense, but I'm out of time to deliberate further since I am begrudgingly following Nikita into the elevator of our hotel.

This is my first elevator ride since that fateful one weeks ago.

The elevator is surprisingly packed for the late hour, though void of anyone who shares the same blood as Andrik.

I scan every face—*twice*—just to be sure.

As I butt shoulders with the lady who hasn't quit eyeballing me for the past seven hours, I slip on the mask I don't plan to remove for a single second over the next four days.

This weekend isn't about me or my stupid ideas of relationships. It is a chance to reacquaint myself with my sister and to make sure my best friend knows there's more to life than endless bills and cruel medical diagnoses.

I plan to be honest, just not until I'm confident my confession won't add more circles to the dark ones rimming Nikita's eyes. Gigi was right. Nikita is one wayward step from burnout, so I need to do anything I can to ensure that doesn't happen.

Nikita is the foundation of our family.

If she topples, we all topple.

After the numerous mistakes I've made over the past six weeks, that's the last thing I need.

"What floor?" asks a woman hogging the elevator panel as if it is made of real gold.

"Shit," Nikita mumbles as she digs into her pocket. "I didn't check the room number the clerk wrote down."

"The ninetieth floor," announces an accented voice from the back of the pack. It is a mix of accents like my mother's, but since it is extremely mannish, my panic remains stagnant.

Nikita can't say the same. When the dark-haired gent I spotted earlier watching Nikita from the Mezzanine floor leans over her to select our floor, goose bumps break across her skin, and the hairs on her nape stand to attention.

I won't tell you what the front of her body does, or you'll no longer believe me when I tell you I have no interest in women.

I wondered earlier if he was the man who had her exiting our flight smelling like a hot hunk of man. Now I am certain.

Tension crackles between the suit-clad stranger and Nikita over the next thirty seconds. It is excruciating and proves that lust is the most potent emotion we own. No amount of muscle can stop two atoms destined to collide. Their collision could create a big bang of energy or fizzle before forcing the shards to move in opposite directions. The impact is inevitable. It is the outcome that scares people the most.

Curious to discover if the stranger is the cause of Nikita's silence, I lean into her side and whisper, "He wants to fuck you." My wording could be better. I just don't have time to pussyfoot around. Our elevator is nearing our floor. I have only mere seconds to play with.

"He did." I assume her tiredness has her muddling up her reply, but she proves otherwise when she adds, "But he doesn't seem interested anymore."

"Because...?" I sound lost. Rightfully so. I am. Nikita is a beautiful, brilliant woman. Any man would be proud to call her his. Unless...

I stop seeking a wedding ring on the stranger's left hand when Nikita sighs heavily. "Because..." Even after an eternity of deliberation, she delivers the worst excuse I've ever heard. "He's a patient's son?"

"And that matters how?"

"Because he... I..."

My head rockets to the side so fast my neck muscles scream in disgust when a voice I'll never forget sounds through my ears. It is more mature than the last time I heard it, though still extremely girlie.

"Zoya?" Worry burns my esophagus when Aleena stares at me in bewilderment. Her mouth is gaping like a fish out of water, and I can only hope the wetness in her eyes is from happiness. "You came?"

I nod, a better response above me.

After what feels like a lifetime, Aleena repeats, "You came!" Her voice is so loud it echoes throughout the elevator she dives into so she can wrap me up in a heart-thawing hug.

I'm not a crier. It takes a lot to make me get teary-eyed, but I'd be a liar if I said my eyes weren't welling with wetness.

She seems happy that I'm here.

Relieved, even.

"I can't believe you came. I didn't think you would. With how late it is, I was certain you weren't coming." She inches back sooner than I'd like. Fortunately for me, it is only to extend an invitation. "We're about to go out dancing. Do you want to come dancing with us?"

"Ah... *Now?* You want to go dancing now?"

Aleena isn't the only one shocked by my motherly tone. She merely hides it better than Nikita. "You don't want to go out? From the stories Mother shared, that is supposedly what you do every weekend."

The sheer innocence in her eyes makes her words not sting as badly as the impact my body prepares for.

"Not every weekend... Just every *second* weekend," I josh.

My joke sails straight over Aleena's head. "Oh." I wonder if she's more like me than her outer shell portrays when she murmurs, "I must have gotten the dates mixed up."

Her bloodshot eyes follow mine to my wrist when I check the time on my invisible watch. I don't want to rain on her parade, but I would barely survive the creeps who come out this late at night, so I refuse to send my baby sister to the wolves unprepared.

"It is too late to go dancing now." When disappointment is the first emotion she showcases, I talk faster. "But I heard rumors DJ Rourke was playing close by this weekend, so I was hopeful we could skip the blisters tonight to ensure we have plenty of gas left in the tank for his show on Saturday."

"You have tickets to a DJ Rourke show?" My question doesn't come from Aleena. It comes from a blonde wearing a bridesmaid sash on her left.

"Uh-huh," I lie. It is only a temporary fib. I'll sell a kidney for tickets if it keeps Aleena looking at me how she is now.

She's grown up so much over the past three years. Her beauty is the perfect combination of sexy and cute. She had a more doll-like appearance on her eighteenth birthday, and the couple of pounds she's added to her svelte frame makes the change-up even more noticeable.

She is so beautiful that I can't help but admire her out loud.

"Do you really think so?" she asks, her voice almost a sob.

"Of course." I back up my pledge with a brisk head bob. "You've always been the most beautiful sister. Everyone says it."

"Because that's what *she* told them to say." It doesn't take a genius to realize who she is referencing when she sneers "she."

"Anything I ever say to you is because I believe it, Aleena." I act as if I can't feel the beady eyes of half a dozen co-riders on me. "It is Mother's praise you need to be wary of. Okay?"

"Okay." The shortness of her reply shouldn't allow it to instigate so much heartache, but it does. It hurts like hell. "Though I'd appreciate if you didn't tell her about this." Her cheeks whiten as a confession spills from her lips. "I wasn't meant to drink. But when I saw you entering the lobby, I got a little nervous, so I rushed back to my room for a nip of courage."

"I think you had more than one nip."

She grimaces before saying, "I think you are right."

When she sways like a crunchy leaf on a deciduous tree at the end of fall, I band my arm around her waist and tug her into my side.

"Not just about how much I drank, but going out too. I don't think we should go dancing. I don't feel very well." Aleena darts her eyes between Shevi and me. "Is this what drinking is meant to feel like?"

Before we can answer her, a burp almost knocks out the five remaining riders in the elevator. She perks back up while everyone around her goes green around the gills.

"Actually, I think I'm okay."

When she stumbles out of the elevator on the top floor, I tighten my grip around her waist and then shoot my eyes to Nikita. She nods in agreement before I can utter a syllable and then helms our slow walk down the corridor to our room.

***

There's no doubt the wetness in Aleena's eyes is from sadness when she watches me pull an oversized college shirt out of the trash bag now housing my clothes. It isn't designer like her clothes and shoes, and it is a stark reminder of how I survived my first two years without a home. Trash bags were once my blankets.

"The baggage handlers got a little dramatic with my luggage. It didn't survive the flight." When my reply pulls her lips a little higher on one side, I continue the honesty route I promised myself I wouldn't start until after this weekend. "The good news is, I got a compensation check that will fund more than a new Frumpy Fran."

"Frumpy Fran?" Since she is well past intoxicated, her words come out slurred. "You still have that?"

"Uh-huh." A nod adds to my reply.

Frumpy Fran was what I called my gym bag during middle school. I can't remember exactly how it started, but it was along the lines of my mother saying that I'd become frumpy if I didn't increase my cardio from an hour a day to three.

"She was a good bag."

"Looks like it," Aleena murmurs through a yawn. Her tiredness is understandable when you realize she spent the past hour bouncing off the walls. "How many hours of cardio do you do per day now?"

I shadow her slow walk to the bedroom I had planned to be mine while answering, "Ah... none."

"None!" Her voice is so loud Shevi and her other bridesmaid I've yet to be introduced to stir. They're hogging one-half of the bed I'm endeavoring to get Aleena in. "How is that possible?"

When she remains staring, demanding an answer, I shrug. "Good genes?"

"Good genes, my ass. I have to work out twice a day to stay fit, for hours each session, and I still don't look like that." After thrusting her hand at me, she crawls across Shevi while mumbling under her breath. "No wonder he looked at you the way he did."

"Who?" I ask, hopeful my daft act will save our exchange from nosediving toward awkward.

Topics of jealousy only ever veer a conversation one way— toward the negative. I've only had an hour of pleasantries. I'm not ready to flip the switch just yet.

Aleena's response is so delayed that just when I think she'll never answer me, she finally does. "The man on the mezzanine."

It takes me a beat, but clarity slowly seeps through the cracks of my exhaustion. "He was looking at Nikita, not me."

"*No...*" Who knew one word could sound like an entire sentence? "Though we will return to how she knows Maksim Ivanov later." She waits for me to nod in agreement before continuing. "I was talking about the man across from him. The one who got so riled up about your stare of another man, he almost blew a gasket." I'm completely lost, so she strives to lessen my confusion. "Dark hair, cropped beard, dreamy eyes."

Her description could describe a million men, but the increase in my pulse during her last feature announces exactly who my thoughts stray to.

I can't deny this, and neither can Aleena.

"Who is he to you?"

"No one," I lie before almost immediately backtracking on it. "If it is who I am thinking, what we had could barely be classified as a fling."

"Had?" she double-checks, as if drinking makes you deaf.

I nod, not willing to lie with words again so soon after my last slip-up.

When she remains quiet, looking perplexed, I pull up the bedding until it sits under her chin like I did when she was little. Once she is as snug as a bug in a rug, I say, "Isn't this weekend meant to be about you?" Her faint smile tugs on my heartstrings before she nods. "Then my idea of fucked-up relationships can wait. Your happiness is far more important."

I tuck her in tight before tiptoeing out of the room like a herd of thunderous elephants could wake her from her drunken drift into sleep.

My world feels complete when my best friend eyeballs the closure of my bedroom door. It finally feels like the pieces of my demented puzzle are coming together as they should have years ago.

"That came many years later than expected, but followed a similar path to what I had envisioned." After filling a glass with a double shot of vodka to settle a handful of nerves the last part of my exchange with Aleena instigated, I spin to face Nikita. "Are you sure you're okay with them staying here with us?"

Her brows furrow as she slowly nods. "I'm sure." She strays her eyes around a living room larger than my apartment. "Are you sure you didn't mix up our key cards with Aleena's? A destination bachelorette party screams old money, and only someone spending their daddy's money could afford this room."

"I'm reasonably sure Aleena's room is on the floor she entered the elevator, but it's hard to get anything out of her when she's a blubbering idiot."

Nikita sees straight through my ruse that Aleena was the only sentimental schmuck during our multiple conversations since our run-in in the elevator.

She smiles at me like it's okay to be happy at Aleena's delighted reaction to my arrival, before saying, "I told you, you had nothing to worry about." After removing my security blanket as of late, she hugs me. "I'm sure she understands why you left." Her words are muffled in my neck, but I get the gist of her reply by the amount of emotion she uses to deliver it. "And if she doesn't, I'm not opposed to convincing her otherwise."

"I love you, Kita."

She inches back and makes an *aww* face. "I love you too." Her hip bump forces me back half a step. "Enough I'm willing to share a bed with you."

I worm my way out of her grip when she drags me toward the bedroom not occupied by my baby sister and her bridesmaids. I'm exhausted, but I am also too wired up to discover if my intuition is right to rest just yet.

Fortunately for me, I have the perfect way out.

"The last time we shared a bed, you humped my leg."

Nikita's mouth gapes open as disgust hardens her features. "That was you!"

I *pfft* her. "Whoever it was, girl-on-girl action isn't on the agenda this weekend."

With a plan devised in under a second, I head for my luggage and remove one of the many gifts I've purchased since I commenced working at Le Rogue. Mars is a vault of information when it comes to sex toys for novices. She helped me find the perfect gifts for Aleena and Nikita.

"And to make sure it stays off, I bought this for you."

A box sails through the air that Nikita catches with the skills of a pro wide receiver.

She shakes it before asking, "What is it?"

"Sleeping pills."

Her confused expression grows as she rattles the box again. "It doesn't sound like sleeping pills."

I roll my eyes before gesturing for her to open her gift.

She does so without pause for thought, and then her cheeks turn the color of beets.

"You bought me a sex toy?" She barely drags in half a breath before releasing it with a ton of words. "How the hell is this supposed to help me sleep?"

"You use it to orgasm yourself into the sexual coma the limp dick on the plane should have placed you in." I move closer, needing less distance to ensure she doesn't try to bullshit her way out of the truth. My lie detector machine doesn't work well from afar. "When was the last time you got a solid eight hours?" I don't give her the chance to lie. "In that little cabin at Kolomna. Demyan had a peanut for a cock but made up for what it lacked with a magic tongue and gifted fingers. I heard your screams from the lake, but I had to wait to tease you about it since you were passed out for eight... whole... hours."

She acts as if a full night's sleep isn't the equivalent of a miracle for her. "I was zonked from the alcohol we drank."

"You never drank when we went out. You didn't want to face the repercussions of underage drinking with your father, and none of the boys we hung out with were stupid enough to give you alcohol. Not if they wanted to live." This is the curse of too much alcohol. I speak before thinking. "I'm an asshole who doesn't dese—"

"You're right," Nikita interrupts, never one to start a fight. "I did wonder what his response would have been, which is exactly why I didn't drink." She holds up the clitoral vibrator. "But I still don't see this helping."

"You won't know unless you try." It sure worked for me. I slept over ten hours the night Andrik snuck into my bed in the middle of the night.

After recalling this room comes with a sofa bed, I remove my "luggage" from the only full sofa in the room before pulling out the made-up bed beneath.

"Look at that, a fancy-schmancy bed solely for me."

Nikita huffs. "Remember those words when you're whining about a sore back in the morning." Her exhausted eyes drift between the sofa bed and me before she asks, "Are you sure you don't want to share a bed with me?" She jingles the sex toy like it's not the cause of the heat on her cheeks. "I could test this out in the bathroom. It seems to be my venue of choice of late."

If I truly believed she'd give up the good stuff she withheld earlier, I wouldn't leave this room for anyone or anything, but since I know she keeps her secrets as well-guarded as her stress levels, I reply, "I'm sure. Sleep well. I'll see you in the morning."

"Okay. I love you."

"I love you too," I reply as she begrudgingly makes her way into the main bedroom of the penthouse suite.

The door barely closes when I race out of our suite. I'm not hunting down Andrik with the hope he will toss me some scraps. It is merely to ensure my side is heard before his father makes out our arrangement is more sinister than it is.

"Is everything okay with your room?" asks the check-in clerk when she spots me milling in the foyer.

"Yeah. Our room is fine, thank you."

She watches me suspiciously when I inch back until I can see most of the second-level mezzanine. I look in the direction where I spotted Maksim over an hour ago before recalling Aleena said the person watching me was opposite him.

My heart thuds wildly when the features Aleena mentioned earlier come into focus a second after peering behind me. A fit body encased in an expensive designer suit, dark locks long enough to run your fingers through them, and soul-piercing blue eyes make up an incredibly appealing package.

They just don't belong to the man who causes my heart to beat in my ears as often as he forces guilt to weigh down my chest.

They belong to his little brother.

45

ANDRIK

*W*hen I detect I am being watched, I stop eyeballing Mikhail guiding Zoya into the lower-level bar of the hotel. It isn't as heated as the glare I issued earlier when I noticed Zoya's arrival in my hometown had caught the attention of numerous men, but it is just as evil.

"Who is she to you?"

I spin away from the floor-to-ceiling two-way mirror of Maksim's office to greet him with a handshake. We've met previously, but this is the first time it is about business.

When Maksim arches a dark brow, conscious I am being purposely coy, I say, "I could ask you the same."

My daggers miss the bullseye when the faintest grin tugs his lips to the side at the same time his nostrils flare.

He wasn't eye-fucking Zoya earlier.

His focus was steadfast on her friend.

How do I know this? He isn't the slightest bit bothered about the visual of Zoya and Mikhail appearing cozy mere feet from his office window. I'm the only one struggling with jealousy.

I wouldn't have sent Mikhail to do my bidding if Maksim hadn't mistaken my arrival at his hotel as me bringing our meeting forward by several hours.

My head would be buried between Zoya's legs.

Unwilling to show more of his hand than he just did, Maksim gestures for me to sit across from him. He is acting courteous because I own the airline Maksim and Zoya flew with this evening, meaning I wasn't solely aware of Zoya's visit to my hometown hours before it occurred, I also know my list of heart surgeons is being minimized each second Maksim exacts revenge.

Maksim killed Dr. Azores mid-flight and then secured my security company's services to doctor the evidence.

I am more than happy to comply with his request, but only after issuing some of my own.

After unbuttoning my suit jacket, I take a seat across from Maksim before getting down to business. "I have names of the people you're seeking. Many of them." When he attempts to interrupt, I speak faster. It pisses him off, but so be it. I have as much, if not more, pull in this town as him. "Your mother didn't end up where she was for no reason. This ruse runs far deeper than Myasnikov Private Hospital's underbelly. To truly make a stance, you need the information my team has unearthed."

I hand him a printout that Konstantine unearthed after a lengthy crawl through the system he hacked into weeks ago. It shows that Maksim's mother is one of many victims. The main target won't be recognized by name. When they mean nothing to you but a means to get off, you don't get their name before leaving a fistful of bills on the nightstand.

Once I'm confident Maksim identifies the face of the woman being carried out of his hotel room clearly inebriated, I place a second photograph over the first.

This one adds a tic to his jaw.

The whore who kept his sheets warm for a night looks starkly different on an autopsy table.

"They took all her organs, including her eyes."

Maksim tosses down the images before leaning back in his chair. "Are these supposed to rattle me?"

"No," I reply, being honest. "But it is a little hypocritical to make it seem as if you're taking down an industry you apparently commenced."

He looks like he wants to slit my throat.

Good. It means he's now paying attention.

"Someone in your operation is working with the federation." His squint announces he's heard of the federation, but his lack of worry shows he's underestimating their potential. "There are numerous paper trails leading back to Ivanov Industries. Including the sale of your mother's organs."

"What benefit would I get from killing my mother?" He sounds like he wants to murder me just for the insinuation, and it adds another point to my tally.

"From the rumors circulating, to reach the top tier of the Fernandezes' ladder."

When my hand digs into my soft leather briefcase for more evidence, Maksim growls out, "Tread carefully, Kazimir. Very *fucking* carefully."

I give him as much information as I can about organ sales on the black market without putting up the roadblocks I did weeks ago when I contacted Matvei.

It places me in Maksim's favor, though not enough for him not to add his own stipulations to our verbal agreement.

"I will consider holding off on certain regions if you give me the names of everyone in the Myasnikov Private ring."

I almost lecture him on how no business should be ran on "ifs," but hold my tongue when I recall his willingness to bend protocols for me is better than any outcome I could have anticipated.

"I'll see what I can do."

"No." His headshake is as arrogant as the balling of his hand when he places it on his desk in clear warning that his patience is wearing thin. "I want them *now*."

Something in his eyes tells me this is as personal as it gets for him as well, but not all of it centers around his mother's recent hospital admission.

Knowledge that the changeup could swing the needle in my favor permanently sees me offering him a rare snippet of leniency. "Tell me the name you want me to exclude, and I'll have my man run it through the list."

His reply isn't as immediate this time around, but it is brimming with angst. "Nikita Hoffman. *Dr.* Nikita Hoffman."

"Running it now," Konstantine announces, talking through the earpiece I've rarely been without over the past two weeks.

His fingers stroke the keyboard a handful of times before he cusses.

Mercifully, he isn't a man I need to pry answers out of.

"She's on the list, but you may not want to announce that."

I pretend I can't feel Maksim's beady eyes on me. "Why?"

"Because Maksim isn't the only one fond of the Good Doctor. So is your girl."

When my phone dings, I remove it from my pocket and then mimic Konstantine's expletive. The image he forwarded is grainy. It represents what I was staring at earlier. Zoya standing next to a brunette woman at the check-in counter of Maksim's hotel.

Even if I hadn't seen her in the multiple surveillance updates Konstantine compiled on Zoya's trek across the country, the image makes it obvious that they're close.

After a deliberation not long enough to truly determine where my loyalties should lie, and a quick scroll through the information Konstantine forwarded about Dr. Hoffman, I lock eyes with Maksim and say, "She is on the list. But..." I've never seen a man more desperate for an out than the one sitting across from me. "Something seems off with her inclusion." My gut announces this... and perhaps the orifice in my chest I thought would never return to is pre-black sludge days.

Maksim appears seconds from demanding answers by the removal of fingers, but I realize I'm not the only one with a bead-like device in my ear when he slants his head for the quickest second before he wraps up our meeting with a quick-worded snap. "I need to take this." When I don't immediately jump to the command in his tone, he adds, "In private."

Since the interruption occurs at the same time I spot Mikhail walking Zoya to the hotel's elevators, I nod in understanding before exiting his office.

Konstantine's deep timbre rumbles through my earpiece two seconds later. "We got someone piggybacking off our feed. Want me to force them out?"

I stray my eyes to Maksim's office for the quickest second before shaking my head. He's so immersed in watching whatever is playing on his laptop that it will take his hacker longer to realize Konstantine is returning the favor than learning our system isn't the one he should be infiltrating.

If his crew wants information, they need to immerse themselves deep in the federation's bowels.

"Are you sure?" Konstantine asks, obviously having eyes on me since I didn't vocalize my reply.

"No," I answer, once again taking the honesty route. "But you should be used to that by now, right?"

I steal his chance to reply by removing the bead from my ear, dropping it to the ground, and then crushing it under my shoe with the first step I take in Mikhail's direction.

Another battle is in my sights, and it is far more appealing.

I just need to settle my brother's confusion first.

Mikhail looks set to unload a lengthy interrogation on me, but since I have far better ways to occupy my time while Zakhar sleeps, I butt in. "Why is she here?"

I assumed Zoya was in this part of the Trudny District for me. She has the gall to put any man in his place—even one as cocky as me. I was proven wrong when her taxi veered west upon exiting the airport instead of south.

Although Zoya is the best person for me to seek answers from, once again, I have better ways to occupy the time I didn't know I desperately needed until I saw her in the flesh for the first time in weeks.

"She wouldn't say," Mikhail discloses, tightening my jaw. "But she seemed genuinely surprised to see me here, so I doubt she knew this is your home turf until I told her." His chuckle pisses me off, though not as much as what he says next. "She wanted me to tell you that she is only here for three nights, and that she will stay out of your hair if you agree to do the same." The remainder of his reply matches the thoughts in my head. "I told her there was a fat chance of that happening but I'd pass on the message."

He looks like he wants to say more, but when several seconds pass in silence, I ask, "Did she mention Zak?"

He shifts from foot to foot before scrubbing at the stubble on his chin. "No. Which seems a little odd."

I don't agree with him. Zoya is loyal to a fault. She's had plenty of opportunities over the past several weeks to air my dirty laundry for the world to see, but she hasn't told a soul.

Not even her best friend knows about us.

My tight jaw firms more when Mikhail asks, "Do you know Dad tried to bribe her to stay away from us?"

I almost say, "From me," but my focus shifts elsewhere when the side profile of a guest sliding out of a blacked-out SUV near the valet registers as familiar. You can't miss the large scar along one side of his jaw.

His name hogs the number one spot on the hitlist I handed Maksim earlier, so why the fuck is he walking into this hotel like there isn't a bounty on his head?

A hundred theories run through my head. Only one is legitimate. He's here because whatever he is seeking is far more important than his life. That can only mean one thing.

He's here on the federation's behalf.

Fuck.

Maksim's glare is the strongest to date when I enter his office without knocking. I don't know the identity of the woman who moans his name a second before he slams down his laptop screen, but it keeps his eyes off the prize long enough for the hired goon in the lobby to peer in our direction. His eyes widen to the size of saucers when he spots my watch before he sprints for the exit faster than Maksim can advise his security team to stop him.

46

ZOYA

I lied when I said there is no better fix for a broken ego than spoiling someone more defeated than you. Meddling in their blossoming love life is far more cathartic.

Even Aleena agrees.

She hasn't stopped snooping for information on Nikita's connection with Maksim Ivanov all morning. She seems more interested in their coupling than her upcoming nuptials. I'd be worried if it didn't make her so happy. She's as obsessed with scheming as I am, and it reminds me that we're more alike than our mother will ever admit.

The hype is also keeping my focus off my disappointment that Andrik sent his brother to do his bidding last night. Mikhail didn't hide the fact that Andrik was in the building with us. He joked that I should take the service elevator to force him out of hiding, undermining my determination to unearth Zakhar's relationship to Andrik with lust.

I've never felt more disappointed with myself.

Fortunately for me, my confidence is about to be slathered with a ton of compliments all bikini competition contestants sign up for.

"Here she comes," announces Aleena, drawing me from my thoughts.

Nikita is hot on the tail of Shevi, Aleena's chief bridesmaid, wearing the bikini we conned her into only minutes ago when she thought we were going for a swim.

She didn't see the brilliance in Aleena's plan as readily as I did.

I wait to hear the click of a lock sliding into place before pulling my best shocked expression. "Oh no. You left our room in only a bikini, and our key card is still inside. Whatever will we do?"

Shevi steps back with her hands in the air, mumbling her innocence when Nikita shoots daggers at her. She can pull off the preacher's daughter's look.

Aleena and I aren't so lucky.

Nikita sniffs out our wickedness in under a second.

"This isn't funny. We're not freshmen anymore. Let me back into our room."

I act as if there isn't an ounce of angst in her words. "I would if I could, but I can't."

"Zoya..." The shortness of her reply announces her lie detector machine is in full operation. We're well past busted, but since this is far more fun than sulking, I continue my ruse.

Aleena's giggles make my heart beat faster when Nikita pats me down like bags of cocaine are strapped to my chest instead of the prize money I am hoping will make up the deficit I caused to Ellis's bribe yesterday.

When her search comes up empty-handed, I add words to the silent acknowledgement hardening her features. "I honestly don't have it."

Since my tone is honest, she shifts her focus to my accomplices.

"Don't look at me," Aleena blurts out, her face as guilty now as it was when we ate a week's worth of chocolate in one sitting.

We had a stomachache for days on end, but the snippet of rebellion it fired in her eyes made it so worthwhile. It was the first time I truly believed she would one day get out from under our mother's reign.

"I only asked if we could host part of the bachelorette party here. I didn't demand unlimited access."

With Aleena's brow full of sweat, I jump back into the conversation before our ruse is busted. A room key card is an easy thing to hide when you have E cups, but since I knew that would be the first place Nikita would look, Aleena stuffed it between her almost as generous breasts.

"Oh poo. I guess that means we'll have to go down to the foyer and ask for another key."

I can't hide my smile when Nikita grumbles, "The foyer wouldn't happen to be next to the bikini competition area, would it?"

"No," I reply, *pffting*. "But the registration desk for the bikini competition is right next door."

As I hit the button to call the elevator to our floor, Nikita folds her arms over her chest and murmurs, "I'll wait for you here."

I enter the elevator, calling out her bluff with the confidence only a best friend can have. "Okay. But if my hand ends up down a billionaire's pants, I won't be held accountable for my actions."

It dawns on me that I was a little light with the information I shared with Aleena while ruminating on our plan when she shouts, "You put your hand down Maksim Ivanov's pants?"

"No," Nikita denies, her voice barely a whisper. "He put my hand down there."

"Get in. *Now!*"

Aleena doesn't give her a chance to back out again. She pulls her into the elevator by the strap of her bikini bottoms, cracking the air with as much energy as the surge racing through my veins.

A bikini competition is a great way to force Maksim to stop

playing games, but I'd be a liar if I said I haven't wondered if it will coerce the same response from another hot-blooded Russian.

Nikita chickened out of the bikini competition, but Aleena has more than enough excitement to keep up the hype. I forget stuff like this isn't the norm for her. That having fun with your girlfriends, drinking like a sailor on shore leave, and being seen as an object of desire for reasons beyond your fertility status weren't meant to be a part of any stage of our lives.

We were raised to act a certain way. Told how to behave, speak, and eat. Etiquette classes never included prancing around in a two-piece string bikini.

The remembrance sees me wolf whistling like I work on a construction crew when Aleena and Shevi work the stage like they were destined for stardom.

If Aleena's husband-to-be thinks he's getting a demure wife, he's about to be taught a hard lesson.

Demure will no longer be associated with Sakharoff women. Aleena's strut assures this, and my upcoming prance will seal the deal.

After high-fiving Aleena on the way by, I burst onto the stage with more gall than I had only two nights ago. The crowd goes crazy, and I eat up the attention. Their catcalls and whistles pull my confidence out of the trench it's been milling in the past few days, surging it to an almost unmanageable level.

I'm having so much fun it takes several prolonged beats to recognize one of the many faces reflecting at me from the crowd. I can't blame alcohol for the sluggish response. My veins are vodka-free. It is the fact that I've sat across from him only once before. Our exchange lasted as long as it took for me to drive him to the other side of town. It was also six years ago. Right around Aleena's sixteenth birthday.

Does Aleena know Bayli is here?

Is he the cause of the extra spring in her step when she leaped off the stage?

Bayli's expression doesn't give anything away. He looks more confused than pleased. But unlike hundreds of men in the audience, his eyes aren't fixated on my chest. He's staring at the curtains Aleena raced through only a minute ago, wide-eyed and baffled.

I'm so eager to learn if Aleena saw her ex in the crowd that I don't realize the hurricane zooming in on me until it is too late. Faster than I can blink, my elbow is seized in a firm grip a second after my foot leaves the stage, and I'm walked out of the backstage area filled with competitors.

I don't need to look up to know whose ugly green head has reared. The zap his meekest touch surged through my body is all the indication I need to know who is accosting me, so I won't mention his numerous mutterings about my body count never reaching six.

Only one clear line of verbiage makes it through the gibberish. "Cover me until I get back." Andrik's grip tightens on my arm before he shouts, "I don't give a fuck what Maksim wants. Cover for me."

After he removes a bead-like device from his ear and crushes it under his polished boot, he stares down at me. His haughty expression displays that Maksim's orders will never triumph his wish to punish me.

I wasn't with a man, but my bikini leaves nothing to the imagination. To a man as dominant and possessive as Andrik, that's practically the same thing.

That doesn't mean I'll let him boss me around, though.

"Let me go. You're hurting me," I lie.

His firm grip on my arm isn't painful. It incites lust so potent that I get drunk off it, and it seems I am not the only one noticing this.

Andrik's nostrils flare as his pace increases.

"I swear to God, Andrik, if you don't let me go this instant, the first place I'll visit when I return to Myasnikov is your overcompensating country estate."

One second I'm being pulled into a poolside cabana.

The next I'm being bent over a double sun lounger and spanked.

"I swear to fucking God, *Лисичка*," Andrik parrots, mimicking my threat, "I don't care if I have an entire kingdom coming after me —if you ever walk around how you are now, I will kill every man stupid enough to look."

The thinness of my bikini does little to cool the fiery burn that spreads across my left butt cheek when he spanks me another three times.

"If you don't believe me, ask the dancers at Le Rogue why their tips were sliced in half last night."

"*If?*" I mock, too stubborn for my own good. "What happened to... *there are no ifs*?"

Despite my best efforts, my last four words come out as moans. They can't be helped. He doesn't just spank my ass when I get sassy. He also spanks my pussy.

Heat hums through my veins when his fingertips hover over the opening of my vagina after its fifth spank. I'm wet and my clit is throbbing so unashamedly there's no way Andrik can mistake how horny his punishment has made me.

I rise, attempting to free myself from the madness.

My inability to follow orders unleashes a beast. Andrik rakes his fingers up my nape and through my hair before he makes a fist.

One tug on my glossy locks steals my smarts in half a heartbeat, so I won't mention how clouded my head becomes when he does another dozen while grinding his thick cock against my ass.

He's hard as a steel rod. I don't get to relish it. As quickly as he pressed against me, he inches back to marvel at the mess he made.

I'm drenched enough to shadow my bikini bottoms, and Andrik doubles their clinginess by spinning me around, spreading my thighs wide, and then dragging his nose down the thin strip outlining the lines of my pussy.

A moan vibrates my lips when he huskily says, "I've missed that smell." He hooks his finger under the edge of my bikini before carefully peeling it back. "But not as much as I've missed your taste."

"Andrik..." I sound desperate. Rightfully so. I am.

I want him to touch me. *Everywhere.*

And he picks the perfect place to start.

He drags his tongue up the seam of my pussy, his pace leisurely. *Ohh...*

I vocalize my moan when his tongue rolls over my clit, doubling the shake of my thighs. He sucks the nervy bud into his mouth before flicking it over and over again.

And I love it.

Lick after lick, thrust after thrust, he throws my body into chaos until the pounding of my blood through my veins overtakes the moans ripping from my mouth.

He fucks me with his mouth until I come undone.

As I arch my back, embracing the orgasm scorching through me, Andrik continues to tongue my clit. He doesn't care that there are hundreds of people mere feet from us or that we could be busted at any moment. He consumes me as if my pleasure is the only thing on his agenda today, sparking a guarantee of back-to-back orgasms.

Pleasure ripples through me as I rake my fingers through his hair to hold his mouth hostage to my pussy. My cruel tugs quicken his pace. He licks me faster before lowering a hand between my legs so he can give my pussy something to milk while my body ripples through an intense climax.

He pumps his fingers in and out of me while he stimulates my clit with his tongue, his teeth, and the tip of his nose. I try to choke back the moans rumbling up my throat, but his talents are too wondrous to ignore.

I moan his name with no care of who may hear it, and it drives Andrik wild.

As he stuffs his fingers in and out of me, he slides his eyes up to my face. I shudder under the intensity of his watch. The anger blistering from his narrowed gaze earlier is nowhere to be seen. There's nothing but lust and admiration. And perhaps love.

My breath catches before my body goes lax. With bucking hips and the cry of a warrior, I orgasm again. It is long and tiring but mindboggling good.

I'm so out of it that the creak of the sun lounger under our combined weight is the first hint that our exchange is going further than it has in weeks. The head of Andrik's cock rubbing against the cleft of my pussy is a close second.

He rubs his fat cock up and down, coating himself in my arousal, before he commences notching in the girthy head.

"Stop," I murmur, rediscovering my voice.

I'm not ending this as per the concerned look stretching across Andrik's deliriously handsome face as he glances down at me in shock. I am endeavoring to make sure no child is forced down the fatherless route Aleena and I endured during our childhood because our mother was in love with a married man.

"We need a condom."

With a smirk that has me on the verge of climaxing again, Andrik shakes his head before he stuffs several inches of his big cock inside me. He doesn't take me to the root, though the several inches he feeds inside feel fantastic.

As he flexes his cock, spiraling my mind more, he murmurs, "No, we don't."

"But... I started fertility medication." I thrust my head side to side, slowing the roar of ecstasy surging through my body. "I could get pregnant. It is unlikely, but it is still a possibility."

He cuts me off with a groan. "I. Don't. Care."

"You may not, but I do."

I whimper desperately when he slowly pulls out. My pussy sucks at him, coercing him to stay like I'm not demanding the immediate removal of his cock until it is sheathed by a condom.

"That feels *so* good."

With one hand, he tilts my hips high while the other presses low on my stomach. "Because there's nothing between us."

I throw my head back and moan when he rams back in deep.

I'm so full, but it feels amazing.

"There will *never* be anything between us again."

He jerks his hips upward, brushing the head of his cock against my G-spot. My body wrenches with every perfect grind.

"Not a condom."

Another body-tingling thrust that bounces my breasts out of my bikini top.

"Not an organization."

Stars blur my vision as the truth in his eyes crests the wave in my stomach.

"Not a wife." My eyes threaten to burst along with my heart when he grunts out, "*Nothing* will ever come between us again. I promise you that."

I slam my eyes shut as he nails me to the sun lounger with frantic pumps to ensure none of my tears escape. I'll never forgive myself if I get emotional during sex.

Andrik coerces my focus back to him with a teasing roll of his thumb over my clit. He toys with the hardened bud while warping my mind with measured pumps of his thick cock.

His endeavor to unravel me is relentless. He takes everything I'm willing to give, and then some. He claims me. Dominates me. He makes me his.

Then, not long after I've surrendered to the fact that no one will ever have me like this again, I lose all sense of control.

I can't stop coming. It isn't back-to-back-to-back orgasms. It is one continuous climax that pulls Andrik into the madness with me.

He fucks me rougher. Harder. More aggressively, until he fully rams inside me and then groans through the release of his hot cum spurting against the walls of my pussy.

47

ANDRIK

*I*t's been clear from the start that I don't have the ability to deny my every want when Zoya is in front of me. She reminded me that I had a heart before Zakhar's condition encouraged me to utilize it.

She's an asset I never saw coming and a conquest I'll never stop rejoicing, but I won't have her at all if I don't fix the mistakes I've made.

The hope in her eyes when I promised not to let anything come between us again... *fuck*.

It cut me like a knife.

My decisions are hurting her, and for what reason? The federation wants me to fall in line. Who better to help me do that than the hellion I crave more than air?

It will be harder to protect her when they learn of the wealth she offers my life, but that'll be easier to achieve since I will no longer have to hide her away.

I also dare them to try. They felt my wrath when I was blindsided by Zakhar's lineage. That won't be one tenth of the hell I'll rain down on them if they try to hurt Zoya.

Mikhail leaves one of the bars dotted around the aquatic wonderland petty criminals were planning to use as their playground when he spots me exiting the pool cabana I dragged Zoya into hours ago.

We didn't spend the entire time fucking. We talked, and I ate—again. It was the most delicious palette I've ever sampled, but it left Zoya so zonked that my numerous attempts to wake her were fraudulent.

Her exhaustion means I have to leave her in Mikhail's care again. The torment isn't as bad since I know it will be short-lived.

"Maksim was pissed as fuck that you left your station mid-stake-out," Mikhail murmurs, his drawl similar to the one he used numerous times during our childhood when he was starting trouble. "But I reckon he might be thanking you now." He grins when I stare at him with a cocked brow. "Konstantine will explain on the way." He tosses me a set of keys and a new listening device before he heads for the cabana I just left.

"Mikhail..."

He doesn't turn around as my stern grumble demands, but he does give me the answer I'm seeking. "I'll leave your note this time. I promise."

Mindful he doesn't hand out promises like candy on Halloween, I tell him I will return shortly, before heading for my sports car parked out front after a brief stop at the giftshop.

The streets are packed, but the joys of owning a high-powered prototype is that you can get anywhere fast. Not as fast as my helicopter, though the rush is almost as blood pumping.

Though I doubt anything will match the rush of euphoria I experience anytime Zoya is quivering beneath me.

Anoushka greets me in the foyer when I enter my home. Since it is warm out, I'm not wearing a coat, so she removes a soft leather briefcase from my grasp and stores it in the coat closet.

"Zakhar?"

One name and her face lights up with fondness. "He is well... *considering.*" She closes the coat room door and then spins to face me to slacken the groove between my brows with words. "He hasn't stopped asking for you all morning. There were numerous comments about a promised treat."

Her smile is as bright as the low-hanging sun when I jingle the chocolates I purchased from the hotel giftshop on the way out. They're dark and filled with creams only old ladies love, but when you've been deprived of sweets most of your life, you don't care how bad they taste. You devour every piece.

"I better refill his *vodka* before waking him. We don't want him up all night with a tummy ache."

Concern colors my tone. "He's asleep?"

When she nods, I check the time. It is late enough in the afternoon to serve supper.

Anoushka's reply weakens the guilt weighing heavily on my shoulders. "He heard you sneak out and refused to settle until an hour ago. He is in good spirits." Her kind eyes say the words my mouth refuses to speak. *If only good spirits could fix his heart.* "Would you like me to wake him now?"

I almost nod, but I can't pledge to stop being selfish only to break it hours later. So instead, I shake my head. "Let him sleep. We will have plenty of time for sweets when he gets a new heart."

There are no ifs or buts when it comes to the last part of my statement.

Zakhar will get a new heart. I will make sure of it.

"Okay." Anoushka rubs my arms in a motherly manner. "I'll be in the den if you need me."

She's halfway there when I ask, "Is Konstantine here?"

Her gesture mimics the one I made moments ago. "He hasn't been back since this morning. Would you like me to reach out to him?"

I take a moment to deliberate before replying, "No. I can handle this."

I also don't want any witnesses. The last thing I need now is my crew thinking I am a spineless leech.

Anoushka's smile is a little more hesitant this time. I understand why when I crank my neck in the direction of her gaze. A long fleet of SUVs are rolling down my driveway. The one in the middle of the pack is flagged.

"Move Zakhar into my room."

While she does that, I call Konstantine.

"She's still asleep," he murmurs through a yawn, not bothering to issue a greeting. "And shockingly, Mikhail is stationed *outside* her cabana."

I sigh in relief before getting down to the reason for my call. "I'm getting an unexpected visit from my grandfather. Is there any chatter on what it could be about?"

Maksim and I commenced plans to take the federation down in a joint operation that will strengthen his crew as much as it will mine, but it is in the preliminary stages. We have multiple lower-valued affiliates we need to coerce under our reign before we can go after the big dogs.

My agreeance was sealed after Maksim promised to keep the black-market organ sales on this side of the country in operation until Zakhar receives a new heart.

Konstantine's fingers fly over his keyboard before he says, "Zakhar's DNA test results are back." He tells me what I already know. "He is your son."

I nod like he can see me.

Knowing Konstantine, he probably can.

"Did Zak's sample match with anyone already in the federation's system?" I talk as fast as the secret service scan my manicured lawns, seeking any dangers lurking in the bushes, unaware I'm the biggest threat to my grandfather's reign.

Another handful of keystrokes before a whoosh sounds down the line. "No. But that's not surprising considering what we know." Konstantine is great at staying one step ahead of our enemies. "I'll commence my own search shortly. For now, where do you want me?"

My eyes flick to the hallway Zakhar's room is located in before they lower to the floor. The person I'm endeavoring to protect as fiercely as my son isn't in the basement. Her ex is since I still haven't had a second to breathe unmonitored.

"Here. Mikhail won't let anything happen to Zoya." That kills me to say, though it is honest. Mikhail protects Zoya like she is the sister he never had the chance to meet.

Konstantine hums in agreement before telling me he's on his way. "Daniil drives like shit, but his foot never touches the brakes."

The smirk his commentary caused slips when my grandfather's demanding voice booms through the entryway of my home. This isn't the first time he's visited me, but he's never displayed glee when he's walked through my oversized front door.

He approaches me with the walk of a nobleman before fanning out his arms. With an inward sigh, I step into his embrace before kissing both his cheeks.

I refuse to acknowledge the hand he holds out.

Hell will freeze over before I will ever kiss the family crest on his pinky finger ring. It isn't the exact design as the one the man I killed weeks ago was wearing, though it still grates on my last nerve. How can you shade your family name with so much controversy but wear its emblem with pride?

"Andrik." He inches back and smiles widely. "I never thought I'd see the day. A great-grandson from my favorite grandson." His eyes are full of fake elation. Even when we followed his rules to the wire, he's never treated us with respect. He rules with an iron fist, and Mikhail and I have been subjected to its fury on more than one occasion. "So, where is the boy?"

When he scans the palatial floors of the living area, I realize he is unaware of Zakhar's condition.

How can that be? He is the federation's number one puppet.

I put my game face on with only a second to spare. My responses aren't being scrutinized solely by my blood. My grandfather has arrived with numerous strangers. There is only one face I recognize in his posse. Kolya, his chief of staff.

"Zakhar is getting ready for supper. He will be down shortly." I gesture my hand to the den. "Until then, shall we have something to drink?"

My grandfather is in his eighties, but he loves a stiff drink as much as every other Russian man. He nods before dismissing the men surrounding him with an arrogant flick of his wrist.

"You, too, Kolya."

Kolya almost argues but thinks better of it when he is subjected to my grandfather's deep rumble. It is a clear sign that he has reached his limit of disrespect.

I wait for him to be seated before showing him my selection for our pre-supper splurge. His eyes drop to the label for the quickest second before he jerks up his chin in approval.

Pricy vodka slips over the rim of a crystal glass when he says, "I wasn't sure if you would be in. Your movements were last placed at a hotel not too far from here."

I don't need to turn around to know the cause of the slap that hits the coffee table. It makes the same noise as the files I used to bribe Dr. Hemway.

"I can understand your fascination, Andrik, but your father has done enough damage to our family name. I can't have you adding more."

I wet my suddenly dry lips before twisting to face him like I've not been endeavoring to keep my relationship with Zoya under wraps for the past eight weeks.

As suspected, a manilla folder sits on my coffee table. Its slide exposes numerous surveillance images of Zoya and me. The top of the stack is me dragging Zoya out of the backstage area of the bikini competition.

There's disappointment in his tone when he says, "Your wife has undergone in-vitro fertilization—"

"Which has been unsuccessful," I interrupt, like Arabella's failings aren't my fault. "Hence me looking elsewhere." I hand him his vodka, then sit across from him. "I did not know of Zakhar's existence at the time, so I still believed time wasn't in my favor."

He nods as if he believes my lies before sipping on his drink. Once his mouth is tingling with the effects of alcohol, he scrapes his rheumy hand across his lips.

"If your wife is not with child, now is the ideal time for you to choose who you want to move forward with your plans. We cannot have another incident like the one we had with your mother. The public wants a love story, not..."—he rolls his hand through the air like he can't think of the word before he eventually settles on— "pornography."

I stare at him in disbelief. He's making it seem as if I can choose whom I wish to marry. That it isn't the federation's choice.

With my surprise too high for me to discount, I blurt out, "Zoya has not been vetted by the federation."

Air whizzes from his nose. "And yet you continue to place her above your wife." His eyes flick up like he knows which room is Zakhar's. "And perhaps even your son. I would say the vetting has already been done."

I want to call him a liar before spitting at his feet, but I can't. I put Zakhar's life at risk because I couldn't stand the thought of anyone seeing Zoya in a bikini. I fucked up, though I honestly can't say I wouldn't do it again if placed in the same predicament. It makes me a horrible father, but cut me some slack. I was thrust into fatherhood without the months of lead-up most men get. I'm still learning. I will make mistakes, just not all of them will be unfixable.

My grandfather freezes with his glass halfway to his lips when I say, "Zakhar is sick. He needs a new heart." My jaw tightens to the point of cracking. "A heart he is being denied because I am choosing love over a political campaigner's idea of an ideal First Lady."

"No," he denies. "They want you to wed. They don't care to whom. Women can be trained to be anything. Your mother—"

"Was forced out because she reached her expiration date."

I'm not the only one shocked by my outburst. I am usually more controlled. As in command as my grandfather when he ends our conversation with the dignity of a political powerhouse. "You have much to learn. I look forward to teaching you." He stands before signaling for Anoushka to fetch his coat. "But not until Zakhar can learn the same lessons."

When he holds out his arms again, I'm not as stingy with my farewell as I was with my greeting. His reply is a roundabout way of saying Zakhar will get the help he needs because he will make sure of it.

While returning my cheek kiss, he whispers in my ear, "Marry who you want but make your decision now. I will not allow our legacy to continue being stained with matrimonial travesties." He inches back before saying a quote I haven't heard in decades. "When you make a promise, you keep it. Don't you, Andrik?"

48

ZOYA

My body is already relishing in the delight of multiple orgasms, but my heart experiences a similar sort of sensation when my eyes slowly flutter open. I'm still on the double sun lounger, but instead of a bikini caressing my skin, a velvet blanket is keeping me warm from the elements, and there is a large glass of orange juice on the side table.

This time, it comes with a note.

I didn't have enough time to answer all the whims you hit me with during your almost comatose state, so I let you sleep. You won't be so lucky tonight.
Wait up for me.
A xx

I grin like a loon while popping two of the pain medication tablets into my palm and swallowing them with the orange juice.

I'm in such a state of euphoria, my heart believes Andrik ordered pulp-less juice this time around because he knows how much I hate the ghastly chunks sliding down my throat. It makes the juice so much more refreshing, and I polish off the entire glass without coming up for air.

Today was magical.

It started with jealousy, and it ended with a heap of mutual understanding and respect.

Zakhar is Andrik's son, but he was as blindsided by his existence as I was when I called Mikhail to demand he speak with his father.

I wish I could say I don't understand how hard that confession hit Andrik. Having a child in the world and not knowing of their existence is a torment no person should endure, let alone someone who will remain childless.

I'm pulled from the dark thoughts of my past when shouted voices break through the cabana walls. I recognize them both, though I wish I only knew one. Mikhail is arguing with his father, and since it sounds like their voices are projecting from right outside the cabana's entrance, I think I know why.

It is cowardly of me to dress in the clothes Andrik left with his note and orange juice and sneak out, but this weekend isn't meant to be about me. I'm in the Trudny District for my baby sister and my best friend. It is time for me to stop being selfish.

I'm so riddled with guilt that I enter a warzone unprepared. Nikita took a walk on the wild side, and I missed her metamorphosis.

"Zoya!" Nikita staggers across a cabana that reminds me of the pool parties we attended in college before she wraps me up in a tight hug. "Where have you been? You missed the celebration." I'm tempted to pinch myself to make sure I'm not dreaming when she stomps her foot. I haven't seen her act this carefree since... forever. "You won! You got twenty big ones." I step back when she looks seconds from barfing. Mikhail isn't the only sympathy vomiter I know. "Well, more like ten after I borrow a tiny bit to fix that." She gestures to something behind me. "They didn't have long, but they almost drank the bar dry. They won't tell me the final tally, but I can't leave all that mess to Maksim's family. Especially because I was acting like a jealous twit. He deserved it, though. He's being weird." She waves her hand across her face, collecting the spit she releases when she *pffts*. "Anyway, you won!"

"Wow." I wish I could give a more enthusiastic response, but my emotions are too askew to offer up more. I feel like I'm in a dream and that if I move too fast, I'll be jolted out of a fantasy better than any reality I've faced.

"Who are you, and what did you do with"—holy mother of God. I didn't know you could be forced out of sobriety by a burp—"my best friend? You sound like Aleena when I reminded her that her wedding is only a few short weeks away." Her sigh hits me with a second bout of alcoholism. "She's not giving off blushing virginal bride vibes tonight."

From the stories Bayli shared during our drive home years ago, pure white shouldn't be Aleena's wedding dress color of choice.

"Where is she?"

"Um..." Nikita drags her eyes over the crowd of mostly women before pointing to the corner. "There." We cringe in sync when her bloodshot eyes announce the level of her intoxication. She is even more gone than Nikita. That is understandable. Aleena is a cheap drunk because this weekend is the first time she's been allowed to drink.

"She's pretty wasted." Nikita huffs out a laugh. "We're all pretty wasted." As she wipes at the bead of sweat on her top lip, she says, "I don't think the eggs in the brownies were fresh. I've been feeling a little off since I ate them."

I take a moment to assess her as if she is a patient and I'm her doctor.

All appraisals point in the same direction.

"Are you high?"

"No. I don't think." Her eyes widen enough to give credit to my theory. "Do I look high?"

"Yeah, you do."

The world tilted more on its axis than I realized during my brief intermission.

Well, I really shouldn't say brief. Countless orgasms and hours of sex will never be considered brief.

"And you smell like a brewery."

"That would be my fault." A man with surfy blond locks leans against a solid wall of the cabana before greeting me with a wave.

Nikita beams with excitement before she drags the stranger inside the littered cabana. Once he's in front of me, she introduces us. "Zoya, this is Riccardo. Riccardo, this is my deliciously gorgeous friend Zoya."

She should never give up her day job. She is the worst match-maker I've ever met. Not only does Riccardo give off creeper vibes, but also, not all of them are directed at me.

He's eyeing Nikita with just as much interest.

With my brain too fogged by a lust haze, I give the oldest excuse in the book. "I'm not looking for anything permanent right now."

"Good, because from what I can tell, neither is Riccardo."

When Nikita slaps her hand over her mouth, the situation shifts to awkward at a record-setting pace.

"I'm sorry for asking you to come back after your shift," Nikita murmurs to Riccardo two seconds later, finally clicking on that I'm not interested. "I could have sworn you were her type." She hugs Riccardo like it's a consolation prize for an almost win. His response assures me he believes the same. "Are you sure there's nothing?" she asks me while fawning over Riccardo's pecs. "Maybe you should feel his chest. It is all rigid and tanned, with only the slightest smattering of dark hairs."

She's more intoxicated than first believed.

Riccardo's chest is whiter than snow.

"I think it's time to call it a night."

"No." Nikita stomps from foot to foot like a child busting to use the bathroom. "It's still early. The sun hasn't even gone to bed yet, so I don't want to either."

"Kita—"

"Please, Z. I promise I'll be good."

I will never be strong enough to deny her every want. She was there for me when I thought I had nothing to live for, so I'll never ignore her puppy dog eyes.

Furthermore, Andrik's note made it seem as if he will be gone for a couple of hours, so why not have some fun with my girlfriends until then?

"How many bottles can you fit under your..." I don't know how I missed the monstrosity she's wearing. It is frumpy and hideous. "What even is this?"

"It is the ugly coverup Maksim told me I had to wear." She plops onto a sofa and cradles her head in her hands. "He didn't like that my ass was showing. Well, he didn't actually say that. Aleena just thinks that is what he meant. He's so confusing. *I want to see you come. You won't leave my fucking head.* Then, the next minute, he pushes me away. I just wish he'd give me a straight answer like you did Riccardo. Not... fucking... interested." Regret darts through her eyes as she shoots them up to Riccardo. "Sorry."

"It's all good," he assures her. "I'd rather be honest than strung along."

Pain fuels Nikita's reply. It is barely heard through her confusion. "That's what he's doing. He's stringing me along like my feelings don't matter." After a quick breath, she says, "And I think I know why." Her eyes are back on me, wet and full of emotions. "I think he's suing the hospital for malpractice. In all honesty, they deserve it. Their plan to diagnose his mother's condition was preposterous. They were stabbing at theories that made no sense for her symptoms, and when that didn't work, they conjured up an even more absurd way to justify their stupidity. Her diagnosis was so simple a third-year resident worked it out in minutes, so how could seasoned doctors not do the same?"

Whoa. She gave me a brief rundown of her exchanges with Maksim earlier today, but this is far more tense than she made out.

The tension hanging thickly in the air thins a smidge when a drunk voice at the side says, "Because their brains are wrinkly lards of flabby skin between their legs."

Aleena's saying could have only come from one source. "You gave her the *men are stupid because their brains are in their dicks* speech, didn't you?" I ask Nikita.

She shrugs. "Maybe. It is my go-to material when someone is feeling down."

"Aleena was feeling down?" Nikita's attempt to make out it isn't as bad as it seems twists my stomach. She would have made out it was nothing if it wasn't bothering her. "What happened?"

"Nothing happened. She just seemed a little—"

She is interrupted by a toast. It doesn't give off the "in love" vibes I experienced most of the afternoon. "To men who think with their dicks."

Aleena holds up her glass in silent encouragement for the room to join her in her salute. I decline Riccardo's offer of a nip of bourbon, too worried from reading the room to join the festivities.

I feel like some of Aleena's angst stems from her past more than her present, and I can't help but wonder if Bayli's reappearance is the catalyst of her slip.

Once most of the room is ready for her to finalize her toast, Aleena says, "And the women stupid enough to fall for their tricks."

When her glass cracks upon collision with Shevi's, Nikita sobers up enough to see sense through the fog. "It's time to call it a night."

My high chest sinks in relief as I race to Aleena's side before she can swallow a shard of glass as if it is ice. "I'll be taking that."

Her lower lip drops into a pout when I remove her drink from her grasp and place it on the bar she's balancing on before I glue her hip to mine.

"I can walk," she lies.

If I weren't holding up her weight, she'd be flat on her face right now.

Partway out of the cabana, she murmurs, "You can go back to whoever you were entertaining earlier. You don't need to worry about me. I'm fine." Even drunk, she's a terrible liar. "I'm getting married to a man who is gorgeous and successful. My life is great!"

When a group of drunk men enjoying the outdoor paradise of the hotel warn her against exchanging vows, she breaks out of my hold and stumbles their way.

"What do you have to be worried about? It isn't like you're going to be faithful, anyway." *Hiccup.* "It's not like any of you *fools* know how to keep your dick in your pants." She spins to face me, stumbling over her feet. "But at least your wives won't need to compete with *that*." She thrusts her hand at me during the "that" part of her statement. "My sister is so beautiful everyone wants her." She looks on the verge of tears. "Even my fiancé."

The world spins as the orange juice I guzzled down threatens to resurface.

What does that mean?

Is she saying what I think she is?

Is Andrik the mysterious fiancé she hardly mentions?

If so, I'm going to be sick.

"Did you know that he asked me to marry him?"

I shake my head, too sickened to consider a worded reply.

"He did. We were young, but we were so in love." Tears burst into her eyes. "Then you drove him home and I never saw him again."

For the first time in almost a minute, I suck in an entire breath. She's not talking about Andrik. She thinks I was occupying my afternoon with Bayli.

"I drove him home, Aleena. I swear to you that was *all* I did."

Her tear-filled eyes seek the truth from my eyes before she adds words to the mix. "You weren't with Bayli today?"

"No. I wasn't. Not today and not at your sixteenth."

She looks relieved—for half a second.

As her eyes bulge, she folds in two and vomits into a bush siding the river pool. I cringe, almost certain I'll join her if I assist her now.

Mercifully, even while under the influence, Nikita has no trouble handling vomit. She pats Aleena's back until all the ghastly liquid in her stomach is expelled, and then she assists me in getting my sister back to our room.

Aleena continues to mumble under her breath throughout the slow journey, but her voice only loudens enough for me to understand her jabbering once we reach the safety of our suite. "They could have love and money. We-we could give them that." Her throat bobs a handful of times before she locks eyes with Nikita. "You just need to tell Maksim the truth. That you'd never intentionally hurt his mother."

"He knows. He was there."

She moves closer to Nikita to ensure she can see the honesty in her bloodshot eyes when she says, "No, he doesn't. They told him it was a ruse"—Nikita's stomach doesn't seem anywhere near as unbreachable when Aleena burps in her face—"and that you knew he was there. They're putting all the blame on you." She hits her with the same pleading look I plan to give her when she's not drunk.

"You have to tell him the truth. They need to be told when they're wrong. They only treat us this way because we let them." My heart beats at an unnatural rhythm when she quotes something I said to her when I was being removed from her party with Bayli. "If we don't like how we're treated, we should stand up for ourselves." Her focus returns to the present. "Tell them to either ship up or ship out. And we should do it now."

"Now?" Nikita and I say in sync.

"Uh-huh." It hurts that she directs her attention more at Nikita than me, but I've endured so much rejection in my life that the knocks are getting easier. "Let's get it out of the way. That way, if he's not interested in what we're offering, we can do whatever the hell we like all day tomorrow. Stuff the consequences."

"Stuff the consequences." I stare at Nikita like I don't know who she is when she says, "I'm going to confront him and give him a piece of my mind. If it weren't for me, his mother would most likely still be admitted." She jumps up too quick for her drunk head but recovers quickly. "*Tomorrow*. I'll talk to him tomorrow."

"No! Not tomorrow," Aleena whines like all her chips are on Nikita. "We need to do this now before it's too late."

My eyes bounce between Nikita and Aleena's rapidly disappearing frame when she charges for the door with Shevi hot on her tail.

"What do I do?" I blurt out, lost. It is usually Nikita chasing me around, demanding I put on my responsibility hat. I've never dealt with the shoe being on the other foot.

"Go with her," Nikita answers just as Aleena disappears into the hallway before she shoves me toward the exit. "I'll be right behind you. I just need to grab my bag. It is the equivalent of a first-aid kit. It may come in handy." When I groan, confident I am treading in waters way over my head, Nikita laughs. "I'm joking. Go. Your baby sister needs you."

The reminder of Aleena's title is all I need to get my feet moving.

I race out the door, shouting to Nikita that I'll meet her in Aleena's room.

"I'm right behind you," Nikita assures me just as our suite door closes with her being the solo occupant inside.

I make it into the elevator with only a second to spare. It jolts into action before I can spin to see which floor Aleena selected. It isn't the forty-fourth floor as anticipated. It is the lobby.

"Kazimir isn't staying here," Aleena says when she spots my stunned expression. "He's at home, with Mother."

After dipping my chin in understanding, I use the remainder of our elevator ride to prepare for the battle we're about to endure. This is no longer about men who think with their dicks. It is about the unachievable expectations our mother placed on us when we were children.

The exodus of fluids from Aleena's stomach must have taken her down the quick route to sobriety. Her strides out of the elevator when it arrives at the lobby are remarkably stable. She glides across the marble floors without a single stumble, only fumbling when the same face that stopped me hours ago presents again.

She stares at Bayli as if she's seeing a ghost.

His watch mimics hers to a T.

If anyone else but my baby sister were beside me, I'd be jealous Bayli can't take his eyes off her for even a second to acknowledge the people unwillingly trapped in their trance. That's how enthralling their stare down is.

Bayli only has eyes for Aleena, and the realization pinches the last of the air out of Aleena's sails. Her shoulders sink the longer she continues her stalk.

Their incensed rise is fully deflated when their stare down is interrupted by Bayli answering his ringing phone.

"Boss?" His eyes flick up to Aleena for the briefest second before he says, "On my way now."

Despite his cocky wink, you can tell he's hesitant to leave. It takes several long seconds for him to jog to the elevator, and he maintains eye contact with Aleena until the brushed steel doors snap shut.

I give Aleena some time to absorb the barrage of emotions hammering her before striving to ease it. "Would you like to take a seat?"

She shakes her head while twisting to face me. I can't read her as easily as I can Nikita, so her apology shocks me. "I'm so sorry. When he left with you and then disappeared, I assumed what she'd told me for years was the truth." She grips my arm as tears flood her eyes. "I should have never listened to her. I'm so sorry, Zoya."

"It's okay. I understand."

After guiding her to a booth in the corner of the foyer, I gesture for her to slip in first before I slot in behind her. She is shuddering too much to remain standing.

She stares into space for what feels like an eternity before murmuring, "What else has she lied about? How many lies has she told me?" Her drenched eyes lower to me. "How many lies has she told me about you?"

"I don't know," I reply, being honest. "But there's a way we can find out." I pull down the long sleeve on the jersey dress Andrik left for me, before running it across her cheeks, clearing her tears. "Ask me anything you want to know, anything at all, and I will tell you the truth. I promise."

After another brief stint of silence, she commences her interrogation.

It doesn't start where I expect. "Do you love the man you were with this afternoon?"

Since I pledged to be honest, I can only answer one way. "Yes."

49

ANDRIK

*M*y blood boils when a voice at the side says, "Whatever you're thinking about doing, I beg you to stop this madness now before it is too late."

I continue watching my grandfather's fleet of SUVs glide down the driveway of my home, before spinning to face the voice. My father looks disheveled, like he's battling more than the demons of his past. Dark circles plague his eyes, and his shirt is crumpled. He looks like shit, but it does little to weaken my determination.

I have permission to pick, and the verdict will only ever land one way.

Zoya Galdean is mine.

Anoushka moves out from the alcove when I lock my eyes with hers. She's not snooping. She merely makes sure she is available to assist no matter the hour.

"Pack Arabella's and Dina's things, and then have them escorted out by security."

"Andrik—"

"Don't," I snap out, turning to face my father. "Don't act like you care, that you've *ever* cared, or I may be tempted to forget whose blood runs through my veins."

He steps up to me like my gun isn't on my hip. "Do you think I want to live like this? That I didn't try to fight the system too? I've loved and lost. Fought and hated. I did *everything* you have done, and I still lost. Your mother—"

"Was constantly embarrassed *by you*! Disrespected *by you*. You didn't love and cherish her. You threw her away as if she were a broken toy the instant something new and shiny was placed in front of you!"

He chokes on a sob, like my words truly pain him. "I fought with the same tenacity as you, the same grit, but the outcome never altered." The sheer remorse in his tone sees the needle going in the opposite direction for the first time tonight. "So not just as your father, but a man who has also lost *everything*, I am begging you to accept your fate before it is too late."

"My fate is with Zoya. My life is with her. She is who *I* pick."

"Then kiss your life goodbye, along with your son's," he snarls through gritted teeth.

Over being constantly manipulated, I yank my gun out of its holster, pin my father to the wall by his throat, then almost singe a hole in his temple with a bullet.

Only almost because I don't want my son to see this side of me, and although Anoushka is quick to pull him away from me like she did me from my mother thirty years ago, he is too close to miss the death of his grandfather.

"My mother—"

"Was not the woman you think she was." Speaking in pretense already pisses me off, so I won't mention how potent my blood becomes when he adds, "She fooled us all." He uses my quick check of Zakhar's location to his advantage. "This is not a battle you will win without losing everyone you've ever cared about. Including Zoya Dokovic."

I inch in the trigger further. I don't want him to speak Zoya's name, let alone associate it with that surname. Even when we wed, she won't take that name. We will create a new surname, one as noble and respected as I had planned to return to my family's before he made the task impossible.

Bile burns my throat when he says, "Why do you think he was so quick to say yes?" His eyes flick in the direction his father just walked. "They want a pure bloodline, and you and Zoya will give them that." I almost turn the gun on myself when he says, "Sibling marriage was historically practiced amongst royalty through pre-colonial times. If you go through with *his* plan, it will become modernized."

"You're lying!"

"No," he instantly denies, shaking his head so firmly the wetness in his eyes almost trickles out. "Zoya is your blood relation." His eyes bounce between mine, full of honesty and shame. "That's why you're so compelled to protect her." As the barrel of my gun scalds his temple from the fury racing through my veins, he stammers out, "I didn't want to believe it either, but you can't deny DNA."

I tighten my grip on his throat when he squirms. He's not running. He is digging for his wallet. I'm just too worked up not to respond negatively. I want to kill. I want to maim. There's just no guarantee my first victim won't be me.

My jaw firms when he pulls a faded photograph of a blonde woman out of his wallet.

My mother was brunette.

"This is Mikhail's mother." The image of Mikhail's mother holding a strip of ultrasound pictures rattles when he moves it closer. "Look at her face, Andrik. Her features." He releases a solidary word with a hot breath. "Identical."

He's not speaking about similarities between Mikhail and his mother. He is highlighting how alike Zoya and his second wife are. Since Stasy is at the age Zoya is now, they could be mistaken as sisters.

He hopes I'm already over the fence, but just in case, he drags me over a little more. "Now look at the dates in the photo and when it was taken."

My stomach heaves when the hundreds of calculations I run through my head after doing as instructed all provide the same result.

Stasy was five months pregnant with a daughter four months before Zoya was born. Her due date was a mere seven days before Zoya's birthday.

I fight the heaves of my stomach when my father hammers the final nail into my coffin. "I ran a sample of Zoya's DNA against Stasy's that was already in the system."

You can't marry a Dokovic without submitting your DNA to the federation's database, so his claim that Stasy's DNA was in their system is legitimate.

I feel like I am sucker punched when he says, "It was a match. Zoya is your half-sister. Her DNA proves it."

With a roar of a wounded man, I redirect my gun and fire simultaneously until all the bullets in the chamber are dispersed and I am certain I am dead.

50

ZOYA

"*I*'m getting married!"

I step back, stunned. My hearing must be playing tricks on me because there is no way those words just came out of Nikita's mouth. She is as straight as an arrow. The only responsible one of our duo. She wouldn't marry someone she's been dating for six months, so a stranger doesn't stand a chance.

"Can you believe it?" She walks straighter than Aleena did when I chaperoned her walk to her room several floors down, her gorgeous lace gown swishing against her thighs.

Aleena needed time to decompartmentalize everything we had discussed, and since I was just as eager for a debrief, I didn't fight her wish for some downtime.

"I guess your ploy worked." When she leans in, I don't smell any alcohol on her breath. "A bikini competition was all that was needed for him to pull his head out of his ass."

Before I can respond, a doorbell buzzes.

Nikita's eyes pop before she strays them back to Maksim, who's standing at the side of the living room, looking a cross between coy and frustrated. "That'll be the event coordinator to set up the aisle."

"You're getting married *now*?"

She nods, smiles brightly, then bolts for the door to let in her late-night guests.

"Keet... I don't think this is a good idea. You hardly know this man." I twist to face Maksim. "No offense."

"None taken," he replies, stepping closer. "But we both agree that this is the best way we can move forward."

With a proud smile, and after letting in a crew of twenty, Nikita cozies into Maksim's side before fanning her hand over his heart. The position would have you convinced they've been married for decades. "I took Aleena's advice. I told him *everything*. He knew most of it, but there were some things I had managed to keep secret"— she playfully slaps his chest—"despite being under surveillance twenty-four-seven." She leans in as if sharing a secret but keeps her voice loud enough for everyone to hear. "You're safe in the bathrooms, though I would steer clear of the bedrooms. Maksim has cameras everywhere."

I swallow the brick her commentary caused before trying to simmer the electricity brewing in the air. "I'm glad you've been honest and that you're happy with the outcome, but are you sure this is the route you want to take? Gigi will have a fit when she finds out you got married without her."

"Maksim says we can do it again in a couple of months. We just need to wait for the heat to die down first."

The gurgle of my stomach accompanies my brief reply. "Heat?"

Nikita looks set to answer me. Before she can, she is interrupted by a florist asking what color hydrangeas she wants on the makeshift altar.

"What am I missing?" I ask anyone willing to listen.

Maksim doesn't seem like the type who enjoys an interrogation, but he gives me a little bit of leeway since it is late and I'm completely lost. "I can't disclose everything now, but this is the best way for me to protect her. By becoming my wife, she won't be just protected by me. She will also be sheltered under mafia law."

"*Mafia* law?" I knew you could tell a man by his suit. Maksim's screams mafia.

As does Andrik's, though we will keep that confession for another day.

I appreciate his honesty when he dips his chin. I just wish the honesty route we're endeavoring to get off the ground didn't leave me open to infiltration.

"But I'll have a hard time keeping her safe if you're not on the same team as her."

I take offense to his claim. "Of course I'm on the same team as her. I'll always be on the same team as her. Nikita is my best friend. I would never do anything that could put her in danger..."

My words trail off when Maksim spins around a tablet he gathered off the couch table. The image on the screen is grainy, but not even poor pixelation can hide the fury in Andrik's eyes as he drags me out of the competitor's area of the bikini competition.

After a quick swallow, I say, "Andrik—"

"Andrik?" Maksim interrupts, his brow arched.

When I nod, he twists the tablet screen to face him, stares down at the image for several seconds in silence, and then tabs across several images.

The surveillance photo he shows me this time around makes more sense of his worry. It is a still image of Ellis goading me into accepting his bribe. I couldn't look more corrupt if I tried.

"He was railroading me, so I said what he wanted to hear so he'd leave me alone. He wasn't meant to show up. But when he did, I learned something I didn't know previously, so I pretended his money was mine."

Maksim twists his lips like this isn't the first time he's hearing my side of the story. "Is that how you paid for this?"

I follow his hand's wave around the penthouse suite before nodding. "I deposited money into Nikita's grandmother's account before using her credit card to order an upgrade. Nikita doesn't know about any of this. I don't want to overwhelm her. She has enough on her plate."

Again, he nods, his understanding a little unnerving. "If you truly want to help lessen her stress, you need to give the money back."

"I know that. I've been wanting to do that. I just haven't had the time..." I stop with the excuses and be honest. "I will give it back. I would do it tonight if I could." I'm not sure how Andrik will feel when I admit to taking a bribe from his father, but I can't demand the truth from him and not give him the same. "I left the majority of the money at Myasnikov."

It is in the cardboard box under Nikita's bed because if I were ever going to rob the rich, I would always give it to the poor.

"How much do you need? I will organize the funds." Maksim stops and furrows his brows. "I can deliver it for you as well, if you'd like?"

"That isn't necessary." I swivel on the spot like a schoolgirl. Innocence is not an act I can pull off. "Andrik is coming here tonight."

"Here?" He points to the floor beneath his feet.

"Uh-huh. We have... *business* to discuss."

Maksim doesn't believe me, but thankfully, he doesn't push me on it. "How much do I need to organize until we return to Myasnikov?" His question matches my sentiment to a T. He will not pay for my mistakes. He will only help me fix them.

"One hundred thousand." I grimace. "Minus this." I swirl my finger around the penthouse. "And two first-class airplane tickets."

Maksim huffs as if one hundred thousand dollars is chump change.

I realize I hardly know the man in front of me when he mutters, "If you're sleeping with the airline's owner, you should have been given an upgrade for free." He punches something into his tablet before locking his dark eyes with mine. "Or better yet, you should have flown in one of his many private jets." An arrogant smirk stretches across his face. "Or perhaps he knew I was watching and wanted to leave this weekend breathing."

I love his cockiness, but I also think he is a fool. He must be to underestimate Andrik's level of dominance. I've only been standing across from Maksim for minutes, but I'm shocked the door hasn't already been busted down. That's how possessive Andrik is.

After a handful more finger punches on his tablet, Maksim says, "I will have the funds delivered with our wedding rings."

I sigh in relief and panic at the same time.

"Is this really happening?" I ask while staring at the people transforming the living room of the penthouse into a wedding chapel.

"Yes," Maksim answers, his eyes on Nikita. "It would have been weeks ago if they hadn't tried to fool me."

I ponder if his level of deception is as deep as what Andrik has endured the past two months but am stolen the chance to ask when Nikita thrusts two swabs of fabric in front of me.

"What color do you prefer?" Nothing but love and admiration shines in her eyes when she lifts them to my face. "You will be the most beautiful maid of honor, and I will be so blessed to have you standing at my side."

She doesn't necessarily ask for me to support her while she weds a man she hardly knows, but the sentiment in her eyes sees me giving the same answer I gave Aleena only hours ago.

"Yes."

51

ZOYA

*N*ikita's wedding was fast but gorgeous, though she seems to have no recollection of it.

"You let me get married!" Her high squeal whistles through my ears. "You let me get married to a man who hates me?"

"I don't hate you."

Her panic lowers to a manageable level from Maksim's pledge, though not enough for me not to try to help her connect the dots she lost while sleeping. "I tried to stop you. But by the time I returned to our suite, you had already decided. You were so determined to go through with it that you organized a late-night visit from a local minister."

"No." One word shouldn't take so long to deliver. "I wouldn't do that. I went to the foyer for a room key and watched you shake your ass, and then I... I... I..." She peers at Maksim like perhaps her memories are more buried than gone before she whispers, "I married you."

"You did," he replies, grinning.

"Because...?" If she wants Maksim to fill in the blanks, she needs to give him a minute to speak. "Strangers don't marry strangers unless they're in Vegas, and they wouldn't tie the knot with someone they don't like. You dislike me so much you walked out when my pants were huddled around my knees and my pussy was exposed."

"I didn't—"

I sling my head to the side when Maksim is interrupted by the last person I expected to see looking bright and chipper this morning. Aleena represents an angel ready to be placed at the top of a Christmas tree. It is a starkly contradicting look to the one she presented last night. "Want to miss out on a big inheritance?" I'm not the only one lost when she enters the room while saying, "When I accidentally let slip to Maksim about your excessive student loans, he mentioned an inheritance he'd never see if he didn't wed. Putting two and two together, I realized how ideal this could be." She gleams with excitement. "You need money, and Maksim needs a wife to get it. This"—she darts her hand between Maksim and Nikita—"fixes both dilemmas."

Nikita sounds as confused as I feel. "Zoya just said I had already decided before either of you had returned to our suite. But now you're saying you helped cook up a scheme that would have me believing marrying a stranger was a good idea?"

"No, that isn't what happened," I jump in, trying to save Aleena before she's trampled by Nikita's lie detector machine. "She... I..." I've got nothing, so I thrust a takeaway cup of coffee toward her. "I brought you coffee."

When Nikita accepts it, she has a Janet Jackson Super Bowl moment.

"Shit. Sorry," she apologizes.

I already knew Maksim was a good fit for Nikita, hence me colluding with Aleena to get them together, but his low growl of disapproval seals the deal.

"You loathe that too?" I backhand his chest like we're lifelong friends. "Aleena is right. You are a perfect match."

"Z!" Nikita shouts.

"What? Don't act like you can't feel the sparks. You've been panting like a dog in heat since we got here."

"And you thought he was married, so you should have muzzled my mouth."

When Maksim glares at me like it isn't Nikita's mouth that needs muzzling around married men, I shift his focus to the cause of Nikita's outburst. "The blonde."

"Slatvena?" Maksim asks, forcing heat to creep across Nikita's cheeks from the provocative way he says her name. "She is my assistant." He sounds more humored than frustrated while adding, "She also wasn't forced to attend yesterday's festivities. She was there for the same reason every other spectator was."

"For charity," Nikita assumes, always a goody two-shoes.

Maksim laughs before putting Nikita out of her misery. "She went to enjoy the view."

"Oh..."

With Nikita still lost, I give the international sign for scissor sisters. Her eyes don't veer lower than my face, but she gets the idea. "*Oh...* Then why not marry her?"

Aleena jumps back into our conversation. "It needs to look authentic." Her nose screws up like a rabbit. "If it doesn't appear legitimate, the inheritance will be voided." Either out of excuses or desperate to wipe the suspicion from my eyes that she appears too adapt in marriages of convenience for me to let slide, she hooks her thumb to the door. "We should probably go. This is a private matter. We don't want to intrude."

I almost shake my head until I see the wish for privacy spreading across Maksim's face. I hardly know him, but I trust that he has Nikita's best interests at heart, so I change my shake to a head bob.

When I hug Nikita, she whispers, "If you leave me now, I'll disown you for life."

"He won't hurt you, Keet. He only wants to help you."

Although I'd sell a kidney to stay and support her through this, Aleena's quick exodus leaves me no choice but to squirm out of her hold and race out of the room, hot on Aleena's tail.

"Leaving again so soon?" I murmur when I notice her heading for the main exit door of the suite, slowing her steps. "I thought we had plans today?"

Her shoulders rise and fall three times before she spins to face me. "We do. I just thought I should wait for you down there."

There could be anywhere, but she doesn't extend her reply even with my expression showing my confusion.

"Is everything okay?" I thought we made good headway in our relationship yesterday, though now it seems as if we're back to square one. Since I think I know the cause of that, I ask, "You seemed pretty knowledgeable in arranged marriages in there." I nudge my head to Nikita's room. "Is that for any particular reason?"

She looks panicked and then relieved. "No. Of course not." My squashed heart gets a moment of reprieve when she steps closer. "I was coming to collect my phone. When I overheard Nikita's panic, I thought a little bit of spit and polish wouldn't hurt anyone. Maksim will be good for her, so I want her to give him a chance. If that needs an occasional lie to happen, I'm okay with that."

"He will be good for her," I agree, "but it doesn't explain how you knew what ruse to run with."

She exhales deeply before gesturing for us to move our conversation to the living room. I wait for her to sit first before sitting across from her. I'm better at reading people when I can see them head-on.

It seems like forever before she speaks. "This isn't my first engagement."

I nod, recalling her saying last night that Bayli had asked for her hand in marriage.

I'm knocked back when she says, "I was engaged last year. The terms were similar to the ones I just stated." Her eyes fall to her hands knotted around her skirt. "The groom called off the wedding the night before." I want to pop my knee into the groin of every man who has ever hurt her when her voice cracks. "He had fallen in love with someone else. She was pregnant and his family would never allow him to have a child out of wedlock, so she took my place at the end of the altar."

"Aleena, I'm sorry."

She brushes off my sympathies as if they're not required. "It's okay. I'm fine with it now. It just stung a little at the time. It kind of knocks your ego being disregarded like you're worthless."

She is preaching to the wrong person, but since this is about her, not me, I scoot to the edge of my chair before squeezing her hand in mine. "But things are different this time, right? This isn't an arrangement. You love Kazimir and he loves you?"

Her sob breaks my heart, so you can imagine my surprise when she acts like everything is fine. "Of course. It's wonderful." When my expression announces that I need a little more convincing, she says, "Last night was nerves. I was getting cold feet and petrified that Kazimir was experiencing the same. But he put my worries to bed last night."

"He visited you last night?" I need to get a second opinion on the medication I am taking. They're making me far too sentimental. I sound like a lovesick fool.

A flare darts through Aleena's eyes as she nods. "Yeah. He made everything better and had me so giddy that if a certain someone hadn't hogged the hotel event planner's evening, she may not have been the only one shacked up and married right now." She bumps me with her knee. "If only we were in Vegas."

I giggle. It loosens some of the tension hanging heavily on my chest. "So we're still on for today? You still want to hang out?"

"Yes," she whispers. "Of course."

"Okay." I squeeze her hand again. "Why don't you go grab the girls and come back here. We have a full itinerary of activities to undertake."

I melt into her embrace when she hugs me before I shadow her walk to the door.

I stare at it for a few moments to gather my bearings. Something feels off with Aleena's story, though I can't quite pinpoint what it is.

It doesn't help that my usually stealth detective skills are lagging this morning. I barely slept last night. It wasn't solely Nikita's abrupt nuptials keeping me awake but also the promise of a man I shouldn't have fallen in love with but have.

I waited up for Andrik as asked.

He never arrived.

I stop staring into space when the creak of a door opening trickles into my ears. Maksim exits Nikita's room looking more disheveled than he did last night. Her memory loss is worrying him as much as it is me.

"I have a handful of matters I need to take care of." When I nod, he continues. "There are two guards stationed at the end of the hall, and my security personnel were briefed this morning. She is safe here, though I would appreciate if you would encourage her to stay on the hotel grounds."

"Most of our activities today are here."

Like all dominant men, he only hears what he wants to hear. "Most?"

"I booked us a spa day at a salon in town. No offense but the prices here are outrageous."

He smirks, amused by my honesty, but remains firm on his orders. "I will have Slatvena cancel the appointment."

"Every girl knows the best cure for a hangover is a spa day. If you want her memories back sooner rather than later, let the appointment stand."

Maksim doesn't seem the type to compromise, though I am delighted when he does. "I will organize for my team to come here." My lips barely move before he gives them no reason to. "At the hotel's expense."

"That would be wonderful. Thank you."

He eyes me for a nanosecond before muttering, "But?"

"But..." He isn't a fan of delayed gratification. "The spa day was in preparation for a DJ gig we were planning to attend tonight. I don't see DJ Rourke willing to do a home visit like your spa techs."

He gives me a look as if to say, *Don't bet on it*, before he pulls out his phone. "What time is the gig?"

"Nine."

He scrolls an overloaded planner on his phone while humming before he says, "That could work. I'll organize security."

My mood perks up. "Great. Thanks."

"But." He isn't asking a question this time. He's about to hit me with a statement. "Nikita won't be able to leave this room with *that* hanging over your head." He nudges his head to the duffle bag I was unable to hand back last night since Andrik failed to show up. "It will be harder to maintain her safety when there are too many variables at play."

"I understand. I just..." Again, morals break through pathetic excuses. "Andrik didn't show up last night, and I don't have a way to contact him."

Maksim almost looks sympathetic.

Almost.

"My offer is still open. I am more than happy to return it to him."

I stray my eyes to Nikita's bedroom door for the quickest second before recognizing the cause of the commotion outside the suite's door. Aleena and her bridesmaids are giddy with excitement about our day, and it reminds me of what this weekend is meant to be about.

"Okay. But on one condition."

He no longer looks sympathetic.

Murderous is more suitable for his scowl.

"Can we keep this between us? I will tell Nikita when the time is right, but I don't want Aleena finding out about it just yet."

I can't discourage my sister for marrying for money when it looks like I am willing to do anything to get it. I also don't want her to know I am involved with a married man. The emotions she displayed when she confessed that she had been cheated on shows her opinion on adulteresses. I don't want her to ever look at me like that. It will ruin the progress that has taken twelve years to initiate.

Maksim collects the duffle bag from the floor, doubling the output of my heart, before twisting to face me. "You looked out for Nikita when I couldn't. For that alone, I will be forever in your debt." I get misty-eyed when he murmurs, "Just don't hurt her. Because that is not something I will ever forgive."

He doesn't need words to hear my promise, so he leaves without them.

52

ANDRIK

"Are you sure you want to do this?" Konstantine scans the information in front of him. "This is bigger than the federation. It is a globally recognized army in the millions. We won't be able to compete if the spark you're attempting to ignite turns into an inferno."

I jerk up my chin, never surer of anything in my life. "That's the point. I don't want to compete against him. I want him to take down the federation *permanently*."

Konstantine waits a beat before breathing out slowly. "All right." He inputs the details needed to spread my ruse into international waters while saying, "Just make sure my grave is dug the standard six feet. I don't want any bears digging up my corpse."

The fact he thinks I'll come out of this exchange alive shows the lack of faith he has in my plan. I'd usually dislodge bullets for the disrespect, but since the steps I'm putting into play are to achieve the exact opposite, I swallow my pride for the hundredth time in the past two hours and impatiently wait for the final pieces to be placed down.

"Is that it? Is it done?"

"Uploaded as per your specifications. I just need to hit send," Konstantine answers, his tone off. I learn why when he murmurs, "I'm still not sure about this. This seems almost suicidal."

He hits the nail on the head, but I can't tell him that. Instead, I take the defensive route because it will favor me as much as the latest ploy we just instigated.

"I don't pay you for your opinion. I pay you to protect my assets." He looks seconds from defending himself, so I talk faster. "Assets that are being squandered to nothing because you left me open to infiltration."

Konstantine's hacking talents are undeniably impressive, but I learn his street smarts are just as on par as his computer skills. "That shit ain't on me. I protect your digital footprint. *That*"—he thrusts his hand at my crotch—"has always been your responsibility." He sinks into his chair, tsking and moaning on the way. "I also ain't falling for your shit. Nor will I fall on the knife for *him*." The way he spits out "him" leaves no doubt as to who he is referencing. He is talking about our father. "If you want to fire me, fire me. But I ain't leaving without an exemplary employment history because I earned that fucking right. Years of dedication earned me that right."

I don't have time to play games, so I get to the point. "You're fired. Your severance will be forwarded to you this afternoon. Don't bother packing your things. I will have someone do it for you."

"You'll have someone do it for me." He huffs out a laugh. "Who? You let them all go. Anouska. Lilia. Mikhail. Zoya." His last name stings the most. "You've thinned your crew down to nothing in hours, so you've got no one left to boss around." He looks like he wants to spit in my face. "But I guess that's the point, isn't it? The fewer attachments, the less carnage. You've just failed to realize you can't do this without me."

I scoff before shaking my head. His cockiness is pathetic. I taught him everything he knows. When you come knocking at my father's door, seeking a handout from a man who refuses to pay a single cent in child support, you learn quick smart that the only thing you will inherit from him is a vigorous hairline and a big cock.

When my glare tells Konstantine he would be nothing without me, he changes tactics. "I'm not leaving. I came into this family with nothing, so I don't care if I leave with the same."

My hand instinctively moves for my gun, doubling his contrite grin.

I hate having my authority tested. I fucking loathe it. But just like my head knew it would never win the battle of my heart if I were to turn up to my pre-arranged meet with Zoya last night, it knows it won't triumph in this fight either.

I shouldn't be surprised. I taught Konstantine everything he knows. The first lesson was that the result of the battle doesn't matter. It is knowing that you've never walked away from one that truly counts.

Another battle presents when I notice a flashy sports car gliding down my driveway. It isn't in a fleet, and there are no flags flapping above the side mirrors.

My jaw firms when Maksim slides out of the driver's side, removes his sunglasses, and then drags his eyes across my home. This is the only property in the name my mother called me. The rest are under KADOK Industries, meaning he shouldn't be here.

"Zoya," I murmur to myself when he pulls a duffle bag from the back of his convertible. It isn't the same duffle bag my father handed Zoya days ago, but it is just as plump.

"Do you want me to get rid of him?"

I shake my head at Konstantine's offer before giving him a look that says our conversation isn't over.

Maksim smirks when I exit the front door of my home. "I guess we got off on the wrong foot." He tosses the duffle bag at my feet like disrespecting me comes with no repercussions. "Maksim..." When I leave his handshake hanging, his smirk doubles. "Our deal is off. If you can't be honest with who you are, I don't want to work with you."

"It is too late to negotiate after the deal is done. You don't pay for an hour, blow your load in thirty seconds, and then ask for a refund. That isn't how it works." With Zoya already in the forefront of my mind, my tactics naturally veer toward her. "You also can't keep the promise you made to your wife last night if you back out now." Maksim hides his interest well. He looks bored. "My son needs a heart." That gains his interest. He knew I was seeking a vital organ, but he had no clue who it was for. "If he doesn't get one, he will die."

"What's that got to do with me?"

He plays the devil's advocate well. It is a pity the numerous surveillance images Konstantine stole from his servers last night show a different man. He will do anything to keep his new wife safe. He will even side with Satan.

"If Zakhar dies, you will hurt Zoya."

He *pffts* me. "She's never met the kid, so I doubt she'll care."

"She will when she discovers they're related."

Maksim's steps to his car slow. "Related how?"

It is the fight of my life to not fold in two. "How doesn't matter. DNA doesn't lie. She is his blood relation, and as such, she will be devastated if she learns that you did *nothing* to help him." I only have him partially over the fence, so I give him a tug. "Another senseless death of the innocent children your wife is endeavoring to save."

"Leave her out of this!" His roar rumbles through my chest. "Or the only heart your son will receive will be yours."

I laugh like I haven't already sought advice on an adult donor's heart being placed into the chest of an almost five-year-old. It was the first thing I researched after picking out the shards of glass that embedded in my cheek when I fired at my reflection.

That's how fucking sick I felt when I couldn't discount the honesty in my father's eyes.

"I will never mention her name again, and it won't be uttered by anyone on my team. But I need more time. My son needs more time."

I don't know if it is the pure angst that gets me over the line or the promise to rid the world of anyone who speaks his wife's name in vain, but I am grateful no matter the premise.

"You have a month. After that, it won't be just Myasnikov Private's gizzards being dissected. This entire fucking rort will be torn down."

Since that is all I've ever wanted, I dip my chin in understanding.

53

ZOYA

*W*hen I spot a familiar face in the crowd, I tell Aleena that I will catch up with her in a minute. Maksim hired a stretch limousine filled with security guards to take us to our concert, so it isn't like our transport will leave without me.

"Do you want me to wait?" Nikita asks when she realizes who has caught my eye.

It isn't the man I've been trying to rile into making contact all day.

It is his younger brother.

"No. It's fine. I'll only be a minute."

"Okay," she murmurs before begrudgingly walking away.

We talked today, so she is aware of some of what I'm going through. She knows Andrik is married or getting married and that I had Maksim return the bribe I accepted from his father. I was just a little light on the reason I can't assist Andrik with his ruse, and how it could have dire consequences on his son if he were to call it off.

I'd never get off her shrink couch if I gave her all the details in one sitting.

"Hey," I greet when Mikhail spots me gawking at him at the end of the bar.

His glum expression switches to glee. "Hot damn, Sunshine. The masseuse didn't force him to pull his head out of his ass, but that dress sure as fuck will."

I curtsy like I didn't purposely wear this dress to coerce Andrik out of hiding before joining him at his side of the bar.

"Does your brother know that you're drinking at a rival's bar?"

I don't know much about mafia men except they wear exceptionally tailored suits, so my assumption that Andrik and Maksim are rivals is pure speculation. Maksim's arrogance after his meeting with Andrik adds to my theory.

"He would if he'd answer any of my calls. He cut me off." His laugh stabs my chest with pain. "Emotionally *and* financially."

I dump my purse on the sticky counter like I have nowhere else to be before plonking my backside on the barstool next to him. "Why? What happened?"

"I have no fucking clue. It finally felt like he was letting me in, then *bam!* I'm out in the cold again."

I wish I couldn't sympathize with how he's feeling.

Unfortunately, I can.

"Do you want to help me pull his head out of his ass?" He looks so desperate for a solution to his dilemma that I don't wait for him to answer me. "We're going out. Booze. Dancing. And enough sweat to intermingle scents in a jealous-provoking way."

Mikhail twists his lips, fighting a grin. "He will kill me."

"He'd have to be standing in front of you to do that."

Now he smiles. "Are you sure you're ready for the consequences this could cause, Sunshine? I won't be the only one in the shit."

"If it gives you a chance to talk some sense into him, I'm all for it." As flashbacks of his argument with his father play in my head, I say, "I don't want whatever is going on between Andrik and me to affect your relationship with your family. I care about you, Mikhail. You're like the big brother I never had."

He noogies my head in an annoying little brother way. "I feel the same, pip squeak. But can we save the declarations of love until we're in an area where a ton of people will hear them? Maksim locked this place up like a vault last night. Anyone would swear the king's jewels are stored in his penthouse."

Since he isn't far from the truth, I remain quiet.

After slipping off his seat and digging some bills out of his pocket, he tosses them onto the bar and then curls his arm around my shoulders. "All right. Let's get this show on the road before I have to woo women into my bed with charm instead of an impressive bank balance."

"Mikhail..."

"I'm joking, Sunshine. My dick reels them in even better than the millions Andrik doesn't know about."

The first several hours of our night are a hoot. We dance, drink, and party like I assume people our age did in 1999. However, we don't see a single sighting of Andrik.

Either he's left town or our dance moves looked as awkward as they felt.

Mikhail is devastatingly handsome, but there is no spark between us whatsoever. It was like a brother and sister dancing at their grandparents' silver wedding anniversary dinner. You do it to appease your parents, but you get no joy out of it whatsoever.

After assisting Aleena out of the stretch limousine, I drift my eyes to Mikhail.

He is as sober as I am.

"Do you want to come up?"

He looks at an almost-passed-out Aleena before he returns his eyes to my face. When he shakes his head, I smile. He hates vomit as much as I do.

"Let me get her to bed, and then I'll join you for a nightcap."

We leave tomorrow morning, so tonight could be the last time I'll see Mikhail for months. I don't want to waste the opportunity to strengthen our friendship for something as unsatisfying as sleep.

He wishes me luck for a vomit-free transition before he heads for the bar to save me a seat.

Nikita and I practically carry Aleena to the elevators.

Nikita laughs when Aleena mumbles how much she loves me into my neck.

"And you thought I was a lightweight."

"You are," I tease before quietly returning Aleena's declaration of love.

I'm not ashamed to admit I love her. I've just never spoken those words to anyone but the woman standing next to us, and the remembrance has me wishing I had a way to contact Andrik. I could ask Maksim, but I don't want to stretch how accommodating he has been.

Furthermore, he's giving Nikita the world, and I don't want anything to risk her accepting his plentiful offerings.

Aleena settles faster tonight than the previous two. It's not hard to crave sleep when you're burning the candle at both ends.

Nikita's head pops up from a glossy magazine when she hears me enter the living room. "All settled?"

"Finally." I flop onto the seat next to her, exhausted. "Today was..."—confusing and cathartic but also what dreams are made of, so I settle with—"amazing." I twist my torso to face her. "Thank you so much."

She brushes off my comment as if it is weightless. "Don't thank me. I didn't do anything."

I smack her in the face with a pillow. "No prenup, baby. So any gift from Maksim today was also a gift from you."

Any knocks my ego endured today become non-existent when she says, "I've seriously had the best day of my life. I never would have predicted that would be the statement that ended my day when I woke up this morning."

"Then what are you still doing here? Why aren't you taking full advantage of the alone time before we fly home tomorrow? I love Gigi, but you know as well as I do that if Maksim makes you scream like you did earlier today, she'll take his head off with a baseball bat."

"Z!"

"What? It was so hot I'm seriously reconsidering my stance on sex club parties." *Next time I might ask Maksim to keep the lights on.* "You don't have to participate, but what are your thoughts on this pose?" I leap onto the couch, arch over it, then shake my tooshie. "Too risqué or tastefully nasty?"

She spanks my ass, adding to the welts Andrik's hand left yesterday, before she leaps to her feet and heads to her bedroom.

"Are you seriously staying here? He had one request, Keet. One!"

She thinks because her back is to me that I can't see her eye roll.

She's wrong.

"It's late."

"Don't act like he isn't awake, awaiting your return."

I hide the burn my prolonged wait last night caused my heart by following Nikita into her bedroom. I almost laugh when she squashes her ear to the wall separating our penthouse suite from Maksim's.

"I don't want to wake him if he's asleep."

"He isn't asleep." When I mimic her snooping ass, I learn there is more honesty to my statement than first believed. Maksim isn't asleep. He isn't alone, either.

"Maybe it's the TV?"

"That isn't the TV." Nikita's voice has an edge of pain to it. "There's nothing but infomercials on at this time of the night, and her voice is too young to be an infomercial host."

I try to recall if Maksim's quick scroll through his calendar this morning mentioned a Raya when he says, "I appreciate you coming, Raya. I know it is late, and you've traveled a long way, but hopefully I made the trip worthwhile."

"Of course you did." Nikita heaves, not missing the ambiguity in Raya's reply. She either wants to fuck Maksim or has. I hope it is the former.

Maksim's deep timbre pulls away from us as he says, "Let me know if you need anything."

He must be walking.

I realize Raya's hoping for the former when she replies, "I wouldn't say no to a chaperon to my car."

When footsteps sound through the door, I lock eyes with Nikita, silently promise her she has nothing to worry about, and then sprint for the entryway of our suite.

I beat Nikita to the peephole. I'm glad. The visual of Maksim walking a redheaded woman down the hall isn't incriminating, but it would turn the gut of even the most confident woman.

Regretfully, Nikita isn't one of them.

A second after I inch back from the peephole, she takes my place. She blinks three times before she sinks away from the door, spins, and then flattens her back against the glossy wood.

I can see a million thoughts shifting through her head before she settles on the one I often land on when trying to work out why Andrik went from meeting me and being married in hours.

"Maybe he wasn't expecting me to give it up so easily."

"No, Nikita. This isn't on you. And we don't even know what this is. She could be an acquaintance? Maybe she helped him arrange all the things he did today?"

"His hand was on her ass. They're more than colleagues."

Maksim hasn't given any reason to lose my trust, so I won't let my insecurities tear him down. "No, it wasn't. It was near it but not on it." When she glares at me, disgusted I am taking his side, I say, "You don't see how he looks at you. He's crazy about you."

"The only thing he's crazy about is thinking I will let this slide. It is two in the morning. No one has business meetings at two in the morning."

When she snatches up a chair from the dining room and wedges it under the door handle, I can't help but laugh. That will keep a man like Maksim out for only thirty seconds. If that.

My smile slips when the beep of a key card being scanned over an electronic lock sounds into the penthouse. The door handle jingles before a commanding yet surprisingly in control voice says, "Nikita, open the door. I know you're there. I can see your shadow under the door." Maksim tests the lock again before adding, "You have twenty minutes. If you're not in my bed in twenty minutes, I will come get you."

I wait for Maksim's shadow to disappear from underneath the door before asking, "What are you going to do?"

Nikita shrugs. "Nothing. I'm not going to do a damn thing."

It takes me a minute, and when the truth finally smacks into me, everything makes sense.

"You want him to fight for your attention. You're disappointed he didn't knock down that door and drag you to his bed."

"Don't be ridiculous. Why would I want to sleep on the same sheets he just messed with another woman?"

"Because you know he didn't do anything." I can't believe I missed the signs for so many years. "I get it. I understand why you feel this way. But you need to stop punishing every guy you meet for something your dad did. He chose to go after the people who hurt your mom, knowing it would take him away from you as well. Maksim—"

"Is a stranger! So stop acting like he isn't!"

When she races to her room, a soft hand shoots out, halting me from going after her.

"It'll be okay," Aleena whispers like she's well-versed on arrogant, dominant men.

She's right. Only seconds later, I hear a manly voice say, "Twenty minutes was far too generous."

My mouth gapes when Nikita's door pops open and Maksim walks out with her tossed over his shoulder and whacking into his back. She kicks and hits him while screaming to be placed down. There's no steam in her fight, no heat, because he is reacting exactly as she had hoped.

"I so want that," I murmur to myself.

My eyes sling to Aleena when she says, "Then why aren't you doing everything you can to have it?" I poke my tongue at her when she giggles. "If that's what you were endeavoring to do when you were air-humping Mikhail's crotch from three feet away, you need to devise another tactic. That was more PG appropriate than having your mother chaperone your prom date." I realize I could possibly be a bad influence when she quotes, "If you want to make a man tick, get him thinking with his dick."

She smiles when I groan. She can. She doesn't understand how jealous Andrik is. When his green head rears, he's like a bull in a china shop. But also, she's right. If I want to coerce Andrik out of hiding, I need more than a risqué hemline and slutty shoes.

As Andrik would say, I have to play this game with the integrity it deserves.

"Drink this." I thrust a bottle of water into Aleena's chest before tossing her pain medication and a vitamin B tablet. "Swallow these. And then wish me luck. I'm going to need it."

"I doubt it," she replies, tripling my confidence. "But I will give it to you anyway." She throws her arm in the air and shouts like a cheerleader. "Good luck!"

I am so pumped with nervous recklessness that I make it to the hotel lobby in the blink of an eye. Have you ever driven the same route over and over again that it is only after you put the car in park that you wonder how the hell you got there in one piece? That's what I'm experiencing now.

One minute, I am racing for the door of the penthouse suite.

The next minute, I'm entering the hotel bar, seeking Mikhail amongst the crowd.

I have the pick of a dozen men, but Mikhail is the only one I am certain will survive my ruse, so I veer my steps toward him.

"Hey, Suns—"

I cut him off by pressing our lips together.

I'm not going to lie. Our kiss is awkward as fuck. There's no tongue. No heat. Not a single spark fires between us. It is the equivalent of kissing Grampies.

It has the effect I am aiming for, however.

Out of nowhere, and with the roar of a deranged man, Andrik rips me away from Mikhail before his fist cracks his little brother's nose.

As the crowd pulls back to create a UFC ring, Andrik plows his fists into Mikhail's face and body. He gets in five or six non-contested whacks before Mikhail realizes what is happening.

I lied when I said Mikhail wouldn't be able to protect Nikita. He gives back as good as he gets, and within minutes, there are as many bruises shadowing Andrik's face as Mikhail's.

"Stop!" I scream when Andrik headbutts Mikhail hard enough to split the bridge of Mikhail's nose.

Blood gushes down Mikhail's face as I endeavor to achieve what the security guards aren't game to attempt.

I place myself between two maniacs.

"That's enough! Stop. You're acting like fucking lunatics."

Andrik shunts me to the side before he gets back up in his brother's face. "I told you I'd kill you if you touched her." He spits at Mikhail's feet. It is as bloody as his teeth. "I don't make threats for show."

His swing rockets Mikhail's head to the side with a sickening crunch. Before he can get in another jab, I shout, "I kissed him. *Me.* So if you want to be angry at anyone, take it out on me."

Help comes from an unlikely source. "She is telling the truth, Andrik." Ellis steps through the crowd, parting the spectators. "Mikhail had no say." With Andrik's fists still ready to punish, he steps between them like I did earlier but more to one side. "He also isn't to blame for your anger. If you want to take that out on anyone, you need to look closer to home."

His reply firms Andrik's fists instead of loosening them, so he shifts his focus to the less hostile one of the duo.

I can't hear what he says to Mikhail. It must be shocking because his pupils dilate to the size of saucers before his eyes rocket to me.

My ego gets bitch-slapped when he looks seconds from vomiting before his hand shoots up to his mouth to scrub away my kiss. He scrubs and scrubs and scrubs until his mouth is as red as the blood oozing from the top of his nose. It isn't enough. After pushing through the crowd, he shoves open the bar's washroom door with enough force to warp the hinges.

"I'll deal with him," Ellis announces, removing Andrik's suddenly remorseful eyes from the swinging restroom door. "You fix *this.*" He glares at me during "this." "Then come home. We have plans to finalize."

He is so confident that Andrik will follow his orders that he leaves after the quickest glance my way. My arm is snatched up in a brutal hold only seconds later.

54

ZOYA

The strong scent of alcohol pumping from Andrik's pores indicates that something is amiss with him, so I won't mention the fact he walks up past numerous solid surfaces more than capable of issuing the punishment he believes I deserve.

The meeting places dotted throughout the foyer of the hotel are empty because only the insane stalk the halls at this hour.

That should have been the first indication that I was about to make a terrible mistake.

Nothing good happens at 2 a.m.

I attempt to yank out of Andrik's hold when he jabs the call button on the elevator panel. I say attempt as his grip is too deadly to dislodge. His fingernails dig into my arm firm enough to mark, and they shred my last nerve.

"I kissed him to force you to react. I wouldn't have done it if I'd known you were going to take it this far. My god, Andrik, you hurt your brother. *Badly.*"

"No," he denies, his grip firming more. "*You* hurt him. Not me. Don't put your shit on me."

After I'm forcefully walked into the elevator, I drink in his confused expression in the mirrored wall. He's angry, downright furious, though that is barely seen through the bewilderment swamping him. There's so much pain in his eyes, so much hurt.

Their pain convinces me that this is no longer about jealousy. It is about something far more sinister than that. I doubt even an illicit affair will scratch the surface of the betrayal he is currently experiencing, and I have an inkling I am the catalyst of his pain.

"I had no intention of taking your father's money. I gave him that date and time because I knew he wouldn't be able to uphold his side of our agreement if I was three thousand miles away. I had no clue he would show up early."

"Because you underestimated him."

He doesn't see my nod. He doesn't need to. He knows the truth because this isn't his first rodeo with his father.

"We *all* underestimated him." He shakes his head as if disappointed with himself. "But I got burned the most because I was closest to the flame." When his glassy eyes drop to my arm, he steps back as if it is ravished with as many bruises as his face and knuckles. "I..." A brutal swallow bobs his Adam's apple and shifts his focus in under a second. "You should have kept his money."

"No. I should have never bartered for it to begin with," I immediately reply, my tone announcing his suggestion isn't up for negotiation.

I screwed up badly spending some of it, but the prize money of the bikini competition meant I was able to recoup the loss of my life-altering mistake.

"He just made me so mad that I fired off a demand before truly considering what I was doing, and then I spent it under the same guise."

He huffs out a laugh before saying, "You should have spent it all.

He owes you far more than 100K, мил—" He stops partway through my nickname, cusses, then jabs at the penthouse suite floor button, urging the elevator to hurry up.

Though the wish to keep our conversation alight is burning my skin, I need time to make sure I don't make another foolish mistake. I also need to think of something to say to fix the mess I created tonight. Don't misconstrue. I'm glad it worked, and it is forcing a conversation we need to have, but the tension feels different from the one crackling in the air during our exchange yesterday.

It almost feels like the start of our ending.

"Andrik—"

"Don't," he snaps out, his tone pained as he guides me out of the elevator and down the hallway. Like Maksim earlier, he keeps his hand hovering above my skin instead of against it. "This needs to stop. We can't do this. I can't..."

With a *pfft*, he swipes a key card over the electronic lock of the penthouse suite and then opens the door, shocking me that he has access to my room.

After placing the key card on the entryway table like he no longer needs access to it, he pulls an airline ticket out of his pocket and places it on top of the room key card.

"I organized you a flight back to Myasnikov. It leaves in four hours. The rent on your apartment is covered indefinitely. If you don't want to stay there, I can have someone on my team organize another location. I told Lilia not to expect you back at Le Rogue tomorrow night. Although you no longer work there, you will be compensated as if you do until you find another position."

I attempt to interrupt the stern rumble I imagine he uses in the boardroom, but I am too shocked to speak.

If this isn't a see-you-later brush-off, the pope isn't Catholic.

"The car in your parking bay at your apartment building is

yours. The insurance and registration will be covered by KADOK Industries."

His dismissive tone ends my silence. "I don't want your money, your car, or your apartment." I hate that my voice croaks during my next sentence. "I just want you."

Andrik's back molars smash together so fast their crack adds extra damage to my heart. "That is *not* a possibility."

"Why?" I ask, following his brisk stalk to the door. "If it is the fertility issues, they can be fixed. I could have an operation to lessen the damage, or we could use a surrogate."

I'm clutching at straws, but I am desperate. Not just to be chosen first, but for him to admit my infertility isn't the reason he is walking away from me.

I know it is more than that.

It has to be.

"Talk to me, Andrik! Tell me what is going on. Please."

He keeps walking, and it breaks my heart.

"You said you would always put me first. That you were going to make things right. How the fuck is this upholding any of the promises you made yesterday?"

His fist lands into the doorframe before he grips the crumbling wood like he is struggling to stay upright. I watch his chest rise and fall as he strives to maintain his anger.

Violence isn't the emotion I want him to display, but it is better than the one he rips through me when he says, "I love my wife. She can give me everything I've ever wanted." When he cranks his neck back to face me, the deceit in his eyes clears away for honesty. "You cannot."

With my devastation blinding, I snatch up the vase next to me and throw it at the door. It narrowly misses Andrik's head as he slips into the hallway and leaves without a backward glance.

When my legs pull out from beneath me, I don't land on the floor with a thud. I fall into the arms of my baby sister, who assures me time and time again that everything will be okay, and that it is now her turn to carry the burden of our birthright.

55

ZOYA

"If you're going to apologize again about this morning, hush." Aleena wraps me up in a hug that warms my cold, dead insides. "I'm glad I was finally able to be there for you as you have been for me for all these years." I roll my eyes, and she giggles. "Not the cards, although I loved that you made them yourself. The words inside them."

"You saw them?" I can't hide the shock in my tone. My cards were returned every year seemingly unopened.

Aleena nods. "Do you remember how we snuck chips and cookies without Mother noticing?" I match her head bob. "Hair straighteners aren't just perfect for resealing plastic seams. They also loosen envelope glue."

Although I love knowing how crafty she is when it comes to deceiving our mother, there's one point I can't gloss over.

How did she get my letters to begin with?

Before I can ask her that, the truth smacks me in the face. "Stasy?"

Her smile is brighter than the sun. "She never let Mother's lies fully sink in. She always encouraged me to seek my own truth." She breathes in the smell of my freshly shampooed hair. "I'm so glad I finally listened." After another sniff, she spins to gather her suitcase before locking her wet eyes with mine. "Contact may be sporadic until the wedding. Mother—"

"I know," I interrupt, not needing her explanation.

Our mother hates me.

No deliberation required.

"But that won't be an issue for too much longer. It isn't like she's going to move into Kazimir's house with you." When she grimaces, I balk. "Right?"

She groans as if nothing is concrete when it comes to our mother before she hands her bag to a driver wearing a driver's cap.

"Bye," I whisper when she waves at me before sliding into the back seat next to Shevi.

I watch her chauffeur-driven SUV drive away, confident this isn't the last time we will speak. If I don't think positively, depression may gobble me up and swallow me whole.

I refuse for my gloomy mood to rain down on Nikita's and Aleena's happiness. They deserve to be spoiled, and I'm grateful I get to witness it up close.

Maksim is a man of his word, and he is repaying his debt by ensuring I am included in every event he organizes for Nikita—even their private jet flight home.

He also offered me a job, so I'll have an easy excuse for my stalking.

I stop following Aleena's SUV's roll through the streets of the Trudny District when dark hairs tickle my elbow a second before my best friend asks, "Are you ready?"

Nikita is so loved up right now I can't help but sway when I spin to face her. "Yep. Just give me one minute to grab something I left in the cabana."

When she arches a brow, I bump her with my hip, certain this is not a conversation we're going to have within the next week, much less today.

"Enjoy the reprieve, Z. You can't escape me when we're thirty thousand feet in the air."

I groan before increasing my pace. The bikini Andrik peeled off me notched me ahead of my competitors because it is designer and pricy. Some people look at labels more than the people hiding behind them.

I'm not one of those people, but I am also not leaving a two-hundred-dollar swimsuit to the racoons.

My stomach doesn't know which way to swing when I enter the cabana Andrik and I occupied for hours two days ago. The scent of multiple arousals is still in the air, but it is also infused with Andrik's cologne since his suit jacket is draped over one of the single sun loungers.

I snatch up my bikini before spinning on my heel. Since I am trying to be the bigger person, I don't take a single step toward the exit.

Good things happen to good people—my best friend's fortunate luck of late is proof of this—so I need to pull up my big girl panties and accept Andrik's decision with dignity.

It won't be easy, though if anyone can do it, it will be me.

My brows quirk when a crinkle sounds out of Andrik's jacket when I snatch it up. It is the same sound as the one his jacket made on my birthday, so I veer my hand to the breast pocket without an objection filtering through my head.

My heart bleeds for a different reason when I read the terms of Andrik's latest contract. His son is sick, and if I am reading his contract properly, he won't get the help he needs without Andrik's original marriage contract being upheld.

Divorce doesn't seem like an option for his family.

I shoot my eyes up when Nikita calls my name. "Z?"

"I'm coming," I reply while shoving Andrik's contract back into the pocket of his suit and racing through the exit.

When she spots my race, her gorgeous face adopts an apologetic expression. "Sorry, I don't want to rush you, but from the rumors I've heard, jets cost thousands of dollars a minute to operate even while idling on a tarmac."

As my eyes pop, I mouth an apology before gesturing for her to lead the way.

———

Our flight was uneventful—much to Nikita's disgust. She remained seated with me in the main part of the private jet while Maksim spent most of his time behind a desk in the bedroom.

I'd be worried the honeymoon is already over for them if Maksim hadn't fired his flight attendant because she couldn't dismiss my underhanded commentary that she wants to sleep with her boss.

I went a little hard on her because I'm now more guilt-riddled than devastated. I don't feel sorry for Andrik's wife. What Andrik is going through is the only thing weighing my shoulders down, and how I almost forced that immense pressure onto his son.

Children need to be protected, not pawned as if they're easily replaceable.

Andrik's family has yet to learn that, just like my mother.

I'm drawn from my thoughts by Maksim's stern rumble. "Get. The. Fuck. Off. My. Plane." As the woman who seems to have taken a page out of my book when it comes to the concept of wedding rings scuttles for the exit, Maksim locks his eyes with a gentleman over her shoulder. "And you can go with her."

"Maksim, Maria was out of line but unaware of your recent nuptials."

Maksim doesn't buy his excuse for a second. "She may not have, but you did. Yet you sat back and watched her belittle *my wife*." He says *my wife* with far more possessiveness than Andrik ever has, and it makes me swoon.

"You are right. I am sorry," the male hostess says, backing down. "I apologize for any discomfort caused, Mrs. Ivanov."

He's out the door before Nikita can get in a second chin dip.

Since I caused the tension, it is only fair I try to dislodge it as well. "If you ever grow tired of him"—I lock eyes with Nikita before nudging my head to Maksim standing firm in the galley of his jet— "toss him my way. There's no such thing as sloppy seconds when it comes to men."

I feel the heat of her narrowed glare when I kiss her forehead like I've witnessed Maksim do numerous times the past two days.

It lowers her annoyance even better than Eskimo kisses.

"Are you not traveling with us?"

I laugh when I unearth the reason for the fret in her tone. "Gigi is going to love him." My tone dips a smidge, but since Maksim is in her realm, her snooping isn't as stellar as usual. "And I've got some matters I need to wrap up before commencing my new job on Monday." I drift my eyes to Maksim. "Ten, right?"

He nods. "I will forward you an official job offer to your inbox later today."

"Great. Thanks."

I add a smile to the words that will never display my full appreciation before I gallop down the jet's stairs.

Nikita and Maksim don't follow suit. The pilots trace my steps across the tarmac minutes later, but I lose them when we enter the main part of the airport.

They head toward the lounge section, and I veer for the bus stop.

A step back in luxury can't be missed when I enter the stinky bus. It smells like puke and another substance I don't want to mention. But the company is good.

"Hey, Mara."

Her bruises have healed so well that you'd have no clue she was assaulted only weeks ago.

"Is that seat taken?" I hook my thumb to a seat two spots up from the one I was about to plonk my backside in.

"Um. No. Yo-you can sit there." She removes her purse from the seat next to her before gesturing for me to sit. "Di-did you move?"

Her stutter is unexpected. I thought it was because she was stammering through survival instincts. I didn't realize it was permanent.

"No. I'm just returning from a trip." When her eyes seek the luggage I am without since Maksim said he would have it delivered to my apartment, I sprinkle a smidge of honesty in my reply. "My bag was ruined by the luggage handlers. I haven't had time to cash the compensation check yet." Hating how easy it is for me to lie these days, I ask, "What about you? You're a little on the far side of home."

"Oh. Um. I-I... ah. I'm also going home."

"You went on a trip too?"

I realize not everyone is as good at lying as me when she shakily nods.

After a beat, she switches her nod to a headshake. "I was meant to-to go, but I chickened out. Now I'm going home."

"Without your luggage?"

She grimaces and then nods. "It's a long story."

"We have thirty minutes." When hesitation is her first expression, I settle into my seat and breathe out a hot breath. "And I'm going to need at least twenty-nine of them to clear the murkiness from my chest."

My conversation with Mara is so riveting that I'm hesitant to get off when the bus arrives at my stop. "I'll store your number into my phone as soon as I get a new one." I walk toward the bus driver before spinning back around. "And I know it isn't any compensation, but your boss is an idiot. You're beautiful and kind. If he can't see that, that's on him, not you."

I feel good when she nods.

My mood continues its uphill climb until I enter Le Rogue via the back entrance doors.

"I'm sorry," Lilia murmurs the instant we lock eyes. "I told him it wasn't his choice. That this is my business. But you know what some men are like."

She confirms what I came here to find out without me needing to speak a word.

This is Andrik's business.

"It's fine," I assure her. "Nothing happening is your fault." *I'm not even sure it is mine.*

My head flings to the side when a girly voice says, "I say screw him." Mars saunters into the backstage area with far more clothing than she usually has on. "What's he gonna do? Kill all our patrons until there's none left?"

Lilia and I swallow in sync.

"I doubt a death threat will keep them away for long." Mars butts shoulders with me. "We've been taking inquiries for private shows all weekend. You'll make a killing in the private sector. I can hook you up with some contacts if you're interested."

I don't give her offer any true thought. I didn't realize how selfish I was being when I coerced Andrik into responding last night. This is about more than us. It is about his son.

"Thanks, but I've already secured new employment." I don't

mention it is with my best friend's husband. I don't want to look like a loser. "I just wanted to swing by and make sure there were no hard feelings." I spin to face Lilia. "I wouldn't have placed you in that predicament if I had known."

"Hard feelings? *Please.*" She brushes off my worry with a wave of her hand. "You brought life back into this place and added some spice."

"Tension. Spice. Almost the same thing."

Lilia laughs into my hair when she pulls me in for a hug. "And I agree with Mars. Stuff him. If you want to shake your ass for some funds, I'm not going to say no. He hid you here because his enemies would never believe a man as possessive as him would let someone he cares about work at a strip club, so he can't rip away your shelter with no real explanation. That would make him a dick."

"Don't bring up his dick, Lilia. Baby girl was already struggling to forget it before she went and got reacquainted with it in a poolside cabana." Mars's hip bump this time around almost sends me flying. "For future reference, cabana walls are useless sound barriers. Your moans are circulating the net."

My cheeks whiten as my stomach flips.

This isn't good. Not for me, and not for Andrik's campaign to help his son.

56

ANDRIK

"For fuck's sake, will you shut that thing up!"

I shoot my hands up to my hair and tug ruefully. Days ago, I would have given anything to hear those moans, to have them shred my eardrums. Now they torment me until I am a mere inch from my grave, begging to fall in.

"I'm trying," Konstantine assures me as his fingers move wildly over the keyboard. "But as quickly as I take down a video, another one pops up." He lifts his eyes to mine. "You should be grateful Maksim put a block on all phone activity during the swimsuit competition. If he hadn't done that, I would have had hours of footage to remove from the net."

He laughs like anything he said is funny. He can because he doesn't know how sick and unhinged those noises make me.

She's my...

I'm fucking my...

Since I can't say the word, I pick up the cause for the anger sluicing my veins and throw it to the ground. For what my toss misses, my boot takes up for. I stomp on Konstantine's laptop and then make a beeline for the bar before I shift my focus from mainframes to people.

"Jesus Christ." Konstantine bobs down to collect the ruins of his laptop. "You could have just asked me to turn the volume down."

I clutch my whiskey glass so hard it almost cracks. It was meant to be easier when she left. I'm meant to be able to breathe now. But I can't. The pain is crippling, and I don't know if I am strong enough to survive it.

When not a single denial roars to life, I mutter, "Accept their offer."

Konstantine's damaged goods are now the least of his worries. "There is stupid, and then there is *stupid*. That is the latter. We will get Zakhar a heart, but not like this."

"They're taking too long. This is an easy solution."

"This is suicide!" he yells back. "That's not a possibility, Andrik. It is—"

"Don't call me that. You're not allowed to call me that! No one is allowed to call me that anymore." *No one except her.*

Furious at my inner monologue, I hook my glass at the shelves across from me. I don't relish how its collision sends multiple awards and priceless antiques tumbling to the floor. I'm too busy sculling whiskey straight from the decanter.

I need to numb the ache, blanket the shame. I need to fucking forget, but she's in every frame. I can't get drunk enough to forget her.

I laugh like a madman when a voice from outside my office trickless through the chaos swirling in my head. "Follow their rules. That is *all* you need to do." My father enters my office like I haven't imagined killing him again and again and again since he shared the secret I plan to take to the grave. It is only one of the few joys I currently have. "Give Dr. Fairmont permission for the insemination."

"No. I can't. I don't want to..." I stop before I say too much. I was going to say I don't want to hurt Zoya like that. That the cruelness I unleashed the last time we spoke is enough for her to hate me for eternity. I can't add more. *Right?*

When the denials come hard and fast this time, I give in. I hand over the strings and let the federation puppeteer me, because at the end of the day, it doesn't matter.

I'm dead no matter what.

"Okay." With my reply too soft for anyone to hear, I repeat it. "Okay."

"Yes," my father hisses like a snake while slapping me on the back. "Thank you." He squeezes my shoulder and leans in close. "Your son thanks you."

I don't need to follow the direction of his gaze to know who he is signaling to. The heaviness it adds to my chest tells me everything I need to know, and it sees me cracking open a fresh bottle of whiskey like the empty one in my trash wasn't opened only an hour ago.

57

ZOYA

I dip my chin in thanks to the doorman of Le Rogue when he holds it open for me. When I spot a taxi, I throw my hand in the air, signaling for him to stop before hotfooting it through the main entrance door.

I'm in such a hurry, I bump into someone entering.

"Sorry," apologizes a voice from above before he bobs down to collect my belongings he knocked out of my arms during our collision.

I didn't have much in my locker, but just like my bikini, I paid for them, so I'll take them with me.

Amusement pumps out of my savior when he takes in the naughty secretary glasses and calculator I brought from home. They don't quite match the sex toys Mars encouraged me to have delivered to work so they wouldn't be stolen by my neighbors. They're on opposing teams—as is my response when my savior lifts his head.

I appear to have acquired a stalker.

Bayli slowly stands like my shoulders are wider than his and my height is just as imposing.

His timid take frees me to ask, "Are you following me?"

"No," he immediately replies, shaking his head. "I come here all the time."

His size should make him intimidating, but it doesn't. I met him before he was officially a man. That changes everything in an instant.

"Who's your favorite dancer?"

His expression stonewalls before he murmurs out, "Ah... Trixie."

It takes me a second to roll through the dancers' stage names before I can call him out on his lie. "We don't have a dancer called Trixie."

"What the fuck?" Bayli replies, balking. "Every strip joint has a dancer named Trixie. Trixie, Angel, and Destiny. You'll find one at every club."

I laugh at his absolute assuredness before scooting past him. "You should have gone with Angel. We have three of them."

I hear his huff before the stomp of his feet echoes off the brick-work outside Le Rogue. "What about Destiny? Do you have one of them?"

"We may, but you'll never find out if you continue following me." I point behind me. "The entrance is back there."

He drags his eyes in the direction I'm pointing before returning them to me. After putting enough distance between us that all my swings will miss, he says, "I may be following you." When I huff and walk faster, he jogs to catch up to me. "Not in a bad way."

"There's a good type of stalking?"

"Depends on who you ask." He laughs at my eye roll before saying, "I wanted to ask you something, but I didn't want to do it in front of Maksim and Doc."

Doc is Maksim's nickname for Nikita. It proves Bayli knows them more intimately than a random stranger, and the knowledge frees me to say, "You have five minutes. I've got shit to do—"

"I don't need to know your bathroom habits." He continues to see my eye rolls as approval of his poor comedic skills. "And I won't need longer than five minutes."

"You will if you keep stalling."

"True. Ah..." A thousand words roll through his head before he blurts out four. "Have we met before?"

His question shocks me. I've been told so many times that I'm unforgettable that I've started believing it.

"I swear this isn't a line to get your number or anything. I just could have sworn we've met before."

With my smarts too clouded with confusion to jump straight into another shit fight so soon after the last one, it leaves Bayli plenty of opportunity to offer an introduction.

It doesn't go as planned.

"Ano. It is nice to meet you..."

Ano? Who the hell is Ano?

When he holds out his hand in offering, I accept it before finalizing his question in a way I haven't in over a decade. "Zoya Sakharoff."

I'm not seeking an invitation back into the Sakharoff realm. I'm trying to trip Ano up because something is very wrong with this picture.

I could have sworn on a Bible that he was Aleena's ex who disappeared not long after her sixteenth birthday party. Even Aleena is convinced they're one and the same.

After working my name through his head for several long seconds, Ano gestures to a bar across the road from Le Rogue. "Do you want to grab a drink?"

"I thought you said this wasn't about trying to secure a date?"

He doesn't give off creeper vibes, but just like Andrik last night, something is off with his demeanor.

Even Ano's dimple-blemished grin is a match for Bayli's shy

smile. "I'm not. I just have a feeling you've got answers to questions I've been seeking for years, but I don't see me asking them without a gallon of vodka priming my veins."

Since he seems harmless enough, I gesture for him to lead the way, hopeful I will get as many answers for Aleena as I will for myself.

58

ANDRIK

*M*y drunken climb up the stairs of my home slows when I hear giggling. It's late. I think. I haven't looked at a clock in hours. I've done nothing but drink—and plot. Both have done little to improve my mood. I'm a grouchy prick, hence my hesitation to head in the direction of the noise.

"Fuck it," I murmur to myself before heading to Zakhar's room.

Fury is the first emotion I feel when I crack open his door enough to see his bed. It is soon replaced with fond memories. Anoushka is tucking Zakhar in by using the same tactic she did when I was a child. She tells him he will be transported to another dimension anytime he sleeps. He's not sick in that world. He can leave his bed and play sports. He can do anything he wants to do.

Before my head can talk me out of it, my drunken heart says, "I hear sweets grow on bushes over there."

Zakhar's tired eyes shoot to me before the biggest grin stretches across his face. "No, they don't. Sweets don't grow on bushes." He laughs, but it doesn't hide his hope that I'm telling the truth.

"It's another dimension, Zak. Things aren't the same there. You can be anything you want to be when you're visiting another dimension."

Anoushka smiles in gratitude that I haven't kicked her out as I did previously before she continues her famous bedtime routine. "What do you want to be, Zak? You have to imagine it now to make sure you get the right world once you're asleep."

As she rakes her fingers through his locks that are two shades lighter than mine, Zakhar's eyelids grow heavy.

"I don't want to be sick anymore." He yawns, muffling his words. "I want to be strong and healthy like Daddy." His reply is already tugging at my heartstrings, so I'm knocked completely fucking down when he whispers, "Then maybe he'll stop being mad at me. He might love me like Mommy does..." He hiccups like he is fighting not to cry. "Like Mommy *did*."

"Your mother loves you, Zak."

He can't hide his tears when he shouts, "Then why did she make me come here? Why did she leave me with people who hate me? I want to go home!"

He clutches Anoushka's shirt like I did multiple times when I wasn't much older than him, hiding his shame.

I refuse to let him.

Not because I'm an ass, but because he needs to know he did nothing wrong.

"She had no choice, Zak."

When he shakes his head, sending more tears flinging off his cheeks, I gently grip his arms and pull him back from Anoushka. I need him to see the honesty in my eyes when I repeat my statement.

"She had no choice. But I do. I have a choice, Zak, and I'm not going to leave you. I promise I will be here with you as long as you'll have me." He looks like he believes me, and it weakens the heaviness on my chest. "But you need to promise the same, okay? You need to keep fighting. Can you promise me you'll do that, Zak? That you will stay for me?"

"I promise," he answers, his voice barely a squeak.

"Then I'll do the same," I pledge before pulling him into my chest so my shirt can soak up more than the black slosh that's been leaking from my heart over the past few days.

"You wonder where I get my stubbornness from," I mutter as I exit Zakhar's room hours after he fell asleep.

"Blood isn't what makes families, Andrik." I cringe over her choice of name, but since it is Anoushka, the only constant solid female presence in my life, I let it slide. "Can I please—"

I cut her off before a single plea in her eyes can be voiced. "You should probably get some sleep. Zak isn't a fan of sleep-ins, and we spent half the night watching him sleep instead of joining him."

She does her best to ignore the thick stench of alcohol leaking from my pores when she hugs me, but the lines sprouting from her nose when she inches back make her efforts fraudulent.

"I need to shower."

"You do," she agrees, smiling gently before she squeezes my hand. "It will get better. You just need to take it one step at a time."

Her reply announces that she doesn't know the full catalyst of my downfall.

Since I want to keep it like that, I reply, "It will," before walking away from her.

It won't be easier, but there is only one way you can go when you've hit rock bottom. Up.

A peculiar smell plumes into my nostrils when I enter my room. It isn't unappealing. More unexpected. It smells feminine and sweet.

An odd fragrance considering I've never welcomed a woman into my home, much less my bed.

"It-it's me," stammers a voice with a bird-like tweet. "Don't shoot."

My hand stops reaching for my gun when Arabella steps forward, moving out of the shadows the light outside my room causes. She's dressed in a mesh negligee with an in-built bra and a high split in the thigh. It clings to her skin so perfectly that it doesn't take a genius to realize she is without panties. I can see the lines of her bare mound and the dots of perfume she sprayed on her chest. That's how sheer her nightwear is.

"What are you doing here, Arabella?" This is the first time I've seen her since she left for her bachelorette party. I'm not the best company in general, but I've been a bear with a sore head for the past several days.

"Dr. Fairmont recommends a hands-on approach after insemination."

When she steps closer, I realize the perfume spray on her neck isn't the sole sign of wetness on her skin. Her pussy lips are glistening. I don't know if it is because she has a thing for arrogant jerks or if IVF causes excess residue.

In all honesty, I don't care.

"He said it is scientifically proven that the chances of conception are greater if the recipient's womb is"—her eyes flick up for the quickest second before returning to me—"*stimulated* close to the insemination time."

Her negligee is already leaving nothing to the imagination, but the visual becomes more risqué when she slides down one of the straps, sending the scant material floating to the floor.

She is as naked as the day she was born, but instead of kicking her out as per the better judgment of my head, I order her into the kneeling position the submissive held in Mikhail's apartment the day I met Zoya before I spin around to lock my bedroom door.

59

ZOYA

"I'm so sorry," I apologize when the loud shrill of my phone startles the lady in front of me.

We're in an elevator, and I'm riding her ass so closely that she'll need a proctologist to get me out. It isn't that I'm a fan of invading people's privacy bubbles. I just needed a way to sneak into Mikhail's apartment without him knowing about my arrival. I don't want to be removed from the premises like I was when I visited Andrik's family's country estate three days ago with the hope Mikhail was there.

This beautiful woman is as deliciously chunky as she is tall. I wasn't spotted by the doorman, much less the security guard monitoring the new state-of-the-art surveillance camera system installed throughout Mikhail's building.

My inquiries have been dodged left, right, and center since Aleena's bachelorette party. Andrik and Aleena have an excuse for their silence. They're being watched as much as Nikita. But what is Mikhail's reasoning? Yes, I used him to rile Andrik, but he signed up for that willingly, so he has no reason to ignore my calls.

He hasn't returned a single call or text message, and I've reached out to him over a dozen times in the past two weeks.

When Nikita's grinning face flashes up on my phone again a second after I sent her last call to voicemail, I slide my finger across the screen and push my phone close to my ear.

"Hey, is everything okay?"

I told her days ago that I was going to help Aleena with last-minute wedding plans because I didn't want to look like a loser who can't maintain a single friendship beyond ours. She might dump me if she learns how crappy of a friend I am.

My endeavors to make contact with Mikhail weren't as stellar as my attempt to reach Vlad, but cut me some slack. Vlad didn't look like I had vomited in his mouth after we kissed. Mikhail appeared disgusted after our lip lock.

"Hey. Yeah. Everything is fine." My bullshit radar sounds an alarm, but before I can call Nikita out on it, she continues. "I was just wondering if you could do me a favor. You're at home, right?"

"Ah..." I scan the internal walls of the elevator before grimacing. "I can be, if it's urgent." When she sighs, I blow my cover by straightening my spine. "Is it urgent?"

"Kind of." After another deep sigh, she tells me how she made a promise to pay the medical expenses of a child the hospital was refusing to treat since she didn't have insurance, and that she was hoping the money in her box would be enough to cover the expenses.

This is why I love her. She would give you the clothes off her back if you asked. But I'm lost as to why she needs the equivalent of her life savings to pay the bill. Maksim is giving her the world. She never has to penny-pinch again.

"Why are you using the funds you set aside? Maksim gave you a limitless credit card and permission to use it for whatever your heart desires. Use that."

"I can't."

"You can, and you don't have much choice. You have two, three nights' admission max saved."

I'm reminded how daft women become when we're trapped in a love haze when she says, "And?"

"And..." I leave her on hold for a couple of seconds to ensure her head doesn't get too big for her boots. It's what best friends do. "During your two-minute rundown on what happened, you said the clerk announced the Petrovitches were several thousand in debt. I don't think you have that much in your box, Keet. Because if you did, you would have purchased your grandfather's breathing machine with it months ago."

Her sigh breaks my heart. "I don't know what to do."

"Yeah, you do. Maksim gave you that credit card for a reason. He wants you to use it."

"That was before we..."

I follow my co-rider out of the elevator on the seventieth floor before asking. "We...?"

She says the last thing I expect. "We're kind of not on speaking terms."

"Huh?" One word shouldn't relay so much devastation, but it does. If Maksim and Nikita can't make it, there is no hope for the rest of us. "Since when?"

"Since I threatened to leave him—"

"You what!"

Her voice is almost a sob. "Things are complicated."

"Oh, I bet they are. Maksim is—"

"I miss him, Z."

I'd give anything to be in front of her right now. She couldn't say no to some friendly PDA. Not with that much angst in her tone. "Then tell him that."

"I can't. What if I lose him too?"

"Keet..." Nikita is the smartest woman I know, but she has no street smarts whatsoever. "I love you, girl, but sometimes you're so blind you can't see what is directly in front of you. Maksim would *never* put you in that position. He loves you too much to ever hurt you like that."

Her breath catches in her throat. "No—"

"He. *Loves.* You. That's why he is struggling to give you the promise you need to move past your fear that you will lose him too."

I resonate so much with what I'm saying, but this isn't about me or my wish to be placed first. This is about my best friend and how she'd rather be picked last than love and lose.

"He isn't a man who can sit back and let the person he loves be hurt because she wants him to promise not to retaliate. I don't know a single man who could promise that, let alone one who spent most of his childhood protecting his mother."

"He told you about that?" she asks through a sob.

"No. But I know you, and I understand your fear." I give her the honesty she deserves. "And I also understand Maksim's. He doesn't want to hurt you. He wants to love you, but that comes with a prerequisite of protection. Everyone knows that. You just seem to have gotten the criteria a little mixed up since you've forgotten the love a parent has for a child is different from the love of a spouse." I give her a moment before hitting her with the big stuff. "Maksim isn't your dad, but I sure as fuck hope he loves and protects you as fiercely as your father did your mother, because that is the type of love every girl should strive for. That is *real* love."

A stupid tear rolls down my cheek when Nikita murmurs, "Z, I have to go."

"Fuckin' oath you do." I cough to ensure my words come out clear before making sure she doesn't forget who she is talking to. I wouldn't be me if I didn't stir her. "Give him a kiss from me."

I laugh when she grunts. It is either laugh or let the stupid emotions that have been hammering me nonstop over the past several weeks win. I'd rather look like an idiot laughing at my own jokes than cry in public.

After taking a moment to center myself, I reenter the elevator and select the top floor. My arrival has already been thwarted, so I may as well make the most out of the distance between the security officers in the lobby and me.

I ride several floors before a cough forces my eyes from the floor for the first time in minutes. I can only see shadows in the brushed steel panels of the elevator, but I don't need mirrored walls to recognize who the cough belongs to. The prickling of the hairs on my nape tells the story.

"Does he know you're here?"

"No," I reply, unwilling to turn around in case I say something stupid. "Well, I'm assuming he doesn't. I had to break cover to take a phone call. One of your tenants on the seventieth floor is very voluptuous."

Andrik's huffed chuckle tickles the hairs his presence stood to attention. "I hadn't noticed."

"Probably because she isn't of breeding age." I snap my mouth shut, inwardly cuss, then twist to face him. "I'm sorry. I'm an asshole who rarely thinks before speaking."

My guilt worsens when I take in his thick beard, unkempt hair, and sunken eyes. Don't get me wrong. He is still the most handsome man I have ever laid eyes on, but he looks exhausted.

Has he slept at all in the past two weeks?

I step closer, crossing over into the danger zone before asking, "Are you ok—"

I'm interrupted by the ding of the elevator announcing we have arrived at Mikhail's floor.

After tightening his jaw like the gesture pains him as much as his disheveled appearance hurts me, Andrik gestures for me to exit the elevator first.

I do, albeit hesitantly.

We don't need a code to enter Mikhail's apartment. The door has been left wide open, and it smells like someone crawled inside and died many days ago.

"I'll open some windows while you check the bedroom."

Andrik takes my bossiness in stride. He veers through the penthouse living room that looks worse than a frat house after a raging party as I open a window in the kitchen before moving for the massive Constantine doors in the dining room. They open out onto the balcony and the city lights.

I spin to face Andrik when he says, "He's not in there, though he's been here recently. The shower is wet and there are towels on the floor."

"Has anyone checked the Broadbent?"

He nods. "I just came from there. He isn't there either."

"Someone has to be buying all this." I wave my hand over numerous boxes of takeout on the dining room table. "And from what Mikhail told me, that person isn't you. And don't say it was because we kissed. You cut him off *before* that happened." Now isn't the time for this, but I truly don't know if I will ever get the chance again, so I run with it. "If you wanted to backtrack on your promise, you didn't have to make Mikhail your scapegoat. You could have told me that the sex was a good distraction from your son's health battles, but that was all you wanted from me."

"*Good?* The sex was good?" He laughs like he needs a trip to the psych ward. "The sex wasn't good. It was *great*. Blistering. So fucking unreal I can't get it out of my head." He jabs two fingers into his temple so furiously I have no idea how his brain doesn't ooze out of his ears. "Do you have any idea how hard it is to live with that? To act like I didn't destroy everything I've been working toward for the past thirty-five years? You didn't just fucking destroy me, Zoya. You *ruined* me."

"You had an affair. It isn't the end of the world. Men cheat. It's almost second nature, or your family—"

"I didn't cheat!" he roars, scaring the living daylights out of me.

I've never been subjected to so much anger and pain that I'm lost on how to reply. I would take away his pain if I could. I'd accept it in an instant. But since I feel like that means I would have to give him up permanently, I don't know if I can do that.

"Andrik—"

"Go home, Zoya!" He pulls away from me with a sneer and peers out the window before proving he has mind reading capabilities. "If you want to help me, go home and pretend we never met, because that may be the only fucking way I will *ever* survive this."

My words wobble when I say, "Mikhail—"

"Is not your problem. He's *mine*! He has been mine for years, and I'm not willing to give him up for you. Not now." His next two words are whispered. "*Not ever.*"

I keep my reply short with the hope it won't display my heartache. "Okay."

I shouldn't have bothered to hide my disappointment. Even the briskness of my reply can't conceal my devastation. I'm not solely upset about losing Mikhail. I am shattered by the words I must speak next for the sake of a child I will most likely never meet.

"Goodbye, Andrik."

Glass smashing sounds out of Mikhail's apartment as I rush out the door and into the corridor. When multiple jabs of the call button fail to open the elevator doors, I toss open the emergency exit stairwell door and then commence a multiple-floor descent. I don't give up this time. I need sweat to hide the tears streaming down my face. Otherwise I will break the only promise I've ever made to myself.

I'll never cry over a man who doesn't want me for me.

"Hey."

I curse myself to hell when Ano greets me with a grin in the foyer of Nikita's building. My visit to Chelabini had a dual purpose. I was meant to check in on Mikhail before making a dreaded trip home so I could see if Stasy had kept Aleena's Polaroid camera as stocked with film as she did mine during my teenage years.

I wanted to back up my claims that Ano is Bayli with physical proof, but I was so upset after my exchange with Andrik, I drove straight home.

I must have gotten a hundred fines because the speedometer barely dipped below a hundred.

"Are you all right?" Ano asks, eyeing me suspiciously. It is understandable. I also gave him the line that I was going home to help Aleena with her wedding. "You're looking a little frazzled."

"Thanks for the compliment."

He laughs before banding his arm around my shoulders and noogying my hair. That's how tall he is. He doesn't even need to stretch to balance his chin on the top of my head. "I didn't mean it like that. I just figured I'd ease you into asking how much elevator rocking you were subjected to. But since you seem to like it dry and hard, I'll just ask. How perverted are you, princess?"

"Call me princess again and you'll find out." I squash my finger to his lips before the "p" of princess leaves his mouth. "And what elevator rocking?"

"You missed it?" He blows out a hot breath. "I guess I'll bunk with you tonight. You may be the only one saved from his wrath when he learns her moans could be heard from down here."

"He?" I ask, lost.

"Maksim and Doc," he answers like I'm slow. "They made up." I smile, happy. "And they've been hogging the elevator for"—my smirk grows when he checks his imaginary Rolex—"long enough that if Doc charges by the hour, Maksim is gonna wish he had taken out premium health coverage." He nudges his head to the conference. "His four p.m. has also been here for over an hour."

"Did you tell Maksim he has a guest waiting?"

When Ano shakes his head like my suggestion is insane, I whack him.

"What? You can't seriously expect me to interrupt Maksim when he's..." He makes a gesture I am extremely proud of. "You may survive that shit, but I sure as hell won't."

"You're such a chicken shit." Says the lady who hasn't told him about our possible connection because I'm terrified my mother is responsible for the assault that stole his memories. "Where are they?"

"In the elevator. *Duh.*"

I roll my eyes before entering the security office to advise Maksim of his appointment. My brisk pace slows when I spot a Post-it note stuck to the front of my planner. It has a date two weeks from now and a location scribbled across it, but no other details.

"What is this?" I ask anyone listening.

Two guards shrug before a third one pops up. "The caller didn't leave any details. He just wanted me to tell you that that is *the* date." He emphasizes "the" like it should mean something.

"The date?" My heart whacks my chest when the fog clears enough for me to understand the cryptic message. "*The* date. This" —I wiggle the Post-it note in the air—"is *the* date."

When he nods, I stumble back.

My baby sister is getting married in two weeks, and my invite came in the form of a Post-it note.

I guess it is better than no invitation at all.

60

ANDRIK

My jaw flexes as I tug on the stupid designer tie choking me. Its hold is as firm as my hands are itching to compress around Mikhail's throat. It's been weeks, and he still hasn't made contact. Even with me trying to push him away throughout our adolescent years, this is the longest we've been out of contact.

I was pretty fucking adamant when I let everyone go that I'd break his legs if he didn't give me some space, but I was strung out, drunk, and fairly certain I wouldn't see out the week breathing.

I had arrived at Maksim's hotel to make sure he hadn't followed me down the same destructive path. That he knew of Zoya's lineage before he made a fatal error.

I just lost all sense of morality when my entrance into the hotel saw me stumbling onto them locking lips. I should have been sympathizing with how Mikhail would have felt when he found out how fucking sick his feelings for Zoya are. Instead, I was like a bull in a china shop.

My beatdown had nothing to do with smacking some sense into Mikhail. I wanted to hurt him how it hurt me seeing them kiss.

That's fucked to even admit, but it is honest.

When my call is sent to voicemail for the umpteenth time today, I get desperate.

I use my son to gain my little brother's attention.

ME:

> Zakhar is getting a new heart tomorrow afternoon. If you're not man enough to stand by my side through this, man up for him. He's your blood, Mikhail. That'll always be thicker than water.

I wait for my message to be delivered and read before dumping my phone onto a side table and moving to the bar. Tonight is the rehearsal dinner for my wedding with Arabella. Although things have moved fast since my ruse was reimplemented, it has been relatively smooth sailing.

It helps that for the majority of the time there has been three thousand miles between Zoya and me.

I knew our reunion wouldn't be pretty, but it was more brutal since it centered around our joint worry for Mikhail. I could have told her why her feelings for Mikhail are valid, but I'm a selfish prick when I'm being railroaded. My childhood is proof of this. If I hadn't let them use Mikhail to puppeteer me, we'd both be able to move without invisible strings controlling every step.

As I toss back a three-finger serving of vodka, my phone buzzes. I almost stumble moving for it. I haven't drunk any less in the past three weeks than the first. A high-functioning alcoholic can hide his intoxication better than the average man.

A cuss ripples through the air when I read Mikhail's reply. He sent me a thumbs-up emoji without words. That's the very definition of a brush-off, but since I detect I am being watched by more than the media circus about to become a permanent part of my life, I take any contact as better than silence before storing away my phone.

Kolya, my grandfather's chief of staff, enters the living room of the penthouse suite hosting my imminent nuptials. "We have a new itinerary for you to look over." He hands me three stacks of papers for the next twenty-four hours. No, I am not kidding. "Your father was forwarded a copy this morning, so we only require your approval."

I huff. Approval means nothing when you have no power whatsoever.

"What is the media being told about Zakhar?"

Kolya's swallow is audible. "At the moment, nothing." My glare gets him talking almost too fast for his mouth to keep up with. "We don't want the voters to believe his medical condition influenced your reason to marry—"

"Even though that is precisely what is happening."

He acts as if I didn't speak. "So once his operation is a success and he is well enough for the media coverage his birthright will instigate, a press conference will be held to announce his shocking yet much wanted existence." Scheming flashes through his eyes. "If we play this right, your father will take over the reins sooner than planned."

His prediction isn't shocking. I just never considered I would be a part of the operation for my father's presidency campaign. I did everything in my youth to ensure I was excluded from any public appearances during his campaign for office. Tattoos. Piercings. Haircuts no one under the age of sixteen should wear. I've trialed them all, and up until this point, they worked in my favor.

Now I need to wear my dress shirts fully buttoned up to hide my neck tattoos and hire makeup artists to cover what the collar misses and the ones on my hands. I even removed my nose ring and earring for tonight's event. I no longer represent the Dokovic bad boy, more a middle-aged schmuck willing to kiss anyone's ass if it ensures a vote.

I've never been more ashamed, and I thought I'd hit the bottom of the barrel when it came to indignity weeks ago.

Needing to keep my headspace clear for the next thirty-plus hours, I drop my focus to the document Kolya handed me.

After a brief scan of the multiple-page itinerary, I almost give my seal of approval.

Almost.

Only one point stops me.

"We can't move locations. Zakhar is too unwell for transport."

Kolya nods in agreement. "But we go where his new heart goes." My unease weakens when he adds, "And his medical team said he will handle the transport better knowing a new heart is waiting for him at the end of his journey."

His reply returns the thump my heart has been missing for the past few weeks and loosens the strings forcing my movements by a smidge.

It does nothing for the knot in my stomach, though. Carnage is brewing. I just need to hold back the deluge for a few more hours. Zak needs to come first. Once he gets a new heart, I can shift my focus to making the impossible achievable.

61

ZOYA

"*A*rabella?" One of the many gorgeous dresses Maksim has spoiled Nikita with swishes around her slim thighs when she twists to face me. Her daft expression is cute because of its rarity. "Are we in the right ballroom?"

A heated watch answers her question on my behalf. Maksim left our suite early to finalize some plans he's been endeavoring to get off the ground for Nikita for the past few weeks. Nikita has been pining after him the entire time. Apparently twenty minutes is too long for soulmates to be apart.

I'd hate to see how she'd handle the weeks I've endured.

Although she lights up like a Christmas tree when she spots the cause of the goose bumps breaking across her skin, her feet remain firmly planted next to mine. When she makes a pledge, she keeps it —even if it kills her.

"Arabella is Aleena's middle name." After looping my arm around Nikita's elbow, I commence moving us into the room that's had my stomach in a state of turmoil all day.

I'm nervous about coming face-to-face with my mother again,

but the unease making my composure a mess seems like more than ghosts of my past rearing their ugly heads. It feels more present and personal—like a mother's hate isn't as personal as it gets.

Perhaps it is knowing Ano accompanied me here? Even without photographic proof, I'm one hundred percent convinced Ano is Bayli. The timelines match, not to mention the lengths my mother will go to rid the people she deems unsuitable from her daughters' lives.

I just don't know how to break the news to either Aleena or Ano.

When the cause for Nikita's weighed-down steps smack into me, I endeavor to lessen the load. I did a ton of cardio this morning. I don't need more spasms hitting my midsection.

"My mother was only permitted to assign our middle names. She hated the names our father picked for us, so she encouraged us to use the names she selected for anything of importance. College admissions. Pageant shows. Pretty much anything that could result in it being used in print. I ditched her choice around the same time she ditched me."

"Z..."

When the devastation in her voice makes my nose tingle, I hit her with a stern finger point. "Don't. If you start, I'll start, and then we will both be screwed."

She bumps me with her hip. "Lucky our mascara is waterproof."

"I wasn't talking about makeup." I stray my eyes to the side and then arch a brow like any of the heat from Maksim's stare belongs to me. It doesn't, but if a girl doesn't occasionally stroke her ego, she may never build up the courage to give self-stimulation a go.

I am in such a severe sexual rut I'm convinced not even the most powerful sex toy will scratch the surface of my needs, but for some crazy reason, I've not given any of them the chance to shine.

My PG peck with Mikhail must have loosened a few screws in my head.

I've never felt more batshit crazy.

"Maksim will never hurt you," Nikita says, her voice a purr. The cause of its throatiness is exposed when she murmurs, "Unless you hurt me. There are no guarantees then."

"As there shouldn't be." I love how protective Maksim is of her and that she is slowly starting to accept that it is part of the package when you fall in love.

I'm thankful for the excuse to gag when Nikita asks, "So... what's your middle name?"

I'd hate to be seen as a sentimental schmuck while in a room full of people who believe they can buy anything for the right price. The aroma in the air is rife with old money, and that stigma usually attracts reared-for-purpose brides.

It doubles my worry that Aleena is more under our mother's thumb than she portrayed during her bachelorette weekend, but I won't have a chance to check without enduring the tornado racing my way.

My mother has spotted my arrival, and despite being surrounded by powerful men vying for her attention, she doesn't hide her disdain.

"Please excuse me," she murmurs before making a beeline for me, standing frozen partway into the ballroom hosting Aleena's rehearsal dinner.

I don't want to make a scene. It will make my endeavor to speak to Aleena in a calm, understanding manner ten times harder, but I also refuse to be kicked out of the festivities again.

I was invited, goddamn it. It may have been by the means of a Post-it note, but Maksim and Nikita's invitation was very much legitimate, and even if they wish for the opposite a minimum of once a day, we're a unit. We're on the same team.

As my mother's hand shoots out for my arm, Nikita steps in front of me and thrusts out her hand in offering, dislodging my mother's deathly grip before it can clamp on. "Mrs. Galdean, it is a pleasure to finally meet you in person."

The crowd's huff is as loud as mine when my mother barges her out of the way. She just made a costly mistake. One Maksim will not take sitting down. He's at Nikita's side in an instant, and despite Nikita's numerous assurances that she's fine, he looks set to kill my mother where she stands.

I should feel panicked.

I don't.

It is impossible to love someone who has never loved you. That's why I struggle to understand Andrik's suddenly cold demeanor. If he was honest about needing to stay discreet for Zakhar's sake, I would have given discretion a whirl.

After a final silent plea for leniency, Nikita introduces Maksim to my mother. She emphasizes her parental title, hopeful it will calm Maksim enough for him to see sense through the madness.

"She has been out of contact with her daughter for some time, so in her eagerness for them to reacquaint, she *accidentally* bumped into me." Nikita twists back around to face my mother. "Isn't that correct, Dina?"

My mother is as smart as she is beautiful. "Yes. I'm so sorry, dear. I didn't realize how close you were standing to my darling offspring. It will not happen again."

Maksim doesn't believe her, but since he would rather appease his wife than pry the truth from a woman unworthy of his time, he mutters, "Ensure it doesn't." His glare speaks the words he can't say since he promised no more carnage only weeks ago. *Or the next bullet I release will be earmarked for your head.*

Confident his message was read loud and clear, Maksim finalizes our guide into the rehearsal dinner. Yes, *our* walk. He didn't lie when he said I am forever in his debt. He looks out for me as much as he does Nikita.

I'd love it if it didn't announce things are well and truly over for Andrik and me. Maksim's inclusion in Nikita's life came with hundreds of men who see *any* woman with a pulse as fair game —*excluding Nikita. They're horny not stupid*—yet Andrik's lack of contact makes it seem as if I haven't been propositioned a hundred times in the last week alone.

I haven't used my dirtbox since the flight to the Trudny Peninsula District, meaning every *"Hey, baby, wanna fuck?"* and its hundreds of synonyms have been recorded by the state-of-the-art surveillance system Maksim has watching Nikita's every move.

The evidence is there for a war of jealousy. It is the judge, juror, and executioner who are missing.

I'm drawn from my thoughts when Maksim pulls out a chair for me. It is directly next to Nikita and facing the main entrance doors. The kitchen and bar are behind us. He doesn't care what the table plan says. His security team would have plotted the most viable exit before he arrived, and he will implement their strategies to the wire since it will guarantee Nikita's safety.

He won't tell me who is threatening her, just that the threat is viable enough for him to act on it.

"Thank you," I murmur to the waitress when she fills my glass with wine.

The red goblet of goodness offers the perfect distraction to the swishing of my stomach.

Each glass of wine I enjoy over the next hour soothes my stomach's swirls and replenishes the confidence I lost when my mother dug her French-tipped nails into my arm.

The reason for the wine selection makes sense when Aleena finally arrives to greet her guests. Its glossy appearance matches the fiery coloring of the ensemble that makes her appear far more mature than the twenty-two years she has graced this Earth. Her dress is seductive and alluring—a look she can totally pull off. She is gorgeous and naughty at the same time, the perfect combination of sexy and cute.

It is a custom for the bride to show up late to the festivities of her wedding, but Aleena's numerous apologies about her fiancé's tardiness as she does the rounds reveal they've mixed things up this time.

"He won't be too much longer. He had some family business to take care of."

Her dress swishes against her slim thighs as she moves from guest to guest.

"Oh... I'm as eager as you for him to show up, Mrs. Florence. I promise the delay will be worth it when you see how dashing he looks in his tuxedo."

She laughs off one guest's comment on her glowing state. "I'll have you know my dress is white." She leans in close before whispering, "Off-white is still white, right?"

I'm dying for her to reach our table, but our mother delays that for as long as possible. She pulls Aleena from one side of the room to the next that by the time she makes it to our table, the groom-to-be has finally showed up.

He is greeted by his guests with as much, if not more, euphoria as Aleena's arrival instigated, and he's hidden from view for almost just as long. More than his suit is crumpled when Aleena gestures for him to join her.

As he heads our way, he adjusts his wonky tie. He has the swagger that captures the attention of the room, and a suit that showcases every spectacular ridge of his body.

Aleena was right. He looks so dashing in his tuxedo that he's instantly forgiven for his tardiness. There isn't a single eye he doesn't seize during his walk across the room, so you can imagine how hard it is to keep my expression passive when he finally lifts his head.

I know those eyes.

That smoldering smirk.

I've raked my fingers through that dark hair more than once.

But something is amiss with this picture. Andrik's neck tattoos are gone. His hands are void of the artwork that was faded enough to announce that it has been a part of his life for as long as he's been an adult. And his nose ring and diamond earring that scream rebellion have also vanished.

I swear I'm sitting across from Andrik, but it is like the watered-down version of the bad boy I was instantly obsessed with.

I'm in such a state of shock that when Aleena offers an introduction, instead of denying the handshake her fiancé holds out in offering, I slide my hand into his non-tattooed one and whisper softly, "Zoya Sakharoff."

His top lip twitches before his grip on my hand tightens. "Kazimir Dokovic." As his briefest touch rockets a zap up my arm, he works his jaw side to side. "It is a pleasure to meet you, Zoya." He even sounds like Andrik—if not a little less arrogant.

"Likewise," I murmur before sinking back onto my chair, taking my hand with me.

Aleena watches me for a handful of seconds before she introduces Kazimir to Nikita and Maksim. Maksim's expression is furious. I don't know if it is because he, too, is wondering who the hell Kazimir is or because Ano is signaling to speak with him over Aleena's shoulder.

Maksim waits for Kazimir and Aleena to move on to the table next to us before checking if Nikita is okay being left alone. By alone, he means without him. Half a dozen bodyguards keep her safe when Maksim isn't in charge of the campaign.

"Yes. If we leave before you return, we will meet you back at the suite," Nikita replies.

His forehead kiss steals my attention from Aleena and Kazimir. It is as PG as it comes, but anytime he does it, Nikita's cheeks inflame as if he is dragging the tip of his nose down the opening of her vagina.

The raunchiness of their exchange doesn't contribute to its scorching-hot rating. It is how Maksim is unashamed to show how much he loves his wife even when they're in public. Their relationship isn't a hidden dirty secret. It is love not cloaked in shame.

After breathing in the scent of Nikita's hair, Maksim locks his eyes with mine. He doesn't speak. He just gives me a look I've mastered deciphering over the past month. It is one that announces we need to speak, but it won't occur until whatever surprise he is organizing for Nikita is over.

I nod, happy to leave the awkwardness of our exchange on the back burner for a few hours.

I'm too confused to answer the numerous questions he and Nikita are silently bombarding me with since my introduction to Aleena's fiancé. I'd leave it on simmer for eternity if that were an option.

Regretfully, it isn't.

The groom-to-be's arrival is meant to fuel the flames. Kazimir's appearance douses them so well that dessert isn't even served before the hotel staff commences packing down the room for tomorrow's even bigger festivity.

"We can stay, if you want," Nikita offers when I peer back in the direction of the ballroom, my steps to the elevator slow and reserved. "You hardly saw Aleena, and I don't see it improving tomorrow. Kazimir's relatives are very... *imposing.* They don't seem willing to share him with anyone. Not even Aleena." Although she is giving me an out, she stabs the elevator call button with her finger, eager to find out where her husband disappeared to.

Nikita will never admit it, but she suffers from jealousy more than Maksim does. Her possessiveness could give Andrik's a run for its money.

When the elevator dings and we enter, I select the floor for the penthouse suites before asking, "Did you meet anyone in his family?"

Nikita moves in close to allow her bodyguards to ride the elevator with us before shaking her head. "There wasn't a chance. Things were a little tense."

Tense is an understatement. I've never felt more uncomfortable, and I let a stranger strap me to a sex swing in an underground sex club while heavily intoxicated. We won't mention anything I've done with Andrik, as I'm not sure I would survive the guilt it usually entices this time around.

I'm as convinced that Aleena's fiancé is Andrik as much as I am that Ano is Bayli, but where were his tattoos and unapproachable cocky demeanor? Kazimir could be Andrik's twin, but why wouldn't Mikhail mention him? Why would he make out as if it was solely him and Andrik against the world when they were kids? There couldn't have been a third wheel. Mikhail would have told me about him. Our friendship formed fast, but it was founded on honesty.

My interest is piqued when Nikita says, "The woman next to us said his family is extremely powerful and politically motivated. It kind of makes sense. That was..." A million words roll through her head, but none leave her mouth until we're halfway down the corridor of the penthouse suites. "Have the Galdeans met Kazimir previously?"

"Who?" I ask, still deep in thought about my many conversations with Mikhail concerning his family and striving to work out that if Kazimir is Andrik, why the hell wasn't Mikhail and Ellis a part of the rehearsal dinner?

Nikita scans her key card over the lock of the suite she's sharing with Maksim before repeating, "Kazimir. Aleena's husband-to-be."

"Oh... yeah. Him." I try to keep anger out of my voice. I miserably fail. "I don't know. Maybe."

My stomach gurgles when the movie playing on repeat in my head returns to the start of the rehearsal dinner. The welcome sign outside the ballroom confused Nikita because Aleena is using her middle name for the wedding festivities. Who's to say Andrik isn't doing the same?

As I shadow Nikita into the foyer of the penthouse, I run my theory through my head on repeat.

I also give Andrik's possible full name a whirl.

Kazimir Andrik Dokovic.

Kazimir Andrik Dokovic.

K. A. D.

My eyes pop when I recall the last time those initials turned my world on its head.

KADOK Industries.

*Kazimir Andrik **Dokovic.***

They're the same person. My sister's fiancé and the man who drafted a contract to ensure his wife-to-be knew their union wasn't about love are the same person.

But that isn't the catalyst of my anger.

He lied.

Dr. Hemway said Aleena wasn't on Andrik's list. That she would never be on any list where she was valued for her fertility.

He lied straight to my fucking face, yet I bet he will receive Aleena's forgiveness long before me. I slept with her fiancé—more than once.

I also loved him.

I still do.

With my life falling apart in front of me, I seek assistance from the only person capable of pulling me out of the madness relatively unscathed. I need my best friend, but at the moment, she needs me more.

The wetness on her cheeks announces this, not to mention the high-pitched squeal she releases before sprinting for the man wearing a prison jumpsuit and shackles.

"Daddy!"

62

ANDRIK

$\mathcal{I}$ dip my chin in wordless gratitude to a couple offering their well-wishes to Arabella and me. Their faces are unfamiliar, but since a majority of the seats at the rehearsal dinner are filled by the financial backers of my father's latest political campaign, that isn't surprising.

I never mixed business with pleasure.

I can't say that anymore.

They continue their incessant ramblings on how beautiful our future children will be while I guide Arabella into the elevator and impatiently wait for the doors to shut. I didn't offer to walk her to her hotel suite because I am a gentleman looking for brownie points from my future wife.

My thoughts are far more sinister than that.

As the car jolts into action, I lose the last morsel of composure I have left. With the hand I used to guide Arabella into the elevator, I grip her throat and pin her to the mirrored wall. There's nothing pleasant about my hold. Nothing admirable about it. It is the grip of a killer, and it makes her lips an instant shade of fascinating blue.

"You thought you could lie *to me* and that I wouldn't find out?" I tighten my grip more, lifting her feet from the floor. "How fucking stupid do you think I am!" I don't give her a chance to answer since it could possibly mimic what I was feeling when being introduced to the woman who hasn't left my thoughts for a single second over the past month. I get up into her face and scream. "I asked if you knew who she was the instant *she* left us alone!" The way I sneer "she" ensures she can't mistake who I am referring to.

Dina hovered for hours the day we met. I thought it was because she was one of those helicopter parents always looking out for her children. Now I know otherwise, and it makes me furious.

"You said you'd never heard of the name Zoya before, and that it was a pretty name." I drag her forward before ramming her back, stealing the last of the air in her lungs. "A pretty fucking name! That's what you told me while endeavoring to steal her focus!"

"Be-because..." She digs her nails into my palm, striving to loosen my hold. When her fight only has me doubling my grip, she tries another tactic. "Sh-she's my c-cousin. I-I forgot she changed her name."

I laugh off her lie like a madman. "A cousin with identical eyes, skin, and walk. A cousin with the same fantastic tits and sweltering waist but without the cutesy features that lower your praise from gorgeous to pretty. Is that the cousin you're referring to, Arabella *Dokovic*?"

She nods, and it shreds the last of my leniencies.

"I am not a man you lie to and live to tell the tale!" I roar, my thunderous words echoing in the tight confines of the elevator. "Tell me the fucking truth. *Now!* Or I will gut you where you stand."

"But I'm your bloo—"

I steal the words I refuse to hear seep from her lips by fully compressing on her airways. She is seconds from death. "You are *nothing* to me, but you are even more worthless to *them*." I don't need to mention the federation for her to know who I am referencing. My sneer speaks on my behalf. "If you don't learn that fast, you'll only ever learn it one way. In *death*."

Her watering eyes barely bounce between mine for half a second before she murmurs, "Ok-okay. Okay." Tears stream down her face as she gives honesty a whirl for the first time in God knows how long. "They're seeking a pure bl-bloodline. They want a royal lineage like back in the ancient Romanian times." She chokes on her last word, but it doesn't weaken the truth in her eyes. "But Zoya is infertile, so she wasn't a good candidate." As my hope slithers to the abyss, she discloses, "Zoya doesn't know who our father is. They've kept it from her for years. I only recently found out after I tried to..." The shame in her eyes finalizes her reply.

She knows my secret. She knows I fell in love with my sister and that I'm still fucking obsessed with her, because the humiliation in her eyes while recalling the night she tried to seduce me mimics mine to a T anytime I look in a mirror.

She's mortified, but something far more vital than dishonor is keeping her blood pumping through her veins.

The realization loosens my grip. Only by a smidge. I'm too angry to fully let go. I'm not mad that I am being continually controlled. That's been the basis of my existence since birth. It is knowing how much the steps I must take tomorrow to save my son's life will devastate Zoya. She has spoken fondly of her sister often, and that family ties are vitally important to her since she basically has none.

As much as I wish I could comfort her through this, that isn't something I can do.

I don't trust myself around her.

I doubt I ever will.

So instead of placing the entirety of the blame of my fuckups on someone else, I free Arabella from my clutch and step back.

With a sob, she falls to her knees and drags in big breaths that are sharply redrawn when I say, "Uninvite her to the wedding. I don't care how you do it, but I want it done *tonight*."

Her words are husky when she asks, "You still want to go ahead with it?"

It is a challenge, but I nod. "I don't have a choice."

Confident she won't dare second-guess my authority, I exit the elevator on the next floor, bumping into one of Maksim's paid goons on my way out.

63

ZOYA

"Hey..." I swivel on the spot, never more nervous. "I was just on my way to see you. Are you coming or going?"

Aleena sounds as nervous as I feel. "Ah... a little bit of both." She points to a door that leads to the rooftop. "I needed some fresh air, but I didn't want to go all the way down to the lobby, so I thought I'd go up a couple of floors instead." She peers at the door I tore through five seconds after building the courage to confront her. "Did I wake you?"

"No. Not at all. I was awake." *For reasons I don't want to tell you.*

After gripping her hand in mine, I lead her to one of those fancy armchairs that almost looks too regal to sit on. They're more to glam up the boring hallways than for seating purposes.

"I really need to tell you something, and unfortunately, it can't wait. I—"

"Kazimir told me everything."

My mouth gapes and I choke on a breath that was clearing some of the butterflies in my stomach. "He did?"

She wets her lips and nods. "Uh-huh."

He couldn't have told her everything. There's no way. Who in their right mind would be this calm if they found out their fiancé was sleeping with their sister?

My eyes dance between Aleena's when she adds, "And I've forgiven him."

Now I'm convinced she doesn't know the whole story, but I lose the chance to tell her when she blindsides me with a shocking revelation.

"It is the right thing to do. I don't want my child raised without a father being a part of the picture."

Sheer shock colors my tone. "You're pregnant?"

I balk when she nods. "It's early, but I've known for a couple of weeks." As she fans her hand over her stomach, a mothering glint sparks in her eyes. "The timing is a little off, but I truly believe this miracle happened for a reason, and I would like you to respect my decision to give my child the best upbringing I can."

I hate myself the instant my words leave my mouth, but I can't stop myself. "His contract was never about love, Aleena. Having his child won't make him love you."

"I know," she replies, nodding. "And that's okay. I will love the baby enough for both of us."

"Aleena—"

"This is my decision and *my* child. I will not have you ruin this for me." She shoots up to her feet, her footing wobbly. "If you can't support me, maybe you shouldn't come to the wedding." Tears gloss her eyes when she murmurs, "It was bad enough witnessing him fawn over you in the driveway of *our* home. I won't tolerate it in front of our family and friends."

A hundred thoughts roll through my head as she makes a beeline for the elevator, but only one makes it through the deluge.

"If you knew about us, why let me be a part of your bachelorette party?"

Her shoulders rise and fall three times before she cranks her neck back to face me. "I was hoping if you saw how much I loved him that you'd walk away. That you would let me win for once." There's a hint of deceit in her tone until she says, "That you'd finally let me be free of *her*." She doesn't need to say our mother's name for me to know who she is referring to. "I need this, Zoya, and if you've ever loved me, you will let me have it." A knife stabs my chest when she whispers, "You will let me have him."

"Okay," I murmur in defeat, certain my heart is breaking into too many pieces to ever be placed back together. I am not solely devastated about the pure hurt in her eyes. I'm distraught at the thought of Andrik being a part of my life even with him never actually being mine.

I don't know if I am strong enough for that, but for my baby sister, I will try.

Aleena softly smiles in gratitude before she recommences her slow stalk down the hall. When she enters the elevator, I assume I am free to release the tears my eyes are struggling to hold back.

I'm horribly mistaken.

Our exchange had a witness, and his verdict is starkly contradicting since he offers the third standpoint all great stories need.

"You can't let her guilt-trip you into stepping back, especially since I don't believe her fiancé fathered her unborn child." Ano locks his eyes with mine before he adds another hair-raising dip in the rollercoaster I've been riding for the past several months. "I'm reasonably sure that's on me."

64

ANDRIK

The agitation keeping my skin slicked with sweat clears away when I receive a text message.

ANOUSHKA:

Zakhar wanted to say good luck.

Anoushka's thumb finds its way into almost every photograph, but even with its inclusion, I can't miss Zak's big grin in the image she forwarded with her message.

He's wearing a blue hospital gown, and an ugly hairnet keeps his trademark light-brown locks off his face. He's trying to portray excitement, as to no doubt Anoushka's request, but I can tell he is scared.

You're not the only one, Zak.

Today is the day we were waiting for. Zakhar is about to get a new heart. He's prepped and ready for surgery in a hospital eight hundred miles from my location. All he needs to get better is for me to say the vows I've been dreading all month.

Love, honor, and obey.

Could there be three lesser respected words when it comes to this marriage? Fraudulent, immoral, and corrupt seem far more fitting.

When my father signals that it is time for the wedding to begin, I send Anoushka a message to say I will commence travels to the hospital minutes after I've exchanged vows. My helicopter is on the roof of the hotel, waiting for me.

ME:

Don't let them take him in until I've returned.

I hit send before I can tack on the words I refuse to speak: *I don't want to miss out on the opportunity of saying what could possibly be a final goodbye.*

There are no guarantees that Zak will survive his operation, but we're meant to be thinking positively.

It is a hard fucking feat when you feel like your life won't stop circling the toilet.

A *pfft* vibrates my lips when Anoushka replies with a thumbs-up. As quickly as my annoyance surfaced, it clears away. Anoushka's thumb still features in her next image, and so does my little brother.

Mikhail looks like hell. His skin is scaly, his beard is unkempt, and his eyes are sunken, yet he still looks more alive than Zakhar's whitening expression.

That shows he proved right when he chose his location today.

Just like I did when I let Arabella live.

My father straightens my suit jacket when I reach the end of the altar before fiddling with the white rose the wedding planner pinned on in a hurry. I pull away before signaling for the quartet to commence playing the song Dina selected for Arabella to walk down the aisle.

The quicker this is over, the sooner my son will have a new heart.

As I twist to face the people filling the pews the event company donned with thousands of roses and hydrangeas, my eyes instantly land on one face. It isn't hard to spot her in a crowd. She is the most beautiful in the room, and the most feared.

She could ruin everything with two little words. *I object.*

She won't, though, right? I don't approve of the approach Arabella used to scare her away, but a ruse of an absentee father will be the most effective. Zoya is unaware of her lineage because she was raised without a father's influence. To her, he is a shadow. A nightwalker. Someone who only ever comes out when it's dark. She's never seen his face.

Well, she has. She just doesn't know it.

In case Arabella's delivery wasn't convincing enough, I permitted Konstantine to release some information Maksim's team would have never stumbled onto even if they were looking into me. I know they are—that's all part of the plan—but if they don't interfere in Zakhar's procedure today, I have no issue with them using anything they unearth.

I just have to hope Zoya feels the same way, or I'm fucked.

When the crowd *ahs* in sync, I try to shift my eyes to the end of the aisle—to move them to the woman I am marrying. I fail.

I can't take my eyes off Zoya for a single second. It isn't solely her beauty that demands the attention of any man with a pulse. It is how fast her lips move when a man wearing a backward baseball cap butts shoulders with her.

Whatever he whispers in her ear pisses her off and balls my hands.

That should be the end of my reaction. It isn't, however. After slanting my head to hide the movement of my lips from the people in the front three pews, I ask, "Who is he?"

The earpiece in my ear crackles before Konstantine murmurs,

"No fucking clue. I ran him through facials after he approached her at Le Rogue. Nothing came up."

I accept Arabella's hand from her mother before guiding her onto the podium where the celebrant is waiting for us. Her veil and puffy white dress should be enough incentive to let this go, but Zoya's agitation grew the further Arabella walked down the aisle, which means mine tripled.

"What about in the other system we've been utilizing over the past few months?"

"I wasn't sure it was worth the hassle." My jaw tightens when Konstantine says, "You said you were done with her."

"I am done with her. But I still want to know who he is." I glare down at Arabella while saying through clenched teeth, "Since she is my soon-to-be sister-in-law, I should probably look out for her."

Konstantine's shocked huff announces my exchange with Arabella in the elevator last night wasn't monitored. "All right. I'll run it now. It may take a bit."

"You have five minutes."

He calls me an asshole before the strokes of his keyboard are drowned out by the celebrant commencing proceedings. "Dearly beloved, we are gathered here today to witness the legal union of Kazimir Andrik Dokovic and A—"

"I object!"

As everyone's eyes snap to Zoya, the celebrant says, "We haven't reached that part yet, and you better have a very valid reason for the interruption, young lady."

I hope he kissed his family goodbye this morning. The derogative tone he uses to publicly dress down Zoya ensures it would have been for the final time.

"I have a good reason," Zoya murmurs as her eyes shift from her sister to me. "I'm pregnant, and from what I read last night, there hasn't been a Dokovic child born out of wedlock in over a hundred years. I'd hate for my child to be the first."

Although everything she is saying is true, I scoff before gesturing for the celebrant to continue. The "I'm pregnant" ruse is the oldest in the book. I've dodged it numerous times in the past twenty-plus years without incident.

Though it is a little harder this time since I'm aware her next comment is true. "We had unprotected sex more than once. That comes with a risk, An"—Zoya recovers quickly from her near fumble of my name—"Kazimir. One you failed to adequately assess before you decided to *fuck* with me."

"I didn't *assess* the situation adequately because you're infertile," I argue back, hating that she's airing our dirty laundry for the world to see, but too fucking furious she is placing her anger before Zakhar's life not to snap back. "We met at a fertility clinic."

"Exactly!"

Zoya fights to get out of one of my father's goon's hold before Maksim ends her struggle with a threat. It sees the goon stepping back with his hands in the air, confident he is seconds from death.

I hate that Maksim is defending her, but not as much as the turmoil her following sentence instigates. "I was at a fertility clinic seeking treatment. You can ask anyone who has suffered from endometriosis. The chances of conception *increase* tenfold after laparoscopic ablation."

I shake my head, too sickened to even consider the possibility. A month ago, I would have banged my chest. But now... *fuck*. I'll be seen as a mockery.

This is not something I will ever live down.

"She's telling the truth," fires up her best friend. "I've also been pumping her with fertility supplements over the past six months." Nikita shifts on her feet to face a still and slack-jawed Zoya. "I didn't mean to snoop. I just wanted to lessen your pain. I was trying to help."

The crowd loves the tension the sheer honesty in Nikita's eyes offer.

I fucking hate it.

So much so, I dismiss Zoya with an edge of arrogance I am certain she is growing to loathe. "It doesn't matter. I love Arabella, and I want her to be my wife."

I also love my son, and I refuse for my foolish mistakes to end his life.

He isn't even five yet.

He has barely lived.

Why the fuck am I the only one who cares about that?

"That choice is now out of your hands," says a voice steeped in history.

The wedding invitees whisper among themselves when my grandfather stands to his feet and turns to face Zoya. Although he projects his voice in her direction, the sneer of his words reveals who his anger is truly directed at.

It isn't Zoya or me.

It is my father.

"I didn't work so hard to keep our family name in good graces to have a child born out of wedlock. If her claims are true, they will wed. *Today.*"

With a flick of his wrist, he sends Kolya out to purchase a pregnancy test and ends the nuptials saving his great-grandson's life.

65

ZOYA

$\mathcal{A}$s she tears open an early-detection pregnancy test, Nikita whispers, "I really hope you know what you're doing, Z. This family seems a little tense."

She knew what to say when I commenced my ruse because I grilled her last night on how I could make a pregnancy test appear positive even if you're not pregnant. She grew so worried that I had taken a test and was freaking about the results that she admitted she knew of my fertility issues and confessed to supplementing my "vitamin water" with medication I couldn't afford.

It's why Grampies's pharmaceutical bill surged so astronomically high six months ago.

Before I can tell her that I have no damn clue what I am doing, a deep male voice from outside the bathroom says, "Step out of the stall. We don't want the test contaminated."

"Just a minute," Nikita murmurs before she shifts her focus back to me.

"Not a minute. *Now!*"

I slant my head out of the stall before releasing some of my anger onto a person undeserving of my wrath. It isn't his fault my lie forced him into a female restroom to watch me pee on a stick. He also didn't try to force my sister into a marriage that would only end one way—with her death. But I'm too frustrated not to release some of the pressure, so he will be hit with some of it.

"Do you know who her husband is?" The brute jerks up his chin. "Then I suggest you shut your mouth before he teaches you some manners. She's also a doctor. They can't lie even when you want them to." My last statement is more for me than Nikita. I need to have some faith in Dr. Hemway, or my entire plan will go to shit.

With the goon more worried about Maksim's sudden appearance than who is peeing on the stick purchased by political royalty, I tell Nikita to go ahead.

She does so with knowledge I doubt she learned in medical school. "You need to dip this end into your pee midstream." She emphasizes her last word like it has a heap of importance. "Once you've finished, pop the cap back on. A positive result should come up in a minute or two."

"Are you sure it will come up?" My words are so faint I'm surprised Nikita hears them.

She nods. "One of the best treatments for endo sufferers is to stop their cycle. The HCG hormone thickens the uterus, but it also interrupts your period."

"Okay." I breathe out slowly before accepting the test from her and moving to the toilet.

While I do my business, Nikita stands just outside the disabled toilet stall, within eyesight of the goon meant to authenticate the accuracy of my test by ensuring I am the only person who pees on it.

Two lines appear on the early detection test before I've even placed on the cap.

My ruse is full steam ahead.

I should feel relieved, but I'm an odd mix of anxious and

worried. I hate what my objection could do to my relationship with Aleena, but Andrik's son keeps popping up in my mind too. I've never met him, but I don't want him to be hurt by the actions of the people who are meant to protect him.

When I hand the test to the brute, he grunts at the result before he gives it to a second man standing outside the restroom.

I can tell the exact moment the news is shared with Andrik. Glass smashing sounds into the bathroom a second before his grandfather's elderly frame fills the doorway.

"Switch outfits with your sister. Your guests are waiting."

"Aleena... please." I grip her arm before she can leave the dressing room as quickly as she entered it. "I'm not doing this to hurt you. I swear to God." When she yanks out of my hold, I get so desperate that I share secrets with her I'm still struggling to work out. "If you conceived a daughter, you wouldn't have seen the year out. If it is a boy, you'd have a maximum of five years. Less if Andrik's"—I cuss before correcting—"Kazimir's interests strayed."

The information Ano gifted me last night couldn't be misconstrued. Disappearing wives are as regular as extramarital affairs for the Dokovic clan. If I had ignored Ano's information, I would have placed a timer on my sister's head.

I couldn't do that, so I placed my life in the firing zone instead.

When Aleena remains facing the exit but not walking through it, I murmur, "You saw how quickly his grandfather switched us. We're disposable to them. Replaceable. I'm trying to save you and your unborn child from that."

Nikita cautioned me last night that Aleena's pregnancy confirmation could have been a ruse to force me to stay away from Andrik, but my heart refuses to believe it. I know she is pregnant. I'm just skeptical that her baby is Andrik's. The IVF dates in Andrik's contract don't match. The timeline Ano gave me is far more viable.

Aleena's eyes lock with mine, and the wetness in them breaks my heart. "By trapping us with *her*."

"No. I will get you out. I promise."

She wipes at the tear that rolls down her cheek when she shakes her head. "It doesn't matter. I made my bed, and now I must lay in it."

"Aleena..."

She races through the door so fast that my shout bounces off the wall in the hallway three guards are monitoring. They don't belong to Maksim's crew. They protect the Dokovic assets, and that is precisely what I am to them now. A piece of property.

But, as Aleena said seconds ago, I made my bed, so now I must lay in it.

After shoving my feet into the dress Aleena hand-delivered, I yank it up my midsection and then squeeze it past my breasts. Aleena and I are a similar height and build, but more of my breasts spill out of the dress than it holds in.

I don't bother looking in the mirror before exiting the dressing room at the side of the ballroom. I have no one to impress—not even the man waiting for me at the altar.

"Are you sure I can't talk you out of this?" Nikita asks while handing me the bouquet Aleena dumped at the altar before storming down the aisle with our mother hot on her tail.

As she raced after her youngest daughter, my mother said there would be hell to pay for my objection, and that this isn't the last I'll be hearing from her. I haven't seen her since, and although it shouldn't hurt to notice her spot in the front row is vacant, it does.

Nikita draws my focus back to her. "I'm not above asking Maksim to help get you out of this."

"No. I need to do this." I'd never forgive myself if I pulled out now.

The Dokovics' marital traditions weren't the only evidence Ano's hacker friend unearthed last night. He also discovered the cause of the swiftness of Aleena and Andrik's engagement.

If this wedding doesn't go through, Andrik's son won't get the heart he so desperately needs. That's how Ano convinced me to object. He forced me to pick between my sister's life and Andrik's son. I only came to the decision to object when I realized I could save them both.

"Okay." Nikita's exhale fans my sweaty cheeks with warm air. "Then let's do this."

As I join a red-faced and furious Andrik at the end of the aisle, Nikita stays in eyesight the entire time. All I have to do is signal that I want out, and she will relay my every wish to Maksim.

I won't chicken out, though. Not for my unborn niece or nephew, and not for Andrik's son. They're children, and they should be protected no matter what.

"Dearly beloved..." the celebrant starts again. "We are gathered here today to celebrate the..."

There are no objections this time around.

No interruptions.

There is also no kiss.

The instant the celebrant announces Andrik and me as husband and wife, Andrik leaves the altar without a backward glance, shocking our guests and breaking my heart more than my sister's disappointment that I stole her "wife" title.

66

ZOYA

My groggy eyes slowly open when I hear car doors slamming shut and footsteps. Waking up in a strange environment sucks. It takes me a moment to gather my bearings, and when I do, it adds a ton of pressure onto my chest instead of alleviating it.

I didn't catch the name of the middle-aged man who drove me here after farewelling Nikita and Maksim in the empty reception area. The guests piled out soon after Andrik, and I've been left to navigate my new title and surroundings by myself.

I didn't recognize the names of the towns we drove through during our long journey to Andrik's new home base. They ranged in sizes and wealth status, but Andrik's home can only be described one way—cold.

There is no love in his house, no joy, and the conditions worsen when I discover the reason I was jolted awake. Andrik has returned home. He isn't alone. The little boy I assume is his son is cradled in his arms. He's as white as a bed sheet and looks deathly sick.

"Should he be out of bed already?" I follow Andrik through his palatial mansion when he *pffts* at my question before he storms away. "Why isn't he still in the hospital?"

I assumed that was why I was brought to this location, because it was closer to the hospital doing Zakhar's heart transplant.

After Andrik places Zakhar on a bed and gestures for a doctor in the corner of his room to move closer to his bedside, he mutters, "Because you were not *their* pick, my son has to suffer until you have proven yourself worthy of their selection."

"What?" A better response is above me. I didn't realize this was a popularity contest. I thought the only requirement was for Andrik to marry. That's why I took Aleena's place.

When I say that to Andrik, he storms up close to me. More than alcohol bounds off his breath when he shouts in my face. Death is there too. "He had a heart! It was right there, in the operating room, waiting for him! But *they* got word to the surgeon first, and he stupidly believed their wrath would be worse than mine." When he flexes and unflexes his hands, I notice droplets of blood on the cuffs of his dress shirt he hasn't changed since we exchanged vows. "It wasn't."

A chill runs down my spine, shocked he can speak about murder without the slightest bit of remorse. It only lingers as long as it takes for me to lock eyes with Zakhar. He isn't my child, but I would still burn down the world for him. Every adult should do the same.

"Tell me what to do to fix this. I'll do anything you ask."

Andrik's laugh is as painful as it is sadistic. "The only way you can fix this is by going back twenty-eight years and praying your philandering absentee father keeps his dick in his pants."

I slap him before I can consider the consequences of my actions. Andrik's reaction is just as reckless. He pins me to the wall by my throat quicker than my lungs can be replenished with what I am confident will be my last breath.

It isn't a sexy hold this time around, nor lusty. It is the grip of a killer who was on the brink of breaking before I pushed him over the edge.

When my nostrils flare, my body too eager to live to surrender without a fight, Andrik's massively dilated eyes lower to my nose before they drop half an inch lower.

He stares at my lips for what feels like an eternity before his hold eventually loosens enough for me to suck in some miniscule breaths. He isn't pulling back. He just can't maintain the hold he needs to kill me and run his thumb over my lips at the same time. Hurting me while caressing me simultaneously isn't a skill he seems to hold.

The gentleness of his embrace doesn't match the fury beaming from him. His body is shaking enough for its shudder to be felt from a distance, but the way he strokes my lips is almost nurturing. *Loving.*

His actions don't make any sense.

He hates me as much as I am growing to hate him, doesn't he?

Too bewildered not to seek answers, I murmur, "Andrik—"

One mutter of his name snaps him out of his trance as quickly as his anger swamped him with it. His pupils enlarge to the size of saucers before they're stolen from my view by him throwing his fist into the drywall at the side of my head before he quickly exits the room.

I take off after him, too angry and confused to let this go.

"Your original contract said you wanted an heir!" I thrust my hand at the room we just left. "You have one, so I assumed the only requirement today was a wife. *Any* wife."

"You assumed wrong!" he roars, spinning to face me.

"As did you when you picked *my* sister." My wild eyes bounce between his equally furious pair. "Did you know she was my sister when you were fingering me in the driveway of your shared home?" My anger catapults when he looks disgusted by my line of questioning, which means I'll only push him harder. "Did you know she was my sister when you were on your knees pledging that she would never have you like I was about to have you!" I storm up to him to bang my fists on his chest. "Did you know she was my sister when you had her sign on a dotted line that would end her life in five years *if* she was fortunate enough to birth you a son!"

"No!" he screams, snatching up my hands. "I didn't know anything because *she* lied!" His grip on my wrists turns painful. "I went to their home *for you*, but they made out they didn't know who you were. That they had never heard of a Zoya Galdean before."

"You're lying! Aleena wouldn't do that to me. She loves me."

When he laughs as if the idea of my sister loving me is ludicrous, I snap. I yank my wrists out of his hold before directing my hands toward his face. This time, I close my fists.

"You're the lying, cheating piece of shit. Don't try to put that on *my* sister."

I get in two solid hits before he spins me away from him. "Calm the fuck down before I'm forced to retaliate."

Too furious to see sense through the madness, I stomp my foot and throw my head back like I was taught during boxing classes.

Andrik grunts through the pain of his toes being stomped, but he dodges my headbutt by a cat's whisker.

"For fuck's sake, милая," he growls out when I continue to fight.

"Don't call me darling. I fucking hate when you call me that. You only ever say it when you're trying to lie your way into my panties."

Faster than I can click my fingers together, he arches me over the sofa in the den, tugs up my nightwear until it bands around my waist, rips off my panties without the slightest bit of protest from the stiff material, and then narrows his hand toward my ass.

"No," I scream, squirming so hard that he has to pin me to the sofa cushion by splaying his hand across my lower back. "You do *not* get to spank me. Lying, cheating pieces of shit don't get to spank—"

He silences me with a firm crack on my right butt cheek.

"I have *never* cheated."

He spanks me hard on the ass again, this strike more disciplinary based than for pleasure.

"I have no reason to lie."

Another two whacks augment the fire in my gut. They send it from raging with anger to scalding with need.

"And I am not the one who snuck around in the cloak of darkness with no care for who they were taking down in the process." Almost every word he yells occurs with a spank, leaving my ass raw, red, and in desperate need of some TLC, which Andrik immediately commences undertaking while muttering, "That was *my* father." His hand freezes halfway across my burning cheek, his fingertips mere inches from the soaked seam of my pussy. "*Our* father."

As quickly as he bent me over the sofa, he steps away from it.

When he races for a bar at the side of the den, I stand on a pair of wobbly legs. He fills a whiskey glass to the rim with a clear liquid that he downs with one gulp. He drags his hand along his wet lips to gather the leftover liquid on his mouth, its rattle undeniable.

I realize its shake is clattering through his entire body when he spins to face me. He looks as unhinged now as he did while announcing why his son was refused his heart transplant.

There's so much shame in his eyes, so much hurt, I fold on my campaign to burn him at the stake as he was planning to do to Aleena in an instant.

This is about more than a sibling defending a sibling. I'm certain of it.

It isn't even about a father protecting a son.

The fight is completely different when it comes to soulmates.

I only make it halfway across the den before Andrik slices his hand through the air, freezing my steps. "Don't."

The way he looks at me is more painful than his short rejection.

He looks at me as if I am disgusting and that I will *never* be his first choice to mother his children or take on his last name.

His next statement proves my theories. "I went through with the ceremony today because I was hoping they'd keep their word. That they would give my son a new heart. They didn't, so I no longer need to keep my side of our deal either." His eyes fall to the floor. "We will take care of *that*"—he jerks his hand at my stomach—"then file for an annulment shortly after."

My voice cracks when I ask, "My sister?" It wasn't solely Andrik's son's health on my mind when I made my decision earlier today. Aleena's unborn child was right there next to him.

I sigh in relief when Andrik answers, "Will be free to live her life how she sees fit." I wonder just how closely this man has been watching proceedings this weekend when he says, "It came to light recently that she may not be the most suitable candidate for a future First Lady. Integrity is a big part of the role. Conceiving another man's child is not exactly honorable."

Too heartbroken to fight, I nod like I'm not as blindsided by his revelation now as I was when he announced that Aleena made out to him that I didn't exist.

It also confirms my earlier assumption that her unborn child isn't Andrik's.

You only use gimmicks when you have nothing solid to tie you to them.

That was the first trick our mother taught us.

When Andrik commences walking away, I slow his steps by asking, "Will you ever tell me what I did wrong?" I could leave it there, but I'm too hormonal to act pleasant. "Then I can ensure I don't make the same mistake with the next man whose name I want to notch on my bedpost."

He almost bites at the bait I'm dangling in front of him. His hands ball into fists, and I can hear the crunch of his back molars as he grinds them together. But as quickly as my hope rises that the punishment he instigated earlier was just the start, it is flattened.

"There are twelve bedrooms in the east wing. Pick any of them you want."

After releasing his balled hands, he heads in the opposite direction of the way he suggested.

67

ZOYA

"Good morning."

I wait for the middle-aged blonde woman to acknowledge my greeting, before tiptoeing into Zakhar's room. He's awake—barely. I don't believe his exhaustion is of choice. He's so unwell that doing something as simple as keeping his eyelids open is exhausting.

Hope that everything isn't as bad as it seems rains down on me when Zakhar's nanny says, "Don't expect much of a response from him. He only responds to candy. Don't you, Zak?" She tickles his ribs, sending his boyish laugh bouncing around the room.

When I laugh, Zakhar's joyful eyes shift to me. He stares at me with his head tilted to the side and his lips quirked for several long seconds before he drops his focus to my pockets. "Do you have any sweets?"

"I don't." When he pouts, I quickly add, "I could get you some."

His smile blurs when he nods fast.

"Let me," offers the nanny. "I'm dying for some caffeine." She twists to face me. "You?"

I nod as eagerly as Zakhar. "Please."

She smiles in acknowledgement before telling Zakhar she will be back in a minute. "Take care of our guest for me, okay? Her reception was a little frosty yesterday, so you need to be extra nice to her." She squeezes my hand on the way out, then exits, closing the door behind her.

I stop staring at the medical equipment monitoring Zakhar's stats when he says, "I think Anoushka likes you. You must have good karma."

"You know what karma is?"

Brown locks bounce in all directions when he bobs his chin. "Mommy says it is when someone is a good person so they're pre... pre... predes—"

"Predestined?"

Again, he nods. "Predestined for greatness." A fondness twinkles in his eyes. "That's why I was born. I was put into my mommy's tummy because I am pre...pre—"

"Predestined," I fill in again.

He doesn't bother repeating the word too large for his vocabulary. "Mommy says I was born to do great things. That I will restore the rightful order." I sit on the edge of his bed and hold his tiny hand in mine when he murmurs, "I just have to get better first."

Since this is the first time I've sat across from a child since Aleena was little, I'm stunned by the swiftness of the change in our conversation. I forgot anyone under the age of ten can go from heartbreak to euphoria in half a second.

"Once I am better, I'm going to learn to fly a helicopter like my dad. Then I won't have to use my legs anymore. I can fly everywhere. I might even go see my mommy. Do you want to come with me?"

"Um. Sure. Do you think your mom will be okay with that?"

"I think so. She doesn't get to do it very often, but she loves meeting new people." I smile when he murmurs, "She looks a lot like you." The fact Andrik picked Aleena from a selection of many pre-approved brides verifies he has a type, so I'm not surprised by Zakhar's confession.

I can't say the same when he continues. "Except she has lines here." He drags his tiny finger over the corner of my eye before moving them to my forehead. "And here." I laugh when he chokes out with a laugh, "And she has tinsel in her hair even when it's not Christmas." He chuckles so loud the monitors at the side of his bed sound an alarm. "She thinks they make her not pretty, but that isn't true. She is very pretty. She is as beautiful as you."

"Thank you, Zak," I murmur when his cheeks inflame at the end of his underhanded compliment. "You're very handsome as well. I bet your mommy tells you that all the time too."

"She does," he agrees, nodding softly. "But it doesn't count when it comes from her. Mommies are biased." He struggles over his last word.

"Sometimes they are," I say, deepening the groove between his brows. "But your mom isn't. You're the most handsomest little boy I've ever seen."

As the heat across his cheeks grows, he asks, "Does that mean you want to be my girlfriend?"

My heart thuds in my ears as I strive to think of a reply. "Ah..."

"I won't be mad if you want to be my girlfriend, but I might have to check with Daddy first. He likes you more than he likes Anoushka." Before I can correct him, he continues. "He's just confused because everyone keeps saying bad things about you." He folds his arms over his chest and sinks back. "I guess you were right. Not all mommies are biased. Yours isn't very nice. She says bad things about you all the time, and she makes my mommy cry."

I spread my hand over my chest. "My mom made your mom cry?"

Little tears nearly topple from his eyes when he nods. "She told her that she's not a real mom. That she's an incuemabator."

I don't need to correct him on his last word. The devastation in his eyes tells the story he's desperate to share without the need for translation.

My first thought is to seek immediate answers to my mother's involvement in his conception, but there's something far more important demanding my focus right now.

"How many times has your mom told you she loves you, Zak?"

His face lights up. "At least a trillion times."

"A trillion?" My mouth gapes and I adopt a shocked face. "I thought maybe a million, but a trillion? No way! That's crazy."

The pain in his eyes shifts to adoration. "That's how much she loves me. She tells me all the time."

"She must be the best mommy."

"She is," he agrees. "She is the best mommy in the entire world."

"Because she is *your* mommy, Zak. That's what makes her the best mommy."

His smile makes my heart feel whole for the first time in years, and it will free me to exit his room minus the guilt that saw me entering it. I just need a little more time to relish his gooey goodness before instigating a battle hotter than hell.

"He is the sweetest."

Anoushka smiles fondly at Zakhar while tracing my steps to the door. I was only meant to visit for thirty minutes. I spent the entire day with him. "He is. And he has certainly taken an instant liking to you. You have a fan for life."

My chest sinks. "I doubt he'll feel the same when he learns how badly I stuffed things up for him yesterday."

Anoushka hands Zak's care over to a pediatrician before guiding me into the hallway. "There is still time to fix that, Zoya."

"How?" I ask, lost. "I married a man I'm meant to hate but don't because I thought it was the right thing to do. It caused more issues." I breathe out slowly. When it does little to weaken my confusion, I offload it onto Anoushka. "I'm sailing blind. I need help. Help Andrik doesn't seem willing to give. Look at how he avoided Zak's room today. He hates me so much he doesn't even want to share the same air as me."

"That's not true. He's just confused." Her eyes flick up to a camera dangling above us before she moves our conversation down the hallway. "If you want to help him, you need to appease the people controlling both his emotions and actions."

I fan my arms out. *Did she miss the part when I said I married a man I'm meant to hate?* "I've done everything I can. I have no other way to assuage them."

I balk, startled when she whispers, "You could get pregnant for real."

"Whatever do you mean? I *am* pregnant." *And suddenly the worst liar in the world.*

Anoushka rolls her eyes, lowering the age bracket I placed her in from sixties to fifties. "Mr. Dokovic is a shrewd, ruthless man, but he is old school. He would have completely skipped over your friend's confession that she gave you fertility treatment. The federation is far more observant. They would have canceled Zakhar's operation purely on speculation that you lied. If you prove to them that you meant no malice with an *actual* pregnancy, they will reschedule his transplant."

Hope dissipates before I can latch on to it. "I wish I could do that, but I can't. For one, Andrik looks at me as if I am mud under his boot." When she attempts to interrupt me, I talk faster, too hurt to remain quiet. "And two, I can't physically get pregnant. I'm... I'm infertile."

She looks genuinely devastated for me, though it only halts her campaign for half a second. "There are ways you can still get pregnant. Mikhail's mother did IVF many years ago. With modern advancements, I'm sure you have options."

"I do, but they take time. That isn't in our favor. Even now, IVF can stretch from two to twelve weeks. You have consultation appointments, the commencement of treatment, ovulation stimulation, trigger injections, and then the egg retrieval. It isn't as easy as it sounds."

My senses smack back into me ten seconds too late.

I blubber when I'm snowed under, and that was a doozy.

Hating Anoushka's shocked expression, I attempt to smooth it over. "I was extremely hungry, young, and desperate." Nothing but shame resonates in my tone. "I also figured if I had no use for my eggs, why not give them to someone who needed them?" My exhale ruffles Anoushka's hair. "I never saw them as my children. I just saw them as my failures."

Anoushka gathers my hand in hers and squeezes it. "Was the option of egg retrieval never given to you when you were diagnosed as infertile?"

My headshake is weak. I don't want more stupid tears to fall. "No. It was never discussed because I never gave any indication to Dr. Hemway that I was interested in having children."

"That didn't change as you got older?"

"It did, but..." Over constantly taking the easy way out, I murmur, "But I would have had to show up to appointments for him to know that." I stray my eyes to Zakhar's bedroom door. "I also never really thought about it until now. An hour with Zakhar has me craving things I've never wanted."

As did every minute I spent with Andrik, though I keep that snippet of information to myself.

I often dreamed over the past several months how different our relationship could have been if he hadn't learned I was infertile. Would he have picked me? Would he have asked for my help to get the answers he was seeking? I want to say nothing would have changed, but my ego won't allow me.

We had a connection ferocious enough to scald anyone within a five-mile radius of it.

It just burned out far sooner than I had predicted.

"I think I might go lie down. I'm feeling a little woozy. I didn't sleep much last night. With the wedding, and then the..." I hook my thumb to Zak's door. "I'm exhausted." It is more an emotional exhaustion than physical, but once again, that can remain between us.

Anoushka smiles gently, soundlessly announcing she is aware of the cause of my tiredness. "Do you want me to wake you for dinner?"

"No, that's fine. I'm not hungry." I walk partway down the hall so she won't see my cowardly face when I say, "If you see Andrik before me, can you tell him my mother knows Zakhar's mother? They've met previously. Perhaps more than once."

Anoushka's shocked huff rustles in my ears before she murmurs, "I think he'd rather hear it from you."

This kills me to say, but it is honest. "He will believe it more if it comes from you. I'm not exactly deserving of his faith right now."

"And you think he is worthy of yours?" She waits for me to face her before saying, "He's lied too, but that doesn't mean either of you are unworthy of forgiveness." Her eyes glisten. "You just need to forgive yourselves first because that guilt is the *only* thing holding you both back right now."

68

ANDRIK

*A*noushka implements a disappointed stance when I ask, "Were you there when he said that?"

"No." Before I can dismiss her from my office with an arrogance that would have seen my bottom paddled when I was a child, she adds, "But I asked Zakhar about it after she left, and he confirmed what she said. Zoya's mother and Zakhar's mom know each other. From what I can tell, they've interacted numerous times."

My silence agitates her to no end.

"Andrik—"

"I will look into it," I interrupt, willing to say anything for a moment of peace.

My head won't shut down.

My heart won't shut down.

I'm tired and angry. That is a lethal combination. It is *not* the time to mess with me.

"But for now, I need to do this." I fan my hand over the files I had couriered to our new location this morning. "I need to find a wife who can birth the next generation of the Dokovic reign." *A federation-approved heir.*

I fucking hate myself. I hated myself last night when I tried to push Zoya into admitting that she lied about being pregnant by suggesting an abortion. And I hate myself now for acting like her fertility issues are the only reason we can't be together.

There are far more pressing issues as to why I shouldn't think about her the way I do, though none I am willing to share.

"There are ways Zoya can get pregnant."

"No!"

Anoushka pushes like Mikhail does because she knows she will never face the wrath of my gun. "She donated eggs years—"

"No!"

"There could still be some available to thaw. Or you could use a donor."

"No. No. *No!*" I shout, losing my cool. "I don't want to have a baby with Zoya. I don't want to father her offspring. I want to pretend she doesn't exist. That's all I fuckin' want."

Because that is the only way I will be able to keep my promise to Zakhar.

I told him he wouldn't lose me like he will his mother in two short weeks. Acting like Zoya can be a part of our life will only end one way—with my death. That's how much it torments me. That's how much it hurts knowing how badly I crave her but can't have her.

"An annulment is being filed as we speak. She will be out of our hair by the end of the week."

My self-loathing slips into the abyss when a croaky voice outside my office door says, "Then I guess I better go pack. I don't want to outstay my welcome."

Zoya pegs a USB drive at my head, her aim perfect. It smacks me in the brow hard enough to sting before landing on my lap.

"I knew you wouldn't believe me, so I got proof." She walks away before something forces her to turn back around. "And by the way, it is still classed as cheating when you're fooling around on your mistress." She glares at me like she hates me. "Especially when you told her that you hadn't been with anyone since her."

This time, she leaves without a backward glance. It is a struggle to stay in my seat. I want to react like I did last night. I want to bend her over my knee and spank her sass right out of her. But that will make me as unhinged as the depraved thoughts that fill my head when I load Zoya's USB drive into my laptop and fire up the first bit of footage.

It is from a hidden surveillance device Konstantine placed in Zakhar's room at my request when I realized I was only being shown what the federation wanted me to see.

This footage shows Dina standing across from Zakhar, intimidating him with a stern stare.

"What was our agreement, Zakhar?"

His little lip quivers as he replies to her snapped question. "That I'm not to tell anyone about my mommy."

"Because?"

Tears gloss his eyes. "Because then she will have to go to heaven."

Dina moves closer, hovering over him with her tall height. "Is that what you want, Zakhar? Do you want your mother to die?"

"No," he answers with a sob.

Dina's composure doesn't alter in the slightest. She remains as stern as a head nun at an all-girl's school campus. "Then do as we practiced. Who is your mother, Zakhar?"

"I don't know," he answers, clearly ashamed he has to hide her identity.

"Where did you live before you came here?"

"I don't know," he murmurs again.

"Who brought you here?"

His eyes flick up for two heart-thrashing seconds, peering into the eyes of his abuser, before he shrugs. "I don't know."

I can't see Dina's face, though I can picture her smile. Victory is rife even through a hidden surveillance device.

After patting Zakhar's head like he is an obedient dog, she shifts to her right before saying, "He won't break cover. I trained him well."

As the footage ends, I shoot my eyes to Konstantine. "Find out who she was speaking to."

He nods as I click into the second file of footage attached to the drive.

Anoushka's disappointed sigh is louder than the strokes of Konstantine's fingers on his keyboard when "Kneel. *Now!*" sounds through the speakers of my laptop.

Arabella... *Aleena?* Whatever the fuck her name is immediately follows my command. She falls to her knees as swiftly as I spin to close my bedroom door, blocking the visual of my supposed wife-to-be naked and ready to please.

Zoya thinks I cheated on her with her sister.

I wonder if she would be as upset when all the truths of that week are exposed?

I'm close to telling her. I can't live with the torment for much longer. But first, I need to visit my old hometown.

My son was interrogated without a parent present.

That warrants punishment, and I'm the judge, jury, and executioner when it comes to punishing the insolent fools who hurt the people I love.

And perhaps their caretaker. "Make sure she eats today." Zoya skipped both dinner last night and breakfast this morning.

After waiting for Anoushka to agree to my request, I add another task onto Konstantine's never-ending list. "And find out who doctored the footage."

Although Zakhar can't be monitored twenty-four-seven by

Konstantine, there's meant to be someone watching his feed day and night. I have a hunch of who might have coerced the security personnel from their post for a minute or two, but I'm not as trusting of my intuition as I once was, so I'd rather Konstantine check. He is one of only a few people I trust right now.

"Who do you want me to forward my findings to?"

Konstantine's question stumps me until I turn to face him. He knows I wouldn't have anyone to take my anger out on if it hadn't been for Zoya, so he believes she should get some credit for her finding.

Since I don't disagree with him, I nod, wordlessly approving his suggestion.

69

ZOYA

I dunk my head under a heavy flow of water, willing myself to pull up my big girl panties and handle my mistakes myself for the third day in a row. It isn't Nikita's job to continually bandage my boo-boos. And it isn't her husband's either. I objected at Aleena's wedding before running the ruse that I'm pregnant, so I need to suffer the consequences of my actions.

It isn't like I have long. Andrik said yesterday that the annulment will be processed within a week. Then I'll be as free as a bird—and most likely still unable to take the edge off without Andrik's involvement.

After swallowing enough water to drown my wish to squeal, I poke my head out of the heavy flow of water. The wetness clinging to my lashes reminds me that I don't need to carry this burden alone. I objected, but I was coerced into making that decision. Ano is as much a part of this as I am, and he doesn't have my number blocked like Aleena does.

He won't be able to help me with the itch I haven't been able to ignore since Andrik's spanking, but he can offer some comical relief to my overstressed head.

I tried to call Aleena a dozen times today, and over a hundred yesterday when the man in the background of every scene of late announced who lured the security officers out of their nook with a damsel-in-distress routine a Disney princess would be proud of so our mother could interrogate Zakhar.

I'm not angry at Aleena's tactics. She's been under our mother's thumb for seven years longer than I had to endure, and she can make Stockholm syndrome seem endearing. I just wish there was a way I could get her to listen to me without involving Nikita's husband.

Kidnap is not above me when it comes to keeping my promises.

Murder may not even be.

The email I sent last night after unearthing the footage of Aleena on her knees in front of Andrik is proof of this. It made it seem as if money is the answer to everything, but the guilt it is bombarding me with now is horrendous.

Morals have me wanting to say I'm striving to get Zakhar a new heart because he deserves one—no child should endure what he has the past twelve months—but in reality, it is because I don't want Andrik to use Zakhar's health battles to excuse his rollercoaster moods.

I need him to be honest and upfront.

He can't do that with his son's sickness hanging over his head.

I went about it the wrong way, though. Not just for Andrik and his family, but Nikita as well. The email I sent went to someone high up at the hospital where she is undertaking her residency. I don't think she has a clue the board at Myasnikov Private is letting people buy their way to the top of the organ donor list.

She wouldn't work there if that were the case, and she would be looking into the donation of her mother's organs more studiously. It occurred under the name of the doctor I emailed last night.

Needing to make things right, I switch off the faucet, wrap a towel around my body, and then enter the main part of my room. I veer my steps for the drawers closest to the door, mindful I dumped my phone there after exchanging numbers with Konstantine.

"If you ever feel the need to hack my security system again, I'd rather you go through me than my competitors," he said while punching his number into my cell. "We all have to eat." He laughed like his paycheck is more important to him than Andrik. He's a terrible liar. "Even her," he murmured while handing me a tablet frozen on a grainy image timestamped after the footage I'd stumbled onto yesterday.

Aleena left Andrik's room with red cheeks and glossy, dilated eyes. I know her well enough to decipher what her expression meant.

She hadn't been bedded by a god.

She had been rejected by one.

Her devastation mimicked the pain that crossed her face anytime our mother told us we were unworthy of anything more than an arranged marriage. She was hurting, and I witnessed our mother deepening her wounds with a ton of unkind words only feet from Andrik's room when Konstantine hit play on the tablet.

Her dressing-down proved that Andrik didn't touch Aleena. He merely refused to let her leave his room until the people watching his every move believed he had.

Learning that is another reason I am showering earlier tonight than normal. It is hard to remember your objectives when you're being swamped by euphoria.

"Where the hell is my phone?" I murmur to myself when my search of the drawers near the door comes up empty. I swear I left it there before showering, but it is nowhere to be found in any region of my room.

My brows furrow when I realize my phone isn't the only item missing. The laptop I used to hack into Andrik's home security system is also gone, and so are the instructions I jotted down when Maksim's hacker, Easton, showed me how to override the firewall of the home server. It was a simple infiltration since no one expects to be hacked from inside their dwelling.

Konstantine made out that Andrik appreciated my help, so why would he confiscate my belongings as if I am a child?

The theories in my head piss me off.

So much so, I am done playing nice.

After releasing a big breath, suffocating the scream I am desperate to release, I charge out of my room and make a beeline for the west wing as if I am wearing more than a towel. I can't confidently declare that Andrik demanded I sleep in the east wing because it was the furthest from his bedroom, but my hunches are usually accurate, so I run with it.

He wants distance between us. Lots of it, and I will give it to him —*after* I've given him a piece of my mind.

"Andrik?" I call out while trampling over a pricy hallway runner and veering past paintings by world-renowned artists.

Andrik's level of wealth reveals why my mother was so eager for Aleena to sink her hooks into him, and why her ruse seems to have started years earlier than Andrik realized. An average man would struggle to dream of this type of net worth. Yet Andrik achieved it by his thirty-fifth birthday. It almost makes me proud of him until I remember that I am meant to be angry.

"Andrik!" I shout again while opening door after door after door.

I stop dead in my tracks at the last door on the left when my senses tingle. They caution me to slow my roll. I don't listen. I never do. It is a bad trait of being impulsively stubborn.

After another big exhale, I push open the door with force and storm inside. "I want my belongings back. *Now!* They're not mine, and Maksim won't take kindly to you confiscating his things."

As my eyes shoot around a bedroom as manly furnished as the room I saw Aleena kneeling in, I swallow down the bile burning my throat. Nothing happened between them, so that isn't the cause of the bitterness surging from my stomach to my throat. It is the dozens of photos spread across Andrik's bed.

Why does he have multiple images of my childhood nanny?

I step closer and gasp.

Stasy isn't the only person featured in the exposé of my family's secrets. Zakhar is there too.

"Oh, Mother, what did you do?" I murmur to myself when I notice the similarities between Zakhar and Stasy. She looks just how Zakhar said. Me but twenty-plus years older.

Wet hair slides against my back when I jackknife to the left. A noise sounds from the bathroom. It isn't the creak of old waterpipes. It sounds like a man in pain—*or ecstasy*.

Too curious for my own good, and somewhat a sucker for punishment, I step closer to the bathroom.

Trickling water sounds louder the further I walk, lengthening my strides.

I've never been more ashamed of my body's needs when the quickest glance through a crack in the door has my clit beating out a mariachi tune.

A trillion theories roll through my head, though they seem inconsequential compared to the visual of Andrik in the shower, stroking his cock.

The heavy stream of water pumping onto the glass partition means not a single speckle of the awe-inspiring visual is hidden from my sight. I can see every ridge of his cock. Every throb of the vein feeding his fantastic manhood. I can even see the droplet of pre-cum his precise pumps cause to the end of his cut penis.

I should look away, but no matter how hard my brain screams at me to do precisely that, I can't. I drink in the way his manly hand doesn't deter from the size of his cock, and how his lips part more with every strangled pump.

I watch the frustration that crosses his face when he takes his anger out on his cock, and with that, learn that even the most unethical scene can be the most beautiful.

When my eyes lower to the wide girth of his cock pumping in and out of his fist, my thighs press. He must be close to finding release. I'm on the verge of climax, and I am only watching. I can't feel the way his cock flexes when he balances his free hand on the tiled wall above his head before he flutters his eyes closed, or feel the smoothness of the pre-cum he drags down his shaft with his thumb, but nothing weakens the wave building low in my stomach.

Instinctively, my body seeks a way to lessen the tsunami that's been brewing in my core for days.

As I pant along with Andrik, I glide my hand beneath my towel before brushing my fingertips over the opening of my pussy.

Electricity blisters through me when my thumb finds my clit.

I roll it at the same frantic pace Andrik uses to stroke his cock. It is a fast, needy speed that doubles the size of the wave about to crest in my womb.

A soft groan seeps through my lips when I slip two fingers between the folds of my pussy. I'm wet. Actually, more like saturated. I am as drenched now as I was when Andrik spanked me over the sofa in his den.

Slickness coats my fingers, and the undeniable aroma of lust fills the air as the movie of his punishment rolls through my head. It goes a little longer than the actual scene and includes both his hands and mouth soothing the rush of euphoria prickling my skin with goose bumps.

When the raunchy exposé ends, I stuff two fingers inside myself, my pussy needing something to cling to when I return my eyes to the crack in the door. The visual of Andrik's fat cock sliding in and out of his hand increases my recklessness.

After adjusting the span of my thighs, I thrust my fingers inside myself urgently. *Desperately.* I finger fuck myself like they'll achieve the same level of euphoria they would if it were Andrik's hand between my legs.

My muscles pull taut when Andrik's pace quickens like he knows how scandalous his show has become. He bends his knees and then tilts his hips upward, matching the incline my fingers make as they surge in and out of my pussy.

While biting my lower lip to lessen my moans, I pretend my fingers are his cock and that my palm slamming against my clit is the arrow of his fantastic V muscle.

I grip the door handle with my spare hand, too shuddering in a lust frenzy to trust my legs to keep me upright. Tingles race through my core when Andrik adjusts his position until he is almost facing me front on.

The fatness of his cock and how much pre-cum it leaks makes my pumps even more desperate. I stuff my fingers in and out, in and out until the fire in my belly roars to life.

Its burn is brutal, even more so when white streams of cum shoot from Andrik's cock and land halfway up the subway tiles.

But before I can fully topple in ecstasy, the rug is cruelly pulled out from beneath me.

"Arabella..."

What?

I yank my hand away from my pussy and take a step back, certain the name I just heard didn't leave Andrik's mouth.

He wasn't thinking about my sister while he was stroking his cock. Surely not.

They have no spark.

No connection.

He turned her down while she was naked and kneeling in front of him.

He also didn't seem the slightest bit attracted to her. We look the same even though we're different. Our personalities make us different. *Don't they?*

I step back again when the name I would give anything not to hear seeps from Andrik's mouth for the second time. Then I toss my hand over my mouth to ensure the dinner I scarfed down under Anoushka's concerning watch remains in my stomach.

Confident I am seconds from losing the fight not to vomit, I snatch up my towel and sprint into the corridor.

I only just make it into the downstairs washroom before I lose more than dinner.

My sanity exits right along with it.

70

ANDRIK

"You fucking idiot," I chastise myself as the fist circling my cock seconds ago slams into the tiled wall my cum is clinging to. "You're a fucking idiot."

I should be relishing the painful sob Zoya released seconds before she sprinted out of my room. It was the exact response I was seeking when I switched her name for her sister's.

I wanted her to experience the torment I've been enduring over the past several weeks.

I wanted her to feel the pain I felt when my brain refused to function until it took care of the distraction in my pants from going through her personal things for hours before walking in on her in the shower.

Dina's suburban mansion looked like no one had been there for months, but her daughters' essences are very much imbedded in its bones. Zoya's was more hidden than Arabella's, but it was still undeniable. It was in the framed photos stuffed in the attic, and in the polaroid pictures Arabella had in a photo box under her bed. It was even in the clothes in the walk-in closet of a room I'm convinced was Zakhar's.

The room I walked past a dozen times when I made my arrangement with Arabella was concealed by a bookcase. I wouldn't have known it was there if the faintest chime of a snow globe hadn't sounded with precise timing.

I had to kick down the door that was padlocked from the outside. The room had two beds. One was made up like a hospital bed. The other one had a familiar knitted blanket spread across it. It was the same design and color as the one Mikhail's mother had draped around her shoulders in the photograph my father had showed me weeks ago.

I've initiated bloodbaths on less, but the final nail in the coffin was hammered when I found a box of Polaroid photos in the back of the closet full of teenage things someone had left untouched for years. They exposed that my intuition isn't as faulty as believed.

Mikhail's mother is Zoya's mother as my father stated.

DNA can't lie, and neither can genes.

Zoya looks identical to Stasy when she was in her twenties, and her childhood photographs are shockingly similar to how Zakhar looks now. He is just the male version of the Chesterton genes.

I guess that means I inherited more than a big cock from my father. We also have the same taste in women.

After shaking my head to rid it of the disturbing image my inner thoughts paint, I shut down the shower and step out. I don't bother toweling off. The fury that I didn't stop Zoya from joining me in hell will soon take care of the droplets of water coating my skin.

I'm hot all over, as burning now as I was when I couldn't stop my steps after hearing trickling water coming from Zoya's bathroom. I was there to find out how much she knew about Stasy's past, not perve.

I shouldn't have looked when I found her in the shower, but the visual was ten times better than my fucked head could have ever imagined. It took everything I had to walk away, and it was only achievable because of the face that flashed up on Zoya's phone when it rang.

Konstantine has yet to find out any information about the man who sat next to Zoya before she objected, but Zoya knows him well enough to store an image of his cocky smirk under an anonymous listing in her phone.

I shouldn't have taken her things like a jealous, neurotic jerk, but it was either leave her room with her belongings or accept Anonymous's facetime request.

The latter would have resulted in more of a display of ownership than stroking my cock in what I believed would be the privacy of my shower to the image of her wet and enticing body.

It would have handed proof to my competitors that I've completely lost the fucking plot.

Since I can't trust myself with the evidence I brought home with me, I gather up the photos of Zoya, Zakhar, and Stasy and shove them into the desk drawer in my room where I hid Zoya's electronic devices.

I slam the drawer shut before shooting my hand up to my hair to tug it at the roots, hopeful a snippet of pain will stop me from reacting to the brutal heaves seeping through the floorboards.

This property is one of my grandfather's estates. It is old enough to be classed as ancient, but worth millions.

As I slide my feet into some slacks, sans boxer shorts, I hear Anoushka knock on the door of the downstairs washroom. She asks Zoya if she is okay and if there is anything she can do to help.

When she gets no response, she tells Zoya that she is coming in and not to worry. She's handled her fair share of puke in her past fifty-eight years.

My heart launches into my throat when a scream is the next

thing I hear. It represents someone stumbling onto a murder scene and has me panicked as fuck that I took my effort to force distance between Zoya and me one step too far.

I race down the stairwell with no concern for the slipperiness, and then barge Anoushka out of the way.

Zoya is slumped on the floor of the washroom. Blood is oozing from her head.

"What happened?"

I skid to my knees next to her whitening frame before rolling her over. A deep gash starts just below her hairline and merges into her blonde locks, making them red. It is approximately three inches long.

"She stood too quickly and got woozy. I tried to grab her, but she fell too fast." Anoushka's eyes dart between the wash basin and Zoya. "She hit her head on the sink on the way down."

I nod robotically before instructing her to fetch the doctor from Zakhar's room. "Make sure he brings his medical bag. I have a first-aid kit in my bathroom, but I don't think it will suffice."

"Andrik," Zoya mumbles painfully when I pull her into my arms before taking the stairs two at a time.

"Shh. You're okay, милая. I've got you."

After pulling back bedding similar to the one I forced Arabella to sit on for hours so the person controlling her strings would believe her ruse to seduce me had been successful, I place Zoya down and then cover her naked body with the bedding.

Her head wound is so bad blood trickles past her ears and puddles into the pillowcase quicker than the shirt I ripped off in a hurry can soak it up.

"Hurry!" I scream, confident I'll murder everyone in this godforsaken town if their negligence kills Zoya, preferring to blame anyone but myself.

A stout doctor with a chin far hairier than his head wobbles into the room, warping the floorboards more than Zoya's tiny frame did when she snuck across my room to watch me in the shower.

That's when I should have stopped. The instant my instincts alerted me to the identity of my stalker, I should have removed my hand from my cock and ended the madness.

I should not have put on a show that encouraged Zoya to do the same.

"You need to hold her hands down for me." I glare at the doctor like he's insane and barely shake my head when he adds, "I need to stop the bleeding. I can't do that if she fights me at every turn."

I don't get in a second headshake. "What the fuck?" sounds from outside my room before Mikhail races in to fulfill the doctor's demand on my behalf.

"It's okay, sweetheart," the doctor assures Zoya when she groans about him piercing the edge of her wound with a big-ass needle. "This will take away the pain and numb the area so I can close the wound with a handful of stitches." He continues pushing down on the syringe until all the liquid inside is gone before he cranks his head to me. "Is she on any medication? Are there any medical conditions I need to know about? The wound is large, so she may need additional sedation."

"It is a little late to ask now, isn't it?" When Mikhail silently pleads for me to calm down, I shake my head. Its briskness slows when I remember what I unearthed earlier today. "Unless Zakhar's heart condition doesn't affect some siblings until later in life."

"I don't believe Zakhar's condition is hereditary," the doctor advises, straying away from Dr. Makarand's theory. "But I will give her a full workup after I've cleaned and closed the wound." He shifts his eyes to Mikhail, aware he is the more stable one of our duo right now. "Will you give us the room?"

"No," I instantly deny, answering on behalf of Mikhail.

"Andri—"

"No," I reply louder, glaring at my brother. "I'm not leaving her. Her injury is my fault, so I need to make sure she is okay."

Anoushka reminds me that she is in the room with us when she squeezes my shoulder. "She fainted, Andrik. That isn't your fault."

She can say that because she doesn't know how hard I pushed her—how much I hurt her.

When Zoya whispers my name again, her voice as pained as the remorse ripping my heart to pieces, the doctor grants me permission to stay.

It's for the best. He'd be dead at my feet the instant he knotted his last stitch if he had attempted to force me from the room.

"Leave them. I will bring the dirty ones down in the morning."

The housekeeper Anoushka sent up to change the bedding dips her chin in understanding before quietly backing out of my room.

The scent of Zoya's blood seeping into my mattress is the reason I don't want the sheets changed. I need the putrid scent to make it through the night unscathed as much as I need it as a reminder of how badly I fucked up.

When the mattress dips under my weight, Zoya groans before rolling onto the hip opposite her head wound, pulling the sheets away from her body. The doctor doesn't believe she is concussed. She is merely sleeping off the sedation he gave her.

"She will wake when she is ready," he said four hours ago.

I'm tempted to poke her, needing to see her eyes to know she is truly okay, but you can only be an ass every so often or it will become a permanent part of your personality.

I learned that the hard way too.

"Hush. I'm just making sure your wound doesn't join your eyebrow to your hairline," I tell Zoya when she protests to me pulling back the strand of hair draped across her forehead, needing something to distract me from her budded nipples. You would swear she can feel my beady watch for how erect they've become.

The doctor went with stitches instead of glue because a majority of the wound is covered by Zoya's hair. To glue it together, he would have needed to shave her head. He changed his mind when I said I'd kill him if he altered her features even in the slightest.

An unexpected smirk curls my lips when Zoya murmurs, "You hush. I'm trying to sleep over here." Her voice is groggy but sexy as fuck.

I should let her sleep, but as I said earlier, I'm desperate to see her eyes.

"Five hours not enough for you, милая?"

"Depends. Are we still talking about sleep?"

Her lips curve upward when I growl.

Then, two seconds later, I get the quickest peek of her baby blues.

"Hey," I murmur like a soft cock, slipping lower down the mattress so she doesn't have to strain to meet me eye to eye.

"Hey," she parrots. After swishing her tongue around her mouth to loosen up her words, she asks, "What happened?"

I sigh in relief before asking, "You don't remember?"

She shakes her head before whimpering in pain. "Ow."

"Gentle." I pull her hand down from her wound. "You've got a ton of stitches in your head."

"Oh god."

Confident her hands won't be as stabby this time, I release them so she can check her wound. She measures its length with gentle probes before guessing its invisibility powers by dragging her hair forward to cover it.

"I guess it could be worse," she whispers after checking her reflection in a freestanding mirror in the corner of the room. "I could have been forced to wear bangs."

"Bangs would suit you."

She rolls her eyes. "I think you're willing to say anything to lessen your guilt. Bangs don't suit anyone."

When she sits up, exposing more of her luscious body, I say, "Where are you going?"

She forces another groan to rumble up my chest when she replies, "Back to my room."

When she stands and almost fumbles, I shoot out of the bed and catch her before she hurts herself again. My hands send goose bumps racing across her skin. Don't ask me what it does to the rest of her body, or you'll admit me for a psych evaluation.

"You can stay here. I have fresh sheets, and—"

"No," she murmurs, her voice announcing she is on the verge of being sick. "The memories will hurt less in my room."

When our eyes align, shame almost folds me in two. Her memories are back, and they hurt her more than any knock to the head ever could.

"I fucked up—"

I'm saved from forcing my shame onto her by a rush of vomit she can't hold back.

As vomit sprouts from her mouth, numerous assurances from a familiar voice outside my room shout that I've got this.

Mikhail doesn't do vomit. He hasn't since he didn't realize his mother had used a cereal bowl as a vomit bucket. He thought it was porridge. His instincts have never led him so badly astray.

"Take her into the shower," Mikhail shouts from outside my room. "It is easier to stomp down chunks"—gag—"than wipe them up."

After warning him that he'll be cleaning up his own mess if he sympathy vomits, I scoop Zoya into my arms like my sleep pants aren't covered with spew and then walk her into the bathroom.

"No," she whines on a groan when I enter the shower stall and switch on the faucet. "Not this shower. I can smell you in here."

"You're puking enough to cover the scent of my cum, so suck it up."

I almost laugh when her bottom lip drops into a pout.

A groggy Zoya is almost as fun as a drunk Zoya.

I dunk my head under the water that's yet to reach a pleasant temperature to rid my head of the inappropriate thoughts bombarding it.

The coolness sees Zoya clinging to my chest more firmly and sends a second round of goose bumps breaking across her skin. They're not the same type as earlier.

"Are you cold?" I don't give her a chance to answer. I check her forehead for a temperature before sticking my head out of the shower stall and yelling, "Get the doctor! She has a fever."

The doctor's diagnosis this time around hits me like a bag of bricks. "Zoya is pregnant."

"No." If I deny the truth often enough, it will eventually make it untrue, right? "That isn't possible. She's infertile. She has endometriosis."

The doctor pushes his glasses up his blackhead-covered nose. "Which makes conceiving difficult but not impossible. Her uterus is extended—"

"Because her friend was giving her fertility drugs. That's why the test came up positive."

"I thought the same. That's why I did an ultrasound with

Zakhar's portable heart equipment. The fetus is a healthy size for its gestation. She is approximately ten weeks along." He shows me footage of a jelly bean-shaped blob before storing the tablet back into his medical bag. "With her condition, she still has a little way to go to be in the safe zone. Her uterus is badly scarred with fibroids, but from what I saw, her pregnancy looks viable. I will continue monitoring and keep you updated."

Before he can leave, I snatch up his wrist. My hold startles him, though not as much as what I say next. "Is there a way to check if the child has anything... *wrong* with it?"

"You are both young and healthy, so the chances of an abnormality is low."

He can say that because he doesn't know why I'm asking.

Sibling relations ended centuries ago for a reason.

"But there's still a possibility?"

The doctor slants his head. "A *low* possibility."

I continue pressing until I get the answer I need. "But still possible?"

"But still possible," he eventually parrots. "There are tests we can conduct to check, but that won't be for a few more weeks."

"What happens if it brings something up?" I ask, convinced a sick child is my punishment for lusting over my half-sister.

"There are a handful of options at your disposal." When I glare at him, over needing to pry answers from him, he stammers out, "Mo-most couples choose to abort."

"Abortion?"

"Yes." He nods sternly. "The procedure is relatively simple. It can be undertaken at a doctor's clinic, and she will be home within the hour." He steps closer as if our conversation isn't being held in private. "Is that something you're considering?"

"No," my heart answers before my head. "I was just curious."

He smiles. "Good. Because I've already told them they were mistaken earlier, which means Zakhar is only days away from getting a new heart." He slaps the tops of my shoulders before shouting, "You should be celebrating! This is the miracle they've been seeking. An heir and a spare to return the Dokovic bloodline to the glory it once held." He makes a fatal mistake. "And I didn't have to remove your swimmers from your sack under general anesthetic and steal her eggs to achieve it."

"Her?"

His pupils widen so much, even with them not shooting to the door he walked through only minutes ago, I know who he is referencing.

A shocked gasp ripples his lips when an antique statue pierces his stomach well enough for its pointy tip to graze his spleen. Then he stumbles back when I remove the corkscrew-like artwork and aim it several inches higher.

I don't stab him in his heart.

I want him wounded, not dead.

You can't get answers from a corpse.

"I..." He gargles on the blood trickling from his mouth as he falls to his knees. "Please..." He grabs at the instrument he's certain is seconds from being pierced through his jugular before lifting his pained eyes to my face. "I'll... do... anything you ask."

"I don't want you to do anything." My voice is incessant with rage. "But you are going to speak." When his head flops forward, I bob down low, grip the measly strands of hair he has left, and then yank his head back to ensure he can see the sheer honesty in my eyes when I say, "You're going to tell me *everything*. Starting with her..."

He follows the direction of my head nudge before returning his pained eyes to me.

He nods. It is for the best. I may have taken my time with him if he had tried to disagree.

Time isn't in my favor.

It isn't for him either, though he won't know that until he's given me answers to questions I hadn't considered asking until now.

71

ZOYA

When my footing slips, I stab my nails into the moss-coated brickwork bordering the massive gardens of Andrik's family estate. The weather in this part of Russia is as poor as Myasnikov's nine months of winter. It is dewy out, and the denseness of the fog almost had me tumbling out of the window I pried open with a letter opener I'd found on Andrik's desk.

As I take a moment to settle my frantic breaths, I think back to the news Dr. Leverington announced seconds before ignoring my request for him not to share the results with Andrik.

I wanted to tell him myself, under better circumstances.

I didn't want it shared as if it was an asset he was purchasing on the black market.

In a way, I'm glad Dr. Leverington has no respect for women's rights. If he hadn't told Andrik the news, I wouldn't have overheard Andrik organizing an abortion for our unborn child.

I've never read someone so poorly before. Yes, it is sudden, and I'm shit fucking scared of stuffing this up as badly as my mother did, but Andrik's contract with Aleena demanded haste. Immediate steps were put into place so she could fulfill his wish to become a family man, so why is he so quick to disregard the welfare of our unborn child?

I don't have time to sit around and deliberate, so I continue scaling down one of the many rock fence walls that divide massive country estates. I'm wearing a raincoat over the shirt I stole from Andrik's room and rain boots I found in a garden shed on the edge of the pebbled driveway. It is freezing, but the raincoat and rain boots are lined with fleece, so my heart is the only thing needing defrosting.

Untrusting of the people in properties directly bordering Andrik's country estate, I follow the road for several miles before crossing into familiar territory. I haven't been in this part of Russia before, but all projects are the same. They're filled with people more willing to help since it is those who have the least who give the most.

"Thank you," I murmur when a lady with a mouthful of rotting teeth places a blanket over my shoulders. When a banana is thrust my way next, I shake my head. "I'm good. Thank you." I can't take her food, especially not with my stomach as full as it is. "I will get this back to you." I tug on the blanket keeping my shoulders warm. "I promise."

She *sheeshas* off my promise before pushing a cart full of blankets down the street dotted with homeless people. She hands them blankets similar to the one she gave me and smiles a toothless grin when they greedily accept the banana I denied.

When I made my plan to escape, I had no clue which direction I should walk. I can't immediately go to Nikita because that is the first place Andrik would look, though she is also the one person I need to speak with the most.

I lose the chance to deliberate when the bang of a truck's loading doors booming closed break through the quiet. I race to catch the delivery driver before he can slip into the driver's seat. He could be going in any direction, but the symbol on the side of his van has me confident he is heading in the same direction as me.

It is the catering company responsible for feeding Myasnikov Private Hospital patients each day.

"Hey, I was wondering if I could get a lift with..." My words trail off when the face that peers back at me registers as familiar.

Nikita was right. Boris's mother gave him a nickname that matches his bulldog face.

The farce is worse when his features are weighed down with confusion. "Zoya?"

I wipe my riled expression from my face before stepping out from beneath the shadow of the streetlight. "Hey, Boris. What are you doing out this way?"

"Um..." He hooks his thumb to the van. "Dropping off some supplies for my side gig." He nervously shifts from foot to foot. "The hospital doesn't pay enough to cover all my expenses."

"You're preaching to the wrong girl." My underhanded invitation for him to bring Nikita into our conversation works well.

"Is Nikita here with you?" He peers past me like my raincoat and rain boots are designer, and we're on the sidewalk of the hottest nightclub in the country.

"No. She's... Ah... She is..." After a groan of a defeated woman, I snap out, "She's at home with her husband."

Boris gives off creeper vibes, so I can't thrust Nikita under his spotlight no matter how desperate I am.

His eyes snap back to mine. "She is?" When I nod, he stammers. "*Oh...*" He wets his mouth like the knowledge she is at home is more shocking than the news she is married. "I didn't realize she had gotten married."

"Yeah. It was a couple of weeks ago." I have no trouble placing myself in danger, though. "Now I'm the only one single and ready to mingle."

"Oh." This is a different "oh" from his earlier one. It is the one of a man suddenly interested in what I am endeavoring to sell him.

When his eyes lower to my left hand to authenticate my claim as if he's heard differently, I slip it behind my back before trying to remove the diamond ring that's fit so snug I'd have a better chance of removing it if I had a hacksaw.

Boris is smarter than he looks. "I should go. Take care of yourself, Zoya."

I thwart his exit with a shameful plea. "Can I get a lift, please? It's freezing out here, Boris, and you are the only one capable of saving me." I want to gag when my voice is similar to the one Aleena used to convince Andrik's security guards to leave their post, but its effectiveness keeps my cringe on the down-low. "Can you help me, Boris? Please."

"I-I shouldn't. I'm not meant to let anyone know about this gig." He's telling me no even with his actions doing the opposite. He looks seconds from scooping my hand into his and asking if he can keep me forever. "It pays well because the materials I distribute are confidential."

"I won't tell anyone. It will be *our* little secret." When his pants tighten at the front, I scrape my teeth over my lower lip and then fan open my raincoat. Andrik's shirt would look baggy if I didn't have Es. "I'm good at keeping secrets, Boris. You can tell me *anything* and I won't tell a soul... Not even your mother will know all the wicked things we'll share."

The diamonds in my wedding band should announce to him how much of a liar I am, but since he's a mommy's boy who will never stop sucking on her bosom without a woman like me forcing him from her tit, he wants to believe me.

"Okay. But you can't tell anyone about this."

"I won't tell a soul," I promise while following him to the passenger side of the van with my fingers crossed behind my back.

After he removes a handful of invoices that look familiar to the one I paid three nights ago, he gestures for me to enter. Since he is so busy ogling my ass during my climb, I get a glimpse of the "packages" he's delivering. They don't look like produce.

"Eyes to the front," Boris demands when my backside's plonk into the seat returns his focus to his job.

I hold up my hands as if I am being arrested. "I was just trying to latch my belt."

My skin quivers when he finds and latches it for me. He smells funky. It isn't a sweaty smell. It is more chemical based than body odor, and it doubles my assumption that he's transporting more than fruit and vegetables.

"Where to?" Boris asks after slipping behind the steering wheel, startling me. He moved so fast that I didn't hear his steps.

It isn't the time to expose my *I-want-you* act was a ruse to get a ride, so I reply, "I will direct you once we get closer to Myasnikov."

He eyes me for several long seconds before he eventually commences our across-territories journey.

72

ANDRIK

*A*s I exit the basement, I scrub Dr. Leverington's blood off my hands with a rag.

I sense I am being watched half a second before a familiar voice says, "If you tortured him for the whereabouts of Zoya's mother, you're wasting your breath."

I test how much Mikhail knows by saying, "Dina—"

"I wasn't talking about Dina." He arches a brow and stares me dead set in the eyes. "Though she will get hers," he snarls, "when I find her." His expression softens again. "I was talking about *my* mother, the woman who birthed both Zoya and me." He takes in my bloodstained clothes and sweat-dotted hair. "When the pieces started falling into place and I realized how fucked up this situation was, I found her and moved her to a safe location." A scoff rustles his hair sitting flopped across his eye since it is overdue for a trim. "I can't believe all this time she was in the same town as me."

"Not always," I advise, lessening his guilt. "According to him"—I nudge my head to the stairwell of the basement like there is only one body down there—"they moved her from location to location to keep her hidden. She's traveled the globe over the past thirty years and birthed numerous children."

"Including Zakhar."

He looks set to go on a rampage. To hunt down the people who kept his mother hidden from him, but there's more to this story than he knows. Stuff that will flip his life plan on its head. But right now, my focus can't be on him. I have far more pressing matters to attend to, so I keep my reply brief.

"No."

He balks before he sucks in a shocked breath. "She didn't birth Zakhar?"

When I nod before pushing off on my feet, he follows me. "Are you sure, Andrik? He looks identical to her, and he believes she is his mother."

I bite back my wish to retaliate to his confession that he interrogated my son without me being present before saying with a laugh, "For good reason."

I must be in shock. I don't usually laugh after a lengthy torture session. I'm not that insane. But there's no doubt laughter is rumbling in my chest.

Or perhaps it is relief that the concrete slab that's been sitting on my heart for the past few weeks has finally lifted. I honestly don't know, though I intend to find out. Soon.

With Mikhail too shocked to help me move forward with my plans, I say, "Stasy is Zakhar's grandmother."

He chokes on his reply. "What?"

I am definitely in the throes of lunacy. Laughter thunders in my chest before it fans Mikhail's white cheeks.

"Why are you laughing? Doesn't this make things worse for you?"

"No," I reply, smiling. "It makes everything better." *So. Much. Better.*

Still grinning, I make it to my bedroom in record-setting time, throw open my door with force, and then stray my eyes to the bed Dr. Leverington left Zoya resting in after assessing her.

My mattress is as bare as my bathroom.

"Where is Zoya?" I ask when Anoushka appears out of nowhere with a bowl of porridge, a large glass of orange juice, and pregnancy vitamins.

She shakes her head, but before a word can leave her mouth, Mikhail asks, "Who's pregnant?" His pupils blow wide as the truth smacks into him. "Zoya is pregnant!" Since he isn't asking a question, he doesn't wait for me to answer him. "Won't that create... *issues* for the baby?"

His horrified expression exposes that he is as worried as I was last night that our unborn child would have a genetic deformity since its parents were alleged siblings. But once again, I don't have time to sit him down and step him through this.

I have a shit ton of groveling to do, and the woman deserving of my grovel is nowhere to be seen.

After requesting Anoushka to check Zoya's room before her choice of breakfast for Zoya causes Mikhail to hurl, I shift my focus to the voice of reason in my ear.

"No one came in or out of your room since Dr. Leverington left it last night," Konstantine announces, his words as fast as his fingers flying over his keyboard. "Shit."

"What is it?"

He breathes out heavily. "It could be nothing, but there was a breach of an exterior perimeter late last night."

I brush off his worry. If Zoya wanted to flee, she would have done it when she believed I had cheated on her with her baby sister. She wouldn't have stayed for another thirty-six hours.

The cause of Konstantine's worry is unearthed when he says, "It was approximately ten minutes after the shadows beneath your door disappeared."

My eyes shoot to the camera above every door in my family's numerous estates as I murmur, "She heard my exchange with Dr. Leverington."

I'm not asking a question, but Konstantine replies as if I am. "Yes." He doubles the load on my shoulders instead of lightening it. "From the timing of the shadows' appearance and disappearance, she only heard the abortion part of your conversation."

"Fuck."

"What?" Mikhail asks, his gills still green but desperate for answers.

I hold my hand in the air, requesting a minute before asking Konstantine to bring up footage of the security breach from outside the compound's main walls.

The footage is playing on my phone screen before I remove it from my desk drawer. Zoya dodges the camera's focus, but I know it is her sneaking out of a gardener's shed on the west side of the grounds. I'd recognize those curves anywhere.

Mikhail grimaces with me when she almost slips while scaling the stone wall bordering the manicured lawns. We weren't so lucky twenty-six years ago. I split my head and Mikhail broke his wrist.

"Track her movements with any cameras in the area and forward them directly to me." Before Konstantine can hum in agreement, I add, "Be discreet. We need to find her before *anyone* else."

The way I say *anyone* announces who I am referring to. Dr. Leverington's bedside confession ramped up my efforts to stay on the federation's good side, and quadrupled my wish to protect Zoya from their madness.

Aleena was the federation's first choice because the timer on Zoya's head is almost as minute as Zakhar's.

"I'm coming with you," Mikhail says when I remove a gun from the safe in my walk-in closet. "She's my sister too."

As I grab extra ammunition, I mutter, "She's *your* sister. Period."

He wants to ask a million questions, but the urgency of the situation sees him taking another direction. "Once she's safe, we need to talk."

I nod. "We do. But not now. Not until I know she is safe."

His quick check of his gun announces he's on board with my plans, not to mention the wave of his arm across his body. He's giving me the lead and, for once, plans to follow my orders.

He may even kill for me. That's how badly he wants to protect his baby sister.

It is almost on par with the lengths I will go to bring my wife home safely.

"Wait. Hold up," Konstantine murmurs a second before I gallop down the stairs. "You can't go."

"Is she here?" My gut is picking up something, but I can't quite work out what it is. I sense Zoya's closeness, but is that because her son is sleeping only doors down from my location?

"No," Konstantine replies. "But Zak's new heart is."

His swallow matches the heavy sentiment on Anoushka's face as she races to the bottom of the stairs at the speed of a bullet. "We need to go now, Andrik. His new heart is already hours old. It won't hold out for much longer."

I look at Mikhail, then back at Anoushka, lost on what to do.

My eyes veer back to Mikhail when he says, "Go with Zakhar. I will find Zoya, and I will keep her safe. I promise you." He steps closer before sealing my fate with the only pair of eyes ever able to pull me out of the madness until Zoya was introduced to my life. "This is what she would want, Andrik."

I nod, conscious he is right.

"When you find her, tell her I—"

"You can tell her yourself when I bring her home," Mikhail inter-rupts before removing the bead from my ear, stuffing it in his, and then requesting directions from Konstantine for Zoya's last known location.

Whatever Konstantine relays to him gets his feet moving as quickly as the wheels on Zakhar's bed. His medical team wheels him across the foyer of the home I tried to escape more than once when I was his age.

73

ZOYA

*W*ith my intuition screaming at me to get out of Boris's van before it is too late for me to plead innocent, I ask Boris to pull over a couple of blocks away from Myasnikov Private Hospital.

He does so, seemingly relieved.

"Anywhere here is fine," I murmur when he glides further and further down the alleyway.

The van's speed has barely dipped below thirty when he commences removing his belt and unbuckling his jeans. "I've been dreaming about this for hours." He shifts his eyes to me. They're brimming with lust. "But I had to exercise patience. I didn't want us to crash." He wets his lips while eyeing mine. "Your lips look capable of instigating a crash."

I laugh like he's cute.

It is either laugh or puke. I went for the one that causes less mess.

"Uh-uh," I tsk when he flops out his erect penis. It's uncut and smells as funky as the white ooze dripping from it. "There could be cameras here, Boris. You don't want your mother to see what we're doing, do you?"

He tucks his penis away so fast that I wouldn't be surprised to learn his zipper nipped his skin.

"What I need you to do is hop into the back of the van for me. There are no windows in the back."

"You want me to hop in there?" He hooks his thumb in the direction he refused for me to look over the past several hours.

"Uh-huh." I bring back the cutesy sex pot that had him eating out of my palm. "Because I'm really hungry, Boris, but I don't want your mommy to hate me. She will never let me be your wife when she sees all the naughty things I'm going to do to you."

He swallows harshly before nodding. "All right. I can do that."

He nods like he needs more convincing before he climbs through the minute gap between our seats.

While he pushes aside a box leaking a weird watered-down red liquid, I pretend to fluff my hair in the rearview mirror. The instant his back turns to me, I snatch the keys out of the steering column, throw them into an overflowing dumpster at the side of the van, and then hightail it down the street.

"Zoya?" I hear Boris shout when I'm half a block down. "Are you coming back? My mom would really like to meet you."

I increase my speed, my footing stumbling when a loud bang reverberates down the isolated alleyway.

As my eyes pop open, Andrik's threat from weeks ago rings through my ears.

Don't test me on six because I can guarantee neither you nor him will survive the outcome.

He couldn't have found me already.

Surely not.

When I recall how unhinged Andrik has been of late, I push off my feet.

I barely make it two steps before my wrist is grabbed and I'm pulled into a side alley.

"Whoa. Hold on, Sunshine," a familiar voice murmurs when my hand shoots for the letter opener I took with me for my safety, and I stab it wildly through the air.

After stepping out of the shadows enough to display his eyes, Mikhail says, "If you think I'm here to hurt you, you're barking up the wrong tree."

"I'm not worried about me."

His eyes shoot down to my stomach before they return to my face. "I'm not going to hurt your baby, either. I'm not a complete fucking psycho."

"After the way you reacted to our kiss, I'm going to hold my verdict until I've done some *thorough* research." When he looks ill, bewilderment overtakes my fear that he followed me here to force me back to Andrik's chop-shop doctor. "Seriously! It was the equivalent of a kindergarten schoolyard peck. I've gotten more action from Grampies. If I had a father, it would have been like kissing him."

"What about a brother?" Mikhail says, his cheeks suddenly full of color again. "Would it have been like kissing your brother?"

"Yes! It was the equivalent of kissing my nonexistent brother. Happy?"

"Very," he murmurs, winking. "Though I'd rather in the future if we keep our greetings to cheek kisses. I'm still a little traumatized."

I stare at him, mute and confused. *What the hell is he on about?*

"I'd love to horrify you like all big bros should, but we don't have time." My heart gains an extra beat when he murmurs, "Zakhar is getting a new heart." He checks his watch for the time. "From the last update I got, it's probably pattering in his chest right now." He moves for a blacked-out SUV parked a few spots up before spinning to face me. "Are you coming?"

I almost nod.

Almost.

Mikhail balks when I shake my head. "Why the fuck not?"

"Because your brother doesn't have any issues killing babies."

He appears lost—for half a second.

"Send it to me." After nodding to whoever has him talking to himself like a mental patient, he heads my way while removing his phone from his pocket. "Take this as a lesson on snooping. If you don't stay to get the whole story, you may as well not snoop."

He plays a video that makes my blood boil... until it reaches the end.

"Is that something you're considering?"

"No," Andrik answers, loosening the valve in my chest. *"I was just curious."*

Mikhail stops the video before it officially ends and then demands another. "Now play the one from earlier you told me about." I can't hear what his imaginary friend replies, but it pisses him off. The veins in his hand bulge as he works his jaw side to side. "I'll deal with Andrik. Just play it."

This one is from the same camera used to spy on Andrik and Dr. Leverington, but it only shows Andrik's bedroom door.

I lean in close when a faint roar sounds from the speaker of Mikhail's phone. It's soft but undeniable. Andrik is chastising himself. If the faucet shutting off seconds into the footage is anything to go by, it was seconds before I lost my dinner in the downstairs bathroom.

I refuse to let my heart get ahead of itself, though. "Maybe he was angry his only source of relief was his hand."

Mikhail laughs.

He. Fucking. Laughs.

Asshole.

"Mikhail—"

"Don't Mikhail me. I've waited years for this. Let me relish it for a couple of seconds." He sees I'm confused but does nothing to alleviate it. "Come on." He nudges his head to the hanging-open car door. "I'll fill you in on everything I know during the drive home."

I hate how stubborn I am, but it isn't solely my wants I need to consider now. "I don't think—"

"If you want answers, Sunshine, you need to trust me." He twists around to face me, flashing both his dimples and his kind eyes. "You trust me, right?"

I shouldn't, but I nod.

He grins at my grumble as I slowly trudge toward his SUV.

I'm bombarded for the second time three steps later.

Mara looks as if she's seen a ghost, but her focus is on me instead of Mikhail.

"Your fr-friend works at Myasnikov Private Hospital, right?"

I nod, too panicked by the worry in her tone for a worded response or to chastise her for walking the streets alone this late. It is almost dawn.

"What does s-she look like?"

"Brown hair, around this tall."

I hold my hand an inch above my head as Mikhail thrusts his phone into Mara's face. "Like this."

"Th-that's her," Mara shouts, her voice bellowing through the alleyway. "I saw her earlier. She was at our bus s-stop, dazed and confused." My heart pains for her when she says, "I was hesitant to help because of the r-ruse they'd pull." The person who assaulted Mara months ago used the *I'm-hurt* ruse. As she bobbed down to help him, he launched upward with his fists. "She wasn't well. I-I think she was drugged. I tr-tried to call you, but I don't have your number."

"I don't have my phone on me anyway," I blurt out, unsure what to do.

"How long ago was this?" Mikhail asks.

Mara checks her watch. It isn't as fancy or as expensive as Mikhail's. "Around tw-two hours ago. Maybe a little longer."

When my eyes shoot to Mikhail, panting and desperate, he nods like he knows exactly what we need to do. "Get in."

His demand isn't just for me. It is for Mara as well.

"It's okay, Mara," I assure her, feeling her scared shakes from here. "You can trust him. He's one of the rare good ones."

"When you can, tell him I've got her, but that we need to take a quick detour," Mikhail murmurs as he opens the back passenger door of the SUV for Mara. "That's good. I'll tell her." As he jogs to the driver's side, he removes a bead-like device from his ear. "Zak's surgery was a success. His body seems to be accepting his new heart."

I sigh in relief. "That's great. I'm so glad."

"Di-did you say he got a new heart?"

After instructing Mikhail to go around the hospital's perimeter that makes traffic shit no matter the hour, I twist to face Mara. "Yeah. Zakhar has a hereditary heart condition. He's been in cognitive heart failure for the past twelve months."

I'm truly stoked for Andrik and Zakhar, but I can't fully express my feelings until I know that Nikita is okay. Mara made it seem as if she was found at our bus stop, which makes no sense. Maksim would never let her visit that side of town unaccompanied, and why would she be at a bus stop?

"Take Forty-Second Street. It will bypass the nonsense."

Mikhail nods before turning down the street I suggested as I snatch up his phone from the middle console. It is still unlocked from when he showed Mara a picture of Nikita.

"We're going to discuss this." I twist his phone to display the album of photographs I'm referencing before hitting the call button. There are hundreds, and although I feature more than Nikita, I am not okay with his level of snooping.

I suck at interviews, but I am a whizz with numbers. I can remember most by heart. Since I have called Ano's a handful of times since objecting to Aleena's wedding, that's the first number I call.

Ano is Nikita's shadow. He sits in the hospital's underground parking lot for hours every day, watching the live feed of the hospital surveillance. He wouldn't just leave his post.

"Come on, Ano," I murmur when my call rings and rings and rings. "Pick up."

"Hey, you've reached Ano—"

I hang up and try again as a soft voice from the back mutters, "Did you s-say Ano?" When I nod, Mara's cheeks whiten before she shifts her eyes to Mikhail watching her in the rearview mirror. "You should pull over before it is too late."

He does so without interrogation. The sheer panic in Mara's gaze is enough to crumble the knees of the strongest man, let alone what she says next.

74

ANDRIK

I pull off the hairnet flattening my hair and then remove my face mask, unmuffling my voice just as Konstantine answers my call.

"Did he find her?" I ask before he can speak a word.

"Yes," he replies, his pitch high. "But we're fucked." My heart rate surges as erratically as it did when Zakhar's new heart took its first pump hours ago. "I said this was fucking suicide. They're coming at us from all angles. Henry's army is too big. They're going to wipe us out."

"They?"

"The Gottles and the Ivanovs." It sounds like his finger jabs a trigger more than a keyboard. "Zakhar's heart didn't come from the fe—"

Our connection is lost before he can finalize his reply. I don't need his words to understand what is happening, though. It is midday, but even if the sun wasn't bright enough to light up the street, I couldn't miss the swarm of armed men racing toward the main entrance of the hospital.

The front runner is gunning for blood, and that is precisely what I'll give him if he's here for what I think he is.

As I return to Zakhar's room to protect him from the hellfire about to rain down on him, I remove my gun from its holster and point it at Maksim Ivanov's head.

My fighting stance scares away the nurses settling Zakhar into his room after a few hours in the recovery unit, but since their cowardice won't affect Zakhar's rehabilitation, I let them leave.

Machines are no longer the sole thing keeping my son alive. His new heart is—a heart I am suddenly fretful Maksim is here to collect.

Maksim enters Zakhar's room without fear for his life, like I won't gut him where he stands if his sneer is anything to go by.

I understand his cockiness when I recognize the face of the man who enters next. He's bigger than the federation. More feared because his army isn't confined to one country.

He rules them all.

Henry Gottle the Third is the boss of all bosses and the very man I'd hoped would take the bait I dangled in front of him weeks ago. He has the power to dismantle the federation, but at the moment, his expression announces the only head on his chopping block is mine.

Maksim's deep snarl is picked up by Zakhar's heart monitor. "We had an agreement."

"Which I have maintained." My words are for Maksim, but I keep my eyes on Henry since he is clearly the least unhinged of the two.

Maksim scoffs before he signals for a man I swear I've seen before to move forward. He's dressed in the same riot gear as Maksim's and Henry's crews, but he is without a gun. Like Konstantine, he prefers fighting with a keyboard.

Without moving the scope of my gun from Maksim's head, I peer down at the document the dark-haired man brings up on his tablet before silently cussing. The email Konstantine failed to send weeks ago sits in the outbox of my email server. It was forwarded two days ago, minutes before Zoya uploaded the footage she had unearthed onto the USB she gifted me.

She got Zakhar a heart and broke my promise to him at the same time.

I can handle the fallout of her mistake, but only if the crumble of my demise doesn't affect our son. "He is a child. You cannot hurt a child. Have a fucking heart."

"So you admit it?" Maksim shouts, his nostrils flaring. "You admit you ignored my direct order to keep this type of shit out of Myasnikov Private?"

"Yes," I lie, willing to fall onto the knife for Zoya. I shift my eyes back to Henry, once again confident he is the more stable of the duo. "I didn't have a choice. My son was going to die."

"Then you should have given him *your* heart!" Maksim snarls, returning my focus to him. "You shouldn't have ordered the murder of an innocent child—"

"He didn't."

"No!" I scream when Mikhail enters the operating theater from the entrance the doctors used to escape. He didn't get here easily. He's bleeding from an obvious bullet wound in his midsection and his body is housing numerous bruises. But he is standing—just. "Stay out of this, Mikhail. This has *nothing* to do with you."

Blood smears his teeth when he gives me a look as if to say, *She's my sister, so she's my responsibility*, before he throws himself into the fire without the slightest bit of coverage to protect him from an inferno hot enough to melt his skin off his bones. "I sent the email. It was me."

"He's lying," I deny, moving half of the lights dotting up his chest back to me.

He's pissed, and I hear it in his tone. "What reason do I have to lie, Andrik?"

"Because you're trying to protect her like you think you failed to do twenty-eight years ago." His silence speaks volumes. He's also willing to fall on the knife for Zoya. I just refuse to let him. "You didn't fail her, Mikhail. *Your* father did. If you want to blame anyone, blame him."

"Zoya is my baby sister! It was my job to protect her."

"Zoya?" Maksim stammers out, his confusion as paramount as his anger. "What has she got to do with this?"

"Nothing," I snap out before glaring at Mikhail in silent warning to keep his fucking mouth shut. Henry is here to take down the federation. That automatically drags Zoya into the mess because she is a Dokovic as my father announced.

I am the one missing the royal blood the federation was desperately seeking to reestablish when they stole Zoya's eggs.

My father didn't lie when he said my mother fooled them all. She had them so convinced that I was a Dokovic, by the time my true birthright was exposed, the public had already fallen in love with the idea of me being their future president.

My family's reign would have toppled if the secret ever got out, so the federation buried the evidence before putting in plays to eventually smooth out the kink my existence caused.

Aleena's prime fertility record made her their first pick, but just like Stasy, her age went against her. She suffered numerous miscarriages before news of Zoya's egg donation reached someone high up in the federation.

Aleena carried that surrogacy without incident.

Zakhar was stripped from her seconds after birth and given to his grandmother to raise. The parts between his birth and his introduction to my life were above Dr. Leverington's pay grade.

I will get answers, but it will take time.

Time I don't have if the raised voices outside the operating theater are anything to go by.

Law enforcement has arrived, and they don't seem as willing to seek answers as Henry is.

"Bring them with us."

When one of Henry's goons approaches me, I shift the direction of my gun to his head. "Do *not* touch my son."

"Andr—"

"No," I growl, cutting Henry off with the rumble of a madman. "He will die without proper medical assistance." I shift my eyes to Maksim. "The host of the heart you came here to collect is already dead. Don't make my son suffer the same fate." After recalling the promise he made to Zoya before he wed her best friend, I have no choice but to toss her into the fire with me. I will get her out, as I will Zakhar and Mikhail, but when you're clutching at straws, you have to let some guards down. "Don't make Zoya's son suffer the same fate."

Mikhail gasps in shock as Maksim calls me a liar.

He eats his words when I snatch up Zakhar's medical chart and thrust it his way. I told Zakhar the truth as the doctors were sedating him, not wanting him to face the possibility of going to his grave without knowing the true identity of his mother. The nurse updated the parental details of his patient record as he was wheeled into the operating theater.

It is there, in thick black ink for the world to see.

Zakhar handled my confession better than Maksim does. He groggily muttered that he knew there was more to Zoya turning down his offer to be his girlfriend than a difference in age before the anesthetics took hold.

He's been under sedation ever since.

After raking his eyes over my face, Maksim shoots them to Zakhar. It only takes him three seconds to see what I should have seen in a nanosecond. Same eyes. Same facial structure. It is just his mousey-brown hair that pulls you off the scent since Zoya's is several shades lighter than mine.

"He's—"

Before Maksim can finalize his sentence, gunfire rings out.

The putrid scent of bullets shredding through skin streams into my nose as I dive across Zakhar's body to protect him for what could possibly be the final time.

75

ZOYA

*D*on't let my stellar GPA fool you. I'm an idiot—a complete and utter idiot.

I sent Andrik's drafted email because I had no clue Andrik and Maksim had an agreement to keep those types of proceedings away from Myasnikov Private Hospital. I would have never done it if I had known the consequences it would instigate.

Maksim thinks Andrik betrayed him, and he's out for revenge.

I can only hope Mikhail reaches him before my stupidity destroys more than just my friendship with my best friend.

As I ride the elevator to the top floor of Maksim's building, I pray for a nonviolent outcome. Pushing Zakhar's name to the top of the donor list with a bribe isn't the worst thing in the world I could have done to get him a new heart. I'm just unfamiliar with how matters like this are handled in the underworld.

Fingers crossed it involves money. Andrik has plenty of that, and although he'll be pissed when he learns my mistake cost him millions, I doubt his anger will linger long when Zakhar makes a full recovery.

When the elevator pops open, I exhale a deep breath before entering the foyer of Gigi's and Grampies's new crash pad. I've never felt more hopeless. I haven't heard from Andrik or Mikhail in hours. Not even Maksim is answering my calls, and I've been ringing him as regularly as I have the other two.

I'm panicked out of my mind that I've caused irreparable damage to two mafia entities that were once more friendly than foe, but I need to keep a calm head.

Nikita is fretful enough for the both of us, and I've yet to tell her that I instigated a fight that may end with multiple casualties.

Also, I need to remember not all of Maksim's focus should be on Andrik. His crew didn't drug and kidnap Nikita for hours. More than bribery commenced this battle. I'm certain of it. I just need Maksim to answer one of my damn calls to make sure he is aware of that.

"Thank you," Nikita whispers when I hand her the coffee I offered to fetch so I could fight the urge to fall to my knees and plead for forgiveness. She donated her mother's organs when she was killed, so if she finds out a medical unit may have profited from her loss, she will be pissed.

"About last night." Nikita's exhale ruffles the locks I pulled in front of my shoulders to hide my head wound. "I—"

"If you're about to apologize, my foot is about to land in your butt crack."

She smiles.

She *fucking* smiles.

I don't deserve it, but I am going to relish it.

"Don't smile. I'm not joking. I even removed my shoes to make sure I wouldn't get anything nasty on my new pumps."

She is as eager as me to escape the turmoil making her stomach a sticky mess. "You got new shoes?"

"Yeah. Wanna see?" When she nods, I hook my thumb to the elevator I wish was full of as many Dokovic men as Ivanovs. I'll even accept Andrik's father as a co-rider if it guarantees Andrik's, Mikhail's, and Maksim's reappearances. "Follow me downstairs. There's an entire wardrobe of brand-new designer clothes and shoes that look like they haven't been touched." I remind my heart that no news doesn't always equate to bad news before saying, "If my new husband wants to gift me a wardrobe of designer babies, I'm not going to look at a single item priced under five figures." Before she can sink her teeth into the juicy worm I accidentally dangled in front of her, I back out of my ruse with my arms held high in the air. If I open that can of worms, I won't be done for hours. Nikita needs my focus on her marriage, not mine. "Any news?"

With a defeated sigh, Nikita shakes her head.

"He'll be okay, Keet," I assure her, my voice cracking like Maksim's safety isn't hinged on Andrik's ability to protect his son. "You'd need a tank to take him down, and it would have to be the size of a submarine to keep him away from you." I bring back the playfulness she instigated earlier. It reminds me that there are soft sides to even the hardest men. "Not even the four deadbolts I installed on the servants' stairwell door could stop him." When her mouth gapes, I smile. "What? He couldn't use the front door because it couldn't be budged without pounding the living shit out of it, and he knew that would have woken you, so I got inventive."

"Because?"

My thoughts stray to Andrik when I reply, "Because I wanted you to know he wasn't giving up. He was just being a stubborn ass." I mess up her hair because I know how much she hates it. She won't cry if she's angry. "Like someone else I know."

An intercom buzzing ends her eye roll halfway around.

"Mrs. Ivanov, I have two officers here to speak with you."

My throat grows scratchy. Those were almost the exact words Nikita spoke when she told her dad there were two officers wanting to speak with him.

I can still remember the howl Mr. Hoffman released when they told him his wife had been brutally raped and murdered.

It haunts my dreams to this day, and it is the very reason I've kept my focus on settling Nikita's panic more than my own.

Nikita makes it to the foyer of her grandparents' apartment before a heartbreaking sob tears through her.

"If he's... oh god." When she folds in two, gripping her stomach as furiously as nausea shreds through mine, I race to her side.

"I should have never let him go. I should have made him keep his promise. I can't lose him, Z. I haven't even told him that I love him yet."

"You won't lose him. It'll be okay. And he already knows, Keet. He saw it on your face every time you got jealous. Why do you think he loves it so much?"

Again, my thoughts stray to Andrik. I hate how he hurt me by throwing my sister in my face, but there are so many similarities to the way Maksim loves Nikita and how Andrik was with me before his attention waned that I can't help but compare them.

Our time in the cabana... *gosh*. I've never felt more wanted. I fell in love with him on sight, and that afternoon cemented my feelings for him.

Cement is hard to crack.

Andrik has given it his best shot over the past few weeks, but his hits barely scratched the surface. I still love him enough that I can forgive him. He just needs to ask—and perhaps fall to his knees and beg.

I'm immersed in my wicked plan of revenge I am confident I will be given the chance to execute that it takes me longer than I care to admit to learn why the tension is so rife.

Nikita is standing across from a male and a female detective. The brunette seems somewhat polite, but the gray-haired man's aura puts my nerves on edge.

"Do I need a warrant, Dr. *Fernandez*?" he spits into Nikita's face.

"It is Dr. Ivanov," Nikita barks back, her bite just as stern. "And yes, you do. My husband owns this building, so anything inside it is his possession."

"Then I guess it's lucky we're not here for him, isn't it?"

Recalling Maksim's instructions for Nikita if she was ever bombarded like this, I shift on my feet to face Gigi before saying, "Call Raya." When she nods and waddles off, I butt shoulders with Nikita. "What is this in regard to?"

"Are you her lawyer?"

"No." My words are for the female detective, but my scold is for her male counterpart. "But I don't need to be to make sure she isn't railroaded by a chauvinistic asshole who thinks he's tough because he has a gun."

The brunette attempts to take charge. "We're here in regard to your whereabouts between the hours of"—she checks her notepad —"two p.m. yesterday afternoon until five a.m. this morning."

I continue with Maksim's plan. "She was here the entire time."

The male detective exposes part of his hand when he flashes an image of Nikita in the elevator of her workplace during the timeline his colleague mentioned.

"I arrived for my shift at..." Nikita breathes out slowly before murmuring, "I'm having difficulties remembering the exact time—"

"Another lapse in memory? How convenient."

Nikita retaliates to his snarky tone before I can. "I was drugged with a benzodiazepine that causes memory issues, so perhaps instead of wasting your time questioning me about my where-abouts, you should go search for the real criminals ruining this town." I want to slap her back and say, *Attagirl*, when she snaps out, "And that person is *not* my husband."

"Do you know who drugged you or what synthetic they used?" the brunette asks, her interests piqued.

Nikita shakes her head. "No. We took a sample with the hope it would give us answers, but the results aren't back yet."

She flips over the pages in her notepad before asking, "Do you have an approximate time you were drugged?"

"I don't remember much from before I arrived for my shift yesterday," Nikita answers. "I remember driving there, and I think I entered via the underground garage elevator, but I can't be sure. It's all blank."

"Until what time?"

The male detective's voice is as railroading as earlier, but it is too late for him. He lost any pleasantries he seems to think he suddenly deserves.

"I woke around two," Nikita answers, even with her tone announcing she doesn't believe he deserves her assistance.

The brunette jumps back into the conversation. "A.m.?"

When Nikita nods, arrogance hardens the male detective's wrinkly features. "So the alibi your husband's lawyer gave us an hour ago is false. He was not with you at all."

"Th-that isn't what I said. I said I woke at two. But he was with me the en-entire time."

He scoffs at Nikita's reply. "How would you know if you were passed out?"

"Because he sleeps inside her every night." I look him up and down, doubling my wish to vomit. "And unlike the unfortunate women who have slept with you, she couldn't mistake his presence."

"It's actually anytime she sleeps." Maksim enters the frame from stage left, almost pulling my knees out from beneath me as well as he does Nikita's. "But I'll save the details for someone more worthy of my time." He assists me in keeping Nikita upright before he doubles the whiteness of the detectives' cheeks with a commanding glare. "Is there something I can assist you with, Officers?"

The brunette flashes her credentials. "Detective Lara Sonova from Trudny PD. We're here to verify the alibi Raya Hughes gave for Mrs. Fern—" She recovers quickly. "Mrs. Ivanov earlier today."

"Once she finalized her shift, she was here with me all night, as my lawyer has already stated."

"Ah..." Lara flicks through her notepad. "And—"

"And if you have any further questions, they can be directed through my lawyer, as also stated earlier." Maksim's arrogance could give Andrik's a run for its money. It doesn't stop me from seeking any signs of injury on his body, however. "Is that understood?"

"Yes," Lara gives in just as I sigh in relief.

Maksim doesn't appear to have even been in a fight.

After soundlessly apologizing to Nikita for her partner's actions, Lara heads for the elevator.

It takes her colleague another thirty seconds to join her.

The elevator doors have only just shut with the detectives on one side and us on the other when Nikita commences an in-depth search of Maksim's body.

When he laughs, appreciative of her panic, I inhale a lung-filling breath of air for the first time in hours. It has me convinced that everything is okay, that none of the horrid theories I've been running through my head over the past several hours are true.

Only a psychopath could laugh after hurting innocent victims because of someone else's mistake.

Andrik and Mikhail are quiet because Zakhar's recovery is more important than my dramatics. They had nothing to do with the revenge Maksim was undertaking. They're as innocent as the gleam in Zakhar's eyes when he asked if I wanted to be his girlfriend.

I tune back in at the right time.

"Ano?" Nikita asks, her one word full of worry.

I sigh in relief when Maksim replies, "He was found a few hours ago. He is a little groggy and sporting a handful of new stitches, but he's been through worse, so I don't see his recovery taking long."

"Is it...? Did you...?" After a stern swallow, Nikita asks more fluently, "Is *it* done?"

All the relief Maksim's laughter lifted from my shoulders stacks back on when he shifts his eyes to me and narrows them before he says, "The faction working out of Myasnikov Private was more extensive than anyone realized. They weren't just *selling* the organs of *legitimate* donors. They were encouraging harvests."

Oh shit.

When I recall the weirdness of the invoices Boris tidied up in a hurry, I make sure Maksim's focus is on the right people. "With food?" When Maksim nods, I shift my focus to Nikita, praying like hell she will help me shift Maksim's daggers to the right culprits. "That's why you kept bringing up bananas." Hating that I'm being a coward, I return my eyes to Maksim. "Her memories are still foggy, but she recalled seeing a crate of bananas being carried out of the hospital."

A rush of nausea hits me when Maksim discloses, "They were poisoning members of the community through food banks, then plucking a handful of unsuspecting victims from the pile to succumb to the latest gastroenteritis outbreak ravishing the city. Their families had no clue."

He isn't saying what I think he is, is he?

Zakhar's new heart was from someone who *accidentally* died, right?

That's how bribes work. You pay a premium to push a desired recipient to the top of the stack. You don't murder someone for what is meant to be readily available.

Before I can pry the truth from Maksim's eyes, Nikita asks, "Then how did your mother end up on that list?"

I take a moment to breathe through the heaviness on my chest when Maksim attempts to appease Nikita's curiosity. "The man she came to see was a chef. With his business not doing well, he substituted some of his produce with supplies a charity worker was skimming from the food banks."

"The tainted food is why there were so many outbreaks over the past several months."

I'm brainstorming out loud, mindful this is bigger than just Zakhar's new heart, but Nikita doesn't know that. "And also why there was an increase in surgeries." Her eyes widen as her mouth gapes. "I saw bananas. They were being carried out of the hospital. Does that mean...?" My stomach gurgles when she clicks on to the truth half a second before me. "Yulia's father lost his job. He couldn't afford food. He was supplementing his lost wages with produce that was donated to him. That could be what is making Yulia sick."

Yulia is almost the same age as Zakhar.

The same height.

The same weight.

She also has the same blood type. I saw her patient details on the invoice I paid for a blood workup Maksim funded on behalf of her family weeks ago.

Please, no.

When Nikita races for the exit, Maksim grabs her wrists and tugs her back.

She doesn't take kindly to being manhandled, but unlike me, she uses words to announce her dislike. "Let me go, Maksim. I need to help her. There are ways we can reverse the damage of the poison."

"Oh fuck," I murmur on a sob when Maksim says, "It's too late."

"No." The devastation in Nikita's voice cuts me like a knife. Its slashes are nowhere near as damaging as the ones my guilt is instigating. "She can get better. I can help her."

As he stares at me as if I am the professor who threatened to fail Nikita every semester if she wouldn't put out, Maksim says, "My men found her this morning. She was in a room at the back of the loading dock. Her organs had been harvested. There was nothing we could do." My heart breaks along with Nikita's when he says without remorse, "We took down the people directly responsible for her death. We made them pay." A tear rolls down my cheek when he adds, "And I won't stop until *every person* who hurt her has paid."

"Promise me," Nikita demands, unaware she is signing my death certificate.

After a final glare hotter than the sun, Maksim lifts Nikita's tear-drenched face before he murmurs, "I promise." His eyes are back on me, hot and heavy. "No one will *ever* hurt you like this again."

I don't know what compels me to do it, but I nod as if his confirmation of protection isn't a threat.

My agreeing gesture pacifies Maksim enough to put our confrontation on the backburner until he settles Nikita, though it does little to stop my knees from pulling out from underneath me when I'm left alone in the foyer.

I fall to the floor with a clatter and muffle my howling sobs by biting my palm.

76

ZOYA

I've moved past my grief by the time Maksim returns to the living area. I buried it deep in an anger that's so volatile I don't consider the aftermath of my actions when I storm up to Maksim and throw my fists into his chest and face.

He blocks my first two hits, but my third and fourth send his head rocketing to the side and a sickening crunch sounding through the entryway of Gigi and Grampies's apartment.

"Did you kill them! Did you punish them for something they didn't do?" I don't give him the chance to answer. My grief is too strong to see through the madness. "It wasn't them. They didn't initiate the bribe. It was me. *I* sent the email. *I* bribed Dr. Sidorov to put Zakhar at the top of his list because I didn't know about the agreement Andrik had made with you."

Air whistles through my teeth when I drag in a much-needed breath. I'm still belting into Maksim, still overwhelmed with remorse, but I won't stop fighting.

I should have *never* stopped fighting.

Maksim's tattooed forearm blocks my fist before his hands clamp my wrists and he pulls them to my sides. Although his sneer is barely a whisper, I have no trouble hearing him since he tugs me to within an inch of his face before bobbing down low so we're eye to eye. "Admissions like that will get you killed, so if you want any chance of fixing your mistake, you need to shut your fucking mouth."

When my shock renders me silent, he drags me into the servants' stairwell and then shoots his eyes to the door he walked me through only seconds ago.

Satisfied his wife isn't going to burst through it to ask what the hell is going on, he shifts his focus back to me.

He stares at me like he hates me, his nostrils flaring and his jaw tight.

My glare mimics his to a T. He seemed like a fair man. Just. I never considered he would be a monster who'd kill an innocent child for the stupidity of an adult.

"He wasn't even five. His birthday isn't for another ten days," I stammer out when my grief becomes too much.

"And Yulia was only six. *Six!*" he shouts. "Yet you sent her to her grave in the cruelest way possible."

"I didn't know. I swear on Nikita's life I had no clue—"

"Don't bring her into this! Don't use *my wife* to fix *your* mistakes."

He frees my wrists from his hold before he steps back to pace the corridor. I can see the struggle on his face not to retaliate with more violence, sense his struggle. He wants me to pay for hurting Nikita, and I honestly want the same as well.

"This is my burden, so I'll take the shame. I will tell her everything. I'll admit to every horrible thing I've done." I wait for him to look at me before adding with a sob, "But not until you tell me what happened to them." I hiccup. "Did you kill them?" His silence agitates me to no end. "Answer me, goddamn it! Did you kill them?"

"No!" Maksim shouts, his angry roar reverberating in the tight confines of the corridor. "But don't think that was my choice. I promised my wife I would take down the people responsible for hurting her." He stares me up and down and then shakes his head in disgust. "But *he* was right. Keeping that promise may hurt her the most." He hates his next words. His expression announces this, not to mention his tone. "She needs you in her life. I doubt she would have one if it weren't for you. But you're going to tell her the truth. You're going to tell her everything when *I* say she is ready to be told." He bangs his chest when he says *I*. "Do you understand, Zoya? Not a second before and not until I know she is strong enough to endure the pain *your* shame will place on *her* shoulders."

Tears topple as I nod. I am both ashamed and relieved.

Nikita will be devastated when I tell her what I did, but I can live with that shame if it means Andrik, Mikhail, and Zakhar are okay.

After staring at me long enough to ensure he is confident I am telling the truth, Maksim signals to a man at the end of the stairwell to move forward.

"Take her to this address." He hands him a business card and then returns his eyes to me. "That is as far as I can take you. *He's* not exactly welcoming to visitors right now."

He drinks in my solemn head bob for half a second before he spins on his heel and walks away.

He is almost back in the foyer of the penthouse suite when I slow his steps. "For what it's worth, I'm sorry."

It feels like the sun circles the planet a hundred times before he accepts my apology with the briefest chin dip.

I gallop down the servant stairs half a second later.

77

ANDRIK

"*I* don't give a fuck what Henry said. Find my wife!"

I slam down my phone as if it is an old-style rotary phone before smashing it with my fist. Henry has an army of millions because he is a fair man. He looks at the evidence to ensure his decisions aren't based on the wizardry men in our field often use to get their way. His verdicts are swift but accurate, hence Zakhar, Mikhail, and I making it back to our compound relatively unscathed. But I've yet to hear the outcome of Zoya's mistake.

Henry knows she threatened Dr. Sidorov, and that a sternly worded email is sometimes all you need to motivate a coward, but he wouldn't issue a ruling without first speaking with Zoya.

I pleaded with him to let me accept the consequence of Zoya's mistake, that she wouldn't have made it if I hadn't pushed her so hard.

Nothing I said got through to him, so I shifted my focus to Maksim.

He is as stubborn as me, and just as unhinged, so I knew the perfect way to get him to listen.

I used his wife against him.

I told him that she'd never forgive him if he took away the one person who kept her standing when her entire world crumbled beneath her feet, and how Zoya didn't solely sell her eggs for herself. She also did it to buy Nikita textbooks and fund the first round of medication her father's incarceration could no longer fund for her grandfather.

I told him he wouldn't have a wife to defend if it weren't for *my* wife.

He seemed to pay attention, but our conversation was hours ago, and not a single member of my team has laid eyes on Zoya since.

I flatten my palms on my desk just as Konstantine says, "I found a way in." His fingers fly at a million miles an hour. "Where do you want me to look first? I won't have access for long. Henry's hacker is good." We had to go around the federation's system since it no longer exists.

Henry doesn't just dismantle an organization. He wipes their existence from the history books.

"The Chrysler Building. That's where Mikhail dropped her off." My eyes go wild when we see inside the building for the first time in months. Maksim's security is usually too high to infiltrate. "There."

My heart thrashes against my ribs when Konstantine freezes the image of Zoya sprinting through an underground parking garage. Her face is ashen, meaning the tears tracking down her cheeks can't be missed.

"Get the plate, then add it to the traffic cam database."

"Fuck," Konstantine groans. "I'm out. She booted me."

Shockingly, I keep a cool head. "Try again. While you do that, I'll seek another access point."

The click of a safety on a gun being flicked off sounds through my ears when I enter the room next to my office. Zakhar is still sedated, but I'm not here for him. I need the man seated across from him who survived the federation's implosion by the fine hairs on top of his head.

The secret service agent in the corner of the room re-houses his gun when he realizes who is approaching our current serving president. He knows I am no fret to my grandfather because if it weren't for him, I wouldn't exist either.

It wasn't solely the public's admiration that kept me alive. It was also my grandfather's. He loved my mother from afar for years, so in turn, some of that affection shifted to me when I was born.

He rules with an iron fist, but just like Henry, his rulings are fair. He couldn't stomach me being torn from his clutches as numerous of his children were during his prime, so he agreed to be the federation's puppet on the promise that my lineage would be buried as strenuously as his son hid his one and only true love.

My father let them take my mother. He hid Mikhail's.

The knowledge pisses me off until I recall what the outcome could have been if he hadn't loved Mikhail's mother more than mine.

When my grandfather's rheumy eyes lift to me, the shame in them reminds me of the reason for my visit. "I need access to White Eye."

"I don't have access—"

"You do," I interrupt, my tone stern. "You might have been puppeteered as well as the rest of us, but *you* had to input every code, speak every word of their vocal access passwords. You have access; you just need to bring back the fear. The notoriety. You need to continue trying to return our family name to the glory it once held."

He nearly corrects me when I say *our*, but my hand thrust at Zakhar halts his words.

"He won't survive this without her, Andrik." I use his middle name on purpose, knowing his fondness of me may be the only way I will chip through his stern exterior. "A boy needs his mother. I know this more than anyone. Give him the chance to show you he can be great by having the guidance of both a mother and a father." I lower my eyes to his pinkie finger, balking when his family crest ring is nowhere to be seen. Its disappearance fuels my campaign. "We're not robots, Grandpa. We can love you without fearing you." An unexcepted pocket of emotions hits my voice when I murmur, "She could have loved you without fearing you. You just never gave her the chance. Don't do the same thing to Zakhar."

His wet eyes lower from his translucent hands. He stares at them with a brooding silence that displays he is a man of great power. He wants our family name to have the respect it once held. I truly believe that. He's just fighting demons decades older than mine.

"Please," I murmur, not below begging if it ensures Zoya is returned to me safely. "You didn't do all this work to let your family down now. Help me find her. Help me find my wife."

He stares at me for barely a second before he flicks his eyes to the secret service agent standing guard in the corner of the room. "Fetch my briefcase."

"Mr. President—"

"Now!"

I inwardly fist pump when his stern rumble leaps the agent into action. He races for a briefcase my grandfather is never without before placing it on the end of Zakhar's bed not used by his tiny frame.

After dismissing the agents from the room, he squashes his thumb on the finger scanner and then murmurs, "I had to do something. I couldn't let him die." More tears fill his eyes, showing a side of him I've never seen. "I didn't play by their rules for decades to let them kill your mother's only grandson." He raises his eyes to me. They're still glistening with wetness, but the deluge does little to hide his determination to return the respect his family lost centuries ago. "So I made them pay."

When he opens his briefcase instead of revealing the access code that will allow Konstantine to hack into any security system in Russia, he hands me a simple USB drive.

I stop considering the importance of the microdrive when he mutters, "Give it to Henry. He will grant you access to anything you need once he opens the file inside."

I have questions. Many of them. But since I don't have time, I kiss his cheeks without the begrudged groan any affection usually forces from me before sprinting for the exit.

I almost make it into the clear when my grandfather calls my name—my real name. "Andrik." He waits for me to face him before he says, "Tell your father I'm sorry, and make sure he knows the truth." He lowers his eyes to the USB drive. "Everything you need is in there."

"No," I reply, shaking my head, unwilling to do his bidding. "He needs to hear it from you..."

My words trail off when he makes sure there's no possibility of him facing his mistakes head-on. He raises a gun I didn't realize he was holding until now to his head and fires one shot.

"No!"

The scream didn't come from me. It came from someone behind me, and the familiarity of her voice has me spinning so fast my legs almost buckle out from beneath me.

Zoya is standing across from me. Her hair still has a tinge of red coloring from where she split her head, and her clothes are two sizes too big, but I would recognize those curves anywhere. And that face... *fuck.*

Her wide eyes drift from my grandfather, slumped over the edge of Zakhar's bed with a self-inflicted gunshot wound to the head, to me. I assume her cheeks whiten because she's never seen a dead body before, but remorse pulls her in another direction.

"I'm so sorry." She strays her eyes around a mansion now in ruins. "This is my fault. I caused this. I—"

"No," I cut her off, my one word as fast as the steps I take to bridge the gap between us. "This is not on you, милая." I weave my fingers through her hair nowhere near her wound and breathe in her scent before aligning our eyes. "This was *never* on you."

"But—"

"No buts. No ifs. Life is too short for doubts."

She is as stubborn as a mule. It is one of the things I love about her the most. "I—"

"Do I need to take you over my knee, милая?"

I should have known lust would force her from her stupor state before anything else. It blazes through her veins, making her hot, but before I can pretend the casualty of our battle isn't in the thousands, a childlike voice interrupts us this time.

"Daddy."

Zoya's pupils blow wide before her motherly instincts kick in even with her being unaware of her connection to Zakhar. She races into this room and places herself between him and a scene that will scar him for life before his eyes are halfway open.

"You can't open your eyes yet, Zak, or you'll ruin your surprise."

He swishes his tongue around his mouth to loosen up his words but keeps his eyes so tightly shut that wrinkles spread across the bridge of his nose. "You got me a surprise?"

"Uh-huh," Zoya lies before gesturing like a badass mafia boss for me to remove the dead man at the foot of the bed. "But I forgot to wrap it, so I need you to keep your eyes closed for a little bit longer. Okay?"

"Okay," Zakhar replies as Konstantine assists me in carrying my grandfather out of the room. The doctors Henry ordered to monitor

Zakhar's recovery do nothing but stare. I'm not even sure one of them is breathing.

"We're almost ready."

Zoya grunts and groans while using some of the supplies we left the hospital with to clean up the brain matter splattered across the bottom of Zakhar's bed.

Now is not the time to admit this, especially since I am hiding the body of the man who saved my life in the closet of my son's room, but I'm hard as fuck.

I knew Zoya had the gall to take down a kingdom, but I had no clue it extended this far.

"Okay." She breathes out heavily when I return to the room before she scans the stark confines. Henry's crew destroyed ninety-eight percent of this compound, but Zakhar's room is basically untouched. His control shows you can be a man of mass power without being heartless. I plan to mimic his constraint as I rebuild.

After snatching up a clean bed sheet from a stack of many, Zoya curls it around her shoulders before giving Zak permission to open his eyes.

He does, albeit a little hesitantly. He is still in a lot of pain, but he's willing to endure it for the chance of sneaking in some sweets before dinner.

When his eyes land on Zoya to silently demand she cough up the sweets he's seeking, she throws out her arms and jumps in the air. "Ta-da!"

Zakhar clicks on to her ruse faster than me. I'm not surprised. He is as smart as his mother. "You're my surprise?"

"Uh-huh." She steps closer to his bedside, kicking away the gun my grandfather used to kill himself. "I know there is a bit of a difference in our ages, but age-gap romances are all the rage right now. If you can overlook my *future* wrinkles, I can pretend you're a lot taller than you are."

Zakhar sounds disgusted when he asks, "You want to be my girlfriend?"

Unsure of the cause of his suddenly dour mood, Zoya hesitantly nods. When it whitens his cheeks more than the mammoth operation he undertook thirty-six hours ago, she says, "I thought that was what you wanted, Zak?"

"I did, but..." He takes a moment to consider a nicer approach. When his pause for contemplation leaves him empty-handed, he hits Zoya with brutal honesty. "That's a little gross now."

Zoya's shocked huff is drowned out by Mikhail's chuckle. It is the chuckle of a man who no longer has a bullet in his stomach but is still feeling the effects of going against an army alone. "Tell me about it, bud. I'm still traumatized, and she didn't make me."

Gingerly, he enters the room, brushes shoulders with Zoya, and then playfully ribs her out of her frozen-in-shock state.

After taking in three sets of admiring eyes staring at her, she murmurs, "What am I missing?"

Since Zak is too young to know tact, he breaks the news I'm dying to share with her first. "You're my mommy!"

Hours ago, that confession would have added a timer to her head.

Now, it ties her to me for life.

Thank fuck.

78

ZOYA

A familiar aroma stands the hairs on my nape to attention a second before it engulfs my senses. I must have been in a deep sleep, as the paintings lining the hallway I am being walked down are different from the ones outside Zakhar's room.

Andrik moved us to a new location not long after my meeting with Henry Gottle Sr.—the boss of all mafia bosses.

The information his grandfather handed him before taking his life exonerated me of any wrongdoing in Yulia's death. I sent the email warning them of the repercussions if they were to back out of a deal made before Andrik learned of Maksim's interest in the Myasnikov District, but it was Andrik Sr.'s involvement they paid the most attention to. But Andrik didn't want to risk any further repercussions occurring in a territory not ruled by him.

I still feel guilty as hell as to what has occurred, though you probably wouldn't believe me if you saw footage of my last four hours.

Zakhar is my son. My flesh and blood.

I was determined to protect him before I was aware of that, so I can't pledge that I wouldn't have taken as drastic of steps as his great-grandfather did if he still needed a new heart.

The reminder prompts me as to why I fell asleep on a rock-hard chair. "Zakhar…"

A stern rumble doubles the output of my heart. "Is safe. He's resting. Now I need to make sure you're taken care of the same way."

After smirking at my fake huff of annoyance, like I'm not loving his endeavor to ensure I am aware of my importance in his life, Andrik walks us into a manly room at the end of a long hallway.

I don't know whether to laugh or cry when his steps veer us to the bathroom instead of the bed. I feel dirty and gross, but I'm not as fond of bathroom antics as Nikita is.

Mine have always resulted in a negative outcome.

"I—"

"Shh, милая. Not yet. All of that can wait until after I've showered you, fed you, and put you to bed."

Goose bumps break across my skin when he places me onto the vanity a second before his hand shoots down to the hem of the shirt I borrowed from Nikita. His fingertips float over my midsection with a tenderness the agitation in his eyes shouldn't allow.

He's been quiet since Zakhar's blurted confession. I didn't need words to know Zak was telling the truth. The sheer ownership in Andrik's eyes told me everything I needed to know.

I am a mother.

The excitement the remembrance blisters through me is shocking. You could only surprise me more if you told me my mother was responsible for this plot twist in my story I never saw coming.

Although my heart hasn't stopped whacking out a funky tune for hours, it won't stop me from seeking answers. "How?"

Andrik grunts as if frustrated by my inability to follow orders. I may have believed his dislike if he hadn't hardened the instant the first syllable escaped my lips.

He waits for my eyes to lift from the protruding rod in his trousers to his face before he says, "I don't have all the answers yet, милая. I will get them. I promise you that. But I don't have them yet."

With nothing but honesty in his eyes, I nod before raising my hands in the air so he can remove my shirt without hindrance.

A hiss of air escapes his lips when he realizes I am braless. "Jesus fucking Christ, милая. You are going to ruin me."

His eyes lift to my face when I murmur, "I think we've already established that... more than once."

"*Think*?" There's that arrogant, dominating man I've fallen in love with. "Think is a consideration. A doubt. It does *not* belong between us. But this..."

I dart my eyes to the crotch of his trousers, not wanting to miss the impressive outline of his cock when he grips it.

My stare at his cock doubles the hunger ripping through me, though I barely feel its spasms over the surge that electrifies my heart when he falls to his knees before he presses his hands to my stomach.

"This was *always* meant to be between us." He lifts his eyes to mine, full of silent apologies. "I was a foolish, insolent man, милая. I don't deserve your forgiveness. I don't deserve you"—his eyes flick in the direction of Zakhar's room before he returns them to my nonexistent bump—"*any* of you. To be asked to give you up will be death worse than a thousand." Nothing but honesty colors his tone when he says, "It *will* kill me. But..."—that killed him to say as much as it did for me to hear it —"if that is what you want for our family, I will respect your wishes."

I gasp in a sharp breath, shocked by his offer. The sentiment in his eyes ensures it can only be read one way. He's giving me, Zakhar, and our unborn child an out, freeing us from the madness he's endured for decades with no threat of retribution for my choice.

He is giving us the opportunity to walk away.

I don't give his offer any true thought. Who in their right mind would? You didn't see the way he sheltered me when vengeance came knocking, or how mine and our son's needs were more pertinent to him than revenge.

He's putting us first—and now I need to do the same.

"What happened to there are no ifs or buts?" I squash my finger to his lips before he can answer me. "I also didn't sign a prenup, so should you really be giving me an out before you've gotten all the bang for your buck? It is too late to negotiate *after* a deal is done. I thought I taught you that better than anyone."

He laughs, and the heat of his breaths quickly announces that my panties are soaked. Don't judge. The man I desire as much as my lungs crave air is kneeling in front of me, mere inches from my pussy. This could only be hotter if I were riding his face like there was still eight seconds on the timer.

I barely press my thighs together when the voice I became obsessed with in under a second adds to the mess between my legs. "милая... We have much to discuss."

Andrik is telling me no, but his actions do the opposite. After leaning in close enough to force his shoulders between my thighs, his eyes lower to the large gap my unladylike position involuntarily enforces.

He growls when he spots the wetness the high rise of my skirt can't hide before he finally answers one of the numerous pleas my hooded eyes are hitting him with. He puts his hands on me.

"Fuck, милая. Is all this wetness for me?"

He steals my lie by backhanding my clit. The frisky slap doubles its manic throbs and has me finally understanding why he walked us to the far side of his mega-mansion.

He doesn't want my cries of ecstasy to wake our son—because despite our beliefs, sorrow will *never* rank higher than our needs.

I doubt even grief could touch the surface of how much I crave this man.

"Please," I beg when his finger only traces the seam of my panties instead of peeling them away from my weeping sex.

He seems hesitant, like there's a possibility God himself could stop this, but instead of announcing the cause of his worry, he mutters, "Fuck it," before he lifts his eyes to my face. "Please, *who*?"

"*Andrik*. Please, Andrik."

I grunt through the spasms his second growl sluices through my veins. It is as rumbling as the first but without its hesitation.

It rolls through my body like liquid ecstasy, weighing down my limbs as well as his following sentence does. "Their lies couldn't stop me from wanting you back then, so they don't stand a chance now either."

My back arches and my head thrusts back when he sucks my panty-covered clit into his mouth. I shudder through the intensity of his suck as he twirls his tongue around the hardened bud. He toys with my clit until my panties dampen enough to outline every detail of my pussy, and I crumble under the awe of his skills.

Then he does it again—minus interfering panties this time.

"Oh, my sweet милая. Wickedly sexy but with the cunt of a saint. I could eat you for days and it'll never be enough."

Andrik places his mouth back on my pussy, and I ride the storm it causes for all it's worth. As his fingers thrust in and out of me, milking my G-spot, he tongues my clit and swipes at it with his thumb.

Pleasure charges through me as I rest my back on the mirror, needing its coolness to calm the fire raging low in my stomach. I'm burning up everywhere, seconds from a third torrent of ecstasy washing over me.

As he plays at the wetness slicking from my pussy to my ass, Andrik locks his eyes with mine. "Do you have any idea how many times I imagined doing precisely this over the past month?" He rolls my clit with his thumb, stealing any chance of a reply. "I imagined it every day, multiple times a day." He presses down hard on my clit, magnetizing my thoughts so well that I don't give his next sentence any real thought. "They convinced me you were my blood, yet I still masturbated about how good you taste every *single* day."

I shift my hips upward, mashing my pussy with his face as waves of pleasure cascade around me. I'm mindless with need, spiraling and spasming through the jolts rocketing across my core.

I come again and again until a handful of the tremors shifts to twinges of worry.

Andrik is looming over me, wide-eyed and sweaty. I don't know where his trousers went. He lost them somewhere between driving me to the brink of climax over and over again to guiding the head of his fat cock between the folds of my pussy.

As he searches my face for any signs of discomfort, he slowly notches inside me.

"Christ." His cock flexes, and I almost come again. "How did I ever get so lucky? My cock is being gripped by the tightest and tastiest cunt I've ever had the pleasure to know."

He sinks in until the wetness coating his chin slicks the hand wrapped around the base of his shaft. Then, like a light bulb switching on, a desire to claim me as I've never been claimed crosses his face.

After freeing his cock from his strangling grip, he thrusts fully inside me with one ardent pump. Tingles spasm low in my womb when the head of his girthy cock rams into my uterus. It is painful, as anticipated, but also euphoric. I've never been taken so deeply or roughly.

When I moan through the sensation of being so full, Andrik drags his cock out to the tip before he rams back in.

I grunt, loving how unhinged he is. I feel dirty and wicked, but isn't that how sex is meant to make you feel? It isn't purely for conception. Pleasure is very much a part of it.

As is the sensation of being craved.

With every rock of Andrik's hips, he bottoms out against my uterus and produces frantic grunts from my lips. I love how hard he is taking me, how deep, though not as much as what he says while driving me to the brink.

"He made out your condition was worse than it was. That there was no possibility of you conceiving naturally so you'd never be placed on their list." His hooded watch is a mix between jealous and relieved. It announces who he is speaking about without his name needing to leave his lips. "Then he removed your donation from the database and had them stored in case you ever wanted to use them in the future." He fucks me harder. Faster. He reminds me who owns every tremor wracking through my body by commanding every inch of it. "And I almost killed him for it."

His laugh belongs to a madman, and I can't get enough of it.

He said "almost."

That means Dr. Hemway is still alive.

The amount of constraint that would have taken a man as possessive as him is mesmerizing. It doubles the size of the goose bumps breaking across my skin and augments the wave low in my stomach.

"Fuck, Andrik," I moan as arousal ripples through me.

Tears spring into my eyes, and not because of how deep he takes me. It is the sentiment in the air and how he peers down at me as I come undone in his arms.

It is the affection he portrays. The love.

It is how he will always place me first even when I wish he wouldn't.

I dig the heels of my feet into Andrik's ass as a climax bursts through me. My cries of orgasm echo around the bathroom, doubling the speed of his pumps. As I shatter like glass, he continues thrusting into me.

His pace increases with every long plunge until the adoration I'm hitting him with becomes too much for him to bear.

He balances his forehead on mine, aligns our eyes, then sinks in low before giving in to the waves of ecstasy barreling into him.

"Fuck," he shouts as he fights the urge to still his hips.

He continues rocking, pumping, stealing the last of the air in my lungs. He fucks me wildly and recklessly until stars blister for the second time and I'm on the verge of an orgasmic coma.

"Fuck, милая." With sweaty hands, he cups my flushed cheeks and raises my head before pressing his lips to mine. "I knew from the moment I saw you that you were going to ruin me." He drags his nose down the side of my cheek, stopping my heart. "Yet I still signed up for it like a schmuck with half a cock."

As his fingertips tickle the backs of my ears, he breathes life back into my body with a heart-stuttering kiss. He licks at my lips and nibbles on my jaw as I fight not to surrender to the madness so soon again after only recently being freed from it.

Regretfully, I am as stubborn as a mule.

Andrik freezes with his tattooed fingers knotted in my hair when I ask, "What did you mean when you said they made out I was your blood?"

EPILOGUE
ZOYA

One and a half years later...

*H*uge blue eyes find me across the room before they're stolen by the bubble maker Andrik cursed to hell this morning. I swear he was on the verge of firing at it with his gun before Mikhail took over the reins of setting up the decorations for Amaliya's first birthday party.

I'm not upset I am not picked first this time.

Amaliya is obsessed with bubbles. It is almost on par with her father's obsession with me, which pushes my devastation at being disregarded like a broken toy to the background of my mind.

Andrik has been greeting our guests for the past hour, but not a single second has passed without me feeling the heat of his gaze. He watches me as intently now as he did when he aired his family's dirty laundry in the bathroom of one of his many country mansions.

Or should I say *my* family's dirty laundry.

I won't lie. It was a fight not to respond negatively when Andrik explained why he had been so cold and distant after our romp in the cabana, but the attraction that forever fires between us was strong enough to slacken the churns of my stomach to manageable in under a minute.

I was wary of Dr. Leverington's death confessions—conscious some men will say anything to stay alive—but learned soon after our reunion that every secret he exposed was true.

I am Kazimir Ellis Dokovic's eldest daughter, and Mikhail is his firstborn son. My family lineage is centuries long. I have brothers and sisters and dozens of cousins.

Every family member I have unearthed over the past eighteen months has stripped another member from Andrik's rapidly dwindling family tree, yet he doesn't seem to care.

How could he when our son is running across the manicured lawns of his palatial mansion, kicking a soccer ball, while our daughter woos her party guests with her two-teeth grin?

A life no longer under the federation's thumb is all Andrik has ever wanted.

His grandfather gave him that wish, and a newly formed government is keeping it.

The federation didn't keep Andrik's lineage hidden solely to force his grandfather to toe the line. Andrik's wish to return his family's name to the notoriety it once held was founded centuries ago. His mother's direct bloodline with Russian royalty is why the federation shifted Luiza's title from Andrik Sr.'s mistress to his eldest's son's wife.

Ellis and Luiza's union was never about love. It was for an heir Luiza struggled to conceive since she was diagnosed with a heart condition similar to Zakhar's just shy of her eighteenth birthday.

Under the guidance of the federation's chief doctor, she sought assistant from a holistic doctor who specialized in fertility issues. The story gets a little murky from there.

Some say they fell in love. Others say Dr. Holtz was so obsessed with Luiza that he switched Ellis's sperm for his own.

Andrik believes both versions of the story.

To him, love and obsession are the same thing.

I startle when a familiar voice drags me from my reminiscing. "Are these ready to go out?"

A dress with a price tag heavier than its flawless design swishes around my thighs when I spin to face Nikita. Although the USB drive Andrik Sr. handed to Andrik before his suicide exonerated me of any wrongdoing in Yulia's murder, I still confessed my sins to Nikita.

She swears she has never once hated me for the email I sent in desperation, but she isn't as skilled in lying as she is in detecting liars. I felt her disappointment, and I carried it for the three weeks it caused our contact to be sporadic.

The stress of worrying that I had caused irreputable damage to our friendship was enough for my obstetrician to order me to a month of bed rest.

It was my phone call to Nikita for a second opinion that reopened the communication lines. She gasped in bewilderment when I told her I was pregnant before she claimed credit for Amaliya's conception.

I was quick to remind her that a thirty-second leg hump isn't enough to conceive a child but that I was more than happy to give her a chance to prove my theory wrong the next time we had a sleepover.

Her laugh soothed the cracks in my heart no amount of groveling from Andrik could fix, and her reply fortified the flimsy patch job. "I told you it was you."

We've spoken every day since. Sometimes multiple times a day.

The remembrance adds mushy gooeyness to my voice when I answer, "Yes. All those are ready to go out."

When she gathers the plates of cupcakes in her hands, I snatch up a handful of napkins and stuff them into Maksim's chest before telling them I'll meet them outside with the real birthday cake shortly.

Maksim grumbles about being bossed around, but since he is still under Nikita's spell as much now as he was the night they wed, he follows his wife out of my home without further protest.

We have staff who could restock the snacks table, many of them, but on days like today, when we want our home filled with family and friends, we give them the day off.

It doesn't make the shell of our home as echoing as you'd think. Anoushka is here, and so is Konstantine, Lilia, Vanka, Mars, and Daniil. Even the driver who didn't go over twenty when we drove Amaliya home from the hospital has made an appearance.

Everyone of importance is here. There's just one person we're missing.

It isn't Ellis, as you may suspect. Shockingly, he is still a part of our lives. More because he could only react to the lies that were presented to him. He only learned the truth along with Andrik.

Ellis treated Mikhail so poorly because the federation had flipped the story of Luiza's alleged affair onto Stasy. For over thirty years, he believed the one woman he genuinely loved had birthed another man's child. Her alleged betrayal made him a shell of the man he could have been, and Andrik, Mikhail, and I had to suffer his heartache with him.

Although he believed Stasy had betrayed him, just like Andrik, Ellis couldn't stay away. He hid Stasy where he thought she would be safe, underestimating how desperate my mother—who I still struggle to remember isn't actually my mother—was to prosper in the world of the mega-wealthy.

The instant she discovered who Stasy's late-night visitor truly was, Dina exploited her connection for all it was worth.

We still have a long way to go before the aftermath of the federation's downfall will stop cracking the foundations I will never stop fortifying for my children, but we will get there eventually.

Andrik will make sure of it.

The efforts he's put in to fix my relationship with Aleena is proof of this.

There are so many plot twists in our story, but Aleena's forced involvement hurts me the most. I can't imagine how she felt when she was made to carry a child for nine months, only to have him cruelly stripped away.

We've tried to make things right with her. We've done everything we can to take away her pain and replace it with joy, but now the ball is in her court. We could only release her from her shackles. Anything after that is up to her.

"She will be here, милая." Andrik sneaks up on me with the agility a man his size shouldn't have before he reminds me of his mind reading capabilities. "She is your sister and our children's aunt. How could she not come to her niece's first birthday?" After banding his arm around my waist, he tugs me back before pressing his lips to my neck. "They also don't serve медовик until noon. Did you miss the memo that the Romanovs don't do family celebrations without that ghastly dish?"

Romanov is our new last name. It is steeped in history, so it was the perfect choice for a direct descendant of Russian royalty.

"Until she shows up with the curdled dessert none of our guests will wish to share, how about we test page twenty-two's stability on a kitchen counter for the umpteenth time this year?"

I swoon like crazy when he tilts in close. He's hard, and I'm too horny to remember today isn't meant to be about me.

"Do you think you'll have enough time for that?" I ask as the clock in the living room of our family home chimes twelve times. Andrik doesn't understand the definition of a quickie. "You can't leave me hanging. You *must* make me come... *twice*. It's in our contract." When his lips rise against my neck, I breathe out a moan. "A verbal contract is as binding as a written one."

One bite and my question is answered as quickly as my sassy attitude is put to bed. He won't just hold up the agreement we made before a second set of nuptials with the obligatory newlywed kiss.

He'll blow them out of the water.

"I think I'll be done with three minutes to spare."

My body goes lax when he grinds his thick cock against my ass. He's hard as steel, and despite our backyard being filled with our family and friends, I refuse to stop the exploration of his hands as he lowers them down my quivering stomach.

I need his hands on me as much as I need air to breathe, but he'll also kill anyone who steals my dreams from me for even a second, so it is safer for all involved for me to give in to my needs instead of attempting to douse them.

Well, that's what my heart plans to tell my head when guilt that I'm neglecting our guests eventually surfaces.

"Fuck, милая." Andrik breathes heavily into my neck as his fingers brush the opening of my pussy. "Is all this wetness for me?"

He doesn't wait for me to answer.

I'd only lie, and then he'd have to punish me.

There isn't enough time for that.

Not yet.

All bets are off when our children are asleep, though.

Until then, I'll follow Andrik's instructions to the wire.

It is a rarity, but I don't want just a good life. I want an interesting one as well. A quickie with your husband in the kitchen of your palatial mansion with hundreds of guests only feet away isn't life-altering, but it is pretty darn interesting—especially when multiple orgasms are guaranteed.

The End!

If you enjoyed this book, please consider leaving review.

Facebook: facebook.com/authorshandi

Instagram: instagram.com/authorshandi

Email: authorshandi@gmail.com

Reader's Group: bit.ly/ShandiBookBabes

Website: authorshandi.com

Newsletter: https://www.subscribepage.com/AuthorShandi

ALSO BY SHANDI BOYES

Denotes Standalone Books

Perception Series

Saving Noah *

Fighting Jacob *

Taming Nick *

Redeeming Slater *

Saving Emily

Wrapped Up with Rise Up

Protecting Nicole *

Enigma Series

Enigma

Unraveling an Enigma

Enigma The Mystery Unmasked

Enigma: The Final Chapter

Beneath The Secrets

Beneath The Sheets

Spy Thy Neighbor *

The Opposite Effect *

I Married a Mob Boss *

Second Shot *

The Way We Are

The Way We Were

Sugar and Spice *

Lady In Waiting

Man in Queue

Couple on Hold

Enigma: The Wedding

Silent Vigilante

Hushed Guardian

Quiet Protector

Enigma: An Isaac Retelling

Twisted Lies *

Bound Series

Chains

Links

Bound

Restrain

The Misfits *

Nanny Dispute *

Russian Mob Chronicles

Nikolai: Resurrecting the Bratva

Nikolai: Resurrecting the Bratva

Nikolai: Ruling the Bratva

Asher: My Russian Revenge *

Trey *

The Italian Cartel

Dimitri

Roxanne

Reign

Mafia Ties (Novella)

Maddox

Demi

Ox

Rocco *

Clover *

Smith *

RomCom Standalones

Just Playin' *

<u>Ain't Happenin'</u> *

The Drop Zone *

Very Unlikely *

False Start *

Short Stories - Newsletter Downloads

Christmas Trio *

Falling For A Stranger *

One Night Only Series

Hotshot Boss *

Hotshot Neighbor *

The Bobrov Bratva Series

Wicked Intentions *

Sinful Intentions *

Devious Intentions *

Deadly Intentions *

Martial Privilege Series

Doctored Vows *

Deceitful Vows *